PRAISE FOR

The Way We Weren't

"An insightful and compelling read."

—Leila Meacham, *New York Times* bestselling author of *Dragonfly*

"*The Way We Weren't* is so deeply satisfying on every level that it will continue to resonate with you long after you turn the page on one of the most exquisitely perfect endings you are likely to encounter in some time."

—Sarah Bird, author of *Daughter of a Daughter of a Queen*

PRAISE FOR

A Little Bit of Grace

"Secrets, rejection, and betrayal are no match for the powers of forgiveness in this charming novel."   —*Kirkus Reviews*

"*A Little Bit of Grace* reads just like the setting it so wonderfully evokes—sunny, warm, and bright, with healthy doses of adventure and wisdom thrown in for good measure. Phoebe Fox conjures delightful characters in intricate, unusual relationships who populate a story that feels like sifting sand between your toes and is the perfect book to read while doing so."

—Laurie Frankel, *New York Times* bestselling author of *This Is How It Always Is*

"*A Little Bit of Grace* is a deeply poignant emotional journey punctuated with humor, warmth, and an irresistible irreverence. A rare feel-good novel that you'll urgently want to press into the hands of friends and family. I adored it."

—Karin Gillespie, author of *Divinely Yours*

"There are contemporary and controversial issues involved in this story, but there is also the warmth of friendship, forgiveness, acceptance of family, hope, and the promise of love. I absolutely loved the story. Grace and colorful Aunt Millie are characters that will steal your heart away. Highly recommended."

—Bette Lee Crosby, author of *Blueberry Hill: A Sister's Story*

"As the family secrets emerge and Grace reckons with the past, Fox gives her characters convincing depth. This novel movingly depicts Grace's new lease on life."   —*Publishers Weekly*

"A heartwarming story with great characters in Grace and especially Millie (who might be one of the best-written characters all year). You are emotionally invested in the characters and hope for Grace to be able to move on with her life. A great end-of-summer read."   —Red Carpet Crash

"While the setting was beautiful, Grace was easy to root for, there was divorce and heartbreak, and then a potential romance angle, there was also a human element to this book that I thought was very timely and incredibly well written."

—Chick Lit Plus

The Way We Weren't

Phoebe Fox

Berkley
New York

BERKLEY
An imprint of Penguin Random House LLC
penguinrandomhouse.com

Library of Congress Cataloging-in-Publication Data

Names: Fox, Phoebe, author.
Title: The way we weren't / Phoebe Fox.
Description: First Edition. | New York : Berkley, [2021]
Identifiers: LCCN 2021023860 (print) | LCCN 2021023861 (ebook) |
ISBN 9780593098370 (trade paperback) | ISBN 9780593098387 (ebook)
Classification: LCC PS3606.O967 W39 2021 (print) |
LCC PS3606.O967 (ebook) | DDC 813/.6--dc23
LC record available at https://lccn.loc.gov/2021023860
LC ebook record available at https://lccn.loc.gov/2021023861

First Edition: November 2021

Printed in the United States of America
1st Printing

Book design by Ashley Tucker

For Joel

I need to have loved you. I need to have told you so.

—William Dickey, "A Kindness"

We have within us the capacity to manufacture the very commodity we are constantly chasing.

—Dan Gilbert

The Way
We Weren't

Before

~~~~~

t's his hands that let her know everything is going to be okay after all.

Sitting close beside her on the stands, bare but for the two of them with practice having ended almost two hours ago, his empty glove forgotten at his feet, he cradles her hand in his, one wrapped firmly around her fingers as if anchoring her to the hard metal surface currently freezing her butt, the other cupped over it like a baby bird he shelters from the cold bite of the March air.

But it isn't their clasped hands resting on the thigh of his acid-wash jeans, above the rip in the knee that's from wear, not fashion, that solidifies their future for her. Not the sight and warmth and comfort of his wide fingers around hers, his nails short and blunt and chewed at the edges, hers ragged with peeling pink polish the same color as the two lines that have just brought their childhood to a screeching halt.

It's the way he didn't care when her pee got all over his fingers as he took the little stick from her. But also the way he rubbed his hand hard against his jeans before he let himself touch her again. Those two things tell her all she needs to know: that no one has ever loved her like Will does—no one has ever loved anyone the way Will Malone loves her—and that she will do anything to hold on to this boy.

So even though they've never talked about anything further in the future than senior prom, even though they are just kids, with no idea how to even take care of themselves, let alone a baby, she says yes. Because everything is going to work out. As long as she has him and he has her, everything always does.

Marcie

Marcie lay curled on her side like a comma, staring at the drywall texture of the bedroom wall—a "Monterey drag," the contractor called it. It was supposed to be more elegant than an orange-peel finish, but she and Will were sorry they'd chosen it because the taupe paint alternately glopped and skipped over the deep fissures and grooves, and it took three coats to cover the white freckles still showing through. *Now I know why they call it a drag,* Will had joked as their arms started to ache with rolling.

That was how many years ago now? When the house was just built, long enough that a lot of those white pocks had started to reappear where the paint had been scuffed, dinged, and chipped away with wear. They should repaint—they could afford to hire someone to do it now, of course. They were too old for that nonsense, and she couldn't see them undertaking that two-day ordeal again. By the end of it, every inch of them had ached as if they'd done a triathlon instead of home décor.

They'd both been covered in paint, not least because with the carpet yet to go in, Marcie and Will had made a game of practicing different brushstroke techniques on each other (*Nice to know my art classes do have some practical applications*, Marcie teased as she made impressionist streaks across Will's forearm) until it had led to the inevitable conclusion and they'd wound up on a drop cloth on that cold concrete floor, smearing it all over each other's bare bodies.

Too old for that nonsense too. Too old for a lot of things.

She curled deeper into the sheets, listening to the shower run in the master bathroom and knowing she had to get up and get ready too or she'd be late for work. She'd already missed two days at the height of event season at the hotel. Chuck was probably on the verge of going supernova from the pressure of trying to handle everything on his own—not that he'd actually had to do that, since he'd been burning up her cell phone with increasingly frantic messages, most recently about the Frazier-Magnussen reception. Mrs. Frazier was determined that her son would have the perfect wedding she'd never had, and most of Marcie's efforts so far had centered around managing the mother of the groom and gently reminding her that the hotel was simply hosting the reception, and any changes to the menu or décor needed to be run by the Magnussens and their wedding planner. Apparently Mrs. Frazier was inflamed to the point that Mr. Magnussen was now calling to complain that the hotel was helping the woman take over his daughter's special day. Marcie needed to put out that fire before it got out of hand.

Will had tried to confiscate her phone when it kept buzzing with work calls and texts—*You need to rest, and they need to give you a break right now*—but she'd argued that ignoring the crises would only make them worse when she got back, and it wasn't as if Chuck or anyone else at the Bonafort knew why she'd suddenly taken two unprecedented personal days. Marcie and Will hadn't exactly been sharing the joyful news. Will wanted her to stay home a few more days too, not try to jump right back into routine but give herself some time "to process." As if she were an antiquated CPU. Marcie just wanted him to stop hovering over her. He'd been a steady presence ever since they got back from the doctor, pulling the covers over her shoulder, rubbing her arm or bringing her a glass of water or making soup that grew cold on the bedside table next to the tarnished silver bell that was part of the Malone family sterling his parents gave them when they were married, two eighteen-year-olds who used paper plates and plastic forks when they entertained. He'd set it there so she didn't have to get up if she needed anything, but she had yet to ring it because all she really wanted at the moment was a little space.

She'd told him after the procedure that he didn't have to stay home with her. *If I need anything I can call Emily,* she'd said, nodding at her cell phone charging on the nightstand. Her mother-in-law lived just three doors down—they'd all bought at the same time after Will's father died, a new neighborhood where they could be close enough for Will and Marcie to keep an eye on Emily—and she would come right over, but Marcie knew she wouldn't call. Emily didn't know about the miscarriage. No one did, because they hadn't told anyone Marcie was pregnant. They hadn't quite gotten used to the news themselves.

I want to stay with you, he'd replied, and he probably meant it, stroking her arm until she put her hand on top of his, trapping his fingers to stop them.

Just go.

It came out sharper than she meant it to, and the wounded look on his face sent a flash of guilt through her. *I'm just going to sleep,* she'd said as a consolation prize. She hadn't wanted to take time off at all, but the doctor advised her to *take things easy on yourself for a little while* and not try to tough out the pain, though there really wasn't any pain so far. The woman had also offered to refer Marcie and Will to a fertility expert—*this is quite common with older parents*—so clearly Dr. Wilkins wasn't exactly an expert at reading the room.

The shower turned off and she watched the moving shadows in the light seeping under the door as Will finished getting ready. She flipped over and assessed the paint wear on the opposite wall.

The bathroom door shushed across the carpet and she smelled Will's Mitchum deodorant on a wash of humid air. Closing her eyes she kept her breathing steady, hoping he'd assume she'd fallen back asleep, but Will knew her rhythms too well.

The dip of the mattress behind her, that relentlessly stroking hand on her shoulder. So nice and solicitous now that the problem was solved. Her eyes opened.

"Marcie . . . if you want to take another day at home, I think—"

She sat up, tapping him on the shoulder as if tagging him out so he'd make room for her to get out of bed. "Nope. Just getting a slow start. You through in the bathroom?"

He stood obligingly, holding out a hand to help her up that she ignored. He rested it on her shoulder when she got to her feet, stopping her, and she could smell his toothpaste as he held her gaze. "Marce . . . sometimes things happen for a reason," he said as he pulled her in for a hug.

Marcie stood inert in his arms, staring at the drywall pattern over his shoulder and clenching her jaw until she could look at him again. "Okay. I'll see you tonight."

In the bathroom she pulled the door shut despite the steam still swirling from Will's shower, and when she finally heard the garage door grind open, the hum of an engine, the garage closing behind his car, she felt her body uncoil as if a spring had been released.

Her phone rang barely fifteen minutes after she got on the road, her late start costing her when she got stuck in rush-hour traffic just before Spaghetti Junction. She glanced down at the screen telling her what she already knew: Chuck.

"Four Hundred is stop and start, but I'm on my way," she answered.

"Oh, thank God," came her assistant's relieved voice. "The flowers for the McConley anniversary party came in and there are gardenias. Gardenias, Marcie!"

Marcie rubbed her forehead, where a throbbing drumbeat was just starting to pulse. At the last minute she'd tossed Dr. Wilkins's pain pills into her purse and maybe she'd take one after all. The McConley children were celebrating their parents' fifty-year anniversary with a party for nearly a hundred friends and family, and Andrea, the eldest daughter, had been carefully particular about the menu, décor, and even the cleaning parameters for the banquet room: "No strong scents—at *all*. My mom has parosmia and is very sensitive to smells." Gardenias were beautiful and elegant, but they smelled like a French cathouse.

"Did we make sure to note that in the florist order?" Marcie asked.

She heard the clicking of a keyboard. "Of course—I have a copy of it pulled up: 'Only unscented arrangements.'"

She let out a breath of relief. "Great. Just call June and let her know we need to replace the centerpieces asap."

There was a beat.

"Chuck?"

"I'm just thinking of how to say it."

She sighed. Chuck was a fantastic assistant event coordinator—careful, organized, and wonderfully personable—but confrontation of any kind made him squirm. "Forget it. I'll be there in forty minutes and I'll call her."

The sedan in front of her had had its blinker on as they'd crept along for the last mile, and the relentless flashing was making Marcie's headache worse. "Go on, buddy," she muttered as a space opened up in the next lane, but he didn't take it, nor the next two he could easily have slid into. She turned her own signal off and on a few times, the way she'd flash her brights at someone to let them know their brights were on, but apparently that semaphore didn't translate.

Traffic eased up enough once she got inside the perimeter so she could get the car up almost to the speed limit, but at this hour she'd get snarled in it again when she got close to town. Atlanta highways were like the veins of an old man who'd lived on nothing but Varsity cheeseburgers all his life.

She mentally ticked through the day's to-do list. Put out the fires first. Check with the catering staff to make sure everything was delivered and on track for this weekend's events. Follow up with two potential clients she wanted to land—another wedding and a very high-end bat mitzvah—and talk to Monique, the front desk manager, about the wedding party's arrival pattern. Plus the usual fielding of new inquiries, meetings, and supplier calls.

Her pounding head made her wish she could leave Chuck to handle all the interactions and work in the Secret Garden to-

day. It wasn't actually called that—or anything, since techni-
cally it wasn't even an official feature of the hotel grounds, but
that was most of what she liked about it. Renaldo had been
head groundskeeper longer than Marcie herself had worked at
the Bonafort—more than twenty years—and in that time his
pet project had been slowly transforming what had been a
gloomy concrete employee patio where the hard-core smokers
used to huddle, using their nicotine addiction to justify extra
breaks, into a bucolic little hideaway. Now it was bordered by
grass and a profusion of plantings Renaldo had transplanted
from clippings taken from the public-facing areas of the grounds.
A broken fountain they'd replaced years ago served as a bird-
bath that drew sparrows, cardinals, and warblers despite their
location so close to downtown. On especially stressful days
Marcie would go sit out there, letting the Georgia sun soak into
her closed eyelids and drowning out the sounds of cars on
Ponce de Leon by focusing on the birdsong and the croaking of
amphibians Renaldo had lured to the area with his "toad holes."

Frogs and toads are important for a garden, but so fragile, he
told her. *They need somewhere dark and cool and safe to tuck
themselves away from dangers, and a little calm water outside the
door.*

You're an artist, Renaldo, she said as he showed her the
chipped ceramic pots discarded from the hotel displays that he'd
turned upside down and used for the purpose, dotting them
amid the landscaping in pleasing ways. *You take found materials
and make them beautiful, not just useful.*

Mr. Hullender used to say the same thing in her high school
art class: *Art takes the ordinary and makes it sublime.* Everyday
life could use a bit more of the sublime, in Marcie's experience,
but a bunch of stoners and jocks looking for an easy A didn't
really seem to vibe to the artistic groove Mr. Hullender faith-

fully tried to create, and Marcie had long ago learned that art was a luxury of youth. The closest she'd come to creativity in the last twenty years was painting the bedroom.

The blare of a horn startled her out of her reverie and she realized she'd almost missed the Monroe exit. Jamming her signal on, she checked her rearview, but a white monster truck rode her right bumper, cutting her off till it was too late.

Dammit. The throbbing in her head seemed to swell down into the sides of her throat. Now she had to fight in-town traffic all the way to Tenth Street, cutting across Midtown and adding at least another thirty minutes to her commute.

Her phone buzzed with a text—Chuck. Even in her car Bluetooth's flat, mechanical voice, she could hear his rising panic: "Where are you? GenComm coordinator says they ordered snack setups—not in the BEO!! She says it was included in bid and won't pay extra—set up or not?!"

The Tenth Street exit was just a mile ahead, but traffic was more stop than go. She could risk a flat or a ticket by riding on the shoulder and get there, but at this point was it worth the few minutes it might save her? She pictured Mindy Kennedy cornering Chuck outside the conference area she'd booked for her telecom company's sales kickoff, the whites of her bugged eyes showing around the irises in emphasis and her arms pinwheeling around the space, demanding the extra setups Marcie knew perfectly well the woman hadn't ordered. She'd been trying to slide in freebies ever since the company first approached the Bonafort about hosting the event. All Chuck had to do was show her the banquet event order Mindy had signed off on, but he hated contradicting a client.

The line of cars in front of her had come to a standstill again, so she picked up her phone to text Chuck back—no sense calling when Mindy was probably standing right there—

but as she did, the string of brake lights in front of her blinked off, a gap opened up in front of her, and Marcie moved forward, putting on her signal for the exit.

She'd handle Mindy when she got there . . . and then call Mr. Magnussen and assure him that only he and his wife and their daughter were authorized to make changes in the wedding plans and that she'd talk to Mrs. Frazier . . . and then she'd handle the McConley centerpieces—this was strike three with June's Blooms, and Marcie would have to find another small-event floral provider—and put out all the other fires that had sprung up in her two unplanned days off. She'd say the usual things to the usual people and go home and have her usual evening with her husband, and do it again tomorrow, and every day till the weekend, when they'd have the usual Sunday dinner with Emily. And next week she'd start all over again. And the next.

Sometimes things happen for a reason.

The memory came with a shocking wave of fury, and the intensity of it pushed her back in the seat like g-forces. She gripped the wheel, Will's words and the pressure of her fisted hands adding to the drumbeat against her skull.

What was the *reason* she and Will had found themselves unexpectedly, accidentally knocked up at forty-three the same way they had when they were eighteen—and that both times it ended in a miscarriage? What was the *reason* that having children wasn't an option for them?

As traffic got up to speed she almost missed her second exit too, the ramp just now forking off to the right.

Sometimes things happen for a reason. The most inane cliché on earth, especially meaningless said between two practical, logical people who didn't subscribe to the notion of a universal order or an all-powerful deity carefully conducting the random orchestra of life. What a stupid, empty thing for her husband to say to her.

Her car was veering off to the right at her exit when at the last second Marcie flipped her blinker to the left, her tires grinding over the rough tarmac dividing the exit lane, and merged back into 75/85 South through-traffic, watching the sign for the Tenth Street exit pass by the passenger window and then blip in her side mirror before slowly vanishing in her rearview.

As cars peeled off on all the downtown exits, traffic thinned until she was almost at the speed limit by the time she passed under I-20 on the south side of town, Atlanta's messy skyline receding behind her and the pressure in her head finally easing.

And Marcie drove.

Flint

The drunk was still there when the sun went down. Still lying on the sand, in the same position as far as he could tell when he thought to look out his window again. Probably strung out too. Seemed like the whole town was buying or selling drugs these days.

What the hell was it about beaches that made people want to fornicate or pass out on them or both? This morning he'd leaned over to pick up a Slim Jim wrapper and an empty beer bottle and put them in the plastic bag he'd long ago taken to carrying with him on his early morning walks along the beach before the sun rose, before the people came. When his foot hit something solid amid the amorphous mass of clothing lumped on the sand and he'd realized what it was, he'd only barely restrained his impulse to prod the body with his shoe.

Over seventy years he'd been here, except for three of them where he'd been in an even worse shit pile, and of all that had changed, what he noticed the most was the trash. They always left it, the tourists—he spit the word in his mind like an epithet—but over the years it had evolved. When he was a kid he'd found wrappers from Necco Wafers and Love Nest bars, Bireley's orange drink bottles, and condoms, each piece like a character in a story telling him something about the person who'd cast it off. He'd try to picture each item in use—who had been using it, who they were with, where they came from.

Then it was Fun Dip and Space Dust envelopes, Fanta Grape cans, and condoms, now seeming less interesting. Not pieces of a mystery but useless remnants of lives left behind for someone else to clean up. Later empty sandwich bags and plastic six-pack rings and pop tabs and condoms, then bottle caps and more condoms, long after it had ceased to matter what the garbage was and who had left it, only that they had, and littered his beach.

In the early afternoon he'd poured the remainder of his fourth cup of coffee into the kitchen sink as he stared through the window at the drunk still crumpled on the sand beneath the stippled shade of a palm tree. Coffee was about the greatest beverage in the world—with two or three piquant and forbidden exceptions—but after enough of it the tongue grew bitter and coated and the stomach rebelled. When the appeal of coffee paled was still the gut-wrenching time of the day he'd kill his child for a sweet scotch on the rocks.

So to speak.

He'd made lunch for himself—cheese and a box of crackers, with an apple afterward for fiber—and gone back to his book.

He hadn't looked anywhere after that but up into the ass end of the bathroom sink, wedging himself underneath the cabinet till his back screamed at him and his arms felt like they'd break if he tried to keep them up any longer, and still the damn pipes kept up their steady drip, drip, dripping that had already started a cancerous bloom of mold and rot at the back corner of the wood. He finally levered himself out, smelling like mildew and covered in a wet paste of the boric acid he'd put down to keep the roaches out, aching like a damned old woman, the plumbing no better off than before he'd wasted two hours of his life trying to fix what was long past the stage of repair.

When he made dinner later, as the sun grew low in the sky and hovered above the water, the drunk was still there, still in the same spot, and as he ate his soup from the pan he'd heated it up in, standing at the kitchen window looking at its shape on the sand, he began to wonder if the body was, in fact, a dead one.

Wouldn't be his first one of those either, but that was where he drew the line at cleanup. He finished his soup, washed out the pan, and carried the empty can to the recycle bin in the carport on his way back out to the beach.

The first thing he noticed was that the body was a woman— wearing, of all things, a skirt and a flimsy little blouse. The second was that she was breathing, if shallowly, and so he turned around to go back to his house, satisfied she'd move on after she'd slept off whatever crap she'd put into herself the night before.

Unless someone had done this to her. Those damn date-rape drugs had found their way to this beach along with every other kind of poison that laced its deadbeat inhabitants. But that still wasn't his problem. He'd call an ambulance for her and leave her to the people who were paid to help.

He walked back to the woman and bent over her, poking two fingers into the tangle of hair at her neck to find her pulse. You weren't supposed to move people who might be injured. You'd just do more damage. And then you were involved too. He thought all this as he squatted to get his arms under her—she was tiny—and lifted her up despite the twinge in his back. He thought it as he heard a clink as a set of keys fell from her pocket to the sand and squatted again to pick them up, along with a pair of heels—heels!—discarded on the sand, and he thought it all the while he walked back to his house with his latest gathering from the beach.

Marcie

Her head hurt. It wasn't the least of her discomfort, but it was the one Marcie concentrated on as she squeezed her eyes tight, not wanting to open them yet. She could reach out and ring the little silver bell, ask Will to get her an ibuprofen.

But he would hover, smothering her with solicitousness, and wouldn't let her go back to sleep, and that was the only thing she wanted.

Her mouth felt pasted shut, dry and rank, her tongue too big inside it. Her face was tight and hot. Did she have a fever?

"You trying to kill yourself, or are you just stupid?"

Marcie's eyes shot open at the raspy voice of a stranger.

She wasn't in her bedroom. Instead of their heavy damask bedspread (a compromise for the impractical linen she'd wanted), an age-worn blue blanket covered her where she lay on a sofa. An old man sat in a green velvet armchair across from her in an unfamiliar room, staring at her with no expression. His hair was wiry and gray, his face rough and sun-beaten and pulled into a myriad of furrows.

She should get up, something registered in her brain as memory seeped back in. She should shoot to her feet and into a defensive stance. That was what you did when you found yourself in a strange place, a strange situation, maybe a dangerous one. You prepared to fight or flee. But it seemed like a convention from another world—meaningless in this one. This one where she could just curl up on this ratty old sofa and go back to sleep. Let the man do whatever it was he planned to do.

"The hell did you take?" the man barked, forcing her eyes open again.

"Take?" It came out only with an effort.

"What were you *on*," he said. "Do you know?"

She shook her head, wanting to say she wasn't on the kind of drugs he was talking about—wasn't on any kind of drugs at the moment, unfortunately. She'd started dry-swallowing ibuprofen somewhere around Valdosta and again past Port Charlotte with another dose of the hydrocodone, the hours in the car finally bringing on the cramping and pain Dr. Wilkins had promised. But they had clearly long since worn off, and she'd tossed the bottles back into her purse. Which was where? She couldn't remember what she'd done with it and it seemed like too much effort to sit up and look around.

Or to explain to this forbidding old man how she got here. Wherever "here" was.

What would she say even if she did? *Instead of going in to work today I drove straight down I-75 for absolutely no reason. And when I realized I needed gas in Lake City, I thought that as long as I was in Florida I might as well go to the beach, so I kept driving till I wound up . . .* Where? What town had she ended up in? There had been a sign that sounded like somewhere pretty . . . Something Key? She couldn't remember now—by then she'd just wanted to get to the ocean while the sun was still out, so she'd exited and followed the signs hoping for a beach—somewhere she could just sit and *think*.

The road had narrowed from six lanes to four and then funneled her onto a dated concrete bridge, and the Gulf of Mexico spanned out before her gray, flat, and featureless—just one more disappointment. With a dirty bank of clouds shifting over the sun, the sea didn't shimmer with diamond light so much as glint like the glass from a broken car window in the reflected illumination of a streetlight. The bridge dumped her onto a sole potholed road running along the little spit of land studded with run-down businesses and weathered cracker-box houses, a few midrise hotels popping up among them like acne, tiny public-beach access areas tucked away here and there. Marcie had parked the Acura in a vacant space in one of them, turning off the engine and sitting in anticlimactic silence in the car till it grew suffocatingly hot. *Well. Might as well see it.*

She'd walked along the beach for a while in her skirt and blouse, the sleeves rolled up against the stifling moist heat and her work pumps dangling from her fingers, the sand scratching her bare feet like a cat's tongue. The blanket of humidity stole her energy, making her a little dizzy, and when her legs wore out from pushing into the soft sand she sat in the scant shade of some palm trees clustered about fifty feet from the shore, watching the lackluster tide go out, the water gradually seeping away as if down a clogged drain.

As the water started to turn golden and then orange she realized, surprised, how late it was. Will would be home any minute. She'd texted him when she stopped to gas up in Lake City, but all she'd said was that she'd be home tomorrow—it wouldn't be the first time she'd stayed at the hotel after working late—right before she'd texted Chuck, **I'm not coming in this week after all**, and then turned her cell phone off to avoid his frantic phone calls that were sure to follow.

Now she remembered leaving the phone in the trunk of the car with her purse for safekeeping. She'd thought to just rest on the cool sand where she sat for a few minutes—it was still and quiet, the first time she'd felt peaceful in weeks, and she'd wandered farther than she realized and was so *tired*. When she caught her breath she'd walk back to the car and call Will. Explain . . . what? That she'd just been having a really bad day? What had she been thinking? She'd find a decent hotel and call him, then head back tomorrow, though she hadn't brought an overnight bag or even a change of clothes.

That was the last thing she remembered before waking up here, in this beat-up living room.

A loose, sickening fluttering began behind her rib cage, into her stomach. People didn't just leave like that, with no notice, no plan. They didn't pull a spontaneous no-show at work and drive aimlessly till they finally curled up on a beach and woke up in an unfamiliar room with a hostile stranger. That wasn't *normal*.

The old man looked disgusted. "That's great. Just looking for a thrill, I guess. Aren't you thrilled?" He shook his head. "You got a car, or you want me to call a cab for you? You should probably go to the hospital, but I'm guessing you won't."

"No . . . hospital," Marcie managed, her voice peculiar in her ears. How long had she been passed out on that beach?

"Yeah. Okay." He looked at her for a few moments more, then spoke again. "You can use the phone, you want to, you got someone to call. Otherwise, this isn't a hotel."

Oh, God. She had to call Will. He must be worried . . . probably thinking she'd lost her mind. She pushed back the blanket to sit up, her head feeling unanchored, as if it might spin away off her body.

Glancing at the ancient rotary-dial phone on the table beside the worn armchair, she couldn't fathom using it to call her husband in front of the disdainful old man who sat inches away. Couldn't imagine him hearing her sheepishly confessing to Will this stupid, impulsive thing she'd done—confirming the man's contemptuous dismissal of her.

She should ask where she was, though. Who he was. Some remnant of politeness told her she should at least thank him for apparently helping her out. But it all seemed like so much effort, and he didn't seem eager to make any further conversation.

Her keys were on the plain wooden trunk in front of her. She picked them up and pushed her feet into her practical low heels on the floor beneath them. When she stood, darkness swirled over her vision, and for a second she thought she'd fall down. But she held herself still until her sight cleared and she could see the man still sitting motionless in his chair; then she let herself out the battered screen door next to the sofa.

She must have walked farther than she thought, because by the time she made it back to the public-beach access where she'd parked the car—*dear God, was it* yesterday?—the sun was nearly straight overhead, the heat pressing down on her like a sweaty fist. A few vehicles were scattered around the lot, hazed with salt and sand. But the Acura wasn't one of them. Disbelieving, she checked the lot number—Access 23, which had stuck in her mind because it was the day of their anniversary: June 23—and looked around again, but her car had either been stolen or towed.

With her purse inside. With her phone.

She walked to the empty spot where the Acura had been and stood there for a moment at a loss, her breathing coming in fast, short pants. Why hadn't she called from the man's house? Taken him up on his begrudging offer and asked Will to come get her? *You can use the phone . . . you got someone to call.*

The old man said it like probably she didn't. Like she was some kind of trash washed up on shore, a derelict with nothing. She could feel her hair hanging limp against the tight, sun-dried burn of her face, smell her own stench rising from the thin silk of her wrinkled blouse that was stuck to her skin with sweat, and thought how absurd it was that at the moment he was right.

She left the empty space where her car used to be and crossed over the short boardwalk back to the beach. Sinking to the sand and pressing her forehead to her knees, Marcie felt the fervid sun lance into her skin and wished the tide would slowly wash her out to sea.

Flint

The living room was dim—most days in the season he didn't bother opening the curtains, just to be safe—and the artificial dusk combined with the white noise of the AC units had lulled him into a waking trance, his eyes closed and his mind wandering into not-quite dreams.

Jessie was on the sofa opposite him, slumped into one corner like a discarded banana peel. Her skin was wrinkled like the ripples of sand left in a dried-out tidal pool. Only her eyes looked normal—huge in her desiccated head like a china doll's, staring wetly at him.

Fill 'er up, she said from her cracked mouth as if he were a gas station attendant, and his heart slammed against his ribs like a caged madman trying to get out, so loud he could hear it pounding, pounding. . . .

He woke with a sharp sucking in of breath, straightening in the chair, looking frantically around the empty living room in the circle of light the small lamp on the side table cast into the gloom.

Jesus. Jesus braying Christ.

He put a hand to his chest and felt his heart slow, the book in his lap spilling to the floor with the movement. How had he slipped into a fog of half consciousness in the middle of a chapter? Naps were for babies. Or geriatrics. But sleep had been elusive at night lately. It always was, this time of year.

Those eyes.

He hurled himself away from the image of them, leaning over for the book and cursing at the twinge in his back that forced him to remember to go slow.

A *tap, scratch* this time, clearly not coming from his chest, and he realized there was someone at the door. He snapped the book closed with a sharp crack and banged it onto the side table. *Go away. Not buying.*

The slow creak of the rickety screen door let him hope the intruder was giving up . . . but then another knock—delicate and polite, but relentless. A line flashed into his head, one from an old story he'd read out loud so many times he'd memorized most of it—"a knock came so quiet and stealthy as to be scarcely audible." *A rat,* the old man in the story had insisted in a shaky voice, knowing what was on the other side of that door because of his wife's foolish wish on a magical monkey paw. *For God's sake don't let it in.*

But like the grief-crazed wife in the story, Flint pushed himself up and toward the door, dragging back the bolt.

The girl from the beach stood there, looking every bit as bedraggled and pathetic as she had when she'd left a few hours before. A different revenant. It was on his tongue to send her away, to slam the door in her face, when she spoke in that odd, thin voice of hers.

"I don't know where to go," she said. And then she fainted on his doorstep.

This was why you never got involved, he told himself as he leaned down for the second time to pick the girl up from the ground. Now he had this creature on his hands, though he'd have liked to shut the door and call an ambulance to come get her where she lay. Again he was struck by how little she weighed, as though she were hollow.

He put her back on the sofa. She looked like hell—straggly hair, skin burned red and pulled tight from too much sun, lips chapped, clothes wrinkled and dirty. A discarded rag doll.

He could call 911 and let them take her off her hands, as he should have done any number of times already. But he didn't need the questions that might be raised by a girl young enough to be . . . well, she was a grown woman, wasn't she? . . . being medevaced out of his living room, after who knew what had happened to her. It was a mess of his own making, and he couldn't even have the satisfaction of blaming anyone else for it.

If she died on him things would only get worse, so he'd have to at least do what he could for her. He went outside to his scraggly garden and broke off a piece of aloe vera. Inside the house he split it with his pocketknife and wiped its sticky fluid all over her face and lips. The uncomfortable intimacy of it made his hands clumsy, swiping his fingers in jerky movements over her skin, but she didn't move. He went into the kitchen and filled a coffee cup with tap water, then shook his head in disgust at the sulfur smell of it, poured it into the sink, and re-filled the glass from the filtered pitcher in the refrigerator.

She wouldn't rouse when he prodded her, so he palmed the back of her head to raise it up and held the cup to her lips, tipping it into her mouth until she sputtered and swallowed reflexively. She gave a few more weak swallows before he couldn't get her to take any more, and he lowered her back to the sofa. Her skin was hot. He soaked a cotton cloth in the tea he'd brewed earlier, cold from the refrigerator, and laid it over the worst of the burn on her face.

He sat back in his chair opposite where she lay, exactly where she'd been the last time he'd stupidly brought her inside. Like his dream, he realized. He stood back up and took off the now-lukewarm towels, applied more aloe, then made her drink again. Nothing more he could do for her. He picked up his book and went to his bedroom.

The other presence behind the walls at his back created a disturbance that felt wrong, "off," like a footprint marring a fresh-washed stretch of sand, and he realized with a jolt that it had been years since another human being had set foot inside his house.

He knew the kind of drifters who washed up in shithole tourist towns like this all by their lonesome. This one didn't have the look, with her diamond wedding ring and fancy clothes, her brown hair's fake frosted edges, unnaturally white crescents painted on the tips of her shiny nails. What had happened to her?

It didn't matter. It wasn't his problem.

With a sharp creak he snapped his book open and determinedly started to read.

Marcie

She was having the identical dream again—right down to the battered sofa with the threadbare blue blanket over her, a grim-faced stranger watching her from a chair.

I'm not going to have you die here, the man said.

She gasped and opened her eyes to the same living room she'd woken up in once already—same single lamp next to the mangy velvety chair, turned off now, the corners in shadows from the thin streaks of light sneaking in around the edges of the heavy curtains on the room's sole window above her head.

Not a dream.

But she was alone. Had she only imagined the old man? Or had she imagined leaving before, her car vanished?

She blinked, looking around and trying to orient herself, as though that would somehow tell her how she'd wound up here on this sofa again, though she had a vague memory of finding her way back to the squat, sad little house just before the dark edges of her vision had closed in.

There was no sign of the man now, and she took in her sur-
roundings the way she hadn't bothered to before. Everything was
heavy and gloomy, old—surfaces glazed with dust, edges rounded
with age, scarred with use. Against two walls were built-in bookshelves crammed helter-skelter with hardcover books without dust
jackets, their top and bottom bindings faded and bent inward. The
only furnishings were the ancient tweed sofa she lay on, the velvet
chair, the battered end table and lamp beside it, and an old wooden
trunk being utilized as a cocktail table, but the room was small and
gave the impression of being overfull. Her keys once again lay next
to her on the trunk, a coffee cup half-filled with water beside them,
shoes again tumbled on the worn carpet.

The whole room could have fit inside her kitchen. Their
kitchen where right now—what time was it?—Will was probably
freaking out about Marcie's disappearance. If he'd told Emily—
would he have?—she'd be bustling around furiously, uselessly
baking brownies or a cake, not because she thought it would offer
comfort to her son, but because it offered some to *her*. Marcie's
mother-in-law always baked away unpleasant emotions.

Maybe that was what Marcie should have tried.

She pushed herself up a few inches, realizing that she had
to call Will. How would she explain her ridiculous impulse to
drive to the beach, let alone how she'd passed out from . . .
what—dehydration, overmedication, not eating? And been literally picked up off the beach by a total stranger. This was
Will's ultimate nightmare scenario—rash actions that left you
helpless and vulnerable. If he knew the situation she'd put herself in, she'd validate his every cautionary tale.

Suddenly desperately thirsty, she greedily brought the mug
to her lips, some of its liquid sloshing onto her fingers. The water was warm in a room that was uncomfortably cool—it had
been sitting here a while. Where was the old man?

She couldn't wait to ask for permission. With effort she got to her feet and stumbled over to the armchair where he'd been sitting before, the cushion under her concave and sprung, and reached for the receiver of the heavy relic of a phone.

No dial tone. She jiggled the little plastic knobs that held the receiver, bobbling them up and down like a 1950s movie heroine, but the ancient rotary was dead. For all she knew, it was just decoration, an antique put out for effect, but judging from the lack of effort put into anything else in the room it was hard to imagine the old man worrying about clever home décor.

She'd ask to use his cell phone as soon as she found him— but pressure in her bladder told her she'd better find a bathroom first. She thought to call out for her angry rescuer and host, but what would she say? *Old man? Are you there?* They hadn't exactly performed introductions.

Her legs felt untrustworthy under her, so she held a hand against either side of the sole narrow hallway on her left, passing two closed doors as she made her way toward one at the end that was ajar, revealing a sink and a toilet. Maybe the man was behind one of those doors—she'd knock on her way back—but who was behind the other?

She shut the bathroom door and lowered herself heavily to the ancient bowl, a thin blue towel over a rack across from the toilet almost brushing Marcie's knees. The cold tile floor under her bare feet was a faded khaki green, cracked in a dozen places. The shower curtain was the same color, mildew and streaks testifying to its having overstayed its tenure.

She flushed when she was finished and leaned over the sink to wash her hands. Next to an amorphous blob of soap in a chipped dish was a mismatched pile of neatly folded threadbare towels, and Marcie stared at them as she soaped and rinsed her hands, then lifted a washcloth from the top of the stack. Drying her hands slowly, deliberately, she stared in the mirror at the peeling red face of a stranger she wouldn't have recognized twenty-four hours ago, her eyes puffy, her hair lank and dirty. *Jesus.* Will was right—everyone was always just a few bad decisions away from being completely undone. She pressed the damp towel to her hot face.

Out in the hallway, she knocked softly on first one door, then the other across the hall from it, but heard nothing from inside. There was no sign of anyone in the tired old house, like she'd woken up in some B-movie twilight zone, but then she heard an abrupt creak and clatter from the main area.

As she came into the little galley kitchen, with its single window over the sink overlooking a back porch and the flat old-dime glint of the gulf, she saw him standing at the yellow Formica counter, his back to her, pouring from a silver percolator into a chunky mug. The rich scent of coffee overpowered even the base-note smell of the house—a dank must as though something old inside the walls were slowly rotting away—and suddenly she craved a cup of it like air.

Hearing her approach, he turned and stared forbiddingly at her, as if she were an intruder. In the silence, her mouth dry, she sought for the proper words to say when the stranger who'd pulled your unconscious body off the beach found you wandering around loose in his house.

"You in trouble?"

The question, more bark than speech, startled her. She instinctively shook her head.

He kept his uncomfortable gaze on her face. "I got no reason to believe you." He took a step toward her and she registered that maybe she should be alarmed—she didn't know this man, after all, didn't know his intentions toward her. But she found herself just staring back at him.

He turned his back to her again, opened a cabinet at his right shoulder, pulled down a mug and filled it from the pot, then offered it to her wordlessly.

She took it automatically, its warmth and scent instantly comforting. "Who are you?" she rasped out, her voice scratchy.

"Who are *you*?"

"Marcie . . . Malone." She'd caught herself before she ridiculously almost said *Jones*, as if the last twenty-five years had never happened.

"Flint."

Marcie didn't know if that was his first or last name—or a name at all—but she nodded. She cleared her throat to work the gravel out of it. "Is there cream?"

The old man just stared at her.

"Sorry." She took a sip of black coffee that burned its way down her esophagus like a bitter comet, but it felt good. "I was hoping to take you up on your offer to use the phone, but I couldn't get a dial tone . . . ?"

He gave an indifferent shrug. "Could be I missed a bill. Don't have much need for a landline."

"Oh. Well, could I use your cell for a quick call, then?"

"Don't have *any* need for a cell phone."

Good God. The old man lived here in the House That Time Forgot with literally no connection to the outside world? What if someone needed to reach him? What if he had an emergency? She hadn't even seen a computer anywhere, though surely he had at least a laptop secreted away behind one of the closed doors in the hallway. Judging by his sunny personality, people probably weren't lining up to get in touch, but still . . .

"I need to call my husband. I need to tell him"—*that I'm not dead on the roadside somewhere, or abducted, or involuntarily committed to a mental institution, though it's becoming increasingly obvious that maybe I should be.* "I need to check in with him," she redirected. "Is there a pay phone nearby?"

That flat gaze again, as though she were a cockroach crawling across his floor. "Might be. Guess you'll have to go find out."

Her fingers contracted around the mug of coffee, the first thing she could remember putting in her stomach besides painkillers in a couple of days. She'd be fine. She just needed to get to a phone and call Will and everything would be fine. But clearly the prickly old man—Flint—wanted her out of his house, for good this time, and in fairness he'd done more than he had to.

"Okay, then that's what I'll do," she said, stepping close enough to set the mug in the sink beside him.

His face contracted and he pulled his head back. "Take a shower, girl. You smell like a bag of smashed assholes." He stalked out of the kitchen back toward the living room, and a moment later Marcie heard the closing of a door.

She didn't know the first thing about this man, and she was standing in his kitchen drinking coffee as though she were a morning-after lover rather than a complete stranger who hadn't exchanged more than a handful of words with the house's owner—most of them startlingly hostile. She raised an arm and sniffed— *Oh, God.* She couldn't go home like this.

She almost let out a hysterical laugh as the ludicrousness of her situation bubbled up her throat.

What was there to do right now except what the man said—take a shower?

She could only stand the water lukewarm—any hotter than that and it scalded her sunburned face and forearms and calves—but the feeling of sluicing off the sweat and salt and stench she'd marinated in was almost sensual. The ugly green tub desperately needed resurfacing, the grout was so antiquated and dirty she couldn't even hazard a guess as to its original color, and the nondescript bar of soap smelled a little bit like castor oil, but it rivaled the best spa treatment she'd ever had for sheer satisfaction. When she turned the water off and reached for the stack of thin, frayed towels on the bathroom counter she discovered a faded blue men's cotton shirt folded at the bottom. She pulled it on once she dried off, along with the bra and gray pencil skirt that were all she had. The shirt was soft but carried no scent. Her filthy skirt made up for it. She couldn't even bear to think about putting her underwear back on, instead washing it in the sink with the white lump of generic soap and wringing it as dry as she could before balling it up in her fist. Once she figured out what she was doing next, she'd find a way to let it air-dry so she could at least wear it home. She might show up disheveled, dehydrated, sun-fried, and contrite, but by God she drew the line at commando.

The stupid thought made those deranged giggles well up her throat again like soap bubbles.

Clapping a hand over her mouth, she looked at herself in the mirror, her eyes huge and disturbing in her skull, like that horrible doll she'd found at the back of a shelf at a Goodwill as a little girl on one of their trips for school clothes and begged her mom for. Little Miss No-Name, Marcie recalled, a zombie-looking waif in a shapeless burlap sack of a dress that probably gave a whole generation of little girls screaming nightmares. It was so awful Marcie had loved it, keeping the pathetic-looking doll in a place of honor on her bed. With her limp hair and haunted eyes and in the oversize shirt, Marcie looked just like that creepy doll—like a drifter washed up on the shores of some strange town, a piece of flotsam on the beach.

And isn't that kind of what you are at the moment?

That odd fluttering quivered in her belly again, like the first beat of butterfly wings still wet from the cocoon.

She closed her eyes to avoid her reflection. What would it be like to be the terse old man on the other side of the door? Living right on the beach in this time-frozen old house, waking with the sun, nothing expected of him, no demands except what he wanted to do: walk on the sand, read his books, drink his coffee?

It sounded . . . peaceful. The opportunity of that. The freedom. Like being eighteen again, with all the choices still in front of her.

Her eyes shot open. Naked of makeup, her sun-reddened face highlighted a starburst of white creases beside her eyes, a soft tracing across her forehead like the guiding lines of a spiral notebook.

This was ridiculous. She had a husband. A job. Responsibilities. People who would be worried about her. What was she thinking?

Call Will.

Of course she had to call Will. He would track down her car and she could go home and put this ridiculousness behind her.

In a drawer next to Flint's sink she found a comb, a toothbrush, and a tube of toothpaste. She ran the comb through her tangled hair, then rinsed it under the water, dried it off, and returned it to its place. Squeezing a line of toothpaste onto her finger, she did her best to scrub off the funk of two days.

Then she headed out to thank the terse old man and go find a phone.

Flint

The air was heavy with humidity and a marine smell he could never find the right words to describe, a mix of seagrass and fish and ocean. He leaned back in a wicker chair that was coming unwoven, his feet up on the weathered wood enclosing the deck and a book in his hands, open but unread. When he heard the girl open the back door, he snapped it shut and brought his feet to the floor with a clomp.

"Excuse me, Mr. Flint. I just wanted to—"

"Sit down."

She didn't look much better after a shower. Still sunburned and chapped, and swimming in his shirt and that ridiculous impractical skirt, her hair wet, she seemed even more pathetic than she did before. Looking as if she were startled to be obeying, she let herself fully out onto the deck and sat in the only other chair, hard green plastic.

"What kind of trouble are you in?"

"What? I'm not—"

"Bullshit. Don't mess with me, girl. I've been dealing with liars longer than you've been alive. You can tell me the truth, or I'll call the cops and let you explain it to them. Your choice."

She actually laughed, and the sound sent a blaze of fury through him. The hell with this. This was a problem he didn't need. Flint shoved himself up from the chair, biting down on a groan from his twingeing back.

"Wait—I'm sorry."

He ignored her, heading toward the back door.

"I'm not in any legal trouble, if that's what you're asking. I just needed a break."

The explanation was so pedestrian, so ludicrous under the circumstances, that it actually stopped his steps.

Turning around to glare at her, he shook his head. "Jesus. Jesus sunstroking Christ. You needed a *break*? From what, whatever cotillion you were on your way to?" He waved at her fancy little skirt.

Her eyebrows went up. "Yes, I headed here straight from my debutante ball. I'm a late bloomer."

"Don't be a smart-ass, girl. You got any idea what coulda happened to you out on that beach? This isn't the goddamn Riviera. It's a sandpit full of drunks and drug dealers and the occasional murderer. Got shrimpers coming in off the boats who wouldn't think twice about helping themselves to a homeless piece of ass on the beach." He wanted to shock her, with her fancy diamond wedding ring and her coffee with cream and her stupid naiveté, but she just nodded.

"You're right. I don't know what I was . . ." She trailed off, staring out over the sea, her eyes following a bird that had been circling lazily overhead as it suddenly pulled its wings to its sides and shot down into the water like a bullet. The abrupt shift in trajectory seemed to shake her out of her trance and she pushed herself up from the chair, the plastic making a harsh sound as it scraped across the weathered wood of the deck. "I'm going to head back, obviously. I just wanted to thank you for helping me. I'll get out of your hair."

She moved toward the back door, her mouth set in a mix of resignation and determination.

"Slow your roll, fancy pants," he barked. "What brought you here?"

She opened her mouth like she was used to having a quick answer, then stopped with a startled expression. "I don't know. I just needed to get away."

"Well, where you from?" He worked hard to keep the impatience from his tone.

"Georgia. Atlanta. Dunwoody, actually."

Huh. *Dunwoody.* It even sounded pretentious. "You got a family?"

"Yes. No. I didn't really want to go to them."

He was the last person who'd argue with that. "Friends?"

She shrugged. He got that too.

"Someone take your money?"

"It was in my purse. Which is in my car. Which I think got towed."

"What are you running from?"

He'd thought to ambush an honest answer out of her with the abrupt question, but the girl sat silent for a moment, thinking about it, before she responded. "I think my husband."

For a moment he just stared at her, sure he'd misheard. She wore a similar expression, as if she couldn't quite believe the words had come out of her mouth.

"Goddammit, girl—this is all about some marital spat?"

At his raised voice he heard the familiar squeal of hinges, and the nosy biddy next door popped her face out through the crack in the screen door on her back porch. Her mouth fell slack when she saw him standing on his deck with a young woman whose fall of straight blond-streaked hair hung down her back. He knew what she was thinking and he'd put a stop to that.

"Mind your damn business!" he barked with a hard stare.

The girl jumped at his harsh tone, spinning to see who he was shouting at, and as soon as the intrusive old battle-ax saw her face Flint was dimly gratified when she slinked back inside and the door fell shut after her. When would the woman learn to keep her beak out of his life?

When he looked back at the girl she was regarding him with widened eyes. "I guess that's one way to handle a nosy neighbor," she said neutrally.

"What're you going to do now?"

She took a deep, long breath. "I need to call my husband."

He should have been overjoyed, personally ushered her to a phone and out of his life. But her eyes bothered him. Flat and sad, like the light had gone out behind them. A thousand-yard stare.

Like Jessie. At the end.

The memory bothered him. He didn't like a reminder of her in his house, underfoot, within sight, and it annoyed him that this intruder in his life made her cross his mind. He needed to just step aside and let this girl wander on out of here. She wasn't his problem.

"Look, Mr. Flint, I got myself into a bit of a jam and you really helped me. It was nice of you—more than that, actually. Thank you." She tried for a polite smile, as if they were saying their farewells at a cocktail party.

What the hell was she going to do, take herself out of here and go back to a situation that had been bad enough to send her to this shithole town and wind up in the condition she was in? She'd already told him she had nowhere else she felt she could go.

"What are you doing, girl?"

"I'm—"

"Rhetorical question. You know what that means? You don't answer it."

He looked out over the water, which was a muddy silver green like it usually was, filled with the crud sent on from the people upriver who never thought to care about what the garbage they threw into the Caloosahatchee did to the rest of the food chain.

Don't compound stupid with more stupid. He used to tell Jessie that whenever she got herself into a pickle and then made it worse trying to fix things before he found out—like the time she spilled nail polish all over the rug in her room and then tried to clean it with acetone. Next time he went in there the whole place reeked like a toxic dump, and she told him she liked the nightstand in the middle of the room because it was convenient from anywhere. Brazen little thing.

He shook away the memory. That was enough of that.

He didn't know which one of them was worse—this girl for being determined to take herself back to something bad enough to make her run, or him for what he was about to do. But the thought of her out there when she seemed so damned fragile underneath all that guff . . .

"Don't get in my way," he finally said. "Don't talk to me when I'm reading. Don't change things around. You can stay till you figure out something else; then you go. Don't be here any longer than you have to."

This time when he turned to go back into the house he kept going, already thinking he'd made a huge mistake. *Don't compound stupid with more stupid.* Hopefully this girl would show more sense than he had and take herself on out of here after all.

But when he looked out the kitchen window a few minutes later, filling the carafe for yet another pot of coffee, she was still standing where he'd left her, looking out over the ocean.

Marcie

~~~~

The whole point in going back out to talk to the difficult old man—because it certainly wasn't for his peppy conversation—was to take her leave and go find a phone to make a quick direct call: *Will. I need help.*

Because no matter what, regardless of everything else, that was what Will did: He fixed things, took care of them—took care of *her*. Perfect, infallible care of her for her entire adult life—since they were eighteen years old and Marcie's heart had dropped like a brick the first time they saw those two pink lines.

Will had stood guard underneath the stands an hour after baseball practice ended, the sun filtering down through the metal slats of the seats as Marcie peed on the stick. It was the only place they could think of where their parents wouldn't find out—if her mom even saw her buying the tests, she'd have lost her mind.

She'd been so certain the little window was going to be blank, because even though she'd skipped a period, she felt fine—no sickness, no different even. And because bad things didn't happen to her. Not since Will. Will was the good thing that overrode every other bad thing.

But she felt like she was going to throw up as her frozen stare fixed on the little window a few minutes later, as they moved to sit on the bleachers next to the empty baseball diamond, and the two awful pink lines had formed clear as Magic Marker. *My mother's going to kill me* was the first thing that ran through her head. And then . . . *Spain.* She was supposed to leave right after graduation.

Mr. Hullender had encouraged her to apply for a study-abroad program at the Prado Museum—and somehow she'd won one of the internships. Marcie had an eye, the art teacher told her. The kind of discernment that might one day lead her to galleries and museums in the art world as a curator or buyer. She'd had visions of strolling the cobbled streets and plazas of Madrid, lazy afternoon siestas, late nights in smoky bars with painters and sculptors and photographers, talking about art history and theory until the sky turned amber.

We can't afford that, her mother had said when Marcie burst into the apartment bubbling with the news the day she'd found out.

The program pays for everything, Mom. All we have to do is come up with the plane ticket and enough money for food—they even house the interns.

And who's gonna pay for that?

So Marcie picked up as many extra waitressing shifts as she could, even the closing shifts, though some nights it meant she got less than three hours of sleep before school the next day.

Will had been proud of her, but as the trip grew closer she could tell he was worried. *Three months is such a long time where you don't know anyone, and you don't even speak the language.*

Hey, yo parlez *the* español *real good,* she joked. Two years of Spanish for her foreign-language requirement wouldn't lead to any deep philosophical debates, but she was confident she could get by.

But Will didn't laugh. *Is it safe for a woman on her own?*

I'm not on my own—there are six of us, and we're free labor for the museum, so we're probably going to be stuck in the basement twenty hours a day, cataloging the collections. Safer than here. She touched his face. *This could take me somewhere, Will. A credit like this might actually lead to a job in the arts.* Her mother couldn't see the point of dreaming about a career that was so difficult to make a living in . . . but Marcie could.

He'd pulled her close. *Don't forget about me with all those Latin lovers.*

And that was really what it was about, she realized. She wrapped her arms around him, buried her face in the soft skin of his neck. How could she forget Will? How could she ever? *They can't hold a candle to my Southern boy,* she whispered fiercely.

But those dreams were over with those two pink lines. Marcie sure as hell wasn't ready for a kid—all she knew about babies was that they cried seemingly all the time and couldn't tell you why, and that they seemed terrifyingly fragile. Will's parents didn't want him to work to make sure he could keep his grades up even with his football schedule, and they sure couldn't ask either of their parents for money for an abortion. They'd have to use what she'd saved up for Spain.

What felt like five minutes before, her biggest concerns had been getting someone to cover her Saturday hostess shift at

Applebee's so she could make it to Will's tryouts, and whether she could somehow save enough money before her trip so Will could fly out to Madrid and they could travel together through Europe before she came back home, the former probably why the latter wound up not mattering—Will made the team and they were so pumped up that in the primal fervor of their cele-bratory rutting, they hadn't noticed until too late that the con-dom had slipped off and out.

Fat, hot tears had sprung out of her eyes like a hose left partway on.

"Hey," Will said. "Hey. Come on, now." He put one arm around her, covering the stick with his other hand even though it still had her pee on it, blocking it from her sight. "It's okay, Marcie. Everything's going to turn out okay."

"It's not," she said vehemently, the words coming out on a sob. "This changes *everything. Ruins* it."

As if she sat on her other side, her mother's words sounded in her ear: *Men don't stay around when the going gets tough. . . .* It was the litany of her childhood since her dad walked out after another fight when Marcie was eight, leaning down to hug his daughter. *Your mama's making things too hard on me, kiddo,* he murmured with a jaunty wink that made Marcie think every-thing was actually going to be all right, until after a few months she realized he wasn't coming back.

Marcie swore she'd never be her mother, who drowned her-self in bitterness sitting on the sofa, eating her pain away, and the dreams Marcie had for herself sure as hell didn't include a kid. No time soon anyway. But they did include Will Malone—that much she knew with a soul-deep certainty. And getting knocked up in high school was about as tough as the going could get.

But Will took the stick out of her hand and capped it, then leaned back to put it in his front pocket. He wiped his hands along his jeans, back and forth, back and forth, and then he gathered her hands in both of his as if they were precious things that might break.

"Marcie," he said, so calm, "we're eighteen. Adults."

She'd only cried harder. "You don't get it. I wanted—"

He went on as if she hadn't spoken. "We're gonna get married, Marcie. We're gonna have a kid. All this changes is when." He gave that crooked grin she loved, the one that made her heart belong to him the first time she'd seen it. "It's just a little sooner than we thought."

Her throat closed up. He was right. It would be okay. The Prado was for a summer, but Will was her forever. She turned her fingers to clasp his and knew that even if this changed the future she'd imagined, everything would always be okay as long as Will was at the center of it.

So instead of riding the train through Europe, they got married in his parents' backyard right after graduation two months later. Her mother had sat perched uncomfortably on a metal chair at one of the patio tables the whole time, her lips pinched white, her head shaking gently back and forth during their vows like a metronome. Their friends from school clustered together near the drinks table after the brief ceremony, looking uncertain in ties and heels, turning their backs in twos and threes, which Will and Marcie knew concealed the quick tipping of flasks into plastic cups of punch.

Emily and Dick gave them the sterling-silver bell that had been in the Malone family for generations, carried over to America on a boat when Dick's great-great-grandparents had come from Czechoslovakia. Her mother gave them a thirty-dollar gift card to Rich's department store, and pulled Marcie aside as she was leaving the reception to press a savings passbook into her hands.

"There's a hundred bucks in there, and it's in your name only," she'd muttered from the side of her mouth like a Dick Tracy villain. "I know you don't think you're gonna need it now, but if you're smart you'll keep this to yourself for when you do."

Marcie still had that savings account, though she'd never told Will—not for the reason her mother suggested, but because she couldn't bear for him to realize the woman's total lack of faith in him, in them. She'd never added to the account either, and the balance it carried with the paltry interest her mother's hundred dollars had earned in twenty-five years had formed the entirety of her inheritance when her mom finally succeeded in fully closing up her arteries six years ago.

When Marcie's bleeding started just days after the wedding, she'd put in a tampon mechanically before she realized what was happening, freaked out, and called Will at Southern Bell, where he'd taken an entry-level technician job as soon as they found out about the kid. He left work immediately and took her to Planned Parenthood, where the nurse drew her eyebrows together when Marcie showed her the bloody pad, and bolted for the doctor.

They hadn't told anyone about being pregnant. So there was no one to tell when she wasn't anymore.

She hadn't felt any ache of loss. It was as if the tissue attaching to her womb had been tethering her instead, binding her more and more securely onto a path she hadn't chosen with every day it developed. Already living at the bone, two teenagers playing house on their minimum-wage salaries—that wasn't the vision she'd had for their lives. She didn't want to be some *Jerry Springer* cliché, the redneck girl who got knocked up in high school and then just kept popping out children.

So when the embryo broke free, it was as though Marcie had shed an oppressive weight along with the little mass of unformed tissue. Not having a child felt like a life sentence had just ended in surprise parole. Possibilities opened up again. A different future was back on the table.

I'm sorry, Marce. I'm so sorry, Will had said, stroking her hair back from her face when he'd come into the recovery room afterward.

And she was too—but not about the pregnancy. She'd missed out on Spain and the Prado internship for nothing.

The memories seemed like another lifetime as she looked out at the glinting, featureless Gulf of Mexico—impossible to imagine that boy as her partner twenty-five years later in their eddying dance around each other in the empty chill of the second pregnancy they'd lost, as if both of them were trying hard not to create any disturbance in the surface for fear of waking whatever lurked underneath.

Flint's brusque invitation had been as ludicrous as it was unexpected. Stay with him. The idea had almost made her laugh, but remembering the way his whole body had stiffened when she laughed at his threat to call the cops, she kept it tamped down—this clearly wasn't a man with a broad sense of humor. He'd been sincere in the offer; that much was obvious. But even as she walked the length of the main—the only—road bisecting Palmetto Key's narrow peninsula looking for a pay phone, she couldn't imagine what had prompted it. If ever she'd met someone who embodied the term "misanthrope," the sour old man was it. He exuded a leave-me-alone vibe so tangible it was almost a force field.

And yet when she went back into the house to retrieve her shoes and her now-useless keys from his living room to go call Will, to get back where she belonged, the man was nowhere to be seen—but she'd found twenty dollars sitting beside her key ring, and a house key. She took the money—it would take some time to locate her car and retrieve it from impound, and she needed something to eat—and left his key next to the percolator in the kitchen, noting his street address as she let herself out the door. Once she got home she'd wash his shirt and send it back, along with repayment.

Palmetto Key must once have been charming. Its only main road, Marea Boulevard, was lined with houses like Flint's—small single-story bungalows that sat directly on the sand, not on stilts as with newer beach towns. Most of the hotels that dotted the road were clearly leftovers from the fifties and sixties, just a few stories tall, the architecture squat and square, with an old-fashioned tacky cheeriness provided by their signs: hula dancers whose neon skirts blinked from side to side; Art Deco palm trees with perfect round coconuts; big happy orange suns. It all felt tired. Sad.

Here and there a slightly newer hotel towered above its modest neighbors, its streamlined beige or gray exterior jutting up like an insult to the blowsy excess of the buildings around it. But the spare postmodern architecture couldn't combat the overall ambience of Palmetto Key as a blue-collar paradise on the lee side of its heyday.

What it didn't seem to have was a pay phone.

She'd been walking for nearly half an hour, back toward the eruption of little shops near the bridge that linked the peninsula to the mainland, and despite her skirt and the man's loose-fitting top she was moist with sweat. Eleven in the morning and already the air stuck to her skin like a layer of nylon. She hadn't seen a single pay phone anywhere up the entire strip amid the shops hawking cheap, brightly patterned tropical wear, seashells (at the beach!), and tourist garbage like T-shirts and waxy chocolate shaped like alligators and plastic back scratchers and snow globes (in *Florida*). Outside the Sand Weiner—which promised a ninety-nine-cent hot dog anytime, day or night, but had long since been shuttered, boards peeling away from the windows and revealing a threatening blackness inside that rendered the sign's promise unlikely—she found only one scratched-up and tagged metal post that once held a public phone, wires spilling out of it now like entrails from a gutted animal.

She was hot and tired, her feet screamed in the ridiculous pumps, and she hadn't eaten anything in . . . how long?

Tucked behind the main strip of businesses fronting the road, a beat-up shack sprawled over the sand with a crooked sign out front—TEQUILA MOCKINGBIRD—and she trudged up the battered wooden steps onto a deck that overlooked the gulf. Food. And then maybe someone there would loan her a cell phone so she could call Will and track down her car.

A younger woman popped out from the sliding glass doors to the restaurant and handed Marcie a menu. "Sit anywhere," she told her disinterestedly before heading back inside. Marcie took one of the weathered picnic tables alongside the railing that separated the restaurant from the beach.

The water gave only the faintest of background noise, the lull between tides making it almost as still as a lake. A volleyball net was set up next door, and one lone little boy batted a volleyball into the air over and over. His parents—Marcie assumed—were sitting on low beach chairs a few yards away, the woman sprawled with her head back, sunglasses shielding her eyes, the man tapping on his phone. So secure in their little family they could ignore one another.

Farther down the beach, near a pier that jutted out over the water, there was a smattering of bodies, but the small family and two teenage girls walking the shoreline were the only other people nearby. If this beach town had ever had a heyday it was long in the past.

"You know whatcha want?" The woman was back, standing next to the table in denim shorts so tight it looked as though her thighs had been extruded from them.

Marcie looked down at the menu, which she hadn't even glanced at. She'd felt as if she were starving just moments ago, but the list of fried, blackened, breaded options made her stomach turn in on itself. She pointed to the local gulf shrimp cocktail, twenty-five cents each until six p.m. "I'll take these, please. Ten of them."

The girl eyed her. "They come by the dozen."

"Oh. A dozen, then."

"And to drink?"

"Just water. Can you bring two glasses of it?" Her tongue felt fat in her dry mouth.

The server sighed like a leaky tire and turned to go back into the restaurant. Marcie worried about the circulation to her legs.

Will would have laughed if he were here. He'd say something like, *I don't think she's wearing those for her vascular health, Marce,* or, *Bigger tips trump future varicose veins.* He had a way of joking about people that never sounded mean.

Suddenly Marcie missed him with an aching immediacy that cramped her stomach. *Will.* What was she *doing*? She stood from the faded gray picnic bench and walked into the restaurant, where her server had gone. A middle-aged female bartender with a shaggy frizz of blond hair and skin tanned to leather sat on a tall metal cooler behind the bar, watching a sports program on the television overhead. There were three other customers, all men, all older, dotting the chairs around the bar at irregular intervals, their eyes also trained upward at the screen.

"Hello," Marcie ventured. "Is there a phone here?"

The bartender moved only her eyes to look at her. "What, like a pay phone?" Marcie nodded and the woman grinned, revealing a missing tooth at one side of her mouth. "Seriously? Wow, darlin'. You are a back-to-basics kinda gal, ain'tcha?"

"Do you have one?"

Now all three of the men around the bar were looking at her too, as if she were a curiosity.

"Well, sure, there's one up by the alley by that old wiener place next to the Shark Bar. Doubt it works, though. Phone's missing. Petey here saw some guy yank it off the other night, right, Pete?"

"Yup. Right clean off the wire. That was one pissed-off guy." The man who spoke had a couple days' worth of glinting silver beard growing in and wisps of white hair on top of his head that swayed back and forth in the hot breeze of the fan.

Marcie's gut hollowed out. She was exhausted and hungry and lost and she just wanted to go home.

"Do any of you have a cell I could . . . that I could . . ." To her dismay her throat was closing up, her eyes prickling with tears she was too dried-out to cry, and Marcie suddenly was certain these people were about to watch her have a full-fledged breakdown.

"Hey. Hey, miss—ma'am!" The voice came from over her shoulder, a hoarse tone that barely carried over the low reggae song piped into the place, and Marcie turned to see one of the older men standing behind her, the one with the Art Garfunkel halo of tight white curls against light brown skin spotted like a banana, holding out something in a callused hand. "Here you go," he said encouragingly when she only stared at him. "You can use my phone." He held it out farther, his arm nearly straight.

She knew she should thank him, but it felt as if any sound, even just those two single syllables, would open something up she might never get closed again. She only nodded and took the cell phone, their fingers brushing as he released it into her hand. The man smiled at her, kind and soft, but she could only nod again, clutching the phone close to her chest.

"You just bring it back whenever you're finished, miss," he told her gently, and reached awkwardly forward to pat the side of her shoulder.

She took the old flip phone out the door and around the corner, to the side of the outside deck where no customers sat. No internet on this antique, obviously—what was it with old men and phones on this island? She'd have to tell Will about the car so he could find it.

He answered on the first ring in sales-call tone, his brusque "stranger voice."

"Hi. It's me."

"Marcie? What number is this?"

"I don't have my phone at the moment," she said, skirting the truth.

"Where are you?"

"Uh . . . I'm at the beach."

There was a silence so long she thought she'd lost the connection, and then: "What? I thought you had to work today because of the McConley party."

Guilt bit her. "I drove down to Florida."

"You went to *Florida*?" He sounded incredulous. "Why?"

"I just . . . needed to get away."

In his disbelieving silence Marcie heard how idiotic it

sounded. Two days after her miscarriage she left for work and instead drove to the beach?

Wait till he heard the rest of the story.

The boy on the beach had his arms extended, his hands clasped together, and was bouncing the ball on his locked elbows—once, twice, three times.

"When are you coming home?" he asked finally.

She took a breath. She had to tell him. "Well. Funny you ask that. That's actually why I'm calling—"

"This is about the lima bean, isn't it," he interrupted, sounding tired.

Her ribs tightened, her jaw tensing. That was what she and Will took to calling the pregnancy the second time around. Not "the baby," or even "the embryo." The lima bean, as though it were just a little morsel of something inanimate neither one of them ordered.

"Can we not talk about that right now? I need you to—"

"Marcie, I know this has been hard on you. But we'll get through it. I'm sorry. You know how sorry I am. But running off down to the beach isn't exactly how we can fix it."

On the beach below her the little boy had grown bored with his solo volleyball game and now lay facedown on the sand, the ball underneath his stomach, rolling back and forth over it, his face heedlessly bulldozing the sand. Marcie let out a short laugh at the bizarre game.

"This isn't funny," Will said stiffly. "Not to me."

"No, it's not remotely funny."

"Marcie, come home."

She almost laughed again at her predicament but wisely held it in. "I'm not sure I can, actually."

"What are you talking about?"

Where to begin? Now that she was actually talking to Will it was harder than she thought to tell him how stupid she'd been.

But he plowed ahead before she could figure it out: "What the hell, Marcie—you just take off without telling me where you are for two days? I thought you were at *work*, for God's sake. And you just had surgery, no less, so should you even be—"

Her throat felt hot and swollen, her hand clenching the outdated phone. "I'm fine, Will. I just need—"

"I know things have been hard for the last few weeks, but we don't just walk out on each other like that—if something's wrong we talk about—"

"Will!" she said sharply, and he stopped. She closed her eyes, took a breath, opened them. "Can you just look something up for me, please? I've had a little issue and I could use your help."

There was a silence, and then, "Of course I will. What do you need me to do for you?"

Helpful Will. Always so helpful. She remembered him bustling around the bedroom after they lost the pregnancy, unable to do enough for her. So very helpful once he got what he'd wanted all along.

"You know what?" she said calmly. "Never mind. I think I'm going to stay a little longer. I'll be home in a couple of days."

"Marcie . . . just come home and let's talk about this."

"There's nothing to talk about."

"You're upset."

Dispassionately she scanned her feelings. "No. I don't think I am upset. I just want a little time to myself." She would find an internet connection, track down the car, and once she got it out of impound she could get a hotel room, buy a bathing suit and a few other things, and spend the weekend relaxing on the beach before going back to work Monday. It sounded wonderful.

"Marcie . . . come on. This isn't how we handle problems. We talk them out. We work through them together."

"Do we?" she asked, watching the little boy run over to his mom so she could spray more sunscreen on him. "Do we really?"

She didn't wait to hear his reply before she snapped the folding phone shut.

Marcie

arcie pressed her left hand, the phone still in her right, up against the side of the weathered gray building until she felt splinters pierce her skin.

What had she just done? She'd been calling Will so he could help her get home, and then . . . something happened. She wasn't even sure what, couldn't pinpoint what he'd said that made her change her mind, hang up.

The irritable server walked out the sliding doors and stood at the table where Marcie had been sitting, holding a clear glass plate of shrimp and looking around. She turned and saw Marcie around the corner, set the plate on the table so abruptly the shrimp jumped, and then spread her hands— *Well?* Marcie could only nod, and the woman shook her head, gave a visible sigh, and stalked off. Marcie couldn't blame her. Waitressing was a thankless job.

Picking out two little bits of wood embedded in her palm,

she rounded the corner to go back inside, placed the phone on the bar in front of the man who'd given it to her.

He put it back in his pocket, looking a little uncertain. "Miss, are you okay?"

"Do you know where there's a library nearby?" All she needed was an internet connection and she could find the car herself.

The old man nodded and gave her directions—walking distance, thank goodness, and just a few streets down on the main thoroughfare of this dinky little beach town—and Marcie thanked him again and turned to go back to her table, her waitress almost bowling her over at the sliding glass doors, storming out from the kitchen and untying her apron with furious, jerky movements.

"This is bullshit, Darla."

"What the hell, Sadie . . . ? Loosen up your knickers, there, hon . . ." the yellow-haired woman behind the bar said.

That seemed like solid advice, considering the way the poor girl was crammed inside her shorts, but then Marcie realized the bartender was simply trying to calm the waitress down.

"Second weekend in a row I get all day shifts? Forget it." She slammed the apron down on the bar with a muted thud. "Keep your crappy-ass job."

The woman and all three men watched the girl walk out, silently staring after her as the door swooshed shut behind her.

"That's a record, huh?" said one of the men at the bar. "A week?"

The bartender shook her head and lifted a mug to the tap to draw a fresh beer. "Nah. I had one here for half a shift once. Her boyfriend came in and they made up and she didn't need the job anymore." She took a pull from the frosted mug.

"Huh. Beach people," said one of the other older men, short and slight and shriveled like overcooked bacon.

Marcie sat down where her lunch lay on a wilted iceberg lettuce leaf over a bed of melting ice.

Not long after their first miscarriage Marcie started working overnight front-desk shifts at the Bonafort. A nineteen-year-old who hadn't yet learned the hotel etiquette of sophisticated yet deferential detachment, she'd filled the lonely hours of the graveyard shift no one else wanted by chatting with guests who lurked in the lobby in the small, quiet hours of night, fellow restless souls postponing the solitude of an impersonal (if tastefully decorated) hotel room.

One teenage daughter of a family staying the week for a local reunion slipped down every night, trapped in a room with her eleven-year-old brother, who made a poor companion for a gregarious eighteen-year-old insomniac who wanted to talk with someone her own age about her upcoming gap year traveling Europe. "You should do it too!" she'd urged Marcie, as if they were girlfriends planning a trip together. "They really value English speakers in the hospitality industry over there."

Suddenly her high school dreams of Spain felt within reach again. Carried along on the girl's enthusiasm, Marcie came home bubbling with her own. "We wouldn't make much money—mostly just living expenses," she told Will. But what money did they need right now? The miscarriage left their futures wide open—they didn't have to settle into responsible adulthood quite yet after all; why not do something crazy together?

But Will had caught the eye of a supervisor at work who wanted to fast-track him into management. And they'd signed a two-year lease on their apartment they were only halfway into, and breaking it would cost them their hard-scrounged deposits—money they would need if they weren't making more than room and board abroad. And what would Will do there? He had no background in hospitality, no skills that might make a monolingual entry-level communications tech desirable overseas. Was this the best time?

Every point was valid. Marcie hadn't thought it all the way through—she'd gotten sucked into the oblivious enthusiasm of a privileged teenager bored out of her mind in the adjoining room of her parents' luxury suite. The girl's situation was vastly different from Marcie's; that wasn't their life.

But she'd made the mistake of telling her mother about it, and Jeanetta gave a scornful *hmmmph* that set Marcie's teeth on edge. "That's what marriage gets you. Nothing you want. Everything he wants."

"That's life, Mom," she'd argued. "It's a *relationship*, being practical and making choices that are best for both of you, for your future as a family."

It was why they had worked so well as a couple for so long— she and Will heard each other's complaints out, worked hard not to criticize, avoided dismissing the other person's point of view—there was no right or wrong if someone felt a certain way; feelings were feelings, valid whatever the facts. As young as she'd been at the time, Marcie still remembered too many of her mother's angry, contemptuous attacks on her father before he walked out. *Your mama's making things too hard on me, kiddo.* She hadn't had to ask her dad what he meant, and she wasn't going to make the same mistakes in her own marriage. So she didn't finish the rest of her thought aloud to her mom: that Jeanetta obviously couldn't understand that kind of compromise and consideration for someone else or her father wouldn't have had to leave to have a chance at having his own needs met.

But now she wondered whether she'd been overcorrecting for years against the cautionary example of her mother's inflexibility. The transfer to a sister property in Santa Barbara they'd decided she had to turn down after Will's dad died and Emily

needed them . . . the luxury-cruise-line VP who'd been so impressed with Marcie's handling of his daughter's extravagant
antebellum wedding reception that he'd offered her a position
with his company as event manager. Marcie had mentioned
that one to Will almost as a throwaway, a wow-can-you-believe
opportunity they both knew was impractical—the job required
80 to 90 percent travel—and Will lauded her on the compliment of the offer without even considering it as something serious.

Had Marcie been bending herself too far to fit herself into
someone else's mold? Was she the only one who bent?

Maybe she was through compromising. Maybe Will could
be the one who bent for a change.

She tore the head off her first shrimp and tucked in, suddenly ravenous.

Marcie

T he good news was, finding where her car was turned out to be surprisingly easy: She walked right by the lot where she'd parked the Acura and realized the towing company name and number would be on the posted signs—which it was. At the library she looked up the address and asked the woman at the information desk if she would mind calling her a cab. All she had to do now was get her purse from the trunk, pay to get the car out of impound, find herself a change of clothes and a decent hotel, and then she'd treat herself to a nice dinner—if there was one to be had anywhere around here—and maybe sleep until she had to drive back Sunday night.

The bad news was that this frustrating backward little town apparently subcontracted its towing services to morons.

"Hi, I'm here to pick up my car," she told the attendant behind the nicked laminate counter. "It was towed on Wednesday. Or Thursday."

"License and registration?" The bored clerk barely looked up from his monitor.

"I don't have it on me—it's in the car."

"Next." There was no one else in the grubby little waiting room.

"I can get you the paperwork," she explained patiently, "but I need to get into the car."

He scratched a little constellation of pimples by the side of his mouth and pointed at the sign on the wall over his head with the other hand without looking up from his computer screen. NO ACCESS TILL YOU PAY.

In her line of work Marcie met lots of people like this kid—parents of the bride who made themselves feel important by ordering around the hotel staff; despotic food-and-beverage directors barking dictates at their waitstaff; disillusioned middle managers reveling in calling the shots for their company retreat. People who lacked power in some aspect of their lives and so wielded their fragile authority like little dictators when they were awarded some.

She pulled out her event-planner smile, the one she'd actually practiced in a mirror to make sure it carried no trace of frustration or condescension. *Acknowledge the concern. Redirect. Offer an incentive.* "I agree; it's a little unusual, isn't it? I'd locked my purse in the trunk for safekeeping, and it was a bit disconcerting to find out it got towed with the car." She gave a smooth laugh. "But the good news is, this is an easy fix: If you'll show me to the car, I have the keys." She held them up with another work smile. "And then I can show you everything you need and pay you—as soon as I get my wallet."

He sighed, finally looking up but pointedly over her shoulder rather than into her eyes, as if to imply a nonexistent long line of people behind her. "Lady, rules are rules. You don't think everyone in here would like me to bend 'em? Next."

Marcie gripped the keys so tightly she thought they might cut into her palm.

Jesus. Millennials. If this was what Will was picturing for their kid's future, no wonder he'd been so reluctant.

There was a phone in the corner of the waiting area on a three-legged table (that had once had four but now used cinder blocks for the missing one), and Marcie called the cab company back. She couldn't bring herself to give up and go home, to admit that Will was right and she'd been foolish. She'd solve this problem on her own—for Christ's sake, that's what she *did*. She'd go back to the library and contact her credit card companies to get replacements overnighted to her.

Despite the heat she waited outside—she couldn't be certain what she might say to the officious little apparatchik behind the counter—but it wasn't so easy to escape thoughts of Will.

About six years into their marriage, when finances weren't so strained and a lot of their friends were starting their families, Marcie and Will had decided, sure, why not? Let's give kids a go. Except for stopping birth control they didn't worry too much about it, and after a while they both actually kind of forgot they'd been open to the idea.

Marcie wasn't one of those women who always knew she was meant to be a mother. It was one possible path her life might take, *their* life, but one among many, and they were young, so neither of them worried. A year or two later she went back to school to get her degree, which ate up every spare moment she wasn't working at the hotel.

She'd been thinking about art school again, but Claus, the

hotel owner, told her that if she pursued a hospitality degree he'd pay for half of it. It didn't make sense not to accept his generous offer—and the job security it implied. And there sure wasn't the space to add an infant into the mix.

By the time their friends were having kids, Marcie and Will were both focused on building their careers and working long hours—Claus was clearly grooming Marcie for a bigger role in his chain of boutique hotels, and hospitality had no holidays; and Will was working insane hours on telecom-system installations, often pulling overnights during cutovers.

Then their friends complained about their sweet little angels having turned into sullen, angry teenagers they could barely control, and the two of them had started congratulating themselves on their odd stroke of luck. They spent relaxing vacations at the beach while their friends took their kids on chaotic, fraught family trips. They saved money for themselves, their future, rather than college, as they watched so many of their friends argue, separate, divorce.

They could see a doctor to check Will's sperm count and Marcie's eggs, a friend at work suggested as thirty-five crept toward forty. Try fertility treatments. A sperm or egg donor, if it came to that, the woman told her. She should leap at that, Marcie remembered thinking as they lay on the sofa one night, watching yet another sitcom about some wacky happy family. With Will's career finally on an even keel and Marcie having been promoted to head of events at the hotel, they were doing well now; they could afford to seek out medical options. Shouldn't she be so desperate at this point to have children that she'd do anything—anything at all—to have them?

But she wasn't, she'd realized as she rested her feet in his lap. Despite a twinge of disappointment, Marcie wasn't crushed. They'd simply missed the boat, and although a part of her was sad for the family she and Will would never have, she had no interest in tackling diapers and bottles and sleep deprivation and chasing a toddler around. What they had was enough.

"We already have a family," Will said when she spoke her thoughts aloud. "You're my family." Not everyone was cut out for children. Not every marriage needed them.

When she'd missed a period seven weeks ago, she thought it was early menopause and it was almost a relief to have a definitive answer. It wasn't until two glasses of wine at dinner one night had her hurling into the toilet that she wondered. Almost as an afterthought she stopped into the drugstore on the way home from work, grabbed an EPT, took it home, and peed on the stick, flashing back more than twenty years and absently thinking what a hilarious bookend this would be to their fertile years.

Two pink lines. Again.

And out of nowhere a cliché washed right over her like a tsunami and dragged her under: an unexpected rush of protectiveness, of territoriality, a bizarre, aching thrill so intense it almost hurt. The balance of her life tipped in that moment from feeling like the weighted end was behind her to whole worlds of experience sprawled in front of her, the hourglass sand top-heavy once again. Saving for retirement? That was eons away, their child's entire lifetime. Their *child*! Every reason she was grateful they didn't have children disappeared as the future seemed to open like a flower. She charged downstairs almost giddy with new possibilities, holding out the pregnancy test with its two pink lines— and flashing back to being a teenager holding out the same stick in her hand to the same man, just a boy at the time.

Will looked bewildered and asked why she was handing him a pen, and then she saw the exact moment he realized . . . and the way his face fell in on itself.

He hid it quickly, leaning in to grasp her in a hug, but her heart sank to the bottom of her stomach. "Congratulations!" fell inanely out of his mouth, as if she'd just won first place in a beauty pageant.

Marcie could read Will like a road sign even with his best poker face. His expression looked as if it had frozen, and the smile he pushed out was a fissure.

The picture was as vivid in her mind as if it were happening in front of her, that image of the two of them standing there together in the living room like the last frame in a film before it jumped the sprockets and started to stutter and jump and eventually slithered off the reel completely, leaving only a flickering empty white screen.

"Hey, lady, you call for a cab?"

The driver barely looked old enough to have his license—Marcie almost asked to see it. The backseat of the lime-green sedan smelled like root beer as she let herself in, and she rolled down the window.

"Yeah, all right!" the kid said, grinning into the rearview. "Most snowbirds like the A/C. How about some tunes too?"

"Sure," she said agreeably. "What do you like?"

"Aw, I love the oldies." And he wasted no time cranking up Nirvana to a volume too high for conversation. Which suited her fine—this kid made her feel about eighty.

That was Will's main concern—they were too old for kids now. They'd recently started a monthly dinner club at friends' houses now that their kids were old enough for them to have more freedom; they had season tickets to the Alliance and the Fox Theater; went to the Atlanta Food and Wine Festival every September, the Jazz Fest at Piedmont Park, the Dunwoody Art Fest. They worked out regularly at their gym, where they each had a personal trainer. A child would upend all of that, right when they finally had the time and the resources to do it all.

They'd be sixty years old when the kid graduated high school, he said, and then doddering grandparents who'd become a burden right when their child was trying to start a family of his or her own, if they were still around by that time at all. Emily was nearly seventy-six, too old to help with child care—raising a child without that was hard, and expensive. And the reason they had so little extended family to help was because she and Will were both only children—back when kids had been a distant consideration they'd both vehemently agreed that they'd never inflict that on a child of their own. They'd have at least two or none at all.

And none at all had turned out to be just fine. Until it wasn't. At least for Marcie.

But they'd been open to having children before, she reminded him. Older parents were more and more common, and aging wasn't like it used to be; they could reasonably expect to be healthy and hearty well into their seventies and beyond. They'd been able to make wonderful strides in their retirement savings and were well ahead of most people their age, and they could afford to hire a nanny.

And yes, having a child meant curtailing some freedoms, but it wasn't as though they traveled much now, taking their vacations for the most part with Will's mom at the same place every year, the resort on St. Simons Island off the coast of Georgia where Emily and Dick had taken Will all his life. They were smart, stable, open-minded people who would make good parents for any child they happened to have. It would be an adventure, she said. A last-minute chance at a chapter of their lives together they thought they'd missed. Leap and the net will appear.

Yes, Will agreed. She was right on all points. But . . .

This was why they ended up butting their heads against the

dead end of the maze over and over again, every time they broke the pained silences that grew between them and tried to talk it out—because every rational argument made complete sense. Because she could completely see Will's point of view—had shared it right up until she saw those two pink lines for the second time. And he could see hers too—even if he didn't share it.

They were the model of rational empathy for each other. But with cells multiplying inside Marcie at a dizzying rate every day, every second, it brought them no closer to an answer as the need for one grew more and more urgent.

But for the first time in their marriage, Marcie found she couldn't give ground. Not one inch.

It was an adjustment, that was all—as he got used to the idea, as this became their new normal, Will would come around. He was too good a man, too loving—and fathers often didn't feel that direct, immediate connection right away like mothers did, she'd read in online forums. But they did. Eventually they did.

At their first ob-gyn visit—early because of some minor spotting—Will went with her; for now they'd "proceed as if," as the self-help books said. In the waiting room he stared straight ahead toward the receptionist desk, ignoring the magazines strewn over a corner table: *Parents*, *American Baby*, *Highlights* for the kids that some of the women in the other stiff-backed orange chairs had with them. Marcie watched those women monitoring their energetic children with one hand on their rounded bellies, a palm cupped reflexively over her own. When Will heard the heartbeat, she thought . . . when it became real . . .

In the ultrasound room she lay back in the chair while Will stood next to the window, close enough to touch but not touching. The gel was warm when the woman spread it over her belly, the paddle cool against her skin. And up on the screen . . . a little lima bean–shaped blob that looked exactly like every image she'd seen of a first-trimester baby online. When they heard its faint, fast heartbeat, she couldn't stop smiling.

Will studied the screen as though it were a telecom schematic, and he laid his hand lightly on her shoulder and was silent.

"Congratulations," the receptionist said as they checked out after her exam, handing Marcie a slip of paper with *AMA* scribbled at the bottom—"advanced maternal age"—with a card for the genetic specialist she'd need to set up an appointment with as a high-risk "geriatric" pregnancy. Marcie laughed out loud at that—"I'm forty-three!" she said, turning to share the ludicrousness of it with Will.

But he was looking at the receptionist. "Do you guys keep a bar next door for the fathers?" he joked weakly.

The woman had smiled politely and made no comment as Marcie clutched the images the ultrasound tech had given her.

On the way home they stopped for an early dinner. She probably should have picked a different restaurant, but they went to their favorite pizza place—an old mill that was on the Historic Register and had been in the same family since it was built. The naked-beam ceilings and stone walls made it feel more special than the simple family restaurant it was, but it was their pizza that had won Will and Marcie's loyalty.

They were seated beside a family of five, with two boys around eight or nine who might have been twins. The girl—younger by a few years, and dressed princess pretty in jeans and a tutu—sat like an angel in her seat, using her fork and knife to eat her pizza, like a miniature Emily Post.

The boys couldn't sit still, kicking the base of the table, flicking pizza toppings at each other, and at one point conducting what seemed to be a fencing match with their pizza crusts. The parents wearily scolded each infraction, but the boys didn't seem to hear them.

Marcie started talking about the pregnancy, trying yet again to see it from both sides—the excitement and adventure of being parents that seemed so clear to her; the difficulties that seemed to be all Will was seeing. "It really is like a lima bean," she said, diplomatic and conciliatory. "It's like, we didn't ask for it, wouldn't have thought to actually crave it, but once it's on the plate you realize it's not bad."

Will wasn't really listening, though. His face tightened with every yelp and shrill exclamation from the rowdy boys at the next table, and finally they'd had half their pizza boxed up and left. They tried to talk about it a little when they got home, but he looked beaten, exhausted, and nothing she said was going to make a positive out of what he only seemed to see as an oppressive looming negative.

That was when Marcie understood that no matter what happened, one of them was going to have to make a terrible sacrifice.

She went to bed shortly afterward—eight thirty, ridiculously early. While Will stayed downstairs watching television on the couch, she lay under the covers, curled onto her side, tears wetting the pillow in a steady flow.

It was the first time she'd ever wondered if they'd make it through as a couple.

The next morning she'd woken up to a shifting of the bed, saw Will sitting on the edge. He'd brought her coffee and she sat up and took the mug.

"I know you need me to get behind this, Marcie. And I will. I'm trying."

Marcie had burst into tears. The lima bean wasn't something he wanted—he couldn't pretend to her that it was. But he'd try—for her.

When nausea began to hit, Will made emergency store runs for ginger ale, ginger tea, ginger candy. She was tired all the time, her usual energy deserting her to leave her limp and sluggish on the sofa as soon as she got home every night, and he took to making dinner. What little she ate came right back up a few minutes later, and he'd brush her hair off her sweaty forehead when she was perched in front of the toilet, waiting for the next bout of heaving.

Until the night they'd been sitting on the sofa side by side, watching some stupid sitcom with a family trading snappy one-liners, and Marcie laughed and said, "That's going to be us."

But Will didn't laugh, and when she glanced over at him, he looked wrecked.

"Marcie," he said in a ragged voice, "are you sure about this?"

She was just weeks away from her second trimester, had been giddily planning how to tell Emily, her friends, Chuck and Claus and the rest of her staff—had been adding items to a baby registry online, for God's sake—and he asked this now?

She kept her voice carefully neutral. "I thought we were both on board with this, Will."

His face was twisted up in what looked like pain. "I want to be, Marcie. I know you are, and you need me to be. But I . . ."

She'd pulled her feet off his lap, sat up, hands pressed under her thighs. "But you can't. Is that it?"

"It's not that I can't, Marcie. It's that I don't want to."

The words seemed to ring through the house, through her bones.

She'd choked on the hopelessness of it. Weren't his feelings valid? Shouldn't they be? Just because two people loved each other, it didn't mean they always wanted the same things.

But this. *This* thing.

Marcie had wanted things before too—the art-study program in Madrid, the cruise job, Santa Barbara. She'd wanted them and she'd turned them down anyway because Will didn't—because she knew that marriage meant sometimes you sacrificed a little bit for the good of your relationship, the thing that was bigger than either of you alone. Sometimes you had to compromise.

But apparently she was alone in that thinking. Or Will was okay with marital compromise as long as he was getting what *he* wanted.

And that was when her rage had started to smolder.

For the first time Marcie found herself across a divide from the man she'd known as well as herself for more than half her life—the man who'd always been next to her, on her side of it. Or maybe she'd always gone over to his.

After that there was no more to say—they'd examined every angle, heard each other's every viewpoint, exhausted every avenue. That was when the silences between them grew longer, charged. Marcie felt as if something was expected of her—that the only way to break the uneasy stalemate they were in was for one of them to give. And hadn't it always been Marcie?

When the bleeding started, for the second time in their lives he rushed her to the doctor, at her side the whole time. In the hospital room she'd turned to find Will's hand and caught a glimpse of his face.

There was fear, yes. For her. But under it . . . relief. Marcie was almost dragged under by a fierce wave of pain—but on its heels rode a shocking rage. And that hot, acrid fury had started to bloom like a toxic cloud, seeping into every pore of her body until she was putrid with it. As careful as they'd tried to be, somehow they'd lost each other after all.

Sometimes things happen for a reason.

When he'd said that, something that had been stretched tight inside Marcie finally hit the breaking point, snapped. That was why she'd kept driving. It was why the thought of leaving, of going back home, felt like a weight on her chest that kept her lungs from inflating.

As the cab came over the bridge leading back to Palmetto Key, the gulf spreading before them, Marcie made a snap decision.

"Hey, Jacob," she said, reading his name off the license displayed on the dash. "Can you drop me off somewhere else?"

It was a good thing Marcie had cut the drive back to Flint's short—even stopping the mile or so closer at the run-down restaurant took the last of the money the old man had given her.

Inside, the three old men still sat at the bar with the scrappy blond woman behind it like Marcie had left minutes ago, instead of more than an hour.

"Excuse me," Marcie said to the woman. "I saw that you lost a server this afternoon. I can wait tables."

All three of the men at the bar looked over at her, seeming to have forgotten who she was. "No kidding?" said the woman.

It was crazy—filling in at a waitress job in this fading town in this dive bar—but no more irrational than anything she'd done in the last forty-eight hours. "No kidding. I can work today if you're shorthanded. Cash?"

"You bet your bippy, baby," the woman said, reaching below the bar and then plopping an apron on it.

"Hey, how 'bout that, Darla?" said the man with the leathery hide.

"Damn, Darla, you have the luck."

The wild-haired blond bartender gave that gap-toothed grin. "I'm Darla. And you're hired."

Darla—who was also the owner, she told Marcie—pulled down a new T-shirt from a shelf over her head, and said she could start immediately.

Marcie carried the shirt to the bar's tiny single bathroom to change, and tied on the apron as if she'd done it a hundred times.

When she came back out, the restaurant was still empty except for Darla and the three men hanging over the bar like fixtures. Darla reached into a cooler and pulled out a fresh beer mug, then filled it from one of the taps in front of her. She set the beer on the bar and pushed it toward Marcie.

"What's your name, newbie?"

"Marcie."

"Marcie. Marcie what?"

"Marcie . . . Jones." This time it felt right on her tongue.

"Everyone here's got a story, Marcie Jones. So what's yours?"

What was her story? *I have the perfect life . . . or I thought I did. But apparently I've recently decided to blow it all up with absolutely no plan and just see what happens. Is that fun or what?*

Marcie picked up the mug, which was heavier than she expected, and took a tentative sip. It was icy cold, shockingly good. "I don't have a story. I just need the job."

The woman eyed her, slumped against the cooler, arms crossed in front of her. The men at the bar weren't even pretending not to be listening—they were leaning back in their chairs in poses similar to Darla's, crossed arms and expectant faces. "No story," she said to them, as if Marcie had let her down. Then she turned her eyes back to Marcie. "Fair enough, Marcie with the generic last name. You wanna hear mine?"

So Marcie drank a beer in the middle of the day with the odd woman, and three men who looked like they'd washed from the sea right up to the bar years ago and hadn't budged since, while Darla told her about her four ex-husbands, a stint in jail for forgery, and winning the restaurant in a game of craps seven years before. The other men nodded along, as though they'd heard the tales many times before.

Customers trickled in all afternoon. A family of five who asked for virgin piña coladas all around, which made Darla roll her eyes and give a great tragic sigh when Marcie brought her the order. Two women in sarongs and bikini tops who drank Corona from the bottle—"Where's our lime?" Five teenagers who sat in a corner on the deck, slouched over, who all wanted a slow, comfortable screw. It wasn't until she went to Darla for advice about handling the harassment that she realized it was a drink.

"Plus they're too young. You card them?"

"You mean ID?"

"If they're twenty-one I'll eat my Birkenstocks. Bring me their licenses—I can spot a fake from a mile away."

But they were gone when she got back to their table, and Darla called her back over to the bar.

"Where'd you say you waited before?" she asked. The regulars were still planted at the bar, and they eyed her from behind their tumblers.

"Applebee's. It was . . . a while ago. Most of my experience is in hotels."

Darla raised a white eyebrow. "Hotel bars?"

She didn't have a lie in her. She reached to untie her apron. It had been worth a try.

"Hey, hey, hey . . ." Darla waved a hand in the air toward her. "It's no problem. You're doin' okay."

That was a stretch, but Marcie took her hands off the ties at her back. "I'm a fast learner."

~~~

As the day wore on and the stringy woman seemed rooted behind the bar, lifting mug after mug along with her regulars, Marcie began to suspect the entire bar and restaurant was just a handy excuse for Darla to have drinking buddies.

Every time she went back and forth from her tables to the bar, she got better at differentiating the three men planted there. Pete was the one closest to the tap—"First in line," he'd crow when it was time for refills. He had wispy white hair that danced back and forth on top of his head under the fan, like a line of anemic hula girls.

Bink was skinny and red, with a nose swollen with drink and slits for eyes when he smiled, which was almost nonstop. Marcie quickly learned not to ask follow-up questions of Bink in conversation, because any show of interest was license for him to go off on a monologue that was almost impossible to break once he started. More than once Darla had had to bark at her to check on a table when Bink was bending her ear for too long, but Marcie thought the woman was trying to help her extricate herself more than she was actually worried about the patrons.

Arthur was the one who'd offered her the phone. Soft-spoken and gentlemanly, he stood every time Marcie approached him, as if that cloud of white curls were constantly trying to return skyward. After a few instances of this, she finally thanked him for his chivalry, but suggested giving him a blanket pass from then on, since his perch was right beside the servers' area where Darla filled the table drink orders, and Marcie was back and forth almost constantly. She worried he'd slip a disk if he kept shooting off his stool and onto his feet.

The three men were full of fish tales both literal and figurative, punctuated by wheezy, coughing laughs and the occasional

"Bullshit!" thrown out when the storyteller stretched credulity too far.

There were apparently other perks to working at Tequila Mockingbird besides cash and no questions asked. There was a daily staff meal, Darla told her—today she was frying up fresh-caught grouper she'd bought from a local, and she plated up a portion for Marcie. The fish was perfect—flaky and tender with a slight crunch at the edges and simply but perfectly seasoned—and Marcie wondered who Darla was before she came to the beach and let her hair grow long and her memory grow short.

Midway through the dinner rush muscles Marcie didn't know she had ached—her lower back was on fire, throbbing pain between her shoulder blades. She'd forgotten what waiting tables could take out of you—or how demanding it could be.

When the dinner rush started, the other server—Hannah— had to bail her out frequently when Marcie forgot things, or misordered, or—one embarrassing time—dropped a tray that brought the restaurant to instant silence as every patron turned to stare at the middle-aged woman who couldn't seem to master a job that college kids could do in their sleep. When the first slow, sarcastic clap sounded, starting a wave of mocking ap-plause, Marcie wondered whether she could work here long enough to earn her car back or if she'd wind up having to call Will for help after all.

But as the evening wore on, muscle memory kicked in and she remembered there was a formula to it, a rhythm, just like running a hotel event: smile and greet, take the drink orders, turn the ticket in to Darla and greet another table while she waited for the bartender to fill it. Pick up the tray of drinks, set them down at the table as the guests told her what they wanted, post the order for the kitchen and deliver to another table what-ever food was up. It was nonstop and constant motion, but once she finally had the routine down, it required very little mental effort. If it hadn't been for a table of teenagers who walked out, leaving Marcie to eat their thirty-five-dollar bill, she'd have had enough to get the car.

"You'll catch on, newbie," Darla said in her wheezing voice after closing as Marcie settled her tabs at the register. "Tomorrow's another magical day."

"Is there a shift open tomorrow?"

"You betcha. Be here by eleven. You want your shiftie?" Darla was generous with postshift beers for staff.

Marcie untied her apron and folded it into thirds. "No, thanks," she said wearily. "I'm just going to head out."

"Well, here," Darla said, brandishing an open bottle of red wine from a misorder this afternoon. "I'd drink it, but it isn't beer."

Marcie took it—a glass of wine would be heaven—and left Darla in her usual position, leaning behind the bar with another beer in front of her, a couple of the grizzled regulars still hanging out to keep her company.

Flint

When the girl had come out on the deck after washing up, no makeup, her hair wet and limp, and wearing his oversize old shirt and the skirt she'd had on when he picked her off the beach, she looked like what she was—a lost soul waiting for someone to take care of her.

Stupid him, he'd ponied up for the chore. He'd known it was a mistake the second the words spilled out of his loose mouth.

Who was the idiot now?

If she was going to be underfoot for a couple of days, he'd have to make a place for her. She couldn't stay burrowed up in his living room like a mole. That was where he read, and he didn't want her big sad eyes on him while he was trying to bury himself in a book.

So he was in the spare room, trying to clear out enough space to house a helpless waif of a girl he was sorrier every minute he'd picked up off the beach.

And that was one more thing to hold against her, because he hadn't been through these boxes in years, and he didn't want to sort through them now. Just a bunch of useless crap he'd never need: posters of bands and singers he'd never heard of, and knickknacks and bric-a-brac and gewgaws that had been all over the dresser and desk and shelves. He'd left it all alone for a long time, the door closed. Finally it had seemed stupid to let it sit out collecting dust, and it was easier just to box it all up.

The boxes were where he'd packed and taped them shut years ago, piled into neat columns in the meager floor space around the twin bed, now stripped of its bedding. The A/C unit was still on the floor underneath the window where he'd pulled it out—no sense cooling off a room no one used—and the blinds were closed. The room smelled funny, like an underground tunnel where the sun never hit and the air sat still and unmoving.

It took some doing to navigate around the obstacle course of boxes to the window, but he managed it. When he yanked open the blinds, dust mushroomed out and swirled in the sunshine that poured in. It made him cough, and he opened the window to clear it out, but that only sent more of it dancing in the air in the slight gulf breeze that wafted in.

The house wasn't big enough to store anything unnecessary. He probably needed to donate the stuff to someone who could use it—the clothes and shoes, books, some of the dolls and toys Jessie hadn't touched in years even when she was here. She wouldn't get rid of them, though. Kept them up on the shelves above her desk, lined up like an audience facing her bed. Kid never threw anything away.

He'd move the boxes out of the way for now, till he had time to truck them to the Goodwill, leave the girl some sheets and a blanket. If she wanted it clean she'd have to put some elbow grease into it herself. This wasn't a hotel.

The boxes were heavier than he remembered. Or he was older. How could one kid accumulate so much junk in such a short time? Seventeen years . . . that was hardly any time at all. He thought to stack them in the closet, but when he forced open the balky louvered doors he saw that Jessie had beaten him to the same idea, boxes of her old things stacked on the shelves and the floor against the back wall like soldiers awaiting orders, pushed to the corners top and bottom, so there'd been a little space in the middle to hang her clothes.

Ignoring the loops of her handwriting facing out, identifying the contents of the boxes she'd packed but wouldn't let go of when he'd insisted she pare down, he stacked as many boxes as he could fit in the space that was left, then yanked the doors closed in stutter stops along the rusted track. He carried the rest of the boxes he couldn't jigsaw in there out to the hallway, setting them on the floor along one side. Still in the way—but he wasn't making a special trip to the mainland just to get rid of useless stuff.

The room was still small—whole house was small—but at least you could move around in there now. The girl would have a place to sleep, stay out of his way. He brushed off the mattress where dust had collected like a quilt, brought in a set of sheets and the old blue wool blanket he'd spread on the girl when he found her—too hot for it, but she hardly had any meat on her frame, not enough fat to keep herself warm. She could make her own damn bed, though—he'd already done more than she should expect. He set the folded bedding on the mattress, then tugged the vacuum cleaner in too—the carpet was shades darker where the boxes had been resting and the dust couldn't settle—and set some cleaning supplies on the dresser.

Nothing he could do about the purple walls and the purple carpet—like living on the inside of a grape, he used to tell Jessie.

Before he left the room he lifted the air conditioner back into the window. It was ancient, probably didn't even work anymore. But summer was ungodly hot, and if the girl sat there all the time with the window open, she'd let in so many mosquitoes they'd both get malaria. He braced it on the support arm, closed the window and the blinds tight against it, plugged it in. There. That was all he was doing. Too bad if it wasn't good enough. If she didn't like it, she could move on.

By the time the sun disappeared and sucked all the light down after it, he'd pretty well decided she wasn't coming back—she'd left the key after all. Good. But while he was in the living room, reading, he heard that same timid little scratch she'd used the first time she turned back up on his doorstep.

He yanked the door open. "Give a real knock, girl, so I can hear it."

She was carrying an apron and an uncorked bottle of wine, and wore a T-shirt with a cartoon on it, a bird holding some pink umbrella drink, and the words TEQUILA MOCKINGBIRD. He knew that place, right on the beach, as much a locals' hangout as a tourist attraction. How about that? The little princess actually found herself a job. A shithole, but she could've done worse.

"I was hoping I could take you up on your offer to stay here for a couple of days?" she said.

"Take the damn key already and quit bothering me."

"I'm going to be working a couple of shifts at Tequila Mockingbird, up the beach. Just till I get enough money to get my car out of impound."

"Society is no doubt eternally grateful to support one less freeloader." He picked up his book from the table beside the armchair. Looked around for his glasses. He always forgot to wear them when he read, and it gave him a headache. Hell with it. He turned to go back to his bedroom.

"Here." She held out something in her free hand. "They were on the cocktail table."

He snorted. *The cocktail table.* His old army trunk. *Jesus.* He snatched his glasses out of her fingers, which were curled over the lenses, getting her oily fingerprints all over them.

"There's some sheets on the spare bed," he growled. "It's a dust bowl in there. Cleaning supplies're on the dresser."

She might have murmured something else after that, but he didn't stick around to hear it.

Marcie

The old man—Flint—let her in with his customary scowl and a grunt when she knocked, but at least he was letting her stay—and a spare bedroom . . . that was a bonus. She'd been prepared for another night on the uncomfortable sofa.

After his growled admonition about the key, she found it where she'd left it this morning, on the kitchen counter beside the silver percolator, and slipped it into the apron.

She opened a couple of cabinets, looking for a wineglass, but found only the ubiquitous coffee cups and a single jelly glass. She pulled the glass down, filled it with the wine, and took it, along with a twenty from her apron almost as an afterthought, down the hallway past a trio of boxes along it that hadn't been there this morning, leaving the money on the floor outside the closed door she assumed was Flint's, where he'd see it in the morning.

Purple hit her like a slap as she flipped on the light switch

inside the other room, whose door was now open: walls, carpet—
the only thing spared was the ceiling, dingy white with a water
stain in one corner. A rattly grinding noise came out of an A/C
unit in the room's sole window, along with a wash of freezing air.

The old man had left a few cleaning products out on the
dresser, where clean rectangles in the thick layer of dust indicated the boxes in the hallway had once rested there—a yellow
can of Pledge with a rusty top that clearly hadn't seen action in
some time, a half-empty bottle of off-brand Windex, paper towels, and a cloth rag.

She was much too tired to clean tonight, but she couldn't
sleep on that bed—the mattress really should be taken outside
and beaten to get all the years of settled dust off it or, better yet,
put out on the curb, where it should probably have been left a
long time ago. But after she brushed and brushed the top and
finally couldn't see any more dust motes jumping off every time
she touched it, Marcie shook out the sheets Flint had left her,
soft and faded almost to lavender from years of washing, and
made up the tiny bed.

It was a child's room, clearly—a girl's room—but she couldn't
picture Flint as any kind of father. And if there was a daughter,
where was she now? Where was the wife? She couldn't see him
married any more than she could see him as a father.

Behind the chipped purple doors of the closet, boxes were
stacked on every inch of the floor, including on the shelves
above the empty wooden rod. Most were marked in a loopy girlish hand with labels that pricked Marcie with amusement:
"Clothes—these still FIT! Do NOT throw away! Styles cycle
back," and "Keepsakes (NOT 'clutter,' like some people think),"
and "PERSONAL. Yes, this means you, Dad."

She pulled the grease-streaked, sweaty T-shirt over her head
and hung it on one of the empty wire hangers, giving up on

closing the rickety louvered door when it screeched along the rusted aluminum track. No telling what the old man would do if she roused him yet again. That probably ruled out a shower too till the morning, so she pulled on the clean shirt he'd loaned her, realizing she was going to have to buy at least a pair of cheap shorts and flip-flops tomorrow morning. She couldn't work another shift in a skirt and heels.

Marcie crossed to the dresser and opened the drawers one by one.

Empty. Whoever purged this room—must've been Flint—had been thorough. Whatever personal items might have been here had been taken away. Probably hidden inside one of the boxes, but she wouldn't bring herself to go as far as tearing one open. She glanced around the bare purple walls.

Last August she'd wanted to repaint their bedroom a bold deep red—*It'll be sexy,* she told Will. *Like a bordello.*

Or a slaughterhouse, he'd joked. *Red's a serious commitment— if it's too much, think how much Kilz it'll take to cover it up even just to get to where we can start over.* So they kept the neutral taupe.

The tide of anger rose up again, and Marcie chased it back down with a long sip of the cheap red wine. Tiptoeing into the hall, she pulled her door shut behind her in case the light woke him up. But Flint's light was still on too, though behind the closed door his room was silent.

She refilled the jelly glass with wine and then clicked on the small lamp on the piecrust table beside his chair in the darkened living room. There was no television, she realized. For all the man's strangeness, that was the thing that struck her as oddest of all, even more than his lack of a phone or computer. She'd never seen a house without a TV in it.

She scanned the shelves bowed out of shape by the weight of the books stacked tight to the ceiling, spying a familiar title—*Of Mice and Men*—high on one of the less crowded shelves. In school she'd been assigned that one several times, and had made admirable grades on papers about the book off her CliffsNotes reports, though she'd never actually gotten past the first few chapters. But she'd liked the movie. She stretched onto her tiptoes and tipped its spine until it fell into her hand. It was old, the hardcover faded and slightly nicked at the corners.

She set her glass on the side table and sank onto the armchair, cracking open the book's weathered blue cover. It smelled like age and dust and something else, a nice leathery scent.

She'd gotten lost in Lennie and George and the one-handed swamper when something fluttered down onto her legs, startling her into snapping the book closed. A twenty-dollar bill lay in her lap.

Flint stood beside the chair, looking down at her with a fiercer-than-normal glare.

"What the hell is that?" he barked.

She sat up straighter, feeling like she'd been caught shoplifting. "I was repaying you."

"Didn't ask you for that. Save it and get out of my hair." He barely glanced at her before turning and stalking into the kitchen.

She folded up the twenty and got to her feet, debating whether taking the book back to the bedroom would set him off or if it was better to just slip it back onto the shelf, when Flint stomped back into the room.

"If you're gonna drink that stuff, drink it properly."

He held her wine bottle in one hand, and in the other a

stemmed glass, beaded with water. He held it out to her, and she reached for it without thinking.

"Don't drop it," he admonished her, then tipped the bottle to the lip, spilling its purple-red color into the wineglass and its perfume into the room. He tilted the bottle back to read the label. "This is shit, you know."

"It was free."

"Well. Then it was worth it."

Had the man just made a joke?

Politeness made her ask, "Would you like some?"

"Mind your business."

"Okay." Marcie started for the hallway, happy to get out of his way and abide by the terms of their agreement.

"I don't drink," he said.

It was the first piece of personal information he'd offered. She turned around. "Oh."

"Anymore."

"Listen . . ." she said after an awkward moment. "I'm not in any trouble. Just so you know."

"Yeah." It was agreement, not disbelief.

"My husband and I . . ." She looked down at the glass, its sharp, full scent filling her nose. "We had a miscarriage. And I left. I don't even really know why. I just need some time to myself."

It didn't even scratch the surface, but it seemed to be enough for the old man.

"Happens," he said in a grunt that lacked his earlier edge.

Something about the way he looked at her, his eyes a pale blue and watery with age, like a still pond offering her her own reflection, eased the tightness in her chest infinitesimally. She nodded. "Thanks for letting me stay here."

"You wanna be a little more careful with that one," he said, turning to leave. "It's a first edition."

She ran a finger gently over the pebbly surface of the book's cover. "Good night," she called after him.

He didn't pause his uneven gait as he walked down the hall.

She let out her breath after he shut his door and, after a few minutes, sat back down in the armchair, opened the book again—carefully—and continued to read.

Flint

The money had pissed him off. He never asked for a thing—just for her to get on with her life and to get out of his. If she had enough to spare to pay him back, then she had enough to get the hell out and find a place of her own.

He hadn't expected to see her in his chair, reading one of his books. One of his better ones. That should have pissed him off even more, but for some reason it didn't. Books were meant to be read, and too many of his had sat on the shelf for years because he could get through only so many, or he'd finished them years ago and couldn't get back to them again when there were so many others he hadn't cracked yet. Since Jessie had been gone, it seemed like a whole lot of them just sat there collecting dust, and that was as much a shame as a beautiful woman sitting alone at a dance.

He'd read Jessie *Of Mice and Men* when she was what . . . eight or nine? Maybe older—he had a hard time remembering stuff like that. She used to like him to read to her even long after she'd become a hell of a reader herself—fast as lightning. So fast it worried him at first that she was just skimming over the words. But when they'd talk over what she'd read, it was obvious she absorbed every detail. Even so, she always asked him to read something with her at night.

He'd sit on the bed next to her, hardly able to fit his whole frame on the little twin, and she'd curl up alongside him, one hand resting on his chest.

"I like the way your voice rumbles. It helps me go to sleep," she told him.

He had to watch what he read to her, though, because some of the stories kept her awake—the good ones, where she lay there wide-eyed and rapt, and when he closed the book she'd demand, "No! What happens next?"

That was the mark of a worthy story, and Jessie always had fine taste in books—Steinbeck, yes. But Melville too—after they finished *Moby-Dick,* weeks of reading, sometimes he'd hear her up at night, and he'd peek in her bedroom door and see her staring out the window, looking for the white whale, she told him. Hawthorne outraged her—"It's so unfair!" she'd said, ever the feminist even as a little girl. Or not so little then—had she been thirteen when they read that, fourteen? Old enough that he'd felt okay telling her about adultery, and immorality, and dishonesty.

He'd worried so much after her mother left that he was going to screw it all up. That he'd do something stupid or, worse, *not* do the things a parent should. But they'd done okay together. For a while anyway.

God, it had been hard after she was gone. The house felt empty—worse than empty. It felt lifeless. But after a while he got used to it, and he'd started to appreciate the privacy, the solitude, the peace to do any damn thing he wanted without worrying about someone else.

Until this girl came anyway. Now he had to stay in his room more than he would have liked. He couldn't sit on the porch in peace, feet propped up on the rail, the susurration of the waves a perfect background for reading because it didn't claim the attention, just provided a soft, soothing sound track, white noise. Now he felt conscious of things he never worried about, like the fact that he usually ate standing up at the sink. Seemed expedient before—but her presence made him aware of how it looked. And it made good sense to eat from whatever pan he cooked in, use whatever he'd stirred it with to feed himself—conserved both water and effort. But he'd feel funny about it if she came into the kitchen while he was doing it, like he was some kind of weirdo, one of those crazy hermit people you read about sometimes in the paper.

Not that he gave a crap what she thought. Who was she? Just some failure he'd found on the beach, a freeloader and a drifter.

Except . . . she wasn't those things, he had to admit. She'd found a job immediately, and he could tell by her dragging steps down the hallway that she'd worked a long day. Didn't seem like an addict—and he knew about that.

She was here to get away from something. "We had a miscarriage," she said. And that was shitty, for sure, but it happened, didn't it. And people dealt with it. But not this girl. She'd taken off and was out of her element, a little yuppie princess if he ever saw one, but she was choosing to live like one of the lost souls that found their way to beach towns all over the world and never left.

It took a lot to make someone walk out on everything. He ought to know. And a tiny part of him wondered what it had taken to make her do it.

Marcie

The house was empty when Marcie woke up, light streaming through the salt-rimed window of the purple bedroom. In the kitchen she found coffee in the percolator, still hot, and helped herself to a cup before taking a quick shower and reluctantly pulling on the T-shirt and her work skirt. Flint still hadn't come back by the time she left the house at nine.

Her first stop was the island's lone grocery store up the street from Flint's house, where she bought two pairs of shorts off a sale rack that featured sunscreen and boogie boards and Styrofoam coolers and souvenirs—they were knee-length and flowered, but it was better than the only other choices: tight short shorts that would barely skim her rear end.

She kept moving through the store, throwing into her cart a pair of cheap off-brand Keds, red plastic sunglasses (40 percent off because one lens was scratched), a mortifying three pack of bulk panties, and a Wet n Wild blush and lip gloss. At least she wouldn't look like a derelict.

Darla's daily staff meal meant that was one less thing she had to spend money on. Hopefully she'd earn enough today to pick up her car Monday morning—she'd need to call Chuck and let him know she'd be out till Tuesday.

When Marcie made it to the restaurant, the three men were still sitting at the bar as if they'd spent the night there. Marcie ordered a grouper sandwich from Darla, changed in the bathroom, and then hovered at the service bar, listening to Bink deep in a story about working on some film—the highlight of his postretirement avocation as a film extra in Chicago was apparently being tapped to be a stand-in for Paul Newman in one of his movies.

"We've heard this one, Bink," Darla said. "For Christ's sake, Newman's been dead for thirteen years."

"It's always hard to lose a colleague," Bink said solemnly.

Darla and Pete hooted out loud laughs, and even kindly Art couldn't suppress a snort.

"Shut up, ya jealous so-and-sos," Bink muttered. "That's a great story."

"No, a great story woulda been if you worked on that Liz Taylor movie he did—what's it? *Cat on the Roof*," Pete piped in, his long legs bent froglike out to the side. He gave a whistle. "Whoo, that girl could wear a nightie like nobody's business. Whaddaya call 'em? Negligees?" He pronounced it "neg-li-jeez."

Darla looked wistful. "That was back when breasts were breasts." She nodded in Marcie's direction. "No offense to the lady." Darla apparently forgot that she herself wasn't actually one of the boys. And Marcie had been under the impression that breasts were still breasts.

When her food came up she took the plate to a deck table as the four started a lively debate about old-fashioned God-made bosoms versus the surgically enhanced models of modern Hollywood.

Most of mastering the skill of waitressing was pattern recognition, just like in event planning. Locals were the easiest—if she kept the beers coming and checked in now and then to make sure they were okay, then they were friendly, polite, easy to wait on—and good tippers. But tourists were something else again. Families on vacation came in with kids tight-strung from too long in the sun, tired from playing on the beach, irritable and cranky and noisy about it. Babies made circles of scraps around their high chairs—anything put into their hands wound up on the floor, and none of the parents ever cleaned up after them. The trick there was to act like she was on vacation too—as if nothing could be more fun than refilling sippy cups and picking up food their demanding kids tossed down over and over again. If she could keep the perky smile on her face, she could usually count on what she considered an apology tip from the parents.

She was surprised to discover she liked the work—it demanded enough focus that it halted the steady stream of thoughts ticker-taping through her head. When a server called in for the evening shift, Marcie offered to work straight through—she was finally getting the hang of things and one more shift should net her plenty of cash to ransom her car.

Around eight o'clock Darla offered live music—the Beach Monkeys, a long-haired cover band who seemed to travel with their own groupies, kids who looked barely legal. A table full of girls got tipsy and loud and danced sloppily together, asses hanging out of their shorts; tight, tan bellies exposed; breasts pushed up so high, it made Marcie wince. They drank piña coladas and rum runners and daiquiris and hurricanes—frozen drinks Darla hated making and that took forever to get from the bar.

The boys hung together like a gang, made overly bold by too much testosterone and the strength of their numbers. They leered at Marcie and Hannah as though their shorts and the loud, baggy Tequila Mockingbird shirts were a thong and pasties, and made meaningful eye contact while they ordered shot after shot—drinks with names like Rocky Mountain bear fucker, or slippery nipple, or alien cumshot.

When five more of the type came through the door, shoving one another, laughing so loud the lead singer paused from writhing against the mic like an overeager exotic dancer in his fervent rendition of "Sweet Child o' Mine" and glared, Marcie sighed when they settled at one of the picnic-style tables on the deck, in her section.

"What can I get for you gentlemen tonight?" she asked at their table.

"Hey, darlin'." Their spokesman was tall, good-looking—smooth olive skin and knowing, heavy-lidded eyes and thick, careless hair—the type of guy she used to avoid like the plague in high school even before she met Will. Boys like that were too sure of themselves, too prideful and entitled. "I tell you what we're in the mood for tonight. We'd all like"—he leaned forward, as though he had a special secret just for her—"the best muff ever."

Bingo.

His friends cracked up, as though they couldn't get over the cleverness of their buddy's zinger.

"Okeydoke. Can I see some ID?" She kept her tone flat as

they loudly complained about being carded, but each one produced a legit driver's license before she turned back toward
the bar.

The drink was all liquor, she saw as Darla rolled her eyes at
the order and made the round of shots while the regulars looked
on. Darla had a savantlike knowledge of obscure cocktails, and
without consulting anything she poured vodka and rum, Jack
Daniel's and Johnnie Walker. *Jesus*. These little brats were already obnoxious. Marcie could just imagine how they'd act after
a few shots of solid alcohol.

"Keep an eye on those guys," Darla said as she placed the
shot glasses on her tray. "They don't need too many of these."

"They don't need any of them," Marcie said under her breath
as she headed back out to where they sat. A breeze was blowing,
but it brought only hot air.

She stood alongside their table and started setting the shots
in front of each of them. All five had gone suddenly silent as
she'd approached, except for snorting sounds coming out of one
of them—the scrawny, pimply one sitting next to the railing.

"You gentlemen need anything else right now?" she asked as
she leaned over to put the last two glasses on the far end of the
table.

The little skinny one made a grab for her breast.

Marcie reared back, and without thinking she smacked the
bottom of her empty tray sharply on his head, snapping, "What
are you *thinking*, sonny?"

Sonny? played through her mind incongruously. *Really?*

"Ow! Hey!" The kid sat all the way up, hand on his head.
"What's your problem, bitch? I was reaching for my drink and
you got in the way!"

"That is *not* what you were doing. You were copping a feel.
Save it for the prom, kiddo."

The music stopped suddenly, and Marcie felt every eye in the restaurant on her back. Her face prickled. The ringleader stood, tall enough to cast a shadow over her from the light sconce behind him.

"Did you just *hit* a customer?" he said in a tone of disbelief.

"He grabbed me. You saw that."

"That was not a grab, ma'am—all due respect." The kid's tone was oily, overly familiar. "My friend's hand slipped, unfortunately into your personal space."

"Your friend's hand *slipped* ten inches in the air above his drink." But her words were losing steam. *Did* he reach up deliberately? Now she wasn't sure.

The kid shook his head, like a parent disappointed in a child's poor grades. His eyes slid to his buddies, who had all emptied their shots while she'd been talking to the tall one. "I'm afraid we're going to need to talk to your manager."

Are you kidding me, bucko? she wanted to say. This snotty postadolescent kid was going to turn her in to her boss? Choking, impotent outrage closed off her throat. This wasn't supposed to be happening. She was forty-three years old; she was a respected, competent professional. What the hell was she doing in a tacky dive bar on a third-rate beach, about to get in trouble thanks to some shitty little pervert who tried to paw at his cocktail waitress?

"Fine. I'll get her," she gritted out. She turned to head back inside and she could hear the boys break out into barely smothered snickers behind her. She hoped they choked on their own spit.

"Darla," Marcie said at the bar, and she heard the edge in her own voice. Art must have too—his watery brown eyes softened in concern as he looked up at her.

"That's my name; don't wear it out," the bartender said.

"Table outside wants to see you."

Darla raised one bleached eyebrow. "Oh, really? Friends of mine?"

"No," she said tightly. "While I was serving their drinks, one of them grabbed me. I reacted without thinking and, um . . . rapped him on the head with my tray."

She heard Bink let out a snort, but Darla looked grave.

"Hah. No shit. Well. Yeah. Gotta address that, for sure." She came out from behind the bar. Laid-back Darla might have tolerated Marcie's total incompetence at the job, but even she wasn't about to let a waitress hit a customer, for God's sake. "You wanna come on out here with me, Marce?" Darla said over her shoulder, walking toward the deck.

Marcie's cheeks flamed. It would either be he said/she said, or she was just about to be humiliated.

"Problem, gents?" Darla said as they came out onto the wooden planking.

The tall kid shot a quick look at Marcie, a smug smile, before drawing on a grave expression for the owner. "Your waitress assaulted my friend over there, ma'am, hate to tell you."

"She did?"

The kid nodded sadly. "Afraid so. Tristan was reaching for his drink and accidentally brushed by the, er, young lady, and she just . . . snapped. How's the noggin, Tris?" he called over.

The pimply faced brat moaned and pulled his fingers away from his head toward his face. "I can't tell if it's bleeding."

The tall kid shook his head with that disappointed-parent expression again. "Hopefully that won't need stitches," he said.

"Oh, right," Marcie snapped. "You'd better check for a concussion too. And try not to get brain matter on the table, okay?"

Darla frowned at her and held up a hand. "Marcie—no call

for that. What would you gents like for me to do about this is-sue?" she asked the kid.

He was openly smirking. "Well . . ." He seemed to be con-sidering it. "We'd rather not take any legal action—it's not really your fault if your servers are on a short fuse."

"True story, my man."

The boy heaved a sigh. "Tell you what. How about our tab's on the house tonight, and we call it even?"

Darla nodded somberly. "That's what'll square things up for us here, huh?" She turned to regard Marcie, then looked back at the boys. "Or—hang on—what about this?" Darla took a step closer to the kid, who stood a good half foot taller and twice as wide as the stringy bar owner. "How about you and your gropey pals there pay your tab and get the hell out of my bar, and if you tip Marcie here well enough on your way out, there's a chance I won't call the cops on you for sexual assault and then beat the shit out of you while we're waiting on the sirens."

Marcie froze in shock—along with every patron on the deck.

"What the . . ." the ringleader said.

Darla was still smiling, but it was not a friendly expression. "I don't see you digging for your wallet, boy."

"You can't—"

"Fellas?" Darla said, and until then Marcie hadn't noticed that every one of the regulars who spent most of Tequila Mock-ingbird's operating hours sitting at the bar had assembled in the threshold of the sliding doors that opened onto the deck. They were doughy from drink, and they had the sag and wrinkles of men far past their fighting prime. But they carried an air of menace that the five kids were decades away from matching.

The leader was faltering, and his buddies knew it. They shifted awkwardly, getting to their feet.

"Hold on there, my friends," Darla said mildly. "Marcie—their check."

"That's twenty-seven fifty," she said, pulling the ticket from her apron. The kid reached for his wallet and pulled out plastic.

Darla crossed her arms and smiled even wider. "You're kidding, right?"

The kid glared, and she heard a rustling from the men lined up behind her. A couple of the other customers scooted back on their benches, two women got up and beelined inside, and Marcie had a moment where she thought things might get really, seriously ugly.

Then the kid broke eye contact and nodded to his gang. "Who's got cash? Pay her."

Two twenties landed on the table, and then the boys filed out, the seething knot of regulars right behind them all the way to the entrance.

"Don't come back now, ya hear!" Darla called out cheerfully to the retreating backs of the bullies.

Marcie heard a slapping sound, and turned to see where it was coming from, and then it was joined by another, and another, until suddenly she realized the entire restaurant was clapping, and not with the sharp edge of mockery when she dropped a tray. Darla was hamming it up—bowing and curtsying and blowing kisses. Then she held one arm out to Marcie and joined in the applause, nodding until finally Marcie turned to the crowd and gave a tiny curtsy of her own, and the clapping grew louder, and someone whistled, and she heard, "Attagirl!" from somewhere out on the deck.

Darla cut her from the floor around eleven. "Good job, newbie," the bartender crowed, and the casual praise felt as good as any raise or bonus she'd ever received. Marcie was worn out from the long day, her pockets bulging with cash—but when Darla held up an ice-cold mug of beer dripping foam, she sat and had a shiftie at the bar with the owner and the ubiquitous regulars to celebrate her triumph.

Darla didn't want her walking home alone that night—just in case, she said—and she took money from the register and handed it to Marcie when she finished her shift. "Take a cab," she said. "Have the cabbie wait till you get inside, 'kay? I gave you some extra to tip him big enough so he'll do it."

She couldn't believe how kind the grizzled old bar owner was being to a total stranger who'd worked a few impromptu shifts at her restaurant. For all her rough edges she was really very sweet, Marcie realized. They all were—the men who sat at the bar like they'd set down roots there, the kind of men she'd probably have dismissed as barflies at home, if she'd even noticed them at all. But tonight they'd come to back her up, every one of them.

"Thanks for everything, Darla," she said, standing to leave after turning down the offer of a refill. "The boys," as Darla incongruously called the desiccated old men, called out, "You take care, honey," and "Good job tonight," and Marcie waved good-bye with an unexpected pang.

"Hey, newbie," Darla called out, and Marcie stopped on her way to the door and turned.

"We're shy a server for the lunch shift tomorrow. You think you might want to help out?"

Marcie walked back over to the bar. "Sure," she said, reaching for the apron she'd left there. "Why not?"

She waved good night, feeling like part of their circle.

Flint

~~~

ven when the girl wasn't here, the house felt different: an extra coffee mug washed and upside down in the drainboard, a second towel on the rack in the bathroom. And it smelled different too—not unpleasant, nothing he could identify, just . . . different.

At some point Flint had gone from resenting her intrusion into his life to liking the feeling of a house with someone else in it, another heartbeat.

He thought he'd left that desire behind a long time ago.

Since the girl got here memories of Jessie had started breaking through the surface, like a shark's fin telling you you'd better damn well get out of the water. Instead he'd waded on in, even though he knew better—knew it was smarter to move past pain, seal it off, live in the reality you had now. Flint learned that from his first commander, a former POW who told his men that the ones who survived in his camp were those who accepted their situation as their new reality. Lingering in the past, mourning all that you'd lost—that was a short trip to a shallow grave. Isobel had always told him he needed to "work through it" . . . "make peace with the past" . . . "find a way forward." But she was wrong—you could never get back something precious once you'd lost it, and parsing out all the ways you failed would never undo what had been done. What *you* had done. And no one else could fix it for you either.

Even Isobel figured that out finally and stopped trying to hold on to something that could never come back any more than Jessie would.

Marcie wasn't anything at all like Jessie. She was quiet and unassuming, and for the most part kept to herself. But Jessie, even if she had her nose buried in a book, would no more let silence take over the house than she would wear a pink tutu and a tiara. His daughter always had some noise going on— usually the stereo blasting at all hours, not only loud enough that he couldn't think or read or concentrate, but that he was pretty sure anyone within a one-mile radius couldn't either.

"It's too loud!" he'd bellow.

"You're too old!" she'd fire right back.

Mouthy kid, that one. Always with the quick comeback. He'd try not to smile at her sass, but it was hard sometimes. She had a tongue on her—and a will of iron. Wonder where she got that.

The one good thing that came out of Marcie's bivouac here was that he finally had reason to deal with all his daughter's stuff he'd been holding on to all these years. Clutter was bad for the brain, even the kind you shoved into corners you never went into. It was still there, mucking up your mind with useless crap you let occupy the same space as you. It was long past time he got rid of it. And with Marcie apparently gone for the day to that sandpit she worked in, there was no time like the present.

~~~

He felt guilty letting himself into the room—as if it belonged to Marcie now. She'd cleaned a bit, he saw, but other than that, the only evidence that someone lived in there again was the fresh bedding, neatly tucked at the edges and pulled smooth.

He yanked open the louvered doors of the closet so hard, one jumped the track, and that took five stupid wasted minutes to get back where it belonged. What few things Marcie had were stashed in here, staying out of the way as surely as she did his. He pulled down one of the boxes on the shelf, then another one, stacking them, carrying them together outside. The boxes made a loud thunk as he dropped them into the trunk, his car buckling under the weight with a creak before bouncing back up on its shocks. Flint winced at the noise.

He'd wanted to wait till full dark—he could only imagine what the nosy biddy next door would make of this—but he didn't know what time Marcie would be back. What if she came inside and discovered him rummaging around in her room?

His room. His house.

The next box wasn't as bad. "Fragile!!!! Best stuffed animals!!" was scrawled over and over on every visible surface in Jessie's still familiar childish handwriting. The hell did she save those for? *Probably eaten up with cockroaches and moths by now,* he thought, but as he shoved it to the back of the trunk along with another one—"Clothes—do NOT throw away!"—he noticed with reluctant approval that Jessie had carefully taped every single seam so that there was no way in for any marauding critters. Smart girl.

Three trips took care of the boxes up top; he was running out of room in the trunk and the rest would have to get stacked in the backseat. Better just to throw it all out, but there was no sense wasting things that maybe someone could use. His shoulders were starting to ache, unused muscles in his back fluttering a protest as he clean-and-jerked two more—Jesus Christ, had to be books—and carried them out.

The flimsy aged cardboard gave way just inside the front door and its contents rained down on his feet like little missiles: random figurines and a few books, notebooks and stacks of cards and papers. He cursed, furious, as he dropped the other box to the floor, leaned over to stack the fallen items on top of it. He didn't even take time to look at what it all was, just wanted the damn things out—out of his house, out of his life, out of the way—then wrapped his arms around the whole carefully balanced pile and lifted.

He'd bent over wrong, jerked up too quick—he knew it as soon as he felt something give in his back. The pain shot up his spine and into his neck, and the boxes and the top one's exposed contents toppled back to the carpet. He stood gingerly, a hand to the small of his back.

Goddamn girl—one more reason taking her in had been a mistake. If it weren't for her, he wouldn't be messing with this crap, wouldn't be in a mood that had him forgetting how the hell to lift—with your legs, not your back, basic training, for God's sake. He'd be quietly reading a good book, or sleeping, or doing any number of other things.

There were reasons you stayed out of other people's business, reasons you minded your own. He didn't want to worry about anyone else. Didn't need anyone to worry about him. That was what freedom looked like—he'd learned that the hard way.

Goddamned old age. Time to give it a rest for now before he did himself a real injury. The torn box gaped open, revealing a bundled stack of letters he remembered saving for his daughter at her strict command, Jessie's handwriting facing up at him like a mute accusation. He went to the kitchen for some tape to seal the damn thing shut, and as he leaned over the box to retrieve its spilled contents, his back injury—a faulty D ring fifty feet up a rappelling rope decades ago—flared again. Something tore, and he fell to the floor in an agony so white-hot, he couldn't find breath to scream.

Two hours and seven minutes after he'd collapsed to the floor—Flint had ticked the passing seconds off in his mind to distract himself from the pain and the moldy smell of the ancient flattened carpet that told him it needed to be ripped out—he heard the key in the lock, which meant the girl had finally come back. He wanted to roll out of the way of the door but he couldn't, and she eased it open just a few inches before it bulldozed the spilled papers and books along the floor and butted up against his side. He felt the pressure as she pushed gently, and wanted to bat the wood right back at her.

"That's far enough."

"Flint?"

"You don't have to whisper. Who the hell else is here?"

"What's . . ." There was another slight pressure on the door—he assumed she was trying to open it wide enough to poke her head through.

"Knock it off, girl—you want to rupture my spleen?"

"What are you doing?" Her tone was bewildered, her volume still low.

"Yoga, what do you think?"

"Are you okay?"

"I'm fine."

A pause, the door hovering in the space between his body and the jamb. It was almost funny to watch it waver there as she tried to work things out in her mind.

"I'm going to go around the back, okay?"

"Whatever you gotta do."

The door closed and a few moments later he heard her footsteps in the kitchen. Then she was standing in the room beside him.

"That's not yoga."

"Good eye. Too bad you're not so slick at spotting sarcasm."

"What happened?"

He didn't answer for a long moment, half hoping she'd just go to her room and spare him the indignity. But she wasn't budging, and finally he grunted out, "Back. Happens sometimes. I just need to lie here awhile and it's fine. Go on."

She stood there, and he could feel her eyes on him even though he wasn't looking at her face, her gaze running over the dropped boxes, contents splayed across the carpet like entrails. She shifted her weight back and forth, then finally said, "Call me if you need help."

He just snorted, and watched her feet retreat down the back hallway. He heard the door to her room shut, open again, and then the bathroom door. Heard running water, a flushing toilet. The door opened and another one closed.

Seventeen minutes. He rolled, just a little, trying to get fully onto his back to relieve this throbbing ache, and the spasm the movement caused made him gasp and bite back a shout.

Six minutes. He heard the door open again, her footsteps down the hall and another door open and close, and then back along the hall seconds later. Then she was kneeling beside him, her arms full of bedding.

"You wouldn't ask me for help if you were bleeding out,

would you?" she said, dropping the pile and spreading open a blanket that wafted over him like a settling parachute.

"The hell are you doing?" He tried to wriggle away from her, but the bolt of pain made him clench his jaw and go still.

"If you're going to stay here all night, you might as well bed down. Don't be an ass about it."

He looked directly at her for the first time, at the flyaway strands of her hair escaping its bobtail. "That's some bedside manner you got."

"You're not exactly a model patient. And I know," she added, cutting off his reply. "You didn't ask to be anyone's patient. Can you lift your head?"

He did, slightly, and she glided the pillow underneath. He sank back onto it, the angle offering an instant shard of relief.

She stood up, taking a handful of the linens into the kitchen. He heard her banging around in there, and four minutes later she was back beside him.

"I crushed the ice so it'll lie flat. Heat might be better, but if you can move enough for me to get this underneath you it may help."

He looked at the wrapped towel in her hands, its edges tucked like hospital corners to keep the ice in. She was looking right back at him, no trace of the mouse now. Ignoring the split carcass of the box, its obsolete contents that were none of her business, and for that, at least, he was grateful.

Slowly, carefully, he eased one arm to the floor and put just enough weight on it to lift himself away from the carpet. She slid the towel under him so deftly he barely felt her skim his clothes. "What's got into you, girl?" he muttered, settling gingerly back down.

"My name's Marcie. I know you know that."

He shot a glare at her, but it didn't even seem to faze her.

"How does that feel?"

He grunted. "Cold. There's a heating pad in the hall closet. Top shelf."

She pushed up to her feet. "Logistically that doesn't seem the smartest place for an isolated guy with a bad back to keep it."

He wasn't sure he liked this new attitude of hers, but she had a point. "Some pills in the medicine cabinet in the bathroom," was all he said. "Prescription bottle."

When she came back she was holding the bottle and a cup of water, the heating pad tucked under one arm. She set everything down and plugged the pad into the wall beside him, waiting patiently while he slowly lifted himself again so she could swap it for the towel. "Can you sit up to take this?" she asked, taking one of the pills out of the bottle.

"Two," he said. "Don't need the water."

"This says, 'Take one every six—'"

"You gonna make me wrestle you for it? Give me two, dammit."

She returned his glare, and for a few beats they sat there staring each other down. It was more direct eye contact than they'd had since she'd shown up on his doorstep. Then she deliberately shook a second pill out, looking at him again with a familiar expression he couldn't place . . . until he realized it was the look he used to fix on Jessie when she was pushing it.

"Open up." She placed the pills on his tongue and he swallowed, grimacing at the bitterness. Then she settled back onto her ankles, her knees folded in front of her in a way Flint hadn't been able to contort himself in years. This new version of her was unsettling. The girl . . . Marcie . . . had been much easier to deal with when she'd seemed shell-shocked.

She stayed there next to him in her uncomfortable-looking squat. "So what do you go by?" she said finally. "I'm not calling you Flint."

"That's my name."

"It's the name of a rock. So I'm guessing it must be your last name. Right?"

He stared up at the ceiling.

"This isn't the army. I'm not calling you by your last name. So what else you got?"

"Fine." It came out on a hiss, like a bellows. "You're so hung up on names, it's Herman."

One corner of her mouth was quirked up. "That what your friends call you?"

Was she *messing* with him? He turned his head back up toward the ceiling again, ignoring her. Finally she got to her feet, and now her gaze flitted over the boxes he'd stupidly dropped, his private things strewn out for her to dissect.

"What's all this?" she asked, leaning down.

"Leave it. I'll get it."

She raised her eyebrows at him as if to underscore the ludicrousness of his doing anything right now but flopping around like a fish on the ground. But she straightened, doing as he asked. Well, demanded. She didn't go back to her room and shut the door and leave him in peace, though—instead she reached down to the pile of bedding she'd brought in and stretched a sheet over the sofa.

"The hell are you doing?"

She didn't answer, just plopped a pillow against the arm and opened up another blanket.

"Girl! What are you doing?"

She kept her back to him. "I don't know who you're talking to."

Dammit. Goddammit. "Marcie." He gritted it out between a jaw clenched tight as a sphincter. Stubborn little creature.

She turned around with an expression as if he were an old

friend she'd run into at a party, instead of the stupid old cuss who'd brought an irritating homeless derelict into his house in the first place. "I'm going to bed down in here tonight. In case you need anything. You can just . . . ask." From the amused look on her face, this time he knew she was messing with him.

She kicked her sneakers off and slid them neatly underneath the sofa, then crawled in under the blanket. Reaching behind her, she clicked off the lamp. With the windows covered it was pitch-black, and in the blessed darkness he didn't have to see her smirking at him anymore.

"Good night, Herman," she said softly.

He didn't reply. How the hell was he supposed to sleep with the sound of someone else in the room breathing?

He stewed about it for eleven minutes before the pills kicked in and he lost count of the passing seconds and drifted off into unconsciousness.

Marcie

Did he mean to take the boxes somewhere else for safe storage? Or just keep the girl's things in the car to get them out of Marcie's room? Before she could ask, the pills had taken effect and he was out cold.

So she lugged the heavier box to his car, put it in the last available space, and closed the trunk. She picked up all the items that had spilled out of the burst box, but its cardboard was too age softened and flimsy now to bother trying to put it back inside, so she took the box itself to the garbage bin at the side of the house—the concept of municipal recycling didn't seem to have made it to Palmetto Key yet.

She wasn't sure what to do with what had been inside the box. The car doors were locked, not that there was a good place to secure everything inside anyway, and she sure as hell wasn't letting herself into his bedroom. So she brought the pile of papers into her room and tucked it into a dresser drawer.

She told herself it made sense—they were his daughter's

things, and so she returned them to his daughter's room for safekeeping until Flint woke up and could tell her what he wanted to do with them.

But if she were honest with herself, she knew that wasn't where he'd have wanted her to put them. Knew he wouldn't have wanted her to see any of it at all.

The papers must have once been tied together with purple ribbon, but the fall had jostled the stack free and the bow lay slack around just a few obedient envelopes, the rest gathered into a sloppy pile where Marcie had hastily stacked them: old report cards—good grades—and school papers with circled red A pluses at the top; ticket stubs for sporting events and movies and a few concerts, most of the bands B-list even in the eighties; a pile of folded papers, all different sizes and types.

She pulled the stack back out of the drawer—to neaten everything, she told herself. To tie it all safely back together. But the justification came even as she was unfolding one of the papers. Her eyes flicked to the date line—July 23, 1993.

Dad,

Things are great here. I am having a really great time.

That's not true. I am NOT having a good time. The lake we saw in the brochure is a POND, and it's got algae all over it at the shoreline, and the water smells like old lettuce. Swimming lessons are boring. No one here really knows how to swim at ALL, so the counselor—who I don't think is a very good swimmer herself—is starting from the VERY BEGIN-NING, like, kicking and dog paddling. I could swim about eighty laps by the time they figure out how to float. I miss the gulf.

Also, would you please send me some more books? At night
everyone sits in a circle and tells stupid ghost stories, and
they aren't very scary, and they aren't even very good stories. I would rather be reading.

Please go kiss a shark for me. We don't have any here. And don't
just eat soup, okay? Make dinner once in a while. I want you
guys to figure out some good new recipes and we'll all make
them together when I get home, which I hope will be SOON.

Love,
Jessie

Marcie's laugh was loud in the silent house, and she covered
her mouth with two fingers. The girl's personality jumped off
the page, right into her face. Flint's daughter was sassy. How
marvelous to imagine the sour old man navigating a firecracker
of a little girl.

You guys, she'd said. And something about all of them cooking. Her mother? As if drawn by magnets she reached for another letter that had sat just below the first.

Dad,

Ignore the last letter. (Except about my books and cooking
dinner. And the shark.) This place is AWESOME. Yesterday
we learned archery—that's bows and arrows, I'm sure you
know—and it turns out I'm really good at it. I bet I could
shoot an apple off your head, like William Tell and his son (ha
ha, if you trust me!). Today we went on a canoe trip, which I
really like, except I think it would be more fun if I didn't have
to worry about the other people in the boat not knowing

how to row. I bet I would rather kayak. Let's all get kayaks when I get home! You and Isobel can get a two-seater but Berto and I can handle our own.

Everyone's pretty nice, which is good. I met one girl who is from Miami, and it's like she doesn't even know anything about the ocean! I don't think Miami people even notice that they live right next to one. But I'm teaching her some stuff, and she's teaching me Spanish.

Hasta luego, Papá. Te veo pronto!

Con Amor,
Jessie

Who was Isobel? A stepmother? A sister? Was Berto the girl's brother—Flint's son? Where would another child have lived in this tiny two-bedroom house? Marcie couldn't picture even a young boy sharing this overpoweringly purple room, and there was only the single bed.

Who was Flint back then, when his daughter filled his house with the kind of spunk and vibrancy that filled these pages?

Marcie needed to stop. This wasn't her business. These letters weren't meant for her.

Shame wrapped tentacles around her conscience even as she pulled another letter from the drawer, this one from farther down the stack—the date line was from 1995.

Dear Dad,

I know I didn't want to go away again this summer, but I'm going to be honest—this is probably the best camp we've ever picked. (That doesn't mean you were right, just for the record. It just means things turned out okay even though you made me go.) We get to work on all kinds of writing, and there are teachers here who are published, like for real—in magazines and newspapers, and two of them even have actual books of their own, like with their name on the cover and everything! (I asked Ms. Fontana, our Ethics in Reporting teacher, if I could have a copy of hers with her autograph, and she said of course but not to tell anyone else because she had only a couple of copies with her and couldn't give one to everyone. But I'm telling you because I had to tell someone!)

Living in the dorms is kind of fun, but I'm not sure about this when I go to college. Everyone shares ONE BATHROOM. It's bad enough with you and me trying to fit around each other—can you imagine thirty girls all in there together? It's a lot bigger than ours, at least. And I don't really like sharing a room either, but at least I like my roommate—her name is Andromeda (I think that's pretty), and she's from Port St. Lucie, so she loves the beach too, and she wants to be a novelist. I told her that I can write the Pulitzer Prize–winning article about her when she's famous. ☺

I'm worried about Isobel. Are you making sure she's okay? I've been writing her every day, but I haven't heard back, and you know that's not like her. Please make sure she's eating—even if she has to eat the stuff you cook. (Ha ha— I'm just kidding.) I think about her a lot—there's a girl here whose little brother died when she was just like six or something, and she says her mom was never ever the same, like she never got over it. And that kid was just a baby. It must be so much worse for Isobel because she loved Berto for nineteen years, not just one. I miss him all the time, even here.

Anyway, I know you're probably reading this on the back porch, so wave at the gulf for me. I miss you guys. And please make sure you're eating too when you feed Isobel, because she and I both think you look weird when you get too skinny. :P

Love you, Dad,
Jess

Marcie carefully folded the letter back along the creases. Even without her knowing who Isobel was, the idea of the woman losing her nineteen-year-old son made her chest ache. Had she ever told Will that in her mind the amorphous little shape they'd seen in the ultrasound tech's office was a girl? A little girl who would one day argue with them both about cutting her tangled hair; who would dress up as Wonder Woman for Halloween, or Black Widow, or hell, Spider-Man if she wanted to; who would make runny messes of broken egg on the countertop, standing on a step stool and insisting on "helping" Will's mom bake the cakes she was always bringing over from next door?

Marcie had lost a dream, her vast imagination of an untapped potential, the possibility of a road they ultimately never actually traveled. But Isobel had lost a *child*, a nineteen-year-old boy—man—she'd given birth to and raised to adulthood. Had Flint loved the boy too? Raised him along with his own daughter? Was that what had made him so closed off and bitter toward the world? They lost the boy, and then they must have lost each other too, or the woman would still be here with him, wouldn't she?

And where was his daughter now?

Flint

When he woke the sofa was bare, blankets neatly folded at one end, and his back blessedly quiescent. He didn't want to move, didn't want to even turn his head to see where the girl had gone, afraid the slightest motion would bring the pain flaring back to life.

Pills had done their job, though—normally even the sound of the stealthy brush of cotton socks against the linoleum brought him to total abrupt awareness from the soundest sleep. As a teenage Jessie had discovered to her frustration more than once. The image of her frozen figure in the hall when he opened his bedroom door and caught her sneaking out, face a comical study in found-out guilt, almost made him smile. Until he remembered he hadn't caught her every time. He hadn't caught her when he should have.

Muffled clinking from the kitchen told him where the girl was. He shifted and his back warned him to stay put. He slammed his eyelids closed again when the sounds stopped and he heard her coming toward the living room.

"I know you're awake. You might as well have your coffee."

He opened his eyes and saw her standing above him like a Valkyrie, instead of a spear in her hand a thick ceramic mug with a straw sticking out of it. "I'd still be sleeping if it weren't for you banging around in there."

She settled herself carefully on the floor beside him. "No, you wouldn't. You never sleep past dawn, and it's nearly eight."

Eight o'clock? How the hell had he slept that late? He started up, carefully, but intent on getting the hell off this floor.

"Easy," she said, setting the mug down and reaching behind her for the pillow she'd used the night before. "Just push up slowly and I'll prop these up for you to lean on."

"I'm not going to lie around and sip out of a straw like some vegetable. You want to be useful, help me up."

She was leaning his pillow and hers together against the bookshelf beside him as if he hadn't spoken, moving the heating pad aside—she must have clicked it off at some point, because it had gone cold—neatly wrapping the cord.

"Okay, all you have to do is push up to a sit and scoot over." She held out one arm near him as a lever in case he needed it, but Flint ignored it. "A caffeine headache on top of everything else won't make you feel any better."

"I didn't ask you to do any of this." He knew he was being an ass, hateful and ungrateful. He could hear it in his own voice, the bitter, lonely old man who shook his fist at neighborhood kids—if there had been any anymore—and yelled at them to get off his lawn. A caricature.

"I know." She said it quietly and without inflection. Just a statement.

"Well. What are you doing it for?" But he only muttered it.

She seemed to know he'd asked it for form's sake, and ignored him, handing him the mug once he was resting back against the pillows—and sitting was an agony, but already he could feel his back calming in the new position. Slow and gradual was the ticket, he knew from other occasions. He took a sip and relished the heat and bitter bite.

Marcie pushed back to her feet, and Flint debated asking her to try to leverage his weight so he could pull himself up. She didn't weigh more than a minute, but if he could grit his teeth through the worst of it, it might be enough to at least get him mobile. Get him somewhere besides the godforsaken floor. But she'd already left the room—finally. Good. He'd just sit here till the coffee was gone and then he could work his awkward way to his feet in privacy.

But she was back—like a bad dream, like a case of the clap. Was she going to stay here all day, hovering over him like a damn mosquito? This time she held a plate, a fork in her other hand.

"If you think you're feeding me like a goddamn baby bird, you're outta your mind."

"Of course not. You're not helpless." She leaned down to plop the plate onto his lap, dropped the fork on top of it, straightened. "I'm going to get ready. If you want help up, you've got about thirty minutes to let me know." And she left the room again, this time disappearing down the back hallway.

The heat seeping from the plate onto his thighs snapped him out of watching after her. What the hell? Normally he could shut her down in an instant with a barked word, get her to back off, leave him alone. Suddenly she wasn't so much as flinching, yapping right back at him. He hadn't had to deal with anyone's lip since—

Didn't matter. It was no concern of his whether the girl grew a pair or not—except it made it easier for him to get her out of his hair. Hard to kick her out when she seemed like a walking casualty, just waiting to be victimized.

He ate the eggs because he was starving—he hadn't had dinner last night before his damn back hobbled him. And he had no intention of spending any more time sitting here on his floor like an invalid.

Trouble was, there was no way to lever himself up without wrenching his back around in a way it screamed at him that it didn't intend to move. Damned old age. Not one good thing about it. Your own body betrayed you one increment at a time, until you were living in a useless husk you had no control over. And the world kept studying every disease known to man to find ways to keep extending people's lives so they could live even older. What the hell for? Let 'em die once their useful life was over, just like every other natural thing on the planet. When his own works finally quit, it wasn't going to be a bad thing. He'd been done for a long time.

By the time the girl came out, dressed in that ratty T-shirt she wore to her shithole restaurant, he'd long since finished the food and shoved the plate, the empty mug on top of it, the few inches away he could reach. She came and stood nearby but said nothing and made no move to help him.

"Think you got enough leverage in that puny body of yours to lend a hand?" he growled.

"I'm stronger than I look." She put down her apron and extended both hands toward him, crossed over each other, palms facing out. He clasped them with his own, and they felt strange inside his, small and soft and delicate in a way he'd forgotten all about. She'd never get him off the ground.

But when she curled her body into a C and pulled backward, he was surprised at her solidity and force. It hurt—hurt like a bitch—but with her help he slowly, agonizingly pulled himself to his feet. His back stabbed him at the change of position, and he gritted his teeth through it.

"Where to?" she asked, coming around beside him. Her shoulder barely reached his chest, and he cupped a palm over it instead of wrapping his arm around her.

He needed so many things—the heating pad, his pills, more coffee—but he'd figure out a way to retrieve it all once she was gone, not looking at him with her big deer eyes and watching him struggle. He grunted. "Chair."

Somehow she knew to give him something to brace himself against the whole way down to the armchair, bending herself awkwardly until his seat was planted and she could bow out from under his arm. He let out a harsh breath he'd been holding. The deep cushion wasn't the best place to be, maybe, but at least sitting in a chair he felt like a human now, instead of a discarded toy thrown to the ground.

"Hang on." She went back over to the pillows on the floor and brought them over, propping them behind him until all he had to do was rest backward just slightly and he could stay right where he was, feet planted, and take some of the pressure off. She brought him the heating pad and plugged it in close enough to reach, putting the control in his hand. "Lean forward just a little," she said, sliding it directly behind the pain. She brought his pills next, setting them on the piecrust table beside him, loosening the irritating childproof cap. "I don't need to portion these out so you don't get carried away, do I?" she asked.

He might be ready for it to be over, but there was no damn way he'd throw in the towel himself. "Don't be stupid."

"Don't be such an ass."

He almost cracked a smile on that one.

She bent to retrieve his dirty dishes. "There's more coffee. I'll get you a refill."

"That'd be nice," he said quietly, after a beat, but she was already out of the room.

He flicked on the heating pad and in a few moments felt its soothing warmth start to make headway into the pain. He closed his eyes. Back when this used to happen when Jessie was around—not as often then, and only when they'd really over-done it with body surfing or volleyball or something, never from something as stupid as moving boxes—she'd hover all over him like a mother hen. It was like she loved the turn of the table, when she got to be the one in charge, the one taking care, boss-ing him around like a miniature drill instructor. After the first time he let her help him, she remembered just what to do. Such a smart kid. Such a good kid. She would have been an excellent mother.

His head grew tight and pounded, and his back flared with a fresh spear of agony. He fumbled for the pill bottle, shook three out, thought of the girl's sarcastic comment and put one back and the other two in his mouth. His mouth was dry as paper, his tongue almost too thick for him to swallow.

When he opened his eyes some indeterminate time later, the girl had left—he could feel the difference in the empty house. On the table beside him were his book, the bottle of pills, a plastic pitcher, and a glass of water on a makeshift coaster—a paper towel folded into fourths—and he reached for the glass, feeling absurdly grateful.

He was halfway through a chapter before he realized the spilled boxes were gone.

Marcie

~~~

The old man—he was right; Flint suited him much better than Herman—had been in no shape for her to ask him about the letters this morning, if she'd even dared, and by the time she came out of the bathroom, showered and ready to go, he was conked out.

When she let herself quietly out the front door, the nosy next-door neighbor was standing on the raised front porch of her own house, lofted a story higher than Flint's on stilts. Marcie wondered whether she was leaving too, but the woman simply stood there watching as Marcie locked the door, her gray head tilted to one side as if assessing her.

"Everything okay?" the woman called out.

"Fine, thanks."

"I mean with Herman," she said. "I thought I heard him shout last night." She leaned against the weathered wooden railing of her porch, as if trying to get closer without actually leaving her property.

"Oh, he's fine," Marcie said. "I didn't realize you actually knew him."

The woman's eyebrows lifted, and a smile raised indents alongside her mouth. "We've both lived here for more than forty years. You could say we're acquainted."

Considering the old man's crankiness toward his longtime neighbor, it was a wonder the woman cared at all about his well-being.

"He's okay," Marcie said. "Injured his back. I think it's happened before, so he knows how to take care of it."

The woman nodded. "Yes, it's happened before. It's lucky he had you here to help him. Isn't it."

She was peering closely at Marcie across the few yards of sand and gravel and patchy St. Augustine grass separating them, as if waiting for her to say something more. But Marcie figured she'd already told too much of Flint's business to the neighbor he seemed to have an old grudge against, so she waved a quick good-bye and headed toward the restaurant.

The heavy, humid July air draped her like a blanket, and she knew that by the time she reached Tequila Mockingbird she'd be wet more from the condensation against her skin than from sweat. She was almost used to it now, though.

By night the buildings along Marea Boulevard cloaked their flaws in darkness, gaily colored spotlights glinting off dancing fountains and silhouetting rustling palm fronds, highlighting only their good features, skipping carefully over the bad. In the sunlight the little houses and restaurants and hotels showed their shabby edges, like a well-dressed woman with unraveling hems: crumbling stucco, mildew creeping up faded walls. But it felt comfortable—a place where nothing was expected of her. No one even looked at her as she walked down the street in her comfortable shorts and Keds, face bare of makeup, hair tousled into messy waves by the humidity and trade winds and salt air. In a couple of days she'd flat-iron it into its neat bob, put on one of her stylishly tailored but never flashy dresses, smooth her sun-stained nose and cheeks and her freckles with foundation, and add just enough makeup to look polished but never cheap—in the hospitality business, appearances mattered. Well, they did at the upscale Bonafort in the Highlands anyway. Even thinking about the routine felt exhausting.

So far when she'd walked to Tequila Mockingbird she'd taken the street route—she didn't want to show up for work with her feet covered in sand. Although it hadn't taken long to realize *everything* was covered in it in Palmetto Key—the plank floorboards of the deck, the concrete inside the restaurant, rough grains on the backs of the chairs, lining the edges of every table. Her hands stayed sticky with salt, regardless of frequent washings, and the restaurant's ketchup bottles and saltshakers always had a soft white film on them no matter how often she wiped them down.

The beach route was so much more beautiful. From the street the town was tired, sad, used up, but along the water it was a vibrant, different place every day. She hadn't really noticed it at first, used to the showier Atlantic with its more assertive waves and fancy seaside homes and hotels, the kitschy obvious charm of the St. Simons lighthouse looking out for boats. Palmetto Key needed no pretense of a watchdog for watercraft—the smooth, flat gulf hid no dangerous reefs underneath.

Along the shoreline Palmetto Key revealed its true colors, literally: the subtle gradations of blue and gray and green in the placid, amiable waves lapping at the sand. The wildly varying verdant tones of the vegetation: cordgrass and sea oats and railroad vine, mangroves and sea grape—and palm trees, so many types of palms. Shockingly bold hibiscus flowers: vivid red-orange, saturated yellows with delicate pink throats, hot pinks and peaches with creamy yellow edges, white ones with fiery scarlet centers, and even one she swore was periwinkle. Even the sand was specked with pointillist dots of color—translucent tangerine shells thin as glass, silver-green sand dollars, tiny perfect coquina in every hue imaginable—and Marcie couldn't resist dipping down repeatedly, like a sandpiper, to pick up the most extraordinary of the ordinary treasures, slipping them into her pockets.

From this vantage point she noticed businesses she never saw from the street—a thatch-roofed hut that seemed to serve mostly frozen drinks and nachos with squeeze cheese; a battered-wood shack whose cool shadowed recesses held beach-rental equipment: chairs, umbrellas, boogie boards, and paddleboards.

And one coral-painted building she'd dimly registered from its street-side storefront but hadn't paid attention to; because it was always dark even in daylight, she'd assumed it was another of the abandoned businesses that dotted the strip. From the back, though, a rustic wood-burned sign over the beach-facing door read ART, and the turquoise door stood slightly ajar, some kind of reggae music streaming out over the sand.

Was it a gallery? An art shop? A studio?

She veered closer, plodding over the looser sand away from the shoreline, sunlight glinting dully off a rime of salt and dirt caking the window and concealing whatever was in the darker interior. Marcie moved over to the door, reaching for the knob, when the door flew open—directly into her face.

"Ow!" she hollered, cupping her aching nose.

"Oh, crap! I didn't see you standing there. Are you okay?" A man stood in the doorway looking stricken.

"I don't know." She dabbed a finger under her nostrils to see if there was blood.

"You wanna get some ice on that so it doesn't swell up. Let me grab some."

"I'm fine," she said, more irritated with herself than with him. That was what she got for being nosy.

"I've got a fridge in the shop with an ice tray. Just come on in and let me at least put some in a paper towel for you."

He was young, maybe early thirties, long hair tied in a pony-tail, humidity making a soft halo of frizz around his face. He had what would be a beard in another couple of days—Marcie wasn't sure if he was growing one in or just hadn't bothered to shave—and smears of drying white plaster dotted his hands, the hair on his arms, and the side of his nose. Will would say it was dangerous to go into an unfamiliar building alone with an unknown man, but he certainly didn't look like a serial killer—and she could feel her nose swelling up.

She followed him inside and the scents hit her first, instantly taking her back to Mr. Hullender's room in high school, with its irresistible mix of smells: the wet, earthy scent of clay; the subtle tang of acrylic paint; chalky gesso and ashy charcoal; the mint and lanolin of Masters Artist's Soap; an underlying acridity from chemical solvents. Her eyes watered, but not from the smells. Twenty-five years and it all came back to her like yesterday.

She didn't know where to look first—her eyes had too much competition for focus, and the overall impression was of vivid chaos. Brightly colored pieces of pottery were scattered in every corner of a main room about five hundred square feet: on shelves against the wall, on top of wooden tables pushed to the center of it, and all along a glass countertop that looked like it had once been a point-of-sale area in a past life as a retail shop.

Strewn around every flat surface not covered by the pottery was
an array of random detritus: flat marbles in every imaginable
color, like the kind that held kitschy candlescapes and flower
arrangements; pastel chips of sea glass, some worn smooth and
some rough-edged and chunky; shells and beads and dried
flowers, snarls of colored thread, what looked like flakes of
shiny aluminum and brass, even sequins.

A reflexive smile stretched the sun-tightened skin of her
face as her eyes took it all in.

The pottery was like nothing she'd ever seen: bowls in off-
kilter shapes that seemed to have grown up from the table's
surface, vases that looked as though they'd formed by dripping
downward from the neck, asymmetrical plates, some of them
dotted with the flotsam of random materials scattered everywhere, lending those pieces a rough, nubby texture that begged
to be touched. Marcie almost reached out to do so, but caught
herself and pulled her hand away.

The man leaned in the doorjamb, silently watching her taking in the space.

"It's okay if you want to pick one up," he said. "That's what
they're supposed to make you feel."

So she did, hefting a fat-bottomed vase with a narrow neck
and full, balloonlike body. Thick ridges of what looked like sol-
dering wire looped across the surface, like the ropy veins of an
old woman, but their shine and texture lent an oddly alluring
feel to the piece. It was solid in her hands, a little gritty, warmer
than the air. She rubbed a thumb over its nubby surface, enjoying the way the rounded base filled her cupped palms. Careful
craftsmanship was evident in every curve.

"I love it," she said, putting it carefully back on the table.

"Good. I made it."

"You're a potter?"

He laughed. "That sounds awfully colonial. Clay worker at the moment, I guess—well, multimedia lately. I'm trying some new stuff."

"It's . . ." She couldn't find the right word, and the lift of his eyebrow told her he thought she was trying to find a way to be tactful. "No—I mean it's wonderful. Unexpected. Impactful." The little shop enveloped her in a familiar sensory brew of potential and possibility, the way Mr. Hullender's art room always had.

He didn't answer, just turned and vanished through another doorway, and Marcie wondered whether she was meant to follow. The door led to a small back room that was the polar opposite of the front one, tiled in institutional white linoleum like the locker-room hallways in the high school gym, the ceiling cheap speckled acoustical panels, the walls bare, the only furnishings two white plastic patio chairs, flattened boxes stacked leaning along one wall with a huge clear garbage bag filled with packing peanuts, and an enormous kiln in the corner. The man snagged one of the chairs with a sandaled foot and pulled it closer, offering it to her before opening the door of a dorm fridge near the door and bringing out an ice tray. He bundled several pieces into a strip of paper towels he tore off a roll on top of the refrigerator, then twisted it into a bunch before bringing the makeshift ice pack over to Marcie.

"Careful," was all he said as she sank to the chair and he guided her hand with the towel in it toward her aching nose. He kept his hand over hers, helping to hold the ice in place, creating layers of cold and warm sensations.

"Nice smack," he said, still crouched in front of her, and she realized he was older than she'd thought—near her own age. His eyebrows were forked like a satyr's, canopying eyes she saw now were an unexpected shade of gray.

She shifted her knees to create a little space for herself; he seemed too close. "This your shop?"

"Studio, yeah. It's not ideal but I got a smoking deal on the rent—apparently this space has been a Bermuda Triangle for businesses."

"Well, it doesn't look like much from the street." She caught his raised eyebrows. "Sorry."

"No, you're right. It was originally a house and they were less concerned about curb appeal than this spectacular back-yard." He gestured to the wall fronting the back, even though it had no window to illustrate his point.

He stood and went back to the fridge in a shambling, un-hurried gait, opening it and pulling out a bottle of Coke. Uncap-ping it he tilted it toward her, an offering. She shook her head and he tipped it to his own mouth, and suddenly the soda looked very good after all.

"It would make a great storefront to sell your work," she sug-gested, though it was so obvious surely he'd realized? He didn't seem set up for retail, though—the front room was unappeal-ingly dark from the grimy windows and the solid front and back doors shut tight, the space's potential exhilarating but its chaos off-putting for browsing. She hadn't even seen a register.

On their honeymoon on St. Simons Island, she and Will had found a little art shop like this tucked away on a small side street. All by local artists, the grinning proprietor had assured them as Marcie fingered dreamy watercolors and silk scarves saturated with color and pieces of jewelry made from shells and stones and gems. "This one," Will said as she lingered over a chunky ring set with tourmaline, in awe of the filigreed silver-work and the uniqueness of the design. "We'll take this one."

"We can't afford that," Marcie whispered, mortified as the owner cheerfully boxed and bagged the ring.

"We will someday," Will murmured back, lips close to her ear, hand warm on the small of her back. "And by the time we can, you'll already have it. . . ."

She still had it, but it sat somewhere at the bottom of her jewelry box. She hadn't worn it in years.

The clay worker looked amused at her suggestion. "Yeah, I guess it would," he said. "Can't spare the time, though, and I'm not really into peddling my work to the tourists. Most of this is headed for festivals, art shows, that kind of thing."

"So why rent a beachfront space in a touristy beach town, then?"

"Who doesn't like the beach? I like to move around. See new places. Inspiration comes from everywhere, doesn't it?" He gestured into the store. "What's your medium? I recognize the look."

"Oh . . . I'm not an artist. I mean, I used to mess around with making collages back in high school, but that's not really art."

That twist of amusement leaped back to his full lips. "Yeah? Well, don't tell that to Man Ray. Or Picasso."

"They made collages?" she said, surprised.

"They did everything—more or less well, depending on your taste. But yeah, both of them did collage art or incorporated elements of it into their other media."

"What I liked to do wasn't like that, though. I just pieced things together—images or words out of printed materials, magazines and newspapers and store flyers. Maybe the occasional unavoidable library book . . ." His eyebrows rose along with the corners of his mouth, and she acknowledged her petty vandalism with a smile. "Or I used stuff I found, buttons and pieces of fabric, chips of glass, natural materials—leaves and pebbles and bark. It was more like crafting."

"That's called assemblage. And it's more like art. At least I hope so—I've been working on incorporating materials like that into my clay work—hence the bedlam." He waved an arm through the doorway where he was leaning toward the other room, and Marcie pictured the beguiling drifts of odds and ends on the tables and counters.

"Well, you make it sound more impressive than it was—when I did it anyway."

"I hate to be the one to break it to you, but you're still an artist, friend. You can try to leave it behind, but art doesn't always let you. Not everyone jams to the vibe the way you did when you walked in here."

The man's assessment of her high school efforts was too generous, but she couldn't deny a flare of hot pleasure that this stranger saw her that way.

"I haven't done anything like that in years," she said. "Who has the time?"

"You make the time. If it matters to you."

She bristled, even though his tone was friendly. "It's hard when you have other obligations. Not everyone has the luxury of dedicating all their time to what they want to do." She immediately felt bad for her tone, after he'd been nice enough to invite her inside and tend to her nose. "Sorry. I didn't mean that."

But he only smiled, with a single headshake and a one-shouldered shrug, as if casting off her censure. "Yeah, you did. Don't apologize. You're right. We all make choices about what's important to us, and not everyone chooses a creative life."

"Well, it's not always possible."

He regarded her with that unwavering gaze again. "It is if you want it to be."

"That's easy to say."

"What's more important than what your soul calls out to do?"

Her jaw tightened. "Oh, I don't know—making a living? Paying the bills? Helping the people you care about?" she said, thinking of Will, of Emily. Even, she was surprised to realize, of Flint.

"Okay," he said, holding out his hands like he was gentling a foal. "I wasn't trying to judge. You know what's best for you."

"It's not always what's best for an individual," she said mildly, wanting to defuse the tense atmosphere between them. "Sometimes it's what you need to do for the big picture—the things beyond just your own desires."

"The 'shoulds,'" he intoned in a deep, portentous voice, as if announcing the villain in an old-fashioned melodrama. "The taskmaster wardens of life." He grinned to take any sting out of his pronouncement. Everything seemed to amuse him, but not in a cynical way. He just seemed to enjoy things. "You're right— we don't all want the same things. I don't stay in one place more than a year. I don't have a house, or a family, or a dog. I sure don't have a 401(k)—I don't plan much past the next change of season, let alone into retirement, and I get that not everyone would be happy like that. But for me it frees me up from the 'shoulds,' which I never could stomach. I prefer the 'what-ifs.'"

"The 'what-ifs' motivate me too—but maybe not the same way," she admitted. "What if I lose my job and can't pay my mortgage? What if I get cancer? What if global warming kills all the crops and everyone starves?"

"Heavy," he said. "I can see the aversion."

"I like your way of thinking of it," she said wistfully. "The opportunities instead of the dangers."

He nodded. "Glass half full versus glass broken into jagged edges and about to sever an artery." Marcie laughed and he joined in. "I take your point," he said. "My way makes for a hell of a lot of uncertainty. And a lot of ups and downs. It's not for everyone, at least as a lifestyle. But every now and then it can be exhilarating to jump on a what-if—even if you mostly take care of the shoulds. Don't forget to play."

His grin was infectious, and Marcie touched an imaginary hat brim. "It's good advice. I'll try to remember."

"How's the schnoz?" he asked.

She pressed a finger to it carefully. "Throbbing a little. But probably okay."

"Sure you won't take me up on my hospitality? A cold beverage?" He held up his Coke. "I might even have a bag of Cheetos lying around here somewhere, if you want fancy hors d'oeuvres too."

She laughed, feeling oddly tempted to accept. She stood up. "No, thanks. I'd better go."

He shrugged. " 'Kay. Sorry about whacking you back there. You sure you're okay?"

"I'm fine. Thanks for the first aid," she said, holding up the improvised ice pack.

He followed her back through the other room, Marcie drinking in the colorful bedlam as she moved toward the door.

"Hey, if you ever want a place to work, I've got plenty of room here." He motioned around.

"To work?"

"Your collages." He smiled. "Your assemblage. You're welcome to incorporate some of whatever I've got lying around—I get a little carried away with supplies when I'm experimenting."

"Oh! That's . . ." She swallowed a wingbeat of possibility in her chest. "That's a nice offer. I haven't done anything creative in a long time, though. Decades."

"Well, that is a screaming shame, then. You might do something about that."

She didn't know if it was his tone, the possibility he presented, or the way he held her eye longer than casual conversation dictated in the silence that made Marcie's heart stutter . . . until she realized he was simply waiting for her to leave. "Thanks for the offer." She gave an awkward wave, then stepped out the door and down the two wooden stairs to the sand.

The last glance she gave him over her shoulder showed him outlined in the doorway, watching her, that amused expression still on his face.

It wasn't until she got to the restaurant that she realized they hadn't even given each other their names.

The bar regulars called their hellos with their usual bonhomie when Marcie showed up for her lunch shift, but something seemed to have shifted since last night's standoff with the mouthy boys. There was a sense that she had changed sides somehow; now she was greeted as a fellow teammate, not a visiting player. Darla gave her the deck to herself as her station—the first time she'd had that many tables, and Marcie didn't forget a single order. And only once did she have to ask Hannah to run out a food order for her when it got really busy during the rush. "Wait till season," Darla told her—when the weather started to shift up north and drove the snowbirds down below the tropical line, the place would be like that all the time.

But Marcie wouldn't be here then—she had more than enough money to retrieve her car from its purgatory tomorrow. The thought of it made her unaccountably sad. She'd spent these last few days making plans to get herself back home and now that her return was imminent, she realized she was actually going to miss this place. These people.

She set her empty apron on the bar when the lunch rush was over and Darla cut her from the floor.

"Shiftie?" the bartender asked, holding up a frosty full mug drizzling foam down the side.

"Thanks, Darla—I actually have somewhere I need to be." She wanted to stop at the store and pick up something special for Flint for dinner tonight with her extra cash. Maybe cook up some things he could easily heat up till he was back on his feet—God knew the old man seemed to have eaten poorly enough even before he threw his back out.

"Oho!" Darla crowed. "Lookee there, our little mystery gal has big plans. Who is he, Marce?"

"Awww, look at that pretty blush," Bink said. "Spill, Marcie. Who's the guy?"

"Yeah, someone we know?" Pete chimed in.

"Ease up, fellas," Art murmured, always the gentleman.

Marcie shook her head. "It's not a guy," she protested. Well, not really.

"Hey, fair enough," Darla said, and raised the glass in a toast before downing half its contents. "I get the appeal of equal-opportunity dating—I'd be the last one to throw a stone." She gave a loud cackle, winking broadly at the men. "No one's going to judge you, honey. What is it the kids say these days—love is love? And pleasure is pleasure—am I right, gents?"

Marcie didn't bother to correct her assumption—Darla clearly meant well. And she didn't mind being included in the group's habitual razzing.

"I'm really going to miss you guys," she said as Darla quaffed the beer she'd offered Marcie.

"Aw, hell," Darla said with a glance at the regulars. "We know what that means, huh?"

Pete shook his head. "Another one bites the dust."

"Why's it gotta be one of the good ones?" Bink lamented. Art wore a betrayed expression.

Guilt bit at her. "I'm sorry. I know you're down a server—"

Darla waved her off with the empty mug. "Don't worry about it, Marce. This ain't the Four Seasons, and honestly I never expected you to stick around. You're not exactly the dive-bar type, honey." Marcie supposed that was a compliment, although the comment thrust her firmly back outside the circle of Darla and the regulars. "But you did good here, newbie. You're tougher than you look. Now don't go taking any bull crap from anyone." She winked and a rush of warmth filled Marcie. She would indeed not be taking any more bull crap.

She called out her good-byes through a thick throat as she let herself out the front door. Maybe one day she'd come back, find them still sitting here like fixtures, join them on one of the stools for a cold one. The thought comforted even as she knew it would probably never happen.

Flint

~~~~~

lint lay sprawled on his low mattress, legs dangling over the side, pants pooled around his ankles.

He'd done okay in Marcie's absence—the pills had brought the pain down to a dull roar by lunchtime, when he'd staggered into the kitchen and found a sandwich she'd apparently made and put in the fridge for him, so that took care of that. A few more hours in the chair and a couple more pills and he could get up and brush his teeth, give himself a whore's bath with a washcloth even—he knew better than to try to get into the bathtub when his back was twingey and his footing uncertain.

But now he couldn't even put on his own damn pants. He'd gotten one leg in just fine, sitting on the bed, and then he got cocky and stood up—too fast, sending pain knifing through him, and he fell back onto the bed like a landed fish.

Now he could hear her out there rattling around in the kitchen, and if he didn't figure out how to get himself up and dressed ASAP, she'd probably come nosing around in here and get an eyeful of his skinny white ass in his BVDs.

He gritted his teeth and used one foot—slowly, carefully—to push one pant leg off, then the other, hearing the fabric drop into a heap beside the bed.

He rolled to the side, then to his stomach, easing himself backward onto the balls of his feet, his toes. With a deep breath and a clenched jaw, he gave one careful heave backward, lurching upright, barely biting back the roared curse he wanted to let out. He stumbled a little, but caught his balance, his back stabbing arrows of agony into him.

He opened the door of his closet, gingerly reached for the plush robe hanging from a hook on the inside. When was the last time he'd worn something like this? Probably for about two weeks after Jessie gave it to him on their last Christmas together . . . before he retired the thing to his closet and went back to the T-shirts and drawstring pants he preferred. He eased his arms in, one at a time, and belted it around himself. Not exactly a look he was eager for Marcie to see, but better than the alternative.

He shuffled down the hallway and into the kitchen, where she had something sizzling in a pan on the stove, the scent of garlic reaching his nose, the oven door partway open and what looked like two steaks on a broiler pan on the top rack.

"I hope you're hungry," she said.

He stood watching her movements as she picked up the pan and jostled it back and forth, green stalks of asparagus peeping out over the top as she did.

"Smells good," he said gruffly. "What are we having?"

There was no way his back would let him sit at the table, and she must have realized that, because she helped him back into his armchair, where the piecrust table had been cleared off, a place mat, napkin, and silverware set up on it.

Where's my stuff? was on the edge of his tongue, but he swallowed it, saying instead, "You cater too?"

She pointed to the trunk, where she'd set another place setting for herself. "I thought we could eat in here. And don't worry," she said, reading his mind. "I kept everything in order and I'll put it all back after dinner."

Smart-ass.

They ate sitting across from each other, in an awkward silence. Marcie had cut his meat into little pieces, as if he were a child, but he didn't say a word, knowing that trying to do it himself would only have caused him agony.

"I didn't think about this being hard to eat. Sorry," she said as she set the plate on his lap. "Do you want me to feed you?"

He raised an eyebrow, but from her expression he suspected she was razzing him. "It's fine. What I was hungry for."

It had been a long time since he'd sat down to eat. Since he'd had company for a meal, or had anyone cook for him. The steak was just the way he liked it—seasoned only with salt, the edges crisped up, the center pink, but not cooked through. The problem with raising the levee, though, even an inch, was that she seemed to think it gave her license to pry into his business.

"So . . . do you have family nearby?" she asked him as she poured water for them both.

"You see one?"

The room filled with only the whir of the oven fan, the ticking of the wall clock, the clinking of their forks against their plates. But of course she tried again. "So did you grow up in Palmetto Key?"

"Did you grow up lying half dead on the beach?"

That shut her mouth quickly enough.

But she just smiled tolerantly, like he was a truculent kid. "Did anyone ever tell you that you're a delightful dinner companion?"

He didn't want to reward her cracking wise, but damned if a snort didn't escape him. "Did anyone ever tell you to mind your own beeswax?"

She nodded sagely. "Yes, in fact. When I was six. Little Timmy Scofield was a sparkling conversationalist as well."

He didn't want to meet her eye, let her see his amusement, so he laid the side of his fork against one stalk of asparagus, pressing down as much as his twingey back would allow, finally giving up and forking up another piece of meat.

"Emily Post says this is a perfectly polite way to eat asparagus."

He glanced up at Marcie and saw her holding a piece of her own, biting off the end.

"Well. As long as it's perfectly polite." He picked up a stalk, taking half of it in a bite.

She smiled—and damned if he didn't feel like smiling back. "I wish I'd known about asparagus when I was a kid. No matter how many times I tried, my mom would never let me play with my food."

He nodded. "Yeah, that's what I always told Jess—"

He stopped abruptly, unable to believe her name had almost come out of his mouth, after all these years. His fork clattered to his plate.

"Your daughter?"

It was a ballsy question, considering the way he'd jumped all over her for any personal incursions. But of course she already knew. The damned room she was staying in was painted like a jar of jam. What grown-up would have lived in a room like that? Who else but his willful, stubborn, opinionated little girl would have painted it that way? Jessie's spirit inhabited every inch of that room as if she were still here.

But she wasn't.

"What happened to her?"

"She's gone," he bit out before he could think better of it.

Let it go, he told her silently. *It's none of your business.*

"Gone how?"

He didn't answer.

Pain shifted over her expression. "Oh, God, Herman, did she . . . did your daughter pass away?"

He clattered his plate onto the side table, braced his hands on the armrests to push himself up. And *this* was why you didn't lower your guard. "That's a stupid expression. 'Pass away.' Like someone crossed a movie screen and slipped off camera." He'd storm away from her, but he didn't think he could actually push himself out of this chair. "Died," he grated out without looking at her. "Why's everyone so scared of just saying it? It's just a verb, for Christ's sake. It's not like it's a four-letter word."

"Actually, it is."

A hard laugh burst out of him. "Yeah. Maybe that's it. Just another four-letter word." He shook his head. "Fuck."

Silence fell thick in the room as he carefully brought his plate back to his lap and they resumed eating.

"You're right," she said after a while, almost inaudibly. "I should learn to mind my own beeswax. I'm sorry."

She was looking down at her plate with an expression that made a hard thing inside him shift. She'd lost something too, for Christ's sake.

"Don't apologize to me," he muttered finally. "It's little Timmy you owe an apology to."

Their eyes met for a moment when she glanced up in surprise, and he gave her a nod to let her know it was okay.

"Fair enough," she said lightly. "I'll get right on that."

That night in his room, he popped a couple more pain pills and lay on the bed waiting for sleep to take him. Instead he stared at the ceiling for two hours, mapping the cracks and stains he'd never bothered to notice and thinking of his daughter.

When Marcie asked about her, his whole body had stiffened, braced for an interrogation: *Where's her mother? What happened to Jessie?*

What did you do?

The questions thundered in his head, a thousand images flooding in after the clap of them. Memories that should have been fuzzy from disuse, but were clear and sharp edged as photographs: the little creature he'd been left with that was totally dependent on him—*him*. Brenda walked out when Jess was so young—barely walking—and that was the scariest thing he'd ever faced—including his three years in Vietnam. What the hell had he known about taking care of a little kid, a girl?

He remembered the first time he'd had to give her a bath on his own. She was so tiny and delicate he thought he'd break her, was afraid to take his eyes off her for one second for fear she'd slip under the surface and drown. Afterward he wrapped her up in a towel like a little caterpillar in a cocoon, and picked her up and held her wet, slippery body, which smelled so clean. Cleaner than anything he'd ever known.

She was scared of everything at first, right after Brenda took off. Noises at night, sure, and the dark. But also sudden movements or loud sounds—even the phone ringing would startle her up off the couch while he was reading to her. And being alone. It was weeks before he could even walk out of the room without her screaming and crying and running after him. She used to sit just outside the bathroom while he was in there, making him promise not to shut the door all the way.

She wouldn't sleep alone in her room at first, but he didn't feel right letting her in bed with him, so he brought out his old army cot and set it up next to his bed, and brought in her pillow and her little pink blanket to put on top of it. Then after the first night he took the cot and gave her the bed. It only lasted a month or two—thank God; he'd had all the army cots he ever wanted to sleep on already—and then little by little he coaxed her into her own room at night. That was how their reading started—it was the only thing that calmed her down enough to keep her there and let her fall asleep.

"Promise you won't leave until I'm all the way asleep," she'd demand as her eyes started to get heavy. "Make sure I'm not awake even a little bit."

So he would keep reading even after her eyes fluttered closed for good and her breathing grew deep and regular, until his touch on her cheek didn't bring even a twitch. Then he'd pull her blanket to her chin and make sure the night-light was on, and leave open her door and his, as he'd promised. Some nights she even slept all the way through without coming into his room and needing him to go start the routine all over again.

The memories rushed in like water filling a hole, trying to equalize the empty space.

By the time he watched the numbers on his digital clock flip over past one a.m. he realized sleep wasn't coming anytime soon. It took a muscle relaxant and another pain pill to get him there, but Flint slowly made his way out of bed and quietly let himself out the back door to the deck and lowered himself into his rickety chair, staring out at the water.

For a long time Jessie had suffered from night terrors—her blood-chilling shrieks would draw him out of sleep with a pounding heart and a dry mouth, for a moment flashing back to terrors of his own before he remembered where he was. He'd go in and hold her, gently shake her awake. You weren't supposed to do that, he'd read a while ago. It disoriented a kid, scared and confused them, but it never occurred to him not to chase away whatever demons haunted his child.

Most of the time she couldn't get back to sleep, and while he sat out here after tucking her back in, knowing there'd be no more slumber for him for the rest of the night, he'd hear the creak of the screen door behind him, her soft footsteps, before she'd crawl up onto his lap and curl up like a bunny in his arms. She'd been too old for that kind of thing by then—too old and much too independent—but he secretly relished these moments when his growing girl needed him again for a little while, holding her till she fell asleep even though his arms went numb.

The moon was close to full and the beach was lit up, and if it hadn't been for that he might've missed the tracks entirely, lost in his thoughts as he was. He pushed himself laboriously to his feet, trying to be silent, and moved toward the back steps, close enough to see but out of the way, watching till his eyes could make out the humped shadow near the base of a clump of sea oats, clumsily shifting up and down.

A faint shiver tracked down his arms.

As if he'd evoked Jessie with his memories of her, he heard the screen door squeal open behind him.

"Stay quiet!" he whispered harshly, and the sound stilled.

Craning his neck around wasn't even a possibility, and so for a moment he stared straight ahead at what he thought he'd seen, letting himself indulge in the forbidden fantasy of his daughter standing there again, coming out to join him.

"I couldn't sleep and saw your door was open," came a soft voice behind him. The wrong voice. "Are you okay?"

"Come here," he said roughly. "This is something you don't see every day."

In the moonlight as Marcie stepped beside him he could make out her confusion, but she stood waiting. With a nod he directed her gaze toward the stand of sea oats between his house and the one next door.

He knew when she saw it, because he heard her breath catch. The turtle he'd seen scratching her nest in the sand was now lying motionless atop it, laying her eggs.

"Oh." The sound trickled from her lips on an exhale.

He looked down at her and motioned with a finger to his lips to keep her silent; then he held it up in the air: *Wait*.

The turtle stayed like that for a long time, shifting now and then, her flippers making a squeaking sound on the sand. Finally she moved, pulling herself forward, throwing sand behind her with powerful thrusts of her hind flippers, filling in the indentation she'd created. And then she made her methodical, ungainly way back to the water, inch by inch toward the sea, each stroke gaining her so little ground, her body seeming too large for its limbs, too heavy to make any headway.

But there was something impressive about the animal's movements too—an unswerving determination in the way she plugged ahead, steady and strong, not stopping to rest, intent on getting back to her home.

For a moment they could see the dark mass of her against the gently phosphorescing water, but as soon as the turtle got deep enough to be pulled into the waves, her awkward movements vanished and she dived beneath the surface in one fluid motion and was gone. Flint looked at the girl—Marcie—and saw her shining eyes reflecting the moonlight.

"Thank you," she whispered.

He nodded, oddly glad for her reaction.

She walked a couple of steps toward the far edge of the porch, looking out to where the turtle had gone. He came to stand beside her and pointed out the distinctive trail the creature had left on her journey to and from her nest, like the marks left by tractor tires.

"Turtle tracks. You'll see them all over the beach in the mornings during nesting season, tells you where the eggs are laid."

"And then what?"

"Then nothing. You wait. Group around here checks on 'em before dawn every day, marks 'em off, keeps people from disturbing them. But you gotta watch for insects, raccoons, even dogs. They dig 'em up, kill the whole nest."

"Is that why you walk the beach in the morning? Do you work with that group?"

He shook his head. "Just keep my eye out. One in ten thousand makes it to adulthood. More nests survive, more turtles have a chance."

"So now what?"

He shrugged. "We keep an eye on it."

He hoped she hadn't noticed his use of the word "we."

Marcie

t took her a long time to fall asleep after Flint had shown her the sea turtle's majestic, prehistoric struggle to lay eggs that probably wouldn't survive, her crawling progress back to her saltwater home and away from a world not her own. Did the creature know how high the odds were stacked against her, against her offspring? What must that be like—to make a nest anyway . . . to leave it behind, hoping for the best, that somehow one of yours would be the single hatchling to defy the probabilities? Was it simply instinct, a primeval compunction to propagate, or some kind of divine faith?

She wished she could see the eggs hatch. Six to eight weeks, Flint told her—Marcie would be long gone, back to her job and her home and her husband and her life. She'd already gathered her meager things and planned to head home straight from getting her car from the impound lot.

She'd tucked Flint's daughter's letters into the nightstand, neatly stacked and tied together again the way they must have been before they'd fallen from the box. Flint had been carrying his daughter's boxes out of his house, as if he couldn't bear to share space with her memory anymore, and Marcie didn't have the right to intrude on that decision, but one day maybe he'd find them here and be glad he still had these pieces of her.

His daughter had died, his wife gone—wasn't it common that marriages didn't survive the loss of a child? Hers was floundering and they'd never actually had one. This man had lost everything—more than everything, because whoever Isobel was she'd had a son who also seemed important to Flint and his daughter, and they'd lost that boy too. How did a person recover from that much loss?

Maybe they didn't. Maybe they just closed in on themselves and shut themselves away, shut everyone and everything else out.

Her restless sleep had her up early, and by the time he came out the next morning in his newly shuffling gait, still wearing that incongruously cheerful bathrobe, she'd already brewed a pot of coffee, filling the kitchen with its rich scent, and was setting breakfast fixings on the counter.

"How do you like your eggs?" she asked.

"This a thing now?"

She lifted one shoulder but otherwise ignored him. She'd learned that dealing with the old man was not unlike handling a cantankerous client at the hotel: just let the current of gripes roll by like the tide till the person felt they'd been heard. Now that she understood him a little more, his ire seemed poignant instead of prickly.

"I've already checked on our nest this morning," she said, leaning down to find a pan under the counter.

He made a noncommittal noise.

"Should we mark it? To make sure no one disturbs the eggs?"

His feet made soft scuffing sounds on the linoleum as he moved toward the adjacent living room, anchoring himself on the upholstered back of his chair. "We don't need tourists coming up off the beach to gawp. And I sure as hell don't want people trudging in and out of my backyard to do it." His words were harsh but his tone was mild, and as she turned to face him she saw that his expression matched it. "How's the nest?"

"If I hadn't watched the mama make it I'd never have known it was there, just barely a disturbance in the sand."

He grunted. "There's an organization that marks them. Wraps caution tape around stakes to keep people away."

"Aha. I thought those were crime scenes. Good to know Palmetto Key is rife with turtle nests, not murders."

She braced for another rant about how depraved and crime ridden the little town was, but he just lowered himself slowly into the chair. She fought the impulse to offer her arm, but winced as pain contracted his face. How was he going to get around on his own like this?

But she knew better than to ask. She held up an egg. "Scrambled okay?"

He gave a single nod. "It's fine."

Marcie busied herself cracking several into a bowl, whisking them with a fork.

"We don't turn the front porch light on this time of year." His voice broke the silence unexpectedly. "And keep the shades pulled at night to keep the light from spilling out. Otherwise the hatchlings get confused and troop the wrong way."

"Does everyone do that?" she asked. "All the businesses and hotels too?"

"Most of 'em. Regulations. City finally did something about it when residents complained."

Marcie suspected that Flint had been one of the most vocal complainants.

"Years ago waves of baby turtles would get crushed on the road by passing cars—they hatched and headed the wrong way because of the lights." He shook his head. "We once found tides of 'em in one of the hotel pools, floating dead in the chlorine."

Her ears pricked at his absent mention of "we." He and his daughter, he must have meant, but she didn't call attention to it, as if the word were ancient lace that might tear.

Flint offered to drive her to pick up her car when she told him where she was going.

"I can call a cab," she said, concerned about his back. "You rest."

"I'm entirely capable of sitting on my ass and pressing a pedal. What, you can offer help but not take it?"

He had a point, and that way she could defer her good-bye a little longer. It surprised her how hard it was to think she'd probably never see the old man again. Maybe she could call him sometimes. Her gaze slipped to the useless rotary phone. Well, maybe she could write.

"Touché," she said. "Let's go."

He settled himself carefully behind the wheel of the old sedan, a pillow he asked Marcie to bring supporting his back, and at first silence reigned—no shock Flint wasn't exactly a radio kind of guy.

She didn't mind the long stretches of silence between them—there was something peaceful about it, the freedom to share space with another presence with no expectation to engage. No desire, in Flint's case—although she registered his tiny overtures for what they were; apparently even the most committed recluse felt the primeval drive for human contact from time to time.

It was so different from what she'd felt with Will since the lima bean—the silences that had grown between them felt freighted with Marcie's banked rage, resentment . . . and fear. Fear of what might be said, what might be irrevocably damaged if she broke their uneasy détente. With Flint she felt like she could breathe—his indifference to her had the sunny side effect of offering her the freedom to say anything . . . or nothing.

But it was still a house of loneliness, where what she now realized was the pall of loss hung over everything, filled every crevice. The idea of leaving him alone here, in his solitary toad hole, filled her with sadness.

As they came over the bridge that would funnel them onto the mainland, though, to her surprise he was the one who broke the quiet.

"This used to be a swing bridge," he said. "You know what that is? Swivels out of the way for boats. Stupidly inefficient by modern standards—but a feat of engineering for the time. Something to see when I was a kid."

"You've lived here all your life?" The question was out of her mouth before she remembered she wasn't supposed to ask any.

But Flint just . . . answered. Like a normal person. "Almost all. Except for three years in the army I'd rather forget."

Marcie did know better than to pry into that, from the finality of his tone. Instead she gingerly stepped another toe into the territory he did seem willing to let her venture into: "What was it like here then?"

"Fewer people. More mosquitoes."

Well, he was never going to get hit up by the convention and visitors bureau to be an ambassador for Palmetto Key.

"I'll bet it was pretty."

He grunted. "It was all right. Less crap in the river dumping onto our beaches. Less crap on the beach from tourists. More locals, and they took better care of the place. Appreciated what we had." He shrugged. "Times change."

"Change isn't always good," Marcie agreed, thinking of the lima bean and what it had done to her and Will

She felt Flint's eyes shift to her, then back to the road as they turned off Beach Boulevard toward town. "Not what I'd expect to hear from our plucky young heroine."

"I'm not a heroine. Or all that plucky."

"You got out of a bad situation and looked for a better one," he said as if it were a compliment. "That takes moxie."

"It wasn't a bad situation," she countered, the urge to defend Will as automatic as breathing. "It *isn't*," she corrected herself. Whatever else was going on between them, her husband was a good man to his core. They just hadn't wanted the same thing. In any other area that might have been nothing but a blip on the marital radar. It was just with this—a major, irrevocable, life-changing decision one of them had wanted and one of them hadn't—that their foundation had shifted.

And cracked? Marcie didn't know.

Flint was looking at her, eyes narrowed. "If it was all candy and cake then what were you doing passed out on the sand?"

"It wasn't candy and cake," she said hotly, his tone—and the reminder of her state when he'd found her—irritating her. "It was marriage—it *is* marriage, like anyone else's, like any relationship. Good and bad, ups and downs. We just . . . we hit a 'down' we didn't know how to deal with. And I was afraid that if I didn't get off the road I might run us off it. Okay?"

He didn't answer, his gaze trained ahead out the windshield, but Marcie refused to feel bad for putting out the same boundaries Flint always used to shut her down. She refused to feel guilty for defending her marriage. Her husband. She looked out the passenger window at the thatches of peeling pink trees flashing by at the side of the road, arms cinched across her torso.

"Yeah. I get that." His jaw was clenched, his body stiff.

"You okay? Did you bring your pills?"

"My back's fine."

They rode the rest of the way without speaking, but the flare of tension between them had dissolved. She wondered whether he was thinking about his lost daughter. Who knew what swam under the surface of any relationship, waiting to pull you down unexpectedly? Marcie never really understood that before the lima bean.

The same clerk was on duty at the impound lot, the guy every bit as disinterested and unhelpful as he'd been last time. Maybe disaffected ennui was a job requirement—or part of the training.

"Driver's license and registration," he said in a bored tone, his sleepy eyes barely lifting from his monitor.

"They're in the car," Marcie told him again, stacking her cash on the counter.

The man shrugged sloping shoulders, still riveted on his

computer screen. "You got other ID? Passport? Birth certificate and utility bill? Car title?"

"I don't have access to those documents right now—but I have what you asked for in the car."

"Can't reclaim the car without ID."

Flint, who'd insisted on coming inside, stirred beside her, leaning toward the counter as if to bully the bored clerk into compliance. An outburst from a cranky old man wasn't going to get Marcie her car. She touched Flint's arm with one hand as if in filial attentiveness, hoping he'd get the message to back off.

Marcie forced an agreeable smile onto her face. "I do have ID. In the car. If you just let me get my purse out of the trunk, I can provide it and I'll get right out of your hair. I know how busy you must be," she said, despite the otherwise empty cashier's area and apparently the most riveting game of computer solitaire imaginable consuming his attention.

"Can you get a certified copy faxed to us? That would do it."

Flint bent over the counter again, and Marcie pressed an urgent hand to his shoulder, restraining herself from yanking him away by his worn chambray shirt only out of concern for his back. He didn't resist her, easing off and reaching instead toward his back pocket.

"I think we're gonna be able to work something out," Flint said, retrieving a battered brown leather billfold and plopping it to the counter in front of the man. "Is there some sort of convenience fee we could pay so my friend here can just get the identification you need out of the car? On top of the towing and storage charges, of course."

Marcie's cheeks heated and she wanted to slap a hand over her face—or Flint's. Her last embarrassing amateur attempt at bribery had been summarily ignored, and Flint's Mafia approach was even worse.

But the guy finally tore his gaze away from his monitor, eyeing the open billfold. "Fifty for the convenience fee. Three hundred for the tow and thirty a day for storage. Cash."

"Perfect." Flint reached for the wallet again.

Marcie was horrified; she didn't want him paying for her, and the clerk had brazenly quoted double the towing and storage fees posted on the wall over his head. This was ridiculous—she wasn't letting this man extort her. She could just call Will and ask him to—

"Tell you what, fella," Flint added mildly, deliberately folding the billfold and replacing it in his pocket. "Whyn't you let this lady pay you the posted fees right there"—he pointed to the sign—"and then let her back to the lot to get her purse out of the trunk of her car and show you that ID you've got such a hard-on for, and if you do we won't call the DMV and let 'em know that one of their contractors accepts bribes, inflates charges, and visits porn sites on company time?"

It took Marcie a couple of beats to realize Flint had set the guy up. He hadn't been trying to intimidate the man—he was looking at his screen.

The clerk bristled and raised himself up. Flint's eyes hardened and he went utterly still, like a dog about to attack, and for a moment Marcie could see the dangerous, hot-tempered young man he must have been. But the cashier was decades younger than Flint, even if Flint didn't have a bad back. Her heartbeat tripped as the atmosphere grew charged, but just that fast it dissipated, the clerk glancing at the door behind him as though making sure no one had overheard.

He scowled. "Get your damn purse—if you got keys."

Marcie smiled and held them up, jingling them merrily as the man stood and led her toward the storage yard.

Flint waited until she retrieved her purse, showed the proper documents, and paid the clerk—the posted amount—before walking her back out to her car.

"Gotta speak up for yourself, girl," he said as she opened the driver door. "No one's going to do it for you."

"You did."

She meant it teasingly, as a sort of thank-you—an indirect one she thought was the only kind Flint might accept—but he scowled.

"Well, you can't count on me," he growled. "Or anyone."

He sounded like her mother, who'd made similar comments not quite sotto voce every time she was with Marcie and Will, even as years passed and rendered her warnings ridiculous. Until Marcie finally stopped inviting her over, choosing instead to go visit her mother alone. She wouldn't keep putting Will through that, not when he'd never done anything to deserve it. Not when, despite her mom's dire predictions, Will had never let her down.

Oh, no? Hasn't he? Jeanetta Jones's snide tone wormed into her head, insinuating doubts she'd never succumbed to when her mother was alive.

Don't say I didn't warn you.

"That sounds lonely," Marcie said to Flint, ignoring her mother's imagined voice the same way she'd ignored Jeanetta's supercilious comments in life. "I can't imagine living like that—believing you can't rely on anyone. That we're really that alone."

Flint snorted. "Don't be so damned naïve, girl. We're born

alone and we die alone, and there's no one you can count on but yourself, no matter what anyone else says." And he walked away, back to his car.

Was it losing his little girl that had made him believe something so bleak? Was it an accident, maybe one caused by Flint's negligence? Something like that might have happened to anyone, but no rationalization would ever allow a parent, a husband, to get over being responsible for the death of a child.

She should follow him, she thought. Let him know she was headed back home, would be out of his hair—to take care of himself. Give him her cell number just in case the man decided to join the twenty-first century and get himself a working phone.

But his comments stung. What did the bitter old man know, balled up in his dark little toad hole, pushing away everyone and everything? He'd figure out she wasn't coming back when she didn't come back. Probably be relieved.

Her cell phone was dead in her purse—no surprise after all this time—and she retrieved her car charger from the console, plugged it in. How many messages and voice mails might she find? Hard to imagine she'd only been offline for a few days; it felt like she'd been in Palmetto Key much longer, time taking on that drawn-out beach feeling, as if oozing in sap.

Flint pulled out ahead of her and she followed his car out onto the street, back the way they'd come. She could call Will once the phone caught enough juice to turn on, let him know she was okay, that she'd be home soon.

She reached the T junction where Flint's long, squat sedan sat with his blinker on. She watched him make the left turn, inching forward as the cars ahead of her did the same.

Would he even notice her absence? Would Darla or any of the regulars remember her, the woman who left their lives as suddenly as she'd dropped into it? Marcie doubted it. It wouldn't be long before the placid surface of life in Palmetto Key closed back over the area she'd momentarily displaced, the brief time she'd been there lost in the little town's amorphous past.

She took her foot off the brake and turned right toward the highway.

Flint

Use it or lose it.

The stupid saying had always annoyed Flint—most pithy aphorisms did, actually, the lazy man's shortcut to having actual ideas, thinking for oneself—but as he pinballed around the kitchen with no clear plan of attack he realized this one was true, at least in the case of cooking. It had been a lot of years since Flint had actually made a proper meal and he'd lost the knack of planning so that everything was assembled and prepped, ready to hand when needed. It took almost ten minutes just to find the vegetable peeler; the only utensils he'd required for years were his manual can opener and a wooden spoon. No point cooking a decent meal when there was only him to eat it.

But it wasn't just him anymore, at least at the moment, and after he saw Marcie safely into her car at the impound lot, their exchange kept reverberating in his head on the drive home.

We're born alone and we die alone, and there's no one you can count on but yourself, no matter what anyone else says.

One irritating thing about having someone else around was that you were forced to see yourself reflected in another person's perception of you, and as the lines of Marcie's face had contracted like someone had yanked a drawstring from her nose, he'd heard the barrenness of his own words, seen himself as the bitter old misanthrope he must appear to her.

That sounds lonely. . . . I can't imagine living like that— believing you can't rely on anyone. That we're really that alone.

As long as he was navel-gazing, he might as well admit the truth of her reply. It *was* lonely.

He'd managed to convince himself over the years that it wasn't—or at least to avoid assessing it at all—up until Marcie showed up, with her intrusive invasion of his house and her cooking for two and her bothersome questions. Even without all that, there was a different feel to the house from when he was alone in it, the way you knew you were the only one living even before you felt your buddies' necks for a pulse. He could tell without checking whether she'd left, knew she was back before he heard the rustling sounds of her movements or smelled the odors she carried back from that shithole where she worked.

When he'd found himself stopping at the grocery store just before the bridge back to the island to pick up the makings of a meal for the two of them—it was the only halfway-decent market around, compared to the relic near his house, where the produce was limp and tired and you had to check every expiration date—he'd told himself it was just to prove the girl wrong about him, but the truth was, he wanted to.

He used to love cooking with Jessie—cooking *for* her, especially as she got older. It felt like something he could still do for her, some way to take care of his little girl when she no longer needed him to read her to sleep or bandage her scrapes and bruises or soothe away her night terrors. With his daughter turning into a teenager and preferring the company of other kids her age more and more, meals together became an occasion. Flint knew not to take it personally—it was natural, and he wouldn't make the mistakes his own parents had by holding the reins so tight, trying to force an intimacy Flint no longer felt, that he couldn't get out of their house fast enough, enlisting in the army the day he turned eighteen to get out from under his dad's quick hand and his mother's cloying pretense of a happy family. He offered Jessie meals at home, but he didn't require them, and so when she did choose to stay in with him, he felt like he'd won a prize.

Isobel had helped with that too—well, Berto more than anything, if Flint was honest. Flint always thought he was like a big brother to his daughter—Isobel's son had been babysitting Jessie since she was six years old, even then the most responsible kid Flint had ever seen, and he was so good with her. Jessie never minded when he and Isobel went out by themselves every now and then, because Berto would sit and play with her all she wanted, endless games of Chutes and Ladders or Monopoly or even War, the stupidest card game ever invented. Flint couldn't bring himself to slap down cards willy-nilly in an anarchic, strategy-less free-for-all, even for his daughter.

But then puberty roared in and turned his little girl into a disconcerting hybrid creature Flint had to somehow relearn— like a literal harpy: part female, part bird, sometimes the child he recognized, affectionate and sunny and at least somewhat predictable, and sometimes a screeching vulture who'd turn on him on a dime over some unconscious infraction he'd committed, beating her wings in preparation to try them out. And Berto became her Phineus, an object of fascination that sometimes made her seem so adult it disturbed Flint.

Berto was such a good kid, though—Flint never worried about him. On weekends, when the boy's high school friends gathered on the porch, sprawled like colts that hadn't yet grown used to their spindly legs, Jessie swirled among them like a spinning coquina in a rising tide, relishing her role as their un-acknowledged mascot, the boys' coddling and attention turning her into a harmless despot. Flint and Isobel cooked side by side in the kitchen with the laughter and chatter and music from outside as their sound track, watching out the window to make sure nothing got too rowdy for little pitchers. But Berto always had a watchful eye on Jessie—and on his friends to make sure they treated her right. Such a good kid.

Shame what happened to that boy. Flint didn't know how Isobel had pulled through it. A house felt different when it was empty. Maybe he should've thought of that more when things were falling apart, but he was too buried in his own self-hatred and grief.

When he'd parked in his carport and bent back into the pas-senger side of the car for the grocery bags on the front seat, he realized he'd forgotten to stop at the trash dump on the main-land over off Loma Vista, where he'd planned to leave Jessie's old things. The boxes still sat tucked in the trunk, as if mocking him for getting lost in memories.

He'd unloaded the groceries in the kitchen, lowered himself gingerly, mindful of aggravating his back, to fish out his ancient oversize stew pot from the back of a cabinet—once he'd plopped Jessie's tiny little behind into it and pretended he was going to cook her like the witch in Hansel and Gretel, to her screams of delight—and washed the dust out of it. He pulled out his scarred cutting board and found his favorite nick-handled knife—it had been sharpened—and sliced up carrots and Yukon potatoes and onions and spicy sausage.

He'd thought Marcie was right behind him when they left the impound lot—he actually expected her to beat him home after his unplanned stop—but maybe she had errands to run in town or on the island. By the time she got here he might have everything assembled and waiting for her, if he stepped on the gas a little more.

As the rich scents started to infiltrate the house, Flint realized he was actually looking forward to someone coming back to it. To Marcie coming back.

Marcie

I t was almost odd to be speeding up Highway 75, the spiky saw palmettoes planted all along the median softening to a blur outside her open window, the wind lifting her hair, the rhythmic thunk of expansion joints under her tires notching her steady progression back home. So quickly she'd grown accustomed to the slower pace of Palmetto Key, to the thick, rich ocean scents rather than the unpleasant road odors of gasoline and tar.

Now that she had her car, her purse and ID, her phone—plugged into the car charger—real life came rushing back. Decisions must be made. Aside from the increasingly desperate calls from Chuck that she'd ignored the day she left, most of her missed calls were from Will. Those didn't stop after she'd called him—a flurry of them followed the day she'd used Art's phone, as if he'd been frantic to get hold of her again after she hung up, and then periodically since then he'd kept trying her, apparently unwilling to accept that she needed space from even him. Her voice mails were full—she'd listen to them later—and she had fifty-three texts, also mostly from Will, which was saying something. He hated to text. She'd read those later too.

What did it mean that she wasn't more eager to talk to her husband after days apart, the longest she'd gone without hearing his voice since she was a teenager? More than a quarter of a century together, more than half her life, and it was this easy to just . . . stop? Will *was* her life, the center of it—the fulcrum on which her existence turned. She barely remembered a time before Marcie-and-Will, as if they were a single entity.

And yet the lima bean, that tiny little collection of developing cells and tissues—a possible future Marcie hadn't even known she might have wanted until it presented itself—somehow seemed to have changed everything. Upended Marcie's orientation to her world, as if the water that once held you afloat betrayed you, rushing into your lungs and letting you drown.

Her Bluetooth was dead too, so she got off at the next exit, a coagulation of gas stations, fast food, big-box stores, and strip malls, gassing up at a Valero before she pulled off to the side of the lot, leaving the car running in case the phone didn't have enough juice yet. Then she hit "call" and waited for her husband to answer in a strange limbo, not nervous, not anticipating, not dreading. Just waiting.

"Marcie."

Will said her name as a statement, not a question—and as if held back by a fragile dam, that was when her emotions rushed out. She gripped the phone, hot from baking on the console, and had to swallow and take two breaths before she could find her voice.

"It's me."

She heard him let out a long sigh, as if he'd been holding an inhale for days. "Marcie. How have you been?"

A wild giggle bubbled up her throat until she swallowed it back. *Fine, thanks. You?* It was just so surreal. So ridiculous to be talking to her husband after this unprecedented estrangement as if they were casual acquaintances catching up.

"Well, let's see . . . I got a job." She said it as a joke, wanting to lighten the tenor, but Will didn't seem to see the humor.

"You *what*?" he yelped. "What the hell, Marcie, are you not coming home?"

The old urge to soothe, to assuage—to *bend*—washed over her like a seismic wave.

"It was just temporary. I needed some money."

"Where are your credit cards? Do you need me to wire you cash? Are you okay?"

She let out a chuff of air, frustrated. "I'm fine, Will. I'm . . . just fine." He could take that one of two ways—she was just fine and dandy, or fine was all she was, no more than that. She wasn't sure which way she meant it.

It's all right, Marce. Everything's fine. Just fine.

When the bleeding wouldn't stop and she panicked, Will had immediately taken charge, getting her to lie down while he called the doctor, bundling her into the car as he soothed her with a steady stream of empty platitudes like that, holding her hand as if he could anchor her to the exam table while the doctor bent, grim faced, below her bent knees.

After they got home he'd watched her every move like she was a science experiment. He brought her soup and hot tea with lemon, gave her the pain pills the doctor prescribed, plugged in the heating pad for the cramps and wrapped it in a towel. *How are you, Marcie? Are you okay?*

I'm fine.

"Her hormone levels will be all over the place for a while," she'd heard the doctor tell him at the hospital. "She might be emotional."

But she wasn't. They watched TV at night like they always had, although a swath of territory opened up between them on the sofa. *You need anything, Marce?*

No, I'm fine.

"Fine" was the bandage they plastered over all the broken places between them, and Marcie was sick of it.

"Actually I'm not fine," she said. "I haven't been. That's why I left. And it's why I wound up here, why I got into a bad enough state that I had to get picked up off the beach by a total stranger."

"What are you talking about?" His tone went sharp.

"Not like that. An older man. Old. He was kind to me. But the car got towed and my purse was in it, and so I didn't have any money, and he let me stay with him while I earned enough to get it back."

"Marcie, what are you *talking* about? This sounds crazy. I could have come to get you—at the very least gotten you money to get you home. You *stayed* with this guy? For how long?"

"Well, the whole time. Till just now." It was so startlingly easy to just tell him all of this. Why had she hesitated?

In the silence she thought she could hear his blood pressure rising. "You've been staying with a complete stranger in some strange town for *days*?"

"Herman," she said patiently. "Not a complete stranger. Herman Flint. And not in some strange town. Palmetto Key. I told you that." She pictured the rustling palm trees, the gentle, steady sea outside the back door of Flint's little house. *You should see it. . . . We'll have to come here together sometime.* The instinctive reassurances filtered into her head but floated away before she spoke them.

"Marcie . . . do you have any idea how dangerous all of this was? You were completely cut off, with no money, apparently still feeling the effects of surgery, and at the mercy of a complete stranger. I didn't know where to find you—*no one* knew where to find you if something had gone wrong—"

"Nothing went wrong," she bit out. "Or at least when it did, I handled it. Because that's what you *do*, Will. You take chances and you try things and you live your life, and if things go wrong then you deal with it. Because that's what life *is*. Because if you live afraid of taking any kind of risk then you might as well just be *dead*."

The words fountained out of her, carried along on that rising tide of anger that had almost seemed to have ebbed in Palmetto Key.

When friends asked Marcie and Will the secret of their marriage, how they were still so happy together after so long, one of the things both of them always said was "We tell each other the truth—and we pay attention." It meant not deflecting with a "nothing" if Will asked her what was wrong when something was wrong. It meant he sought for the words to share with her his feelings when he was upset, even though sometimes it was hard for him to nail it down concretely. And it meant that when she and Will had talked out his reservations about the lima bean, she'd listened. That's who they were, what their marriage was.

They'd be the oldest parents on the playground, he said, probably constantly assumed to be the grandparents. By the time the child was ready for college they'd be almost retirement age, and how could they pay for that and still have the retirement they'd hoped for? He worried about everything that could go wrong—"geriatric mother" had hit Marcie with a slap of irritated amusement, but it had freaked Will right the hell out, with the doctor's accompanying warnings about birth defects, genetic mutations, fetal irregularities, and complications of pregnancy that might even endanger Marcie's well-being.

"What if I lost *you*?" he asked, fear raw in his eyes.

"Statistically highly unlikely," she joked, trying to lighten the mood for her analytical, left-brained husband, but Will didn't crack a smile.

His words to her on that long-ago afternoon on the bleachers had echoed in her mind: *It's okay, Marcie. Everything's going to turn out okay.* As long as she had him and he had her, everything always did.

"That's not going to happen," she'd assured him, earnest, a hand to his face. "We'll figure it out as we go. You and I can do this, Will. We're going to be *great* at this."

But as days turned into weeks and he grew no closer to turning some invisible corner into welcoming parenthood, his words had begun to worm through her mind. Will's concerns weren't alarmist; they were valid risks of any pregnancy, more so at her age. And that didn't even take into account the bigger issues of raising a child in today's world, a red tide of her own fears gathering momentum like a tsunami: Global warming. Pandemics. An increasingly fraught political landscape with ever more extreme polarization. Increasing wealth inequality. AI. Superbugs mutating beyond the control of known antibiotics. Failure to launch.

Marcie's certainty started to waver. There were hundreds, thousands of things that could go wrong at every stage of a child's life, and how did you bring a person into the world knowing it was riddled with pending disasters around every corner? How did you ever have another moment's peace of mind once this human being that was a part of you came into existence, constantly vulnerable to its dangers and uncertainties?

Will was right: It was too risky, too much for them to take on when they were far too old for the luxury of naiveté and ignorance of all the world's perils. And how did you bring a child into the world if one parent so fervently didn't want to be one? And what would it do to their marriage if she did?

And so, two weeks before the end of her first trimester, she made an appointment for an abortion.

She'd spent the next week in a state of fraught, frantic unrest, not knowing whether she should keep the appointment . . . whether she should cancel it.

Before she could decide, the bleeding started, and it didn't stop.

She never told Will what she'd done. Despite his undisguisable relief, she knew he'd been beating himself up relentlessly for not being able to want what she so desperately wanted.

And she let him. Even though she'd considered ending the pregnancy herself. Even though she had no right to mourn all the lost possibilities.

Maybe her mom was right—maybe Flint was right, and the only person anyone could really count on was herself.

In the silence she could hear him breathing, and she breathed with him for a moment. "I can't get past it, Will," she said. "I keep trying, but I can't, and I don't know if I ever will."

"Marcie . . ." His voice was rough. "It's not your fault."

It's not yours either, she wanted to say, knew she should say. But she didn't.

She hated the lima bean. Hated the pregnancy that had come between them, that changed everything, that ruined the life they'd had together where they had been happy, where everything, before then, had been enough.

But it wasn't getting pregnant that had ruined everything, was it? That just pulled back the curtain on what Marcie had never had to see before—the limits between the two of them, the reaches to which the love she'd thought they shared didn't stretch. The limits she'd accepted for herself.

"Will . . . I don't think I'm ready to come home yet."

This time the silence felt like a physical thing, thick and soupy.

"What do you mean?" He sounded so young, like the boy she'd known.

"I need more time. I'm so angry all the time. I can't stand it. I'm not angry here, though."

"What . . . what about work?"

"I've got vacation time accrued. Sick leave. I was just out for surgery—they'll understand." She laughed without humor. "Chuck can handle things for a little while, even if he doesn't think he can."

She thought they'd lost the connection, and then:

"Marcie . . . are you leaving me?"

In her palm the phone grew moist. It was unthinkable to picture a life without Will—she couldn't ever have imagined it. And yet hadn't she been living exactly that since she came here?

"I don't know."

Tears heated her eyes, but even now she could do nothing but honor their covenant: That was the truest answer she could offer her husband.

Will's voice was low when he finally broke the painful silence. "Do you remember St. Simons?"

It took Marcie a moment to catch up. "Of course I do. How many years have we gone there?"

"I know. That's what made me think of it. I was just trying to picture where you are."

A fist closed around her ribs. "It's nothing like that here," she said softly. And after a few beats: "Do you remember the

ring you bought me there? At that little art shop? The tourmaline one?"

"I . . . Of course I do."

"Would you send it to me?"

He made a low noise in his throat, as if the breath had been
knocked from him. "Where do you want me to send it?"

She gave him Flint's address—where else would she go? As
hobbled as he was the old man needed her, whether he wanted
to admit it or not, and she owed him that much.

He cleared his throat. "Is there anything else you want?"

She thought about her clothes, shoes, toiletries—things she
once would have deemed essential for even an overnight trip. It
was funny how little she had missed any of it since coming
here. The answers that popped into her mind were things Will
couldn't send her anyway. She had her purse now, her wallet
and credit cards. She could buy what she needed here. "I guess
that's it for now," she said finally.

"Okay."

She couldn't stand to hang up the phone. "Will . . ." But then
the word drifted off into the muggy air.

"Don't, Marce. Please . . . don't."

"I'm sorry. I'm just so sorry." She sounded strangled, shaky—
her, not Will, whose voice was flat and distant.

"I'll have the ring to you in a few days. We'll talk later
about . . . the rest."

He hung up, and Marcie was left holding a cell phone slippery with her sweat, connected to nothing.

She sat in the gas station lot for a long time, feeling shaky
and sick. What had just happened? What had they done?

Her body felt empty, hollowed out as if she had bird bones—but also maybe light enough to fly.

She needed to call work before anything else—Chuck was expecting her back tomorrow morning.

"Oh, my God, you have to be kidding me," he said when she reached him. "Do you have any idea how busy we are here? It's not *April*, for God's sake." Weather in Atlanta could go either way in early spring, and there wasn't much going on in the way of attractions unless you were a golf fanatic, so tourism slowed way down. But July stayed busy.

"I do know, Chuck, and I know it's a lot to handle. But remember the quinceañera you ran last year on your own when I was at the conference in New York? Everything that could go wrong did go wrong, and you were amazing. We got a glowing letter about you from the girl's father." *Acknowledge the concern. Redirect.*

He made a chuffing sound Marcie couldn't interpret.

Offer an incentive. She knew her second-in-command well enough to know what would work. "There's a vendor bottle of Lagavulin and a two-hundred-dollar gift card for Girl Diver in the top drawer of my desk." The Asian-Cajun fusion seafood place at Madison Yards in Reynoldstown was new and hot, two of Chuck's favorite things. "The chefs offered to create a personal tasting menu for us if you call ahead. They're all yours."

Another scoff and then, begrudgingly: "Well . . . fine. But it's still a lot of work for one person, Marcie."

It was true, although she'd run the events staff on her own for years before finally convincing Claus to hire an assistant. But that wasn't what Chuck needed to hear, she realized. "Look, Chuck . . . I know a lot of this is falling into your lap, and I'm sorry. But you underestimate yourself. You're excellent at organization and planning, wonderful with the support staff, and the clients always love you. The only reason you get flustered is because you hate to tell anyone no. But I've never met anyone who can make a no sound more like a yes."

Case in point: Last March Chuck had raced into their office to exclaim in horror that his boyfriend had proposed. He still wasn't sure about the whole marriage thing, he confided to Marcie, but he didn't want to lose Michael. *Well, what did you say?* she asked him. *I told him I was thrilled he was so committed and I was too,* he said. *And then I bought him a silver David Yurman bracelet from Brown and Co.* He'd managed to avert Michael from pressing for an answer for three months so far, but the two seemed every bit as happy as they did before. Chuck might not realize it yet, but he was a master at acknowledge-redirect-incentivize.

"You're really, really good at this job," Marcie told him honestly. "Just trust yourself a little more."

"Yes, I am," he said archly. And then his tone finally softened: "But thanks for saying so. Want me to let Monique know?"

She told him yes—his telling the hotel manager would save her a call—and thanked him and they said their good-byes, but before she hung up she heard his voice again: "Hey, Marcie, wait."

She brought the phone back to her ear. "What's up?"

He gave an intake of breath, the way he did to buy himself time to consider when a client made a difficult request. "Is everything . . . okay with you?"

The warmth that suffused her wasn't entirely due to the blazing sun. "Thanks for being concerned, Chuck. Everything's fine."

Was it? Marcie didn't know, but she was grateful to have a bit more reprieve before she had to figure it out.

~~~

When she'd pulled off the highway to call Will, amid the squat strip malls with businesses like insurance agencies and nail salons and bail bonds offices, Marcie had passed a familiar sign for a chain-store hobby shop.

Well, that is a screaming shame, the clay worker in the little beachfront studio had said of her abandonment of art, and he was right. She liked the image of her he'd seen—not a plain, predictable middle-aged woman but a free-spirited creative soul. An artist. That's who she might have been once—hadn't she? She wanted to be that person again, or at least to try.

If she went back home now, would she still do it? For nearly twenty-five years she hadn't, as though art and real life were mutually exclusive, the barrier lowered only here at the beach in her strange little idyll of time out of time.

So she wandered the aisles of the huge store, the vast variety of artistic possibilities seeping into her like low-grade electricity. She let herself touch the skeins of yarn in a colorful honeycomb along one wall, opened the covers of various sketch pads, and ran the paper between her finger and thumb, noticing the different textures and thicknesses. She let her eyes trail across dozens of tubes of paint in plastic displays, drinking in the rainbow of hues on tiny placards in front of each one.

Eventually she retrieved a red plastic basket from the front of the store and began filling it with familiar supplies—Mod Podge adhesive, atelier matte varnish, a starter set of cheap acrylics and brushes, a fine-tipped ink calligraphy pen. She selected random things that caught her eye—canvases and chipboard, a set of two cheap wood frames, hemp cord, a mesh bag of sea glass in every shade of turquoise that reminded her of the chips the artist had scattered across one of the tables in his shop, along with one of flattened marbles of clear glass, a vial of gold glitter—growing increasingly excited as she walked the aisles, placing in her basket the kinds of items she'd dreamed of having in high school but that her mother never could afford. By the time she'd checked out and gotten back to her car she'd charged nearly two hundred dollars on her credit card and realized she'd been there more than an hour. She'd had no sense of time.

The house smelled different when she let herself in— onions and sage and something richer underneath it, meaty.

"That you?" she heard from the kitchen, and Flint poked his head out. "Hope you like spicy food."

"Oh," she said when she took him in. He held a wooden spoon in one hand, a kitchen towel old enough to curl at the edges draped over one arm like an aging sommelier, an incongruity that would have struck her as funny an hour ago. But as she'd come back across the bridge instead of going home to her husband, to her real life, reality had finally sunk in and a sick feeling coiled in her belly.

"Thanks," she said. "I'm not very hungry. You go ahead; I'll heat something up later."

In the purple room she set her shopping bags on the purple carpet beside the dresser, the thrilling lure of their contents no longer drawing her. Who was she fooling? A few crafting supplies didn't make her an artist. An extended vacation at the beach didn't make her a free spirit.

What did she think—that she could just stay here in this limbo she was in forever? Not go back to her job, her home, stay squatting in the tiny run-down house of a man she hadn't known a week ago, who most of the time barely tolerated her? For the first time in her adult life Marcie had absolutely no plan, no vision of her future, immediate or otherwise, and she'd thought it would feel freeing . . . but instead she felt only adrift.

Heeling out of her sneakers she sat on the end of Jessie's twin bed, facing herself in the mirror over the girl's dresser. The woman staring back at her was a familiar stranger—a face you caught in a crowd with a breath of recognition, only to immediately question yourself: *Did* you know that person? Or did they just look like someone you'd known?

The polished surface of her high-end-hotel persona had muted. This Marcie wore little makeup and her skin showed its imperfections—darker than she was used to, the tint across her forehead, nose, and cheeks from the sun, not a compact. Unconcealed freckles made irregular patterns across her nose, and in the absence of added color or gloss on her lips, her eyes were a startling shock of blue. Her hair had lightened all over, rendering her expensive highlights invisible, but a darker line at her scalp revealed the truth of her; if Marcie stepped closer to the mirror she knew she'd see it half threaded with gray. If she actually stayed here, how long until the slow, inexorable erosion of beach towns wore the old Marcie completely away?

Was she really thinking of staying here?

She imagined Chuck's reaction if Marcie told him she wasn't coming back to work, the way his eyes would widen as they always did when he felt overwhelmed, the rest of his face freezing as though desperately trying not to give away his panic. A startling one-note laugh ricocheted back to her from the woman in the mirror. Poor Chuck had no poker face, at least not with her.

The scents coming from the kitchen had begun to seep under the wide crack beneath her door and pulled her out of her funk—cooked tomatoes and something else, pungent and rich. It was an ordinary, homey smell, and yet it made Marcie realize that until now the only time the old house had carried cooking scents was when she made something. Flint seemed to eat nothing that wasn't heated up from a can or a box or a jar.

She'd had her head so far up her own asshole, as the crusty old man would say, she'd completely missed it: He'd cooked for her. For the two of them.

But the kitchen was quiet when she went out, a covered Dutch oven resting on a cold burner, one side of the sink littered with a dirty cutting board, a knife, a vegetable peeler. The small kitchen table was set with paper napkins folded into triangles, soup spoons holding them down, two filled water glasses at each place, beads of condensation caught by cork coasters she would never have imagined Flint to have. She wondered if this was what the house looked like when his daughter had been alive.

As soon as she opened the back door she saw him, one hand stiff-armed on the railing as the old man slowly let himself down the first step off the porch. Without thinking she hurried to his side.

"Let me help," she said, reaching out a bent arm for support.

"I don't need your help."

"You will if you fall. Think of this as a preventive measure for you to *not* need someone to wipe your ass."

"Nice mouth."

"Is that a stone you're comfortable throwing?"

He grunted but put a hand on her shoulder as they made their way one step at a time to the soft sand, which shifted under Marcie's feet. "Watch your step."

"Something's been at the nest."

Alarm charged through her. "What?"

Marcie had checked on it this morning—Flint taught her how to look for any threats to the eggs: marks in the sand that meant some creature had been snuffling at the turtle nest, or any scat left nearby, or even predatory fire ants—but everything had been fine, the sand untouched.

As they got closer now, though, she could see it: There were fresh animal tracks around the slight depression in the sand.

He bent his knees, trying to look closer at the tracks, and she steadied him. "Raccoons," he said.

Her heart dropped. "Did they get the eggs?"

"Not yet. But they will."

"How do we keep them away? Is there . . . a repellent?"

He turned to look at her. "For a raccoon? Anything you put out is appetizer, dinner, or dessert. They're scavengers—worse than maggots. Eat anything."

"Can we give them something they want more so they stay away from the nest?" As soon as she said it she felt foolish.

"Sure. I'll get 'em cocktails while you put out the hors d'oeuvres." He turned and started lumbering off toward the front of the house, and Marcie stood watching. Fine—let him take his chances on the uneven sand. She relaxed once he reached the packed gravel of the side yard, though, stopping at the trash cans beside his house. "Check that the lid's tight," he told her, nodding toward one while he looked over the other. "And look all over it for rips, holes, anything they can get into it through."

She did as he said. They each examined their bin, the silence broken only by the hard plastic scraping the sand underneath.

"How's yours?"

"Fine," she said. "Nothing torn or ripped."

He grunted. "Yeah. This one too." He stood for a moment, looking around the yard, and then he walked purposefully toward the house next door, Marcie again scrambling to recalculate to keep up with his erratic trajectory. Alongside the little clapboard house was an old metal garbage bin, and one side bore a deep dent—fresh, from the lack of oxidation around it— that kept the lid from sitting flush on the top.

"There it is," he said. "That's what's getting their attention." He pulled off the lid and a sour smell billowed up around them in a rotten cloud of stench. "Goddammit," Flint cursed. He slammed the lid back down and hissed in a breath of pain at the collision, then headed around the yard toward the front of the house.

"What are you doing?" Marcie called after him.

"Telling the owner to get a proper damn trash can. She's lived here long enough. She oughta know better."

"Flint . . . wait." He kept walking. "Wait. . . . Hey—hold it!"

He turned around at her sharp command with a glare.

"You're just going to make her mad," she said. "People don't listen if you yell at them."

"That so?" he said flatly, clearly pointing out it was her yell that had made him stop.

"Well, they don't hear anything you say. They get angry and tune you out."

His jaw flexed as if he were chewing something tough. "You just wanna leave that there, then? Bring more raccoons that're eventually gonna dig up those eggs and eat them?"

"No, of course I don't." Why did she butt in? She didn't know the neighbor, and presumably Flint did. Maybe he'd had this argument with the woman before. Maybe the woman didn't know. Maybe she'd forgotten.

Flint pointed up the woman's steep steps. "Knock on her door. I'll do the talking."

Marcie walked up the flight of stairs to the door of the neighbor woman's house and knocked against the screen, the wood clacking loudly against the doorframe with each rap. The inside door opened quickly enough that she suspected the nosy woman had been watching them circle her property.

Up close she didn't look the way Marcie had pictured her. Her skin was soft-looking, like lambskin worn from years of handling. Brown eyes dipped at the outer corners, as if a lifetime of bittersweet memories had dragged them downward.

"Is everything all right?" she asked.

"Mr. Flint wanted to talk to you." Marcie gestured behind her.

The woman's eyes widened and then narrowed. Without a word she pushed the screen door, Marcie moving back to give her space, and the woman stepped out onto her porch and looked down at where Flint stood, legs spread, arms held away from his sides as if prepping for a fight.

They both seemed to freeze there, and for a long moment the two of them simply stared at each other.

"I'm Marcie," she said to break the awkward silence.

"My niece," Flint barked.

Marcie's gaze shot over to him, but the old man's arms were crossed now as if he were daring her to contradict him.

The woman let out a brief sound that might have been a laugh, and Marcie turned back to her, but the sharp brown eyes stayed on Flint. "Your niece. Is that right?" She moved her gaze to Marcie and her smile turned more genuine, making her pretty and years younger. "I'm Isobel. Isobel Dominguez."

The name jolted her. Isobel? Was this the woman Jessie wrote about in her letters? Marcie had assumed it was a girlfriend or second wife, but was it just a neighbor the girl and her father had been friendly with?

But no . . . it was more than that—the woman had clearly been involved in their lives. If this was that same Isobel, what had happened that these two now seemed to barely tolerate each other, let alone talk?

"Marcie Malone," she finally said, falling back on automatic politeness to defuse the weighted tension that was as stifling as the thick humidity. "It's nice to meet you."

"You need to use my garbage cans," Flint interrupted.

"I beg your pardon, Herman?"

Flint—Herman—looked like he'd swallowed a palmetto bug. "I said, you need to use my cans," he bit out. "For now. Till you can replace the busted one. Or I'll get one for you next time I hit the mainland." He turned to cross back to his own yard, his stiff movements telling Marcie he'd overdone it. "You're drawing animals with that thing, you know," he muttered as he shuffled off toward the side of the house.

Marcie stood where he'd left her, staring after him until she heard Isobel shift. Her smile stayed in place, but her gaze sharpened. "I wasn't aware that Herman had a niece."

Heat flushed Marcie's neck and crept up to her cheeks. "This is my first trip," she hedged.

"Herman and I have known each other a long time. I'm surprised I've never heard about you before." Her tone made it clear that she didn't believe it for a second.

"Well . . . I guess I'd better go," Marcie said. "It was nice to meet you, Isobel. We'll throw out the old can for you, if you like."

Isobel waved a hand. "That's all right. I'll put it out empty for the garbagemen next week and I'm sure they'll know to take it."

"Oh. Okay. Well, good-bye."

"Good-bye . . . Oh, Marcie."

Marcie stopped, turned.

"Thank Herman for me, would you, please? It's been a long time since he's done anything neighborly." And with that the woman stepped back and shut the door, leaving Marcie standing alone on the porch.

Flint was standing just inside the front door when she came back, as if he'd been looking out the window.

"What'd she say?" He turned toward his chair as she let herself in, reaching for the book he'd left there as if the answer were unimportant to him.

"She said she'll put the bin out for the garbagemen."

He stood with one hand on the book, the other supporting himself on his chair, his back to her. "Anything else?"

The question carried sharp edges. She was right—there was something between the two. Something more than feuding neighbors or former friends.

"Like what?" she asked.

"How the hell should I know? Was I there?"

She didn't reply. Just waited. But the trick didn't work with the stubborn old man this time, and he held his silence. "How's your back?" she asked finally, and he grunted.

She stepped past him to the piecrust table and retrieved his prescription bottle. Shaking one pill out into her hand, she glanced a question at him as she hovered the bottle over her palm until he nodded.

"One's fine."

She laid it in his warm, dry hand, retreating to the kitchen and returning with a glass of water. "Did you already eat?" she asked.

"Go ahead."

"I thought we could eat together."

"Thought you weren't hungry." The words were clipped, and she heard the intentional echo of her own earlier.

She met his eye. "I had a hard conversation with my husband this afternoon. But actually I'm flat-out starving, so I'm going to go help myself to whatever is in there that smells so amazing, and if you want me to dish some up for you, we could actually eat simultaneously. Which might be nice."

She thought she heard a snort, but he didn't move.

She'd just spooned up the delicious-looking stew—a rich tomatoey broth studded with cabbage and carrots and potatoes and thick slices of sausage—and settled at the table when she heard Flint's slightly shuffling steps come into the room. He stopped and looked at her.

"How is it?" he clipped out finally.

Marcie didn't say anything for a moment; then she picked up her spoon and took a bite of the hot stew, chewing a chunk of spicy sausage as he watched her.

She swallowed. "It's delicious. I've never tasted anything like it."

He grunted. "Balsamic vinegar—a lot of it. Brings out layers of flavor."

As she spooned up another bite, Flint walked over to the range, ladled a bowl for himself, and brought it back over to where she sat. She watched him carefully lower himself to the chair, pick up his own spoon, and start eating.

Marcie took a breath. "It turns out I'm going to be staying at the beach for a while. I wondered if it would be okay if I stayed with you a little longer." She knew better than to suggest it was to help him out.

Suit yourself, she anticipated, or maybe just an indifferent shrug, or no reply at all. Maybe he wanted her out altogether.

Flint chewed a mouthful of stew, swallowed. "Yeah. That would be okay. That'd be . . . good."

Marcie nodded, startled. "Okay. Well . . . good."

Marcie

In the new fragile peace between them, the heavy atmosphere of the house lifted ever so slightly. Flint stopped hiding from her in his bedroom, and in the evenings she joined him on the back porch, wordlessly watching the tide come in, the sun fall in the sky.

But as he started to get around with a little more ease and she grew more comfortable leaving him for stretches of time, she began imitating his long walks along the shoreline. Her daily pilgrimage looking for tracks in the sand was serenaded by the soft whispers of the gentle surf and the peevish cries of seagulls, distant shouts of the smattering of people who dotted the sand and the shallows as Marcie collected interesting shells off the sand and unloaded her curated treasures onto his daughter's dresser.

This morning she opened up the bags she'd brought back from the hobby shop on the mainland and, scooting the pile of found items to one side, she laid her purchases out.

Here in the purple confines of the small borrowed room, the materials seemed overly ambitious. She'd made the hobbyist's mistake of getting excited about supplies before she'd tried her hand at the actual craft. It was overwhelming—it had been much too long since she'd done anything like this and Marcie didn't even know where to start.

But something was rumbling to life inside her: an invisible tickle, like the filament-thin legs of an insect you barely felt stir the fine hairs on your skin . . . a tiny phantom itch to do something with her strange cache.

Without thinking too hard about it—she'd ponder herself right back into paralysis—Marcie selected a handful of materials— a sheet of chipboard, the tub of adhesive, the marbles, some paints—and tucked them back into one of the bags, scooping the shells into another and nestling them inside before heading back up the beach.

The little art studio was closed up tight, though, the artist nowhere in sight for Marcie to take him up on his offer of work space, so instead she trekked on to Tequila Mockingbird. Marcie missed the gang—if they were there she'd say a quick hello before the lunch crowd filed in.

The regulars shouted greetings as she walked up the beachfront stairs to the porch, fruitlessly wiping sand from her feet on a rubber mat outside the sliders. She waved in at the three men and the bartender, unsurprised to see everyone in position. "I forgot my shoes," she said. Darla probably wouldn't care if she walked in barefoot, but OSHA rules were too deeply ingrained in Marcie to ignore.

"It's a beach bar!" Darla wheezed, a broad smile creasing her eyes almost shut. "No shirt, no shoes—no shit! Get in here, girl, and take a load off."

As another server—someone new, she guessed, since Marcie didn't know him—refilled ketchups on the porch, Darla pulled a frosty beer from the tap and took a long sip. "This one's on you, newbie, for my pain and suffering."

Marcie laughed and motioned toward Pete and Art and Bink. "It's on me anyway—all the way around. Least I can do."

"Oho, our girl's all fancy again," Bink said as Darla obliged with three more mugs. But he didn't ask about Marcie's changed situation, or about anything—none of them did, which was one reason she liked being here, Marcie realized. They all existed purely in the moment.

She settled onto a stool beside Art, who gifted her with a shy smile. "I was wondering if you locals could help me with some identification," she said, spreading her haul of seashells on the bar top.

Between the three men, and occasionally Darla, they came up with the name for each one, which were often as enchanting as the shells themselves: the Florida fighting conch, with its smooth pinkish belly; an orange hoof shell, which looked exactly like it sounded; queen helmet, coffee bean trivia, a dog-head triton, and the marvelously named Humphrey wentletrap. The regulars identified a handful of delicate translucent round shells in shades of orange and cream as jingle shells, but Marcie vastly preferred the colloquial name Darla proffered: mermaid's toenails. One that looked like the offspring of a drill bit and the Guggenheim Museum was ID'd as the boring turret snail, a name that she accused Bink of making up until Art showed her the web page on his phone. "Boring like what it does, not what it is," he explained seriously, and she laughed.

"How do you guys know all this?" she asked.

Pete shrugged. "Not much else to do around here."

"Plus it really gets the ladies going," Bink said, and Darla did a spit take, which set everyone off again.

~~~~

This time the back door was open as Marcie neared the little coral-colored building on her way back to Flint's, music filtering out, something with electric guitar, violin, and—she'd swear—rub board. It was funkier than she would have expected from the unusual mix of instruments, almost zydeco.

The lights in the main area were off, the front windows partially blocked by flattened cardboard boxes leaning against them, casting it into even deeper shadows, but there was enough light to see that except for the boxes, nothing had changed.

Again it made her picture the little St. Simons art shop she and Will had discovered so long ago: one-of-a-kind jewelry sparkling in the glass case, saturated batik fabrics unfurled along one wall, sorbet-hued watercolors and vivid acrylic and oil paintings hanging on every vertical surface and displayed on easels, with prints stacked in racks for art lovers on a stricter budget.

She imagined this space groomed into a similar order, the tables and display cases spread out where patrons could browse their contents. Cleaning the windows and installing better lighting would show off the contents to better effect, and then the bland white walls could be painted a deeper color—something vibrant and alive, like a turned-earth brown or the rich russet of sun-warmed Georgia clay, the better to show off paintings and tapestries and metalwork that could be hung against it. Art was meant to be displayed properly, to be seen and touched and enjoyed.

In her imagination she allowed herself to mount her own work in the mental picture of the art shop too, images created from the shells she'd pulled off the sand or the other wealth of materials she'd bought, the shadows thrown by the collages' raised surfaces adding another dimension to the color and pattern of the pieces.

She could see flickers of the light in the other room that told her the clay worker was back there, and she knocked on the rear doorjamb, even though she knew he wouldn't hear it over the music.

"Hello?" she called loudly.

The music abruptly cut off and his frizzy blond head popped out from the doorway. "Hey, Collage Artist!"

"It's Marcie, actually."

He grinned. "*Mucho gusto.* Jeff."

She held up her bag. "I bought some art supplies to try . . . some things I used to do. I'm just messing around, really, but I wondered if I could take you up on your invitation to work here?"

A slow smile spread across his face and he nodded. "Artists always welcome. Come on in." He disappeared into the back room and the music cranked up again, loud enough to drown out her thoughts.

Marcie set her bag on the counter, cleared a space, and got to work.

She was rusty, no doubt. She spent much too long lining up her supplies, placing random items on the chipboard, trying to get a feel for what she wanted to create, but the moment she opened the Mod Podge, its gluey, slightly tangy smell instantly sent her back to her high school art room, and her fingers started working as if from muscle memory.

The open door let in the warm gulf breeze, the thick salt scent, the hot yellow light of the long summer day. The hypnotic sound of the placid gulf waves loosened something inside her. The ocean imposed its constantly shifting *now* onto those who lost themselves here, slowly eroding all your *befores*, lulling you away from your *nexts*. As the sun lowered slowly toward the waterline, Marcie let herself play: no clear plan, no finish line, just the old familiar pleasure of watching something develop under her hands as she let herself get lost in it.

When she finally got to a stopping point, her neck ached and her shoulders were tight. The counter wasn't an ideal work surface—too high to be comfortable for her shoulders, too small to spread out—and her first effort was clumsy, obvious, but Marcie looked at it with a swell of pride.

She'd forgotten whatever she'd once learned about composition—contrast, proportion, balance, unity—but she'd actually *made* something. It was rough, amateurish, yet the pastiche of found items she'd arranged and rearranged, broken into pieces and tried again, and finally set into the adhesive had resulted in a swirling abstract pattern of color and texture that drew her eye into it.

She left the piece flat on the table to dry, then stretched, realizing the music had long ago shifted to something soft and jazzy, and she hadn't seen or heard the potter—Jeff—in hours.

She found him standing in front of his kiln in cargo shorts and a clay-streaked T-shirt, his hair working to escape its ponytail. The kiln's tiled top was tipped back on its hinges, Jeff's arms taut with muscle as he braced his hands on the edges and stared down into the mouth.

"Come here."

She obeyed without thought, coming up next to him so close she thought the heat she felt against her naked arms was from the kiln, until she realized the unit was long turned off, and it was only the warmth radiating from his skin.

"My favorite moment. This part is literally out of my hands—I don't know exactly how my pieces will finish until I open the lid. It's like a collaboration between me and the kiln gods."

Looking down where his gaze was trained, she saw the brick-lined space inside was packed close with what she now recognized as his distinctive work. He reached in, pulled one piece out, and passed it over to her hands. She felt its familiar sandpapery texture in her palms, a slender, narrow bud vase with its lip turned under in a sensual pout. Billows of fire red and orange and magenta across its surface were shot through with threads of something glittery, like crushed diamonds.

"Oh . . ." Her voice was a breath.

Dipping a hand back down for another piece, he didn't respond. As he pulled out one fat-cheeked pot after another, a frown weighted the corners of his usually smiling mouth, but Marcie couldn't understand why. All the pieces bloomed with the vivid colors that she thought of as his signature, in unexpected combinations and random patterns, some with cratered surfaces like the moon, some splattered interestingly with black or dull brown.

He took out more, examining each with the studied intensity of a dog-show judge before setting it aside on the folding table he'd set up nearby. Marcie watched as he lifted out a ceramic shelf and revealed another layer of pottery—bowls of various sizes, plates, platters with raised edges—shaking his head as he pulled out a handful of broken shards.

"What happened?" she asked.

Jeff unloaded the kiln now as if it were a freight truck, emptying out the contents and transferring them heedlessly to the table, even the pieces that were still whole. "A failed experiment. This whole batch is ruined."

"What?" Running her eyes over the intact ceramics' textures, colors, and sinuous shapes, she wondered if he was one of those hyperperfectionist artists who were never happy with their work, always disappointed that the finished product didn't exactly match their vision. But that was what Marcie loved about art—it was part you and part something beyond you, both intention and accident coming together to create something even you hadn't dreamed of. "They're beautiful, most of them. Don't you expect some breakage, working in a fragile medium?"

"It's not that. I was trying something. Normally when I include other materials, I do it after the firing—you leave a channel or depression before you fire it and . . ." He waved a hand. "Doesn't matter. Anyway, I thought I could figure out how to incorporate semiprecious stones intrinsically—I had a vision of veins of amethyst and tigereye and malachite fired into each piece."

"But it worked, at least with some of them," she said, indicating the unbroken pieces on the table. "The one you handed me was gorgeous."

Jeff turned and retrieved the vase he'd given her, placing it back in her hands. Then he picked up something that looked like a dentist's tool, with a blunt spatulate head at either end, and with one end he gave a brisk tap on the piece she held.

Pieces of what looked like glass crumbled and pattered over her fingers to the floor, leaving an empty crevice where the glittery vein had been, and the vase suddenly cracked into two pieces. Marcie let out an involuntary cry at the ruined work of art.

"That was quartz. Apparently at extreme temps the silica stones shatter and can crack the ceramic." He gestured to the table. "The iron oxides change color; some of the other stones turn black, or explode, or melt away completely. Even the whole pieces lack integrity." He lifted a bowl from the table and set it sharply back down, and it collapsed into four large chunks as if it had just been propped together. "I need to try different stones, different temperatures, other techniques. Working with clay is part art and part chemistry."

"So all this work is wasted?" She waved a hand over the table.

"Not wasted. Most ceramists say you can't do what I want to do because the melting temps of crystals and minerals are different from clay, but I think it can be done—with certain compounds anyway. I just have to figure out how. Now I know what *doesn't* work. But I don't know if I'll figure out what does in time to take any with me."

"You're leaving?" Today had been extraordinary for her—she settled in to work when the sun was high in the sky, and when she finished, its light had gone red-gold as it sank closer to the sea. It felt as if the time had passed in a snap—as if she'd been somewhere else, another realm, and only just reborn into the world.

He met her gaze long enough for her to notice his eyes weren't uniformly gray—dark edges rimmed the light irises, a halo of amber around the pupils—then broke into his easy smile. "It's festival season. I'm taking these to North Carolina. Not for half a minute, though. I'm still building up my inventory. But don't worry, Collage Artist—you can still use the studio."

"It's Marcie," she offered again, relieved to keep her new work space but disappointed he'd already forgotten.

"I know. But you don't look like a Marcie."

"What do I look like?"

He shrugged. "What do you feel like?"

That startled a laugh out of her. When she was in fifth grade, she'd asked her mother if she could change her name—"Marcie" was so ordinary, so plain next to her classmates' lyrical Ashley,

Brittany, Amanda, Jessica. *Change it to what?* her mother scoffed, and Marcie had been ashamed to realize she had no idea.

"I guess I'm just Marcie," she said.

"Well, what's it short for?"

Again she laughed. "Nothing. It's Marcie, can you believe. Marcie Jane Jones." She remembered wishing when she met Will that he had a more exotic last name than Malone that might strip a little of the mundaneness from her own, though anything would be an improvement on Jones.

Jeff seemed to think about that for a moment; then he turned back to the kiln and retrieved another handful of broken pieces and smaller crumbles of ceramic. "Nah. That's not you either. We'll just keep trying." He turned and winked at her, and something fluttered in Marcie's chest.

She pushed away from the wall and moved to the far end of the table with the ruined pottery, fingering the lovely broken shards.

Flint

Flint leaned back in his seat, head resting against the wall of the house behind him, warm orange light from the setting sun painting the back of his closed eyelids.

He heard the screen door squeal and clatter shut and his eyes opened slowly. Marcie handed him a sweating glass of water.

"The prodigal returns," he said, then sipped to clear the gravel from his throat. "You slinging drinks at that ratty dive again?"

A smile pulled at her lips as she sat down—a new one, secretive and smug, like Jessie when she thought she'd gotten away with something.

"I've been making art. A collage. It's something I used to do a long time ago."

"Yeah?" He pushed himself gingerly to sit straighter in the chair. "What'd you make?"

She gave a one-shouldered shrug. "I don't know yet. But I like it."

"Well, let's see this masterpiece, then."

She slid a startled glance to him. "I left it to dry at the studio where I was working. I'll bring it home tomorrow and see what you think."

He rubbed his chin, trying not to seize on the word "home." "Yeah. All right."

Following Marcie's gaze out over the water he noticed a slight darkening at the sea line, a subtle blurring of water and sky. Inhaling deep he smelled it, a faint metallic scent, a tinge of sulfur that could still tighten his nuts.

"Storm's headed this way," he said.

She turned toward him, surprised. "Really? It looks so calm."

"Not tonight. Not tomorrow. Soon."

Too far off to worry about—probably the storm would blow itself out—but he'd never shared the mindless conviction of so many locals that Palmetto Key was somehow magically protected.

A creaking from next door told him that meddling old snoop was sticking her nose in his business again before he even heard Isobel's voice.

"Hello there, Marcie. I see you and your 'uncle' are enjoying this weather before the storm blows through."

Judgy old know-it-all—even with his back to her, he couldn't miss the sarcasm she layered onto the word. Wouldn't she just love to catch him out in his lie. Isobel was smart enough to see what was on the horizon, though. She'd remember as well as he did the storm in ninety-two that stripped out the royal palms that used to line Marea Boulevard and wiped out dozens of turtle nests, the surge of seawater afterward that flooded all the cracker houses, shriveled other vegetation like poison. He'd left the stump of the old avocado tree Jessie had insisted they plant jutting up from the sand in his backyard like a reproachful withered finger as a reminder of how bad things could get if you weren't prepared for the worst. Eleven years they'd waited for that thing to finally fruit, and after a single summer of fresh guacamole it got wiped out in a day.

"Mind your business, you old crow," he called over matter-of-factly.

Isobel had to work pretty hard to make sure her loud *tsk*ing carried all the way to his ears over the shushing white noise of the waves. But it did. Behind his back he heard her door slam behind her as she retreated inside in a snit.

"Sounds like you and your neighbor have a bit of a history together," Marcie said. Her carefully neutral tone dangled a hook he knew she hoped he'd bite. Marcie had more than a bit of the nosy parker in her too.

He didn't answer, just tipped his head back and closed his eyes again.

"She didn't seem to believe I was your niece."

"Not surprised," he said without opening his eyes. "Don't have one."

"Why did you lie to her?"

"Why'd you walk out on your husband?" His tone was mild, but he heard air whoosh out of her lungs. It was a fair question, though, given all the ones she'd asked him. He opened his eyes to see her lean forward, cupping the glass between her palms and regarding it as if it might contain the Oracle of Delphi.

"He didn't want the baby. I thought I did."

"That's no recipe for raising a kid," he said after a long moment.

Now she pressed her own eyes closed, tight. "No. It wasn't. And it turned out I didn't really want it either, I guess. So it shouldn't matter, right?"

The silence that dropped between them stretched so long and taut, he wondered if he should just get up, go inside. What the hell was he supposed to say to that?

"My wife walked out on our daughter when Jessie was barely a toddler."

The words fell out of him before he realized, against his will. That was a door he wanted closed . . . but she'd been sitting with him the way he'd imagined Jessie there a thousand times, and the ache in her voice when she told him how her husband let her down was as familiar to him as breathing.

She was watching him now, the way you'd keep your eye on a bobcat as you slowly edged away. "Jessie?" she finally said—softly, carefully.

He wanted to close his eyes again, to push to his feet and stomp back inside, put a stop to her questions, to the memories. But she didn't deserve it. And that was the easy choice, the one that offered him relief, numbness, and he didn't deserve that.

"What was she like?"

Something like a gasp punched up from his rib cage. It wasn't the next awful, inevitable question he'd been braced for, the penance that must be paid—*What happened to her?*—and the relief of it was fierce as a blow.

"Contumacious," he finally said, the rasp of his voice sanding the word. "Like some other people."

"I don't know what that means."

"It's not a compliment." But it was.

"Nosy?" She was guessing.

"Willful," he corrected, remembering those first few terrifying weeks in the wake Brenda left behind her when she walked out.

Jessie didn't eat certain things at first—he'd had no idea. So he just started cooking stuff and seeing what she'd go for. She liked starches—pasta with only butter, not sauce, and bread, and crackers—and anything with cheese. After he figured that last out, he started melting Velveeta over whatever she wasn't getting enough of—broccoli or green beans or carrots. If he thought she'd eat it he'd have poured cheese over apples and peaches and bananas.

She liked oranges, clamoring for them every day—for breakfast, a snack after school, dessert. He'd worried she'd acidify her insides. And grapefruit, if he cut and sectioned it for her, and sprinkled the top with sugar. Anytime they went anywhere and saw citrus trees with fruit, she'd beg Flint to stop and pick some, even if it was someone's yard. And this was Florida—so they saw them all the damn time. Jessie was so hard to say no to. The thought slid a knife-edge toward the bubble of nostalgia rising in his chest.

"Contumacious means bullheaded. Obstinate. Stubborn," he elaborated, taking refuge in the precision of words. "Never wanted anyone to tell her what to do—had to do it her own way. From the time she was little. Tried teaching her to tie her shoes when she was what—five? Six? Kept brushing my fingers away. 'Let *me*.'"

She'd wanted those Velcro ones that you didn't have to tie—just pull them over and press them down. "No," he told her. "You have to learn."

By then he'd gotten a little bit better at telling her no when he thought it was important—even when she pushed out her lower lip and got that intractable look on her face, pulling her eyebrows down so hard it was all he could do not to laugh and cave in. But he knew when to hold his ground with Jessie—too easy for her to ride all over him if he wasn't careful, get her own way all the time and turn into a little brat. Not his girl.

They went and bought the shoes together, because he thought

he could compromise and let her pick a pair—with ties—that she wanted. But she wouldn't even look at any of them, plopping herself down on a bench with her arms crossed, steaming. So he picked a few pairs he thought she would like, and he made her try them on, her eyes studiously up to the ceiling the whole time, and he bought some that fit—purple, of course, with strips that reflected the light—and they went home and he knelt at her feet to teach her. She didn't even let him get through one demonstration.

"She pushed me away and kept trying . . ." he said, telling the ocean so he could forget Marcie was listening. "Looping the lace and poking her finger through it, and ending up with the laces falling free, untied, or tangled in a knot." He'd sat and watched, not offering to help again. Jessie could ask.

She didn't. She rarely did. Her stubbornness she'd inherited from him.

She'd finally gotten frustrated and he could tell how hard she was trying not to cry. He gave his little girl some privacy, said he was going to make lunch. Watched her struggle on the sofa from the kitchen as she kept working the laces without success.

When he called her to the table they still weren't tied. But she wore them into the kitchen anyway, the laces trailing behind her feet, her face tearstained, and sat and ate her lunch without a word to him. Afterward, he cleared their plates, said, "How about a walk on the beach?" and made a point of picking a pair of sneakers to wear instead of his usual sandals. He stood and propped his feet up on his chair, one at a time, knowing she was watching as he slowly, carefully tied his own shoes.

And then she stood up and lifted one foot onto her own chair, painstakingly copying his movements, and finally got them tied. He didn't say a word, just put his hand on the back of her head and rubbed her silky hair as she preceded him out the back door.

Yeah. Stubborn kid.

"She got it," he bit out. "Eventually."

No, he couldn't do this. Isobel was wrong; it was too hard to face the memories—made no sense, like ripping open a bullet wound that had long since scarred over. He braced his palms on the cheap aluminum armrests, done with this conversation, this subject.

But before he could rise an inch Marcie was braced beside him, offering support if he wanted it. "She sounds . . . singular," she said. "Utterly unique."

He grunted as he gained his feet, a hand on her shoulder. "I know what singular means. And your definition's an oxymoron anyway."

"Don't call me an oxymoron."

He blew out an exasperated sigh. "It's not a . . ." But as soon as he straightened and met her gaze he knew she was teasing him.

"I'm going to check the nest," he said gruffly, tipping his chin toward the sand.

"I always do it before bed. I check on it morning and night."

He slid a glance to her, a couple of feet away now. "Okay. Good girl." Another thing he hadn't meant to say. "That's good, Marcie."

Marcie

~~~

Two days later the scent of bacon woke her up and lured her into the kitchen, where she was surprised to see Flint working at the stove, the coffeepot brewing.

"You're getting around like a champ," she said, retrieving silverware from the drawers and setting the kitchen table.

"That's right, I'm ready to go twenty rounds with Jack Dempsey," he carped, but Marcie was accustomed to the meager wavelengths of his emotional spectrum—he had two settings, hostile and prickly—and let it glance off her.

As they sat at the table and ate breakfast, he told her the storm would hit in the next couple of days. "Could use a hand boarding up later," he said.

"What about your back?"

He raised one eyebrow and arrowed a sidelong glance at her. "Why you think I need you?"

Huh. The stubborn old man finally managed to ask for help. She hid a smile and didn't mention that the skies had been blue

and cloudless for days. She'd grab lunch at Tequila Mockingbird, though, just in case, and ask Darla to tune in the Weather
Channel.

"Best warn anyone you give a damn about to get boarded up
too," Flint warned her when she came back out of her bedroom
after cleaning the kitchen.

Marcie gathered her latest collection of shells to work with
at Jeff's on her way out the door and wisely left out her intention
of verifying his forecast.

When she let herself out of the studio at one thirty—Jeff
wasn't there this morning but he'd taken to leaving a key for
her—it was like wading into a sponge, the air so moist and
warm and heavy it felt like someone else's exhaled breath.

When Marcie came through the sliding back door, Darla
was kicked back behind the bar with her feet up on a beer
cooler, the regulars perched on their stools and engaged in one
of their usual pastimes: trying to stump the bartender on punch
lines of dirty jokes.

"Did you know they just discovered a new use for sheep in
New Zealand?" Petey asked slyly.

Darla rolled her eyes. "Wool. Next."

"What did the elephant say to the naked man?" Arthur
asked.

"'How do you breathe through that thing?'" Darla was leaning back, enjoying herself.

Bink wagged his head in admiring frustration. "What do a
nearsighted gynecologist and a puppy—"

"A wet nose. Come on, guys. Challenge me."

"Anyone stump her at all yet?" Marcie asked, settling onto
"her" stool.

Arthur's face turned a shade darker when he realized she'd come in; the other two men nodded a greeting, unconcerned.

Darla hollered out, "Whatcha got for me, Marce?"

She mentally ran through her limited stockpile of jokes. "Okay. What do you call a drummer without a girlfriend?"

Everyone at the bar shouted in a chorus, "Homeless!" Petey guffawed while Bink slapped the bar top, and Darla let out a long-suffering groan. "Ya gotta at least *try*, Marce!" she said.

"Best I got."

At her request Darla tuned the television to the Weather Channel, sure enough showing a swirling hurricane forming out over the water far southeast of the Florida peninsula.

"Well, I'll be damned," Marcie said.

"We all will, I'm betting, but at least the company will be good," Darla said, winking at Marcie over her beer.

"What is it, Marcie?" Art asked, his forehead wrinkled with concern.

She nodded at the TV. "The man I'm staying with, Flint—Herman," she corrected, although the name never sat right on her tongue. "He was telling me a storm was coming but I didn't believe him."

"Not comin' here," Petey said confidently. He motioned toward the screen. "Look at the projections."

Radar was showing a broad swirl of white almost filling the space between Cuba and the Bahamas, but as she watched, the screen flashed to a rendering of the meteorologists' predictions for the storm's path: paralleling the west coast of Florida well out into the gulf until it began a slow but sure angle toward land near the top of the panhandle—far north of them.

Bink whistled. "That's gonna be a big bastard," he said conversationally.

"I say Panama City," Petey shouted, like a game-show contestant.

"Nope—Pensacola," Bink countered. "I'll lay a dollar on it."

Darla made a scoffing noise. "Ooh, a whole buck. Have some stones, gentlemen. Fifty says it hits Mobile. Alabama's due."

"So this thing could hit anywhere along the panhandle?" Marcie asked, her chin propped in her hands on the bar, watching the report.

Art shrugged. "That's what they're predicting, but they can't really tell. Maybe Tallahassee. Maybe as far over as New Orleans."

"Ah, New Orleans," Darla said, making an approximation of the sign of the cross over her chest and then downing half her beer.

"But maybe here?" Marcie asked, faint alarm fluttering her pulse.

Bink shook his head and pointed to the snaking graphic on the screen. "Uh-uh. We're outta the cone of despair."

"Cone of uncertainty," Art corrected him.

He shrugged. "You call it whatcha want."

"Gulf Shores," Petey honked out as the screen changed to live coverage. "It'll hit 'Bama. The Cantore Factor."

There were murmurs of assent from the regulars, a general nodding of heads.

Marcie leaned back in her stool. "Okay. I'll bite."

"The Cantore Factor," Petey said, craning forward and raising a finger like a lecturing professor. "The theory that holds that when Jim Cantore from the Weather Channel shows up in your town, it's time to bend over as far as you can and kiss your ass good-bye." He waved at the TV, where the weathercaster, wearing a formfitting white T-shirt and a plain black ball cap, was now standing on the sand in front of the gulf, whose waves seemed mockingly placid, just like the ones over Marcie's shoulder. The caption underneath him said, *Gulf Shores, Alabama.* "Presto. Alabama landfall."

"When he pops a windbreaker over that tighty-whitie, things are about to get down 'n' dirty," Darla threw in. "And not in the good way."

"This one ain't our storm," Petey asserted. "It's gonna suck to be Alabama this weekend, though."

"Sucks to be Alabama all the time," Bink quipped, and Petey snorted beer out of his nose.

"Marcella," Jeff greeted her when she got back to the studio, the back door closed this time against the heavy, hot air. He pronounced the name with a "ch" sound and an Italian lilt, and she laughed. "No? Not a good fit?" he said, his lips tilting up at one corner as he continued encasing one of his pieces in Bubble Wrap.

She tilted her head toward the open box on the linoleum floor of the back room. "That for the festival?"

He nodded without looking up, tucking the end of the wrap into the mouth of the vase. "Yep. I'm not headed out for another week but I need to make some room on the shelves."

"You might want to leave a little early. Looks like a hurricane is coming this way."

Jeff gave a lazy shrug. "Projections say it's headed north."

She nodded. "I just saw the report. But Flint, my . . . well, the friend I'm staying with"—"friend" felt ludicrous applied to Flint, but she had no idea how else to describe him—"he's lived here most of his life and seems to think he can smell it coming."

Jeff laughed. "Jesus. Beach folk."

She felt guilty for holding Flint up to ridicule. "Well, anyway, we're boarding up his house this afternoon and I thought you might want to too. Just in case. You don't want to take chances with your art."

Jeff picked another vase off the table—this one swirled in peacock colors—and started rolling it in another sheet of Bubble Wrap. "Tell me about *your* art, Marcellina. Have you been exploring your creativity?"

It was a perfectly innocent question, and yet something about it, the way his tone scraped a raw chord in her, made her shiver. "I have, actually," she said. "I finished a new piece yesterday." She'd shaped a mermaid under the sea using chips of sea glass and different shapes and colors of the shells the regulars had identified for her, along with the crushed mineral fragments of Jeff's failed pottery experiments—almost embarrassingly kitschy, but she'd loved working on it, and it made her smile. That old sizzle of electricity that came from the urge to create something, the itch to sort through items that fascinated her, waiting for that ping of recognition that told her, *This one . . . here . . .* had been growing stronger since she'd actually started doing it: the smell of the adhesive, the give as she pressed a fragment of something into it and then the satisfying firm stop as it settled into just the right place. "Nothing 'high art,' but . . . I like it."

"Don't judge. Just do. I'd like to see it."

Something about his tone, the way he looked at her, made her face heat despite his innocuous words. "I'm married," she blurted.

The words leaped out of her as if of their own accord. It had been years since Marcie had needed to use them—it used to be that some of the hotel guests needed a reminder even though she wore a ring, but apparently middle-aged women weren't so much a hot ticket for an out-of-town dalliance.

But Jeff didn't seem fazed by her assertion. "I know. You have a very light tan line where your ring belongs."

She looked down at her left hand, rubbed the spot where her ring had sat for most of her life, noticing he was right. It was faint, but as permanent as a scar.

"Oh," she said softly.

"Did you lose it?"

"No, I . . ." It hadn't been a conscious action to stop wearing it; every night she took the ring off, and always had. One morning on the way to Tequila Mockingbird she just didn't put it back on and hadn't since. Considering the state of things now, she wasn't sure she should be wearing it.

She couldn't live like this forever—she knew that. This was vacation mind-set, not real life. But just the thought of driving back up the highway, going in to work to handle manufactured crises over minutiae, settling back into her routine . . . all of it clenched a fist around her spine. And going home, into the dead-end silences that had grown between her and Will . . . she couldn't even contemplate that.

Everyone said marriage was hard, but Marcie had never really understood it before. Being with Will had been so easy and seamless from the first that they'd been lulled into a false sense of security. When they did start to struggle, she figured this was what it meant—finding your way through challenges and difficulties without forgetting you were on the same team.

But now she wondered whether they'd ever really known each other at all once they'd grown past the adolescents they'd been at the beginning—from the moment childhood had stopped when they found themselves pregnant and suddenly both of them had to grow up fast.

The naiveté of youth made you fearless—open and brave, immortal and unassailable. Finding a like soul who reflected back to you your deepest, most genuine self—saw it and accepted it, and met it with his own openness and vulnerability—was like a drug, especially if you'd lived a lifetime before that feeling invisible, unknown.

But that raised the stakes too, didn't it? Once you'd finally found that validation, losing it was unthinkable. And so little by little you grew cautious, guarded, careful of allowing the person you'd invested so deeply in to see too much of your secret soul. There was too much to lose.

And so you fell into habit, surface exchanges, because if you revealed too much now and were rejected by this person, the one who finally saw you, really knew you, then what did that say about your worth? And how could you survive it? Never knowing that communion was bearable; losing it once you had it was not. So little by little you began to draw behind your battlements, coasting in safe waters on a wave of inertia: a placid string of *How was your day?* and household budgets and daily logistics.

If Marcie was honest now about her relationship—and why be anything else at this point?—she had to admit that it had never been the same after losing that very first pregnancy. The most open and connected she and Will had ever been was when they were teenagers who knew nothing of the vagaries the world would throw at them. Nothing of the gradual everyday erosion life wreaked on the invisible bond that had once connected your naked, most intimate selves.

She'd been so afraid of losing him that instead she'd lost herself.

That was why going back felt unthinkable at the moment—and yet she wasn't ready to move forward either.

"I'm just figuring some things out," Marcie said finally, knowing the explanation was no explanation at all.

"That's why most of us end up at the beach. To figure everything out."

She'd expected him to dig deeper, and she couldn't decide if she liked it that he hadn't, or if it bothered her. "Is that why you ended up here?"

"At first. Sure. Now I just like it."

It wasn't just Flint, Marcie realized—no one talked about their pasts here. Well, no one except Darla. Everyone else she'd met operated as if they'd sprung up fully formed just as they were now—no histories, no ghosts. Except the ghosts were there—you could tell it in the eyes.

"What did you come to figure out?" She needed to shift the focus away from herself.

Jeff shrugged. "What I wanted to be when I grew up."

"And?"

He pushed up to his feet and moved to the dorm refrigerator, pulling out two bottles of Redhook and popping off the tops. Marcie took the one he handed her, grateful for the sharp coldness against her palm.

"I decided to question the premise instead. Growing up didn't really sound all that terrific if it meant what I saw from most of the people I knew. Spending a third or more of their lives doing something they hated. The rest of the time trying to be what everyone in their life needed from them. Forgetting who they were and what they used to dream of, before they forgot how."

Marcie took a long sip of the bitter IPA. Was that what her life was? She didn't hate her job, but it wasn't any kind of passion. It was secure, paid well, offered her room for advancement. It was a good, solid choice of career, and she enjoyed it. But she counted the hours every week until her off days. Didn't everyone?

"Isn't that the nature of the beast, when you work for a living?" she asked him.

He indicated the shop with a tilt of his bottle. "Is it? Look around you. This is what I do, and it's what I love. Anyone who tells you life's about compromise is saying that because that's what they've done, and they desperately need you to agree with them so they don't have to look at what a waste their lives have turned into."

"That's kind of harsh."

He lifted one shoulder, softening his edict with a wink. "Life's harsh."

She didn't know what to say to that, so she took another long pull of the beer. She wouldn't have agreed with him six months ago. Life hadn't always been a cakewalk, but more often than not it had been pretty smooth. Happily married, a beautiful house, a steady job, and everything they could want. A life filled with contentment and security and stability. A life where their hardest decisions had been how to budget so they could renovate the bathroom.

Everything had changed from the moment the pregnancy had come into existence. As though the future addition of a third soul upset their balance of two. Marcie wished she could step back in time and undo all of it, any of it. That she'd never left . . . that she hadn't miscarried . . . that Will had been happy when she told him about it, instead of miserable . . . that she'd never conceived in the first place. If she could alter one element of the equation, everything would still be okay. She'd still have her husband; they'd still be happy. She wouldn't be standing on the clay-speckled floor of a run-down building in a strange beach town, miles from everything she'd ever known, and living her life without Will.

The blood seemed to recede from her veins at the thought and she nearly dropped the moisture-slick bottle. What if this wasn't just temporary, and she wasn't just taking time to gather herself back together before she went home again and picked up their life where she had abruptly cut it off? What if sometimes there was no way back?

Jeff simply looked at her, waiting, as if he could sense the riot of thoughts teeming in her head.

"Life has its challenges sometimes," she said aloud. "Rough spots. But they don't last forever."

"Nothing does," he said.

Marcie studied his face to see what he'd meant by that, but apparently he'd already moved on from the conversation; retrieving a towel hanging from the edge of the utility sink over the fridge, he ran it under the faucet.

She turned away to collect her thoughts, looking at the shelves that had been so jam-packed until today, now just a few isolated pieces scattered here and there. Her eye caught on one tiny little sculpture: a turtle, small enough to fit into a palm and glazed a soft olive color, its shell shimmering with some kind of gold flakes. It was smoother than the other pieces, like glass, and somehow lighter, less solid than she would have expected when she picked it up.

"I was messing around with some new techniques on that one," he said, and she realized he'd been watching her.

The detail on the tiny sculpture was impressive, a pattern imprinted on the turtle's shell, even its expression delineated, conveying a calm, watchful gaze. She rubbed her thumb over the shell, liking the way the little piece felt in her hand. "It's beautiful," she said softly, thinking of the mother turtle from the other night, the odd nobility to the animal's awkward movements as she painstakingly covered her eggs, throwing sand over the nest with her ungainly flippers before pulling her heavy body back to the water, steady and strong, not stopping to rest.

"Hey, keep that," he said, watching as she continued to run her fingers over the turtle's curves.

"No. I mean, I don't want to take a piece you can sell at the festival."

He laughed. "I'm not taking that one. It was a throwaway."

When she still hesitated, he stepped close and put his hand over hers, turning them both over so that their palms faced upward, the turtle resting inside her palm, which rested inside his like a nest. He curled her fingers around the turtle, the heat from his skin seeming to radiate into hers and warming the little turtle nestled in their joined hands. Her heart thumped uncomfortably behind her ribs.

"Art is only art if it touches someone—that's what breathes life into it. You picked this piece up for a reason, Marcella." His warm breath stirred the hair at her ear with the soft "ch" sound, and she shivered. "Really it's just a piece of clay, something I manipulated to look like something else. But art takes on its full expression when it has meaning to someone else. Now it does. So you keep it. Okay?"

Marcie closed her fingers around the turtle and moved it into her pocket, away from the enveloping warmth of his hand. "Okay," she echoed, her voice low, as if they were discussing something intimate.

He stepped back to the sink and turned the faucet back on. "Okay, cool—then it won't go to waste," he said offhandedly, and Marcie suddenly felt foolish. Foolish and old.

"All right, I'm going to head out for the day," she said. "See you tomorrow?"

He nodded. "There's a get-together tomorrow night down off Little Neck Pass—bunch of local artists and artisans," he said, wringing out the towel. "You wanna go? Firepit, music, a cookout. Around ten."

"Ten *p.m.*?" she said, and he laughed at her incredulity.

"You should come—you'd like it."

Goose bumps lifted on her arms, an odd intimacy shivering through her despite his ordinary words. A firepit by the water, music, a group of people who knew nothing about her, with whom she could be whoever she wanted to be. Not Marcie, a middle-aged hotel event planner and wife for most of her life— but Marcella, a bold, unconstrained artist, like them. One of the pieces of driftwood that washed up on the beach and made a new identity for themselves.

She rubbed her thumb over the line of white that encircled her left ring finger. "That's a little late for me. Thanks, though."

Jeff stepped past her toward the kiln, and began wiping out the inside. "Offer stands if you change your mind."

"I won't. But thank you. And be careful in case the storm does come this way."

Jeff shot her another smile—friendly, no more, and again she felt foolish for her assumptions about him, for her middle-aged cautious warning. "Okay, Martina. We'll be there if you decide to walk on the wild side. I'll keep an eye out for you."

As she left him cleaning out his kiln, Marcie realized she didn't know what Jeff meant—that he'd watch for her to show up, even though she said she wasn't going to, or that he'd watch out for her if she did?

It didn't matter, of course. She wasn't going.

Flint

~~~

Flint had been looking at the house next door for the last half hour, eyeballing his neighbor from his bedroom window like some kind of pathetic Gladys Kravitz, watching her struggle with the slabs of plywood she was dragging out of her garage. Forty-five years the woman had lived on the beach, and she still didn't have proper hurricane shutters. Hard to feel sorry for someone who was determined to be so damn ignorant.

At least she was smart enough to know to put something up, though—that weather was headed their way.

Some of the slabs of plywood Isobel was wrangling with were bigger than she was, warped from leaning up on their edges in the moist heat. She wasn't giving up, though. He watched her pull one by an end, the heavy board jumping crazily behind her on the uneven blacktop of her driveway. She let go suddenly and sent the board flat to the ground, shaking her hand—a splinter. He'd told her years ago to get storm shutters so she didn't have to mess with these old sheets of plywood, but

Berto had cut these for her, and the silly woman had developed some kind of attachment to them. To plain wooden boards.

She went back into the garage, came out a moment later wearing gardening gloves—gardening gloves! Didn't she even own a proper set of work gloves? Picked up an edge and got the board upright again, this time spanning her arms across its length and walking it awkwardly, slowly, around the side of the house and to the patio window. She leaned it up against the house and stared at it.

That's right. It's not a one-person job, is it?

Every time a storm brewed up out in the gulf, handmade signs would appear up and down Marea—ads for people who'd put up your shutters or board you up. Good for the snowbirds, who left their vacation houses unattended most of the summer. Good for the old folks too, the holdouts in the little houses like his who'd literally have to die before they'd let their high-dollar property be snapped up by some developer who wanted to raze it down and put up some generic hotel or beach bar. They got so they couldn't do for themselves, but they stayed living on their own out of sheer stubbornness.

Flint wasn't like them. Not yet. He got on just fine on his own. His back was feeling better—he had to admit that having Marcie around to help out let him heal up faster. He was up on his feet today, almost pain-free. He needed to put up his own storm shutters. It was more than he ought to be doing yet, but nothing for it. Storm was coming on its own schedule, not his. He'd wait for Marcie to come home from wherever she'd gone—an extra set of hands to fasten them in place would be nice.

Isobel had apparently *not* hired one of the opportunists who advertised along the avenue. She'd managed to get all the plywood out and propped up against the windows where each one belonged, and now Flint could almost watch her trying to figure out how she was going to hoist the heavy boards into place and then hold 'em there while she drilled more holes into her house.

Holes. *Jesus.*

Back when Berto was around, he would come out and board up for his mom—well, he and Flint, and Jessie self-importantly handing them screws as fast as they could ask for them. Berto was a good kid, hard worker, looked after his mom, especially after his dad died.

Kid got hit by a motorcycle while walking down Marea Boulevard with some friends one night, though. Skull hit the concrete—"God, my head hurts so bad!" he told his mom with a weak laugh when he woke up in the hospital. Flint could see the relief all over her when the boy woke up and talked to her—she gripped his hand and laughed with him even though tears were spilling down her face. Flint drove her back home after the visit—doctors said Berto needed rest. The boy's brain swelled up in the night, and he never made it to morning. Only nineteen.

He opened the prescription bottle on his nightstand. He'd been tapering off the last couple days, but he popped one of the pills now. He'd like one more, just to be safe, but he couldn't afford to get logy.

The stupid back girdle he wrapped around his torso didn't do jack for support, but it was better than nothing. He fastened it firmly in place over his shirt, then grabbed his work gloves off the toolbox in the closet and headed out the back door.

"The hell are you doing, Isobel?"

She was arched over in a position Flint was pretty sure she was about thirty years too old to manage, one hand pressing the plywood in place hard enough that he could see it trembling from the effort, the veins on the back standing out, the other twisted across her own body somehow with an eighteen-volt drill in it. She was trying to get a screw into a hole in one corner of the board on her back porch, but at the angle her contortions had her in, he could have told her it was never going to happen.

"Herman?" She craned her neck slightly, as if to confirm a sighting, and as she did her grip slackened and the board slipped out of position against the window. Flint leaped forward, the sudden movement twinging his back. He lifted the board back where it went, pushing her aside with his body.

"Christ's sake, woman. That's a good way to knock yourself unconscious—or worse."

Isobel straightened her screw and drilled it through the wood and into the stucco of her house, immediately loading another one from the pouch around her waist. "The boards have to get up one way or another, Herman. Storm's coming this way."

He grunted as the drill whined and the wood drew flush into the window frame. They were cut perfectly to size, at least. "You and I are the only ones who know it." Flint could smell it. People laughed when he said that, back when he bothered to tell them, but it was true. Live alongside the ocean all your life and you became in tune with its rhythms, almost a part of it. The way cats could sense when an earthquake was coming, and dogs hid under a bed long before their humans heard thunder, Flint could feel the subtle changes in the gulf breeze, sense the difference in color in the skies, even feel the weight of the air when it grew pregnant with a coming storm.

He didn't mind them. Nature's scrub brush, far as he was concerned. He still remembered Donna, more than sixty years ago, back when there was hardly anything worth knocking down on the beach, but she did just the same. Did the island a favor—cleaned up all the run-down, neglected beach shacks, ran off the weak. Beachside living wasn't for the fearful. Maybe this would be another big one—Palmetto Key was getting pretty skanky, and he didn't just mean the buildings. But these days all the land developers would probably come in after, put up high-rises, ruin anything beautiful so all the Midwestern snow-birds could have their piece of paradise for the winter, identical condos with their pastel colors and cheap wicker furniture.

Damned shame the storms weren't more selective, though. Be nice if they washed out the trash and left the good stuff in-tact: the beaches, the trees and grasses that held the sand where it needed to be.

The turtles. He'd nearly forgotten—another thing he needed to prep for the storm.

Flint took the drill from Isobel's hands. "Brace it. I'll screw 'em in."

She took his place, pressing liver-spotted hands to the board just firmly enough to keep it from slipping, while Flint reached into her pouch for the screws and quickly secured the other side. If he remembered right, there were about thirteen more windows to go. Isobel followed him to the next one—the sliding glass doors from the patio to her tiny living room. She had somehow managed to wrestle the seven-foot-tall slab of ply-wood up the steep back steps and next to the door, and Flint slid it into place, careful not to strain his back.

"Hand me the drill," he told her, nodding to where he'd set it down on the railing.

"You don't have to do this, Herman." She handed it to him, along with a palmful of concrete screws.

"Who else you got, Isobel?" He ground the words out around the two screws he placed in his mouth. "Wore me out worse watching you about to kill yourself than to just get out here and do it for you." She said something low that he couldn't hear over the yowling of the drill, and he didn't ask her to repeat it.

They worked smoothly and methodically, one window to the next: Flint lifted each board into place, and Isobel would wordlessly move in and brace her body against it, holding it steady while he drilled it in.

She waited until they were on their sixth window before she asked the question he'd bet his entire library she'd been sitting on since he'd walked over to her house.

"Where's your 'niece,' Herman?" He could hear the quotation marks she put around the word.

"Out."

"I see."

She did *not* see. Damn busybody was probably sitting there concocting all sorts of seedy scenarios. Well, let her. He didn't give a damn what she or anybody else made of the way he ran his life.

The drill jumped in his hand at the same time it let out a series of piercing cracks. Goddammit. He'd stripped the screw. He yanked another one from Isobel's outstretched hand and jammed it into the wood just above the ruined one. It went in so far the head sank into the wood and the board groaned its impending split. He reversed the motor, backed the screw out slightly, reached over for another one, and drilled it into the same corner, just in case.

"It's not what you're thinking," he bit out.

"You don't have any idea what I'm thinking."

He snorted. "I never have to wonder for long, Isobel. It's not like you ever kept your opinions to yourself."

She let out a small laugh. "Is that really an accusation you should be making, Herman?"

He drilled the last screw into place and slapped his palm, hard, against the wood. He felt meanly gratified when Isobel jumped at the sharp noise, and he walked away from her and around the side of the house. He had the next board in place by the time she came around behind him and leaned her weight against it.

"I'll be happy to help you with your shutters when we're finished," she said.

"Don't need it."

"Your *niece* will help?"

The drill buzzed. "She's not my niece, Isobel, and you know it perfectly well."

"Of course I do. Thank you for not insulting my intelligence anymore."

He put three more screws in, moved on to the next window, bracing for her to press him further. *Who is she? What's she doing here? What's an old man like you doing with that girl?* Isobel never could leave anything alone. That was what finally did them in, after Jessie was gone. Flint just wanted to forget, to leave it alone—what happened, happened, and dwelling on it wasn't going to change a thing. But Isobel wouldn't let it go, hounding him till he finally screamed at her to get the hell out of his house and stay out. That time, she did listen.

But to his surprise she kept quiet now, handing him screws as he needed them, following him, obeying his occasional instructions without argument. His back was starting to throb, the pain still deep down inside, as if it were waiting to well up and spill over, but for now he could still get by. It got harder every time he bent to lift a board, though, and on the next window he was surprised when the plywood came up much easier—and he saw that Isobel had picked up the other corner.

"Easier with two," was all she said. He didn't argue. He'd only pay the price tomorrow if he was stubborn today.

They finished the rest of the windows in silence, working almost as smoothly as he and Berto used to when they did it together. He remembered what he'd said to her—*Who else you got, Isobel?*—and he could have kicked himself.

When they had the last board in place, he turned the drill around and held it out, grip facing Isobel. "Make sure you charge the battery back up. After the storm passes I'll come help you take it all down."

"That's very nice of you." She took the drill. "Why don't we go get yours up so you can relax and rest your back?"

"I'm fine. Just need a quick rest."

"All right, then. Let's go sit down and I'll bring out some limeade."

"That's okay."

"You'll like this batch," she said as though he hadn't spoken. "Came out extra tart, just how you like it."

"Isobel. Don't worry about it." His tone was sharper than he'd intended.

She turned around to face him, hands on her hips, eyebrows drawn into a scowl. "Dammit, you old bastard, I'm trying to say thank you. Why won't you ever just let anyone do something *nice* for you?"

He glared right back at her. "Well, then, *fine*. Bring out the damn limeade."

And then she started to laugh, a loud, guffawing, irresistible sound he remembered as clearly as if it hadn't been nearly two decades since he'd last heard it. "Oh, Herman," she got out, wiping her eyes, her face slightly flushed, and Flint was reminded that before she'd gotten old and wrinkled like him she'd been a good-looking woman. "God, you *are* a coot."

"You oughta know, you shrew," he muttered, following her around to the back of the house.

They sat inside, because the heat was unbroken by any breeze off the water. "And we might as well enjoy the A/C as long as the electricity holds," Isobel said. The living room was dim, heavy blue thermal curtains pulled against the relentless heat of a midday sun flashing off the water.

She had changed a few things, but not much. Same pastel floral sofa in a style Flint always called Condo Crappy, sprung now into a permanent depression in the center of the right-hand cushion, where Isobel always settled herself against the arm. Same rattan coffee table, sharp edges blunted decades ago by numerous collisions with Berto's toy trucks, but its glass top scrupulously clean, as everything always was in Isobel's house, no matter when Flint and Jessie were there.

That was one of the reasons she wouldn't move in with them when he'd asked. When Berto was alive they never discussed it—neither house had enough room for all of them. But once the boy was gone and Isobel spent so long in a dark place he and Jessie worried she'd never come out of, they'd invited her to just come live next door with them. "I wouldn't last a day in your house," Isobel told them, kissing Jessie on the head where they all lounged on the sofa watching some movie he'd long forgotten, chosen just to distract her. "Either you both would kill me for tidying up all your things, or I'd have to kill the two of you for not letting me." She'd waved around the living room where they all usually ended up every day. "This has been good enough for all of us for years, living next door. No need to fix what isn't broken."

Turned out to be a good thing, too, didn't it. Or maybe things would have turned out differently? No way to know. No point thinking about that.

The built-in dark wood bookshelves lining the walls on either side of a tiny television contained a few books, but mostly knickknacks and pictures—photos that hadn't been changed since the last time Flint had sat here in the frayed blue armchair that used to be Isobel's husband's. Isobel and Robert and a baby Berto in one of those god-awful Olan Mills jobbies, stiff and frozen against the ridiculous painted background of an improbable forest. Robert in uniform, black-and-white, head proudly lifted in a patriotic stare off camera. Berto's school pictures in a sectioned frame that showed him in progression from first grade to twelfth: gappy smile and tousle of curly sandy hair; acne and his father's unfortunate buckteeth; braces and a stupid-looking Mohawk; and last his graduation picture, where he'd finally been growing into his looks. Handsome kid—buzz cut, straight white teeth, clear brown eyes that looked a lot like Isobel's. Had a nice smile.

He was what, seventeen in that picture, eighteen? Berto'd been just about the age he was in this photo when Jessie had started becoming aware of boys as something besides playmates who'd horse around as hard as she did. Funny seeing her start to develop a crush on him, and then not so funny when he'd started dating girls his own age and Flint had watched his daughter go through her first heartbreak.

They'd let her be one of the pallbearers at his funeral. Skinny, coltish little girl amid five big, rugged men. Flint had taken the handle next to her, proud of the way Jessie kept her shoulders up, her chin level, and held on to her tears till his coffin was winched down into the hole. Even then she'd kept her head high, staring straight ahead with the tears rolling down like she didn't know they were there. Like grief had filled her up so completely it had to leak out of her.

Jessie had been attached to Isobel like a remora for weeks after Berto died, always at her side, touching her—a hand tucked into Isobel's palm, a shoulder pressed to her hip as they cooked dinner together, falling asleep with her head on her lap while they all watched the little television in this same living room, silent.

Isobel came back from the kitchen with a bamboo tray with two glasses and a pitcher, a canister of ice and a set of tongs, and a plate of some kind of cookie or cracker. "I made cheese straws last night. Couldn't sleep. Help yourself." She set the tray down on the worn blue velour ottoman in front of Robert's chair.

"Shouldn't have gone to any trouble, Isobel." He took one of the little crackers while she placed ice into the glasses with the tongs and poured their drinks.

"I'd already made them, Herman. I lifted the plate off the counter and set it on the tray. It wasn't a great deal of trouble." Her tone was dry. The cheese straws weren't—buttery and sharp and crumbly. Isobel always could cook.

He shifted, his legs bent awkwardly between the armchair and the ottoman. This chair was once as comfortable to him as his own, but over the years he'd forgotten how to relax in it. Forgotten how to be someone's guest, for that matter. "Thanks for the . . ." he blurted, holding up his sweating glass of limeade. The belated words fell like a sandbag between them.

But Isobel didn't seem to notice. "You're welcome. Take some cheese straws home with you later. I'll be cooking up everything I can find lying around today—be nice to have some good food on hand if we lose power."

He grunted. "Remember last time? The god-awful flies?"

She laughed, the sound setting the stillness of the room ringing. "Lord. It was like a charnel house around here, with the swarms."

He and Isobel and the kids had huddled inside her hall bathroom—tiny for all of them, especially when Jessie had insisted they bring in the stray cat she'd been leaving out food for. The creature had yowled and screeched, its raised fur blowing it up to double size as it hunched in a corner under the sink, Flint sure the wild thing was going to go feral and launch itself at the kids' heads. They'd waited in there together once the sky turned yellow-gray and the winds grew strong enough to topple palms on the beach from their shallow roots, listening to the groans of the wind that sounded like ghouls. He and Isobel made Jessie and Berto get in the bathtub, and they stood beside it, ready to leap on top of them if they heard the roof start to go.

Afterward, they walked outside in a daze, skirting the branches and wires and unidentifiable wood and metal pieces of buildings that littered the yard and the beach and the road. The low concrete-block houses dotting the shore still stood, as did the ones built up on stilts. Others were gone, or sported missing chunks like gaping wounds. It had been August, with record heat, fat flies descending like a plague of locusts in the wake of the destruction to feast on the garbage strewn up and down the island. All the locals helping to clean up learned to come out with long pants and sleeves, closed shoes, netting tied over their heads, overheating preferable to being set upon by the filthy insects.

But that was long enough ago that the population had turned over, and in the storm-free decades since, the newbies had grown sanguine and complacent. "Hurricanes skip over Palmetto Key. It's the way it's positioned on the peninsula." He'd heard idiot know-it-alls offer some variation of that theory for decades. Bullshit. It was sheer luck of the draw.

They weren't going to get lucky this time. He and Isobel both knew it. Funny, though, that neither of them was talking about evacuating. She was a tough old stick; he had to give her that.

"You got water?"

She waved her glass toward the kitchen. "Five gallons clean, bathtub's full."

He shook his head. "That's not enough."

Isobel smiled wearily at him, and for the first time he could remember she looked worn out. "It's enough for me. As you said, Herman, who else have I got to worry about?"

He averted his gaze out over the gulf, but the curtains blocked it from his sight. "I got ten five-gallon containers. I'll bring a few over." His rough tone made it sound more like a threat than an offer.

Flint

~~~~~

Marcie found him in the little storage closet at the front of the carport, wrestling out the accordioned metal hurricane shutters. "I thought you were going to wait for me?"

"My back's fine. I'm not some helpless old man you have to keep babying."

He could see her fidgeting out of the corner of his eye, the way Jessie used to when she was about to explode from keeping something in—she never could.

Well. Except once.

"What is it?" he said irritably. "Spit it out."

"Nothing. I just don't want you to injure your back again. I mean . . . you're not *not* old."

Flint gave a loud *hmmmph*—just like an old man—and lifted out another shutter, and then Marcie was beside him. She wordlessly took the other side, and when he ignored her she bumped his shoulder with hers.

"Come on. Let's do this."

The panels were unwieldy but light, and years ago he'd in-stalled brackets around each window and doorjamb, so putting them up was straightforward. He fitted them into place—after the two of them lifted them together—and then drilled them into the brackets. It was quick work, but hot; the temperature had to be close to a hundred, and the air was thick and still. He'd have welcomed even the hot breeze that usually blew in off the gulf against his sweaty skin, but he'd rather have died of thirst than have Isobel show up carrying a tray of icy limeade. Yet there she stood.

"You both look like you could use something cold." She set the tray on the avocado tree stump in the side yard.

"Just leave it there," Flint said around a screw in his mouth, otherwise ignoring the interfering old biddy—he should have known better than to open that door one inch—but when Mar-cie's eyebrows soared up he appended a muttered, "Thanks."

He took his damn time drilling in the panel, then reached for another one, hoping Isobel would take the hint and go. But of course polite, proper Marcie walked straight over to her.

"This looks wonderful," she said. "How thoughtful."

"Limeade. Always one of Herman's favorites. Get over here and hydrate, Herman, before you shrivel the rest of the way up."

Marcie snorted in the middle of a long drink, spilling her limeade. "Thank you," she murmured, clearly amused.

He continued to ignore her, but that had never been an ef-fective strategy with Isobel; she materialized at his elbow, hold-ing a glass. "Drink, you stubborn old coot," she said quietly, one gentle hand on his arm.

The drink was delicious, as always—tart and tangy and sweet, and so cold it hurt his head. Isobel nodded and refilled his glass from the pitcher. "I had a feeling," she said.

"No need to be smug, woman."

"Thanks again for your help this afternoon." She smiled sweetly, but he knew damn well she was enjoying watching him squirm in front of the girl.

"Yep."

"And thank you for the extra water. Unnecessary, but appreciated."

"All right, Isobel. It was a few gallons of water. It's not like I cured cancer." He caught Marcie's eye and scowled.

"Don't worry—I'm not that impressed with you," Isobel said matter-of-factly. "But thank you just the same."

Marcie was literally biting her lips against a flat-out grin.

All Flint could do was glare, but it seemed to have no effect on either one of them. Women. This was what happened when they joined forces. He pushed his empty glass back into Isobel's hand, then stalked off around the corner of the house to finish his work away from the damn hen party.

Marcie followed him toward the storage closet in his carport to put their tools away when they'd finished the job—she'd come trotting around the corner just a few moments behind him, grinning like an idiot, but to her credit she'd kept her trap shut and let them work in peace. All he wanted after the hot, sweaty work was a cool shower and a fistful of his back pills—it was screaming again from all the exertion. But there was still one last task.

"We need to dig up the nest."

"Dig it up? I thought we were protecting it?"

"We are—from the storm. Hurricane's just as likely to tear up the nests as the buildings. Storm surge will finish them off."

"I saw the system forming on the Weather Channel at the restaurant," she said. "They said it's headed north, though."

Flint shook his head. "I don't think so. We need to move the nest."

"Move it how?" she asked, as if the notion were ridiculous. "Where?"

"I'll show you."

But she didn't budge. "It's okay, Flint—Herman. It's not going to hit us. They showed its whole trajectory—weathercasters can track and predict hurricanes now. If you had a TV—"

He sighed and walked back toward her to relieve her of the drill and the box of concrete screws. "I know about meteorological equipment. I'm not an idiot," he said with admirable restraint. "But I've lived here almost all of my life. I know this sea, and I know the weather. If the island floods it'll wash all the nests away. We gotta move ours."

Indecision still clouded her features. "We can move it if you want . . . but what about all the others?" She waved as if indicating all of Palmetto Key.

Losing all those nests bugged him every time a hurricane blew through, but there wasn't anything they could do about that. "We can't worry about those. It might just be pissing into the ocean, but at least we can take care of our own nest."

He couldn't tell if she believed him or was just humoring him, but finally she nodded.

"Okay. Show me what to do."

He pulled out an old Igloo cooler from the hall closet, Marcie tracking his steps. They went back out to the nest and Flint lowered himself gingerly to the sand, carefully scooping off the top but immediately straightening again, hissing out a sharp breath as the pain in his back flared.

"Here, let me." Marcie knelt beside him.

She had to use her hands, Flint told her—and only the sides, not her fingers, so as not to risk tearing the leathery but delicate eggs with her nails as she dug. He let her scoop out the nest as he supervised, making a mound beside the hole she revealed until finally she gasped, and he knew she'd felt the soft give of the first layer of eggs. They were the size of Ping-Pong balls, and he could still feel the slightly spongy but firm texture of them on his fingertips from the first time he'd ever touched them, as a kid—he'd sworn he'd felt a tiny head pressing against the wall of one.

She set them gently in the bottom of the righted cooler, lined with a few inches of sand to cushion the fragile eggs. There were dozens of them the more she dug, and still more, until Flint counted out the final tally as she verified the nest was emptied—a hundred and twenty-three.

"And only one will make it . . ." she marveled, looking into the cooler where the eggs nestled. Her tone was so quiet he wasn't sure she was even talking to him.

"Maybe one. If they're lucky. If it isn't the birds, it's the fish. Mostly it's people—fishing nets and plastic bags and pollution. Chances are they won't even survive being moved."

Marcie brushed the sand off her hands and eased back to sit, as if her legs were cramped from kneeling at the edge of the nest for so long. "Then why are we doing this?"

"Storm's coming," he repeated. "They've got no chance at all once it hits."

She nodded and leaped to her feet with enviable ease, then turned to help him up, and Flint took her outstretched hand.

Marcie

Working in the relentless heat had left Marcie much too tired to cook dinner. "How would you feel about a really great grouper sandwich?" she asked Flint, and to her surprise he took her up on her offer to drive them to Tequila Mockingbird.

She hadn't counted on the turtles coming with them, but Flint was adamant. The house was too cool for the eggs, and he wouldn't leave them on the porch unattended, so now the Igloo sat underneath their table out on the deck.

Despite its being Friday night, the dinner rush was more of a slow trickle, as if no one wanted to wade through the heavy heat and humidity even to feed themselves. Even the regulars were missing from their usual perches, and there were only two other tables of customers—a tired-looking, sunburned family of four, and a boy and girl barely past puberty from the look of them, huddled together in a corner of the deck, awkwardly vaping. Her too-tiny bikini didn't quite contain the baby fat she hadn't shed yet; he wore oversize swim trunks and a T-shirt that swallowed his skinny limbs. A plate sat on the table between them, nothing on it except smears of ketchup and a crumpled napkin.

Darla came out from the sliding doors and plopped onto the bench next to Marcie. "We may have low standards, darlin', but it ain't BYOB."

"It's sea turtle eggs," Marcie explained. "We're making sure they're safe in case the storm hits."

"Well, I'll be buggered. Hey, this your granddad?" she said, eyeballing Flint, and Marcie had to hold back a laugh at his flummoxed expression.

"A friend," she said, and made introductions. Darla offered a round of beer on the house, but Marcie, mindful of Flint, demurred.

"She planning to get this place boarded up?" he asked when the owner pushed herself up and went back to her usual post behind the bar.

Marcie shrugged. "I don't know. Darla's pretty laid-back. I'm not sure she worries about much."

He grunted. "Beach people." He said it like the words were coated with slime, but Marcie laughed.

"Doesn't that also describe you?"

He opened his mouth as if to argue, but then just shrugged.

When their server showed up—Hannah, who didn't seem to recognize Marcie—she ordered their sandwiches, and a basket of the French fries Marcie couldn't resist; Darla knew her way around a deep fryer.

It was odd to see Flint in this setting, a strange collision of her Palmetto Key worlds. And except for their outing to the tow yard, she realized she'd barely seen him outside his house or the beach.

She wanted to ask about Isobel—about whatever had happened today to make his carapace slip. About who the woman was to him, or had been—though she suspected she was forming an idea—and what happened between them . . . their two dead children.

But the somnambulant rhythms of beach life seeped into her along with the tang of salt air and the plaintive cries of gulls, and Marcie let it lie. Let herself sink into the soothing shallows of the present moment. In a comfortable silence they laid into their sandwiches when they arrived—flaky and spicy and perfect—and watched the sun light up the rippled clouds as it sank into a placid sea.

She hadn't considered that Flint's unwillingness to let the turtle eggs out of his sight meant that they'd be living inside until Flint decreed that the danger of a storm surge had passed and they could re-dig the nest. Which wouldn't have been a problem, except that apparently they had to stay at their optimum temperature—82 to 88 degrees, Flint told her, with fluctuations determining the gender of the hatched eggs; higher temperatures yielded more females and lower ones more males. While that fact was scientifically fascinating, Marcie would have been infinitely happier to let them incubate elsewhere when she let herself out of her blissfully air-conditioned room the next morning and walked into a sauna.

"Dear God, Flint, how can you breathe?" she asked him when she made it into the kitchen and found him standing with his coffee at the open back door, looking out at the gulf. The cooler full of turtle eggs sat on the table behind him. "And how are you drinking hot coffee?"

She walked to the freezer and opened the door, standing in front of it.

"Better shut that. If the electricity goes the icebox won't hold up more than half a day or so."

"That's okay. We can put everything in the cooler. Oh, never mind," she said dryly. She grabbed a handful of ice cubes and dumped them in her mug before pouring the coffee over them. Lukewarm was at least bearable.

When she got back from the studio that afternoon, the house was completely shuttered—yesterday they'd left a few windows to let in some light and so that Marcie could use the A/C in her room, but Flint had buttoned it all up tight in her absence—and inside it was even hotter and stuffier than it had been this morning, unpleasantly dim with only a couple of lamps to illuminate the interior. After the bright sun outside it was like walking into a tomb till her eyes adjusted—and only a little better once they did.

Flint had apparently gone shopping, and the kitchen counter was littered with the detritus of his haul: several jars of peanut butter, loaves of bread, cans of soup and beans. Beside it was a collection of survival tools: a manual can opener, three flashlights and several value packs of batteries in varying sizes, matches and Sterno cans, a camp lantern, and an actual transistor radio. Stacked up along one wall were five-gallon containers of water, and beside them in a paper grocery bag, she found half a dozen cans of bug spray and an array of citronella candles.

"Did you rob a survivalist's bunker?" she asked when he came out into the kitchen.

"You got anything you care about keeping?" he asked without a greeting. "I'm making a pile in case we flood."

All that popped to mind was the stash of his daughter's letters in her dresser drawer, but it didn't feel right to mention them now. They'd sat there for too long when she should have said something, and it would create problems—she knew Flint well enough to know he wouldn't like her having anything so personal.

Besides, the weather reports showed the storm meandering along the Gulf Coast before making landfall well up along the panhandle in Alabama—Bink might win the kitty after all.

"And it's only a category two," Jeff told her before she'd left this afternoon, pointing out the wind speeds on the report—they were maxing out at 98 mph. "That's barely enough to rustle the patio cushions. By the time it hits land it'll start losing force and we'll be lucky if it even cools things off."

Marcie, whose entire stock of knowledge on storms came from *Twister*, deferred to the opinions of the weathercasters.

Not that she'd say that to Flint again. No harm in humoring him—the storm was slowly headed north, and by tomorrow it should be well past them. One night of miserably hot sleep was a small price to pay to keep the peace.

But his question did remind her of something she'd forgotten. Marcie went back to her room and returned with the little clay turtle Jeff had given her.

"I thought he could watch over our nest in the kitchen windowsill," she said, passing it to him, "but since they're in here at the moment . . ."

Flint ran a finger over the figurine's smooth back, turning it this way and that to examine the detail, the hard lines of his face softening. "How about that. You make this?"

She shook her head. "No, Jeff did—the clay worker at the studio I've been working at. I admired it and he told me to keep it."

Flint's eyes narrowed at her words. "You wanna watch out for a man who gives you things. There's always a hidden price tag."

"I think it was just a throwaway piece he made and he was being nice."

Flint frowned. "Well. You be careful."

"I will. But thanks," she added gently. Misanthropic as he was, his protectiveness warmed her.

He set the little turtle in the sill, pointing toward the cooler, which had been relocated under the kitchen table. "We'll just turn him to face this way for now."

While she started dinner Flint set up electric fans he'd scared up from his storage room, angling the manufactured breeze over a bowl of ice to keep the two of them reasonably cool while they ate—all Marcie could stomach in the heat was a cold pasta salad.

Afterward, they took tall glasses of tea packed with ice out onto the porch—it was too unbearable to do anything else—and sat side by side in the cheap chairs, watching the sunset create spectacular shades of pink and orange and red and finally deepest indigo against the array of clouds that had begun to drift in ahead of the storm—some streaky and some billowing, some feathery and others almost flat dashes in the sky. They listened to the susurrations of the surf, the skittering palm fronds, the cries of seabirds, and she let the warm air fill her lungs, breathing in the thick marine scents that came with it, feeling loose.

"I'll tell you what," Marcie said, finally breaking the silence. "If a hurricane *is* headed toward us, it sure is putting on a hell of a light show on its way in."

Flint nodded. "I'd say, 'calm before the storm' if it weren't a trite cliché."

"Can't have those," she said with a wink, and Flint actually cracked a smile. "You think we might have to evacuate?"

Flint shook his head. "Nah. That's for cat fives, and this one's not that strong. Worst we'll get is some downed trees and power lines, maybe a surge. I've weathered worse. Don't you worry. I'll take care of us."

A lump formed in her throat, made the tea suddenly hard to swallow. "I bet you were a good dad," she said gently.

His eyes shot up to hers, his expression thunderous. "What the hell would you know about it?"

His swift one-eighty was like a blow—she'd let her guard down and Flint had jabbed right into her freshest wound.

"You're right," she said bitterly. "I don't know a thing about being a parent."

A hand wrapped around her wrist startled her, Flint's dry, warm fingers so tight she could feel the beating of her own pulse against his skin.

"I didn't mean it like that," he rumbled, meeting her eyes. "I was talking about me. Not you. I was a shitty parent. You would've been a good one," he said gruffly.

"I don't know about that." Shame and guilt spread acid into her chest, her belly, through her joints and tendons and muscles. "Some people probably aren't meant to be parents."

He let go of her wrist, looked back out at the horizon. "No," he said quietly. "No, I guess not. You do your best and try your hardest and do what you think is good, and maybe you're right. Or maybe you screw everything up. You don't really know till it's too late—it's already done."

The dull, flat tone of his voice pressed up against something raw in her heart. She thought of the appointment she'd made. Would she have canceled it if she hadn't miscarried? She'd never know. But whatever had happened to Jessie, Flint had raised her, apparently mostly on his own, and he must have done all right, judging by the tone of her letters to him. Jessie had loved her father—and Flint, for all his hard edges, had clearly loved his little girl. "You weren't a shitty parent," she said. "You couldn't have been."

He looked suddenly foundationally weary. "Marcie . . . I know you mean well. But you just don't know anything about it."

"I do, actually. Look at how you've prepped to take care of the two of us." She waved behind them toward the boarded-up house, thinking of the rash of supplies he'd bought. "How you helped Isobel yesterday. I even see how you take care of a cooler full of turtle eggs that probably won't survive." She took a deep breath, knowing she was risking the wrath of Flint's quick temper, but she couldn't stop, couldn't let him sit there marinating in guilt. She knew what that felt like.

"And I know it from Jessie."

Flint

He didn't understand at first, didn't know why Marcie would say something so blatantly ignorant and then walk back inside the house—except that her stupid comment made him want to take a bite out of her hide, and she was smart enough to know it. But as soon as she came back out moments later, holding a stack of papers neatly held together with a purple ribbon, he knew in a jarring flash, like an electric current suddenly racing through him.

Jessie's letters.

He'd had a fleeting thought about the letters when they never turned up, but then he let himself forget about it, assuming—like the ass he was—that they'd wound up back in a box that Marcie had carried to his car.

Jessie loved to write on the trips he sent her on during the summer months, when she was idle and he was working and she was too likely to get into mischief left on her own—and he'd saved every one, rubber-banded together in the bottom drawer of his dresser.

As soon as she came home she'd demand them, as if she didn't trust him to be the keeper of her thoughts, her memories.

"Why don't you ever write me back?" she'd complained.

"I send you things all the time," he'd countered, and it was true: boxes bursting with everything he knew she loved and would be missing—books, fresh-picked citrus, her favorite peanut butter—and little treats he thought she'd like: a new notebook with a purple cover, or a fancy ink pen.

His daughter had pushed her lips out into a pucker, the way she always did when she was exasperated with him and wanted him to know it—which was often. "Those aren't letters. They aren't your *feelings*."

But she knew—he'd thought—that he wasn't the sort to be able to put down that kind of thing on paper. He could read other people's words, and he drank up Jessie's in the letters and notes and stories she wrote. But writing down his own felt harder than charging into combat with nothing protecting you but your M1 helmet.

Yet here were hers . . . in the hands of a stranger who'd never known her.

"Give me those," he grated out, yanking them from Marcie's hands. "What the hell are you doing with them?"

"I picked them up after your back went out, but the box was ruined so I stashed them in her room. I was going to give them to you, but . . ." She let out a shaky breath. "I didn't mean to keep them."

He curled his fingers around the age-softened edges of the envelopes, not sure whether he wanted to protect them or crush them. "Did you not mean to read them either?" Because of course she had. Of course.

The red creeping up her cheeks confirmed it, but she didn't back down. "You were a good parent. She was telling you that in every single letter she wrote. Look."

She leaned over and gently pulled one end of the ribbon. He sat still, not knowing why he let her, as the stack loosened in his grasp.

"Don't," he managed, but he wasn't sure it was loud enough for her to hear. Apparently not, as she lifted the top one and eased out the note with careful fingers, opening it there on his lap.

Dear Dad . . .

Her familiar girlish handwriting. Her purple ink. Her words. He closed his eyes.

"'You should totally see this place—you would fall down and die.'"

His daughter's words in Marcie's mouth jarred him—her words but not Jessie's impatient tone, her occasional know-it-all sass that made him alternately want to shake her and hug her with pride. Flint snapped his eyes open and pulled the stack into his body, including the one she'd opened.

"Stop."

"She loved you."

"Stop it."

"She says it in all of these letters—and not just with the actual words." She was looming there over him, crowding out all his oxygen.

"You don't know what you're talking about," he wheezed out.

"It's right here, Flint." She leaned closer to point to the blurred words, the heat and the scent of her clouding his lungs like smoke, making him think he was going to suffocate, but she wouldn't back away, wouldn't let him get any air. "You still have pieces of her even though she's gone."

He couldn't breathe—that was the reason he pushed her—she had to let him *breathe*.

"You have no idea what I did!"

He didn't mean to shove her, not so hard, but his shouted words seemed to ring in the air like the jangling, bone-deep vibrations of a tuning fork as Marcie landed sprawled on the wooden planks on her ass, staring at him with wide, frightened eyes.

"Jessie! Open this door, dammit!"

"Not until you calm down!"

Jessie had stalked in and slammed the door, locking it—still against the rules no matter how old she got. His fist hit the wall next to her doorframe, cracking the drywall, the noise echoing in the tiny hallway.

"That's *not* calm!" she shouted from behind the door.

He fought for it, clenching his bruised fist by his side, trying to breathe . . . breathe . . . the way he'd taught Jessie to do when she got so upset she couldn't take in enough air to get out the words about whatever was bothering her.

But it didn't work. His heart was beating so fiercely in his chest he wondered if he was about to have a heart attack, and his head sharp-pounded along with it, and he felt the beginnings of what he'd called the red rage in the war, when his vision literally hazed violent crimson at the edges and killing became not just easy, but inevitable.

"Jessie," he said. "You will open this goddamn door, and you'll do it right now or I will break it the fuck down. And that's a promise."

The dead flatness in his voice scared the part of him that was holding on to rationality. It must have scared Jessie too, because a moment later he heard the lock twist and the door cracked open, and Jessie—always one to face trouble, not run from it—stood there in the wedge of light coming from her room, white-faced.

He wanted to push past her, rage into her bedroom, start going through her dresser drawers and her closet and anything else that might tell him who this kid was who'd violated his teenage daughter.

But he was afraid to let himself do it, afraid to go into the girlish purple room that had nothing to do with the woman who'd come into the house ten minutes ago and told him to sit down, that she had something to tell him, and that he needed to respect her decisions and hear her out. She'd been stone-faced and stoic, but he saw her fingers trembling, because he knew her, his Jessie—knew every tiny detail about her. Or thought he had. Apparently there were some huge secrets she'd been keeping.

An image flashed into his head of his own father, the way he'd corner them in the room if he or his little brother screwed up big enough, cower them down with the sheer bulk of his body before reaching to his belt, undoing it, whipping it from the belt loops with a rhythmic *thwap-thwap-thwap* of leather that was terrifying.

He'd never hit Jessie—he wouldn't have her fear him the way he and Georgie had feared their dad. But he didn't trust himself right now to go into the purple room that reminded him of the innocence she'd had—that he'd thought she still had. He didn't know what he might do.

"Outside," he growled, and made himself turn around, give her his back, walk out onto the back porch. He didn't have to look to see if she followed him. Jessie would take her medicine.

He let the screen door flap behind him, hearing the muted

slap as Jessie caught it with her hand and came out in his wake. He couldn't look at her, just leaned over the porch, staring out blindly over the gulf, his hands digging into the railing so hard he thought the age-soft wood would dent under his grip. They stood there like that for a long time, the only sounds the barely audible susurration of the gentle Gulf of Mexico, the nasal honking of seagulls, and his own thick breathing.

Who? he meant to ask again. It was inexplicably important that he know the father—to give himself something to focus on, maybe. Someone to blame and hate who wasn't his daughter. But instead what came almost pitifully out of his mouth was: "Why?"

She didn't answer for a long time, and he figured she wouldn't. But then her voice came, stripped of its usual vigor. "Because . . . because I'm seventeen, Dad. I'm not a little girl anymore."

His shoulders crumpled—he could feel them collapse. Not a little girl. No. She wasn't, not anymore, and somehow that fact had eluded him until her announcement had slammed it home.

Everything he'd done, as careful and attentive as he'd been, and he'd still let her down. He'd been so concerned with parenting her exactly, perfectly right that he'd forgotten she'd grow up. He'd forgotten she would need different things from him as she got older. He should have talked to her about these things, prepared her for dating and boys and—*Jesus*—sex. He'd just kept treating her as the same little girl he'd been left holding, terrified, as he'd watched Brenda walk out fifteen years ago and wondered how the hell he was supposed to take care of this tiny fragile creature when he was such a goddamn mess himself.

He felt a hand on his back, so light he wasn't sure it wasn't just the breeze blowing the fabric of his shirt against his skin. And then firmer, a touch.

"Jess . . . Jess . . . I'm so sorry," he said to the air. "I fucked up, I fucked up, I fucked up."

"Dad . . . Daddy." She hadn't called him Daddy in years.

He turned around, took both her hands in his, pressed them hard, probably too hard, but he couldn't help himself. "I should've told you. I didn't . . . You couldn't have known about boys . . . what they're like at this age—at any age. I didn't tell you about . . . God . . . about being careful or . . . or—"

"Dad, no. It wasn't your fault. I . . . I'm *seventeen*, Dad," she repeated like a senseless mantra.

"No. I don't . . . No. I . . ." He trailed off, not even sure what he was trying to say, and he let go of his daughter's hands and fell back against the railing and slumped there, broken.

But Jessie closed the space he'd created between them, came close and worked her slender arms under his and wrapped the two of them into a hug, her head on his chest, her hair smelling like rain or sea or cool water. He put his arms around her slender body and held her, his little girl—and the woman she'd become—for the first time since she'd gotten big enough that he only felt comfortable with a hand on her head or a squeeze of her shoulders to show her how much he loved her.

If he'd known then that it would be the last time he'd ever hold her, he wouldn't have let go. He wouldn't have pulled back as soon as he did to take her shoulders, look into her eyes, and decide that he would fix it all for her. He would make it right.

"We'll handle this together," he told her with an involuntary shake of her shoulders. "We're going to get through it."

Her great blue eyes grew tear heavy and relieved. "Thank you, Daddy. I . . . I can't do this without your help."

That was a hard admission for Jessie, he knew. She was so much like him.

"Let me make some calls. I'll go with you. I'll be there the whole time. I'll take care of you. And it's going to be fine, and we'll get through it, and you can still start college this fall just like we planned, and everything is going to be okay, honey. It's going to be okay."

She reared back, away from his grasp, her expression shuttering. "*What's* going to be okay?"

He missed the warning signs completely, too intent on making everything like it had been. "All of it, Jess—the . . . procedure. You'll be fine—"

"I'm having this child, Dad."

"No, you fucking well are not. I will not watch you ruin your life before you've even begun to live it."

He saw his mistake in her face before she said a word.

"Is that what I did, Dad? Ruined your life?"

He wished she'd shouted it, ranted, screamed it at him. But her voice was as cold and flat as her expression. It hit him like a slap, kept him from replying just long enough that he watched his silence echo in her face. She started to turn away and he caught her arm—too hard; it would leave a bruise on her tender skin.

"Jessie, wait— No, of course not. That isn't what I meant and you know it—"

But she shook him loose, not even looking at him, walked back inside, and a few moments later he heard the door to her room slam shut.

She didn't come out again for the rest of the day. He didn't knock on her door.

When he woke up the next morning her door was still closed, and when he got home from work, his heart in his throat because he wasn't sure if his daughter would still be there or if she'd have run away, left him, he took some comfort from her battered old Camaro in the driveway, her dishes in the kitchen, and her wet bathroom towel. They'd be all right. They'd get through this eventually.

And for a while it seemed like they would. There were too many awkward, silent days between them, too many nights when he'd sit out in the living room with his book, hoping she'd come join him as she often did and sprawl on the sofa with whatever she was reading. She didn't, but she'd sit down to dinner when he called that it was on the table, and little by little they eked out small conversations—about her job at the library up the street, the beach reclamation in progress by the county, the number of turtle nests found so far this season. About anything except what they needed to talk about with increasing urgency.

Jessie knew it too—that they couldn't put off handling the problem forever. Choices had to be made—and soon. And in the end she was the one who came out of her room one night before bed and sat uncomfortably on the edge of the sofa, and waited until he looked up from his book and met her eyes.

"I have a doctor appointment tomorrow morning," she told him in a voice that broke his heart with its shakiness. "If you'd like to come with me . . . that would be fine."

He held his breath, afraid to say the wrong thing, afraid to ask, knowing he had to.

"A doctor appointment . . . for what?"

He'd hoped never to see his child wear the look that fell over her face at his question—disappointment and resignation and weary resolve, all mixed together in an expression that made her seem much, much older than her seventeen years.

"My first checkup. My six-week checkup."

He looked down at his book, not seeing the words, and wiped a hand down his face and jaw. He'd been hoping she was thinking about the pregnancy . . . but not like this. He'd wanted her to realize for herself what it would mean for her, how hard it would be, how impractical at this point in her life to commit herself to taking care of another soul, a helpless soul that would depend on her for everything, and keep her from doing all the things she'd dreamed about, that they'd dreamed for her together. Jessie was a smart, focused, driven girl. She had plans for herself, and she was too ambitious to let her whole future get derailed. He'd counted on that.

But . . . God, this was the worst part of parenting he'd ever experienced. The choices between what was good for Jessie and what Jessie wanted had never been this hard. She was an easy kid, and so much like him that they seemed almost always in effortless accord.

But he was a parent first. He had always known that, always honored it. He'd sworn from the day they'd been left alone with each other that he'd take care of her, protect her from anything that ever threatened her safety or happiness.

Even if that meant he had to protect her from herself.

"Jessie." His voice was a raw rasp, odd even to his own ears. "Jess . . . that's not going to happen. You're too young, and you don't understand what this means for the rest of your life as clearly as I do." He couldn't raise his eyes to her—couldn't face whatever was reflected back at him in the way she must be looking at him now. "I'm making a doctor appointment too . . . another kind. And we're going together. You're a minor. I'm the parent. That's the decision I had to make, and the way it has to be."

He heard nothing—not a sound, not a movement. He finally got his balls together and lifted his gaze to her, to face whatever he had to from his daughter.

What he saw tore him up. Jessie hadn't budged, as if she'd been frozen to the edge of the couch. Her face was totally blank, as though she were in shock—except for the steady trail of wetness coming out of her eyes and running down her face. It was disturbing, unnatural, and it scared him more than any explosive reaction she could have had.

He thrust his book aside, not even bothering to mark his place, pushed himself out of his armchair and to his knees in front of her, took her cold, limp hands in his own.

"Jessie . . . Jessie!" He shook her arms a little, trying to get her to focus on him, to come out of whatever trance state she'd gone into. But she just kept staring ahead, not meeting his eyes, her own leaking their constant stream of tears.

"Honey . . . I'm sorry. I'm so sorry. If there were any other way to do this . . . I've thought it half to death, every option— even adoption; even what you wanted—trying to raise this kid together. I'd do it *for* you if I could, but I can't. I'm too tired, too old to do it all again. I just . . . You have so much potential, so much life in you, honey. So many things you want to do. A baby changes it all, everything." He was babbling; he knew it. But he couldn't stop talking, desperate to say the right words that would snap her out of whatever distant place she'd gone to and bring her back to where he could reach her again. "And it's not that I'd wish you away, or that I didn't want to raise you. You're the best thing in my life. The best thing . . . the only good thing I've ever done. But you're different from me. You're better. You deserve every chance . . . every chance in the world to pursue anything . . . everything you want. All I want . . . all I want is to give you that. I—"

"But that's the thing, Dad," she interrupted with no intonation, drawing her hands out of his grasp—slowly, almost casually—and letting one flutter to her abdomen. "*This* is what I want. And if I have to run away from here until it's too late for you to stop me, I promise you that's exactly what I'll do."

That stopped his momentum finally, shut him up. But not

for long enough. Of all the shitty, immoral, unforgivable things he'd done in his worthless life, what he said to Jessie then was the one regret he'd never get past.

"If you leave here, you don't come back. Not ever. You won't be my daughter anymore." His voice was flat, dead, chillingly cold.

Shock registered on her face, and she cried out as if he'd struck her—one short, sharp gasp of pain, her hand flying to her mouth. He wanted to take it back, grab her to him and tell her he didn't mean it. Of course she'd always be his daughter— how could she not? He loved her more than his own life and nothing she could do would ever change that, no matter what.

It was what he should have said, but he didn't. He crossed his arms and sat there, furious at her defiance, waiting for her to cave.

He should have known her better than that.

Jessie pushed to her feet and looked down at him with a blank expression he couldn't read, as if he were a stranger to her. He'd lost her already, he realized—no matter what happened.

"Okay. That's fine then," she said in a low tone that shook only slightly. "That's good to know."

She stepped sideways to get past where he still knelt before her and walked out of the room and down the hallway. He watched her until she entered her own room and shut the door behind her, but she never once looked back.

In the morning when he got out of bed after a sleepless night, her door was open, her bed neatly made. But her car was missing from the driveway, and Flint knew that Jessie was gone.

It felt like something had broken free of his sternum and punched out through his rib cage when he finally stopped talking.

Marcie still sat where she'd fallen—where he'd pushed her—sitting up now, arms wrapped around her upraised knees as if protecting herself, and she just sat there, staring at him.

Good. He didn't care if she looked at him like that—like he was some kind of animal, a beast. He hadn't asked her to poke her nose into his life. *Let* her be afraid of him. Let her run off.

But she didn't.

"How . . ." Her voice cracked like a teenage boy's, and she cleared her throat. "How long ago?"

"A long time. Fifteen years. More."

His daughter would be in her thirties. How the hell could that be? The last time he'd seen her she'd still had the coltish build of girlhood, all limbs and big eyes and curly brown hair she'd gotten from her mother. He tried to picture her with threads of silver in the sable curls, the slightest beginnings of crow's-feet around her blue eyes—laugh lines, he hoped. He hoped she laughed a lot. But he couldn't do it—she always looked in his mind the way she had the last time he'd ever seen her: too thin and fragile, her hair loose and wild around her face, her eyes . . . her eyes shuttered and faraway, huge in her face and wet with tears.

"She's not dead." She wasn't asking.

"No."

Marcie's mouth hung open like that of a beached fish, that infuriating look of certainty she'd worn replaced by bewilderment like a cloud bank rolling in and eating up the sun. She shook her head. "But she's your daughter. Your *child*. You're supposed to *love* her."

Her tone, heavy with dismay, added a weight inside him, one more brick laid on top of a pile of them.

He tried to soften his voice, but it still came out in an abrasive rumble: "Marcie . . . love isn't always worth it."

He'd wanted to say it as gently as he could, but the girl's face crumpled in on itself as he told her that truth.

It *wasn't* worth it. Not even for all the joy Jessie had brought him while he'd had her, a happiness he could never have imagined, never found in a lover or the bottle or a book—only in raising his willful, smart, proud little girl. Because after you did your job, when you loved them as best as you knew how, gave another human being everything in you, every scrap of love, every vulnerability, every heartbreak until you were just one big aching wound, all you were left with was the fading memory of that love and the bitter knowledge that you would never be that happy again.

Marcie

n the silence that fell between them, Marcie could hear her own heart beating in her ears.

She had an image of Jessie now—young and fiery, from his description, headstrong, and so certain. So painfully, misguidedly certain.

What had the poor girl thought when she'd gotten pregnant so young? That first time it happened to Marcie, she'd panicked. She'd been a child herself, not fit to mother another creature, even a dog. If Will hadn't been so excited about it she wouldn't have even been tempted to try—and it had cost her not just Madrid, but the dream of an art career.

But the second time . . . when life had filled in so many of those fears and inadequacies with experience, with more assurance and confidence—in herself, in the two of them—that time she thought she'd known. She'd had the same blind foolish faith Jessie had had—until she hadn't, and the hard rationality of adulthood smothered that idealistic conviction. Doubts set in and once again Marcie had abandoned what she thought she'd wanted.

Love isn't always worth it, Flint had grated out in that sandpaper voice, and although she'd learned to let a lot of the old man's cranky absolute statements roll right through her head like a passing wave, this one stayed stuck, swirling in the eddies of her mind. *It isn't always worth it.*

"How can you say that?" She surged to her feet and squared off like a prizefighter. "About your *child*?"

Instead of the usual quick rage she'd grown to expect, his face softened, like butter left out too long. "You can't understand, Marcie. What it's like."

Heat surged up through her chest and her limbs and into her eyeballs, making them throb. "Why?" she said in an animal voice she didn't recognize. "Because I'm not a parent?"

His answer was a defeated shrug that might as well have been a detonator.

"Neither are *you*," she bit out. "Donating sperm doesn't make you a parent. And your job's not done when you don't feel like parenting anymore." She got right up on him, close, drilling three fingers into his chest like a pile driver on every charged word she spit in his face, hard enough to bruise. Flint sat motionless, letting her hurt him, his body shifting limply with every fierce blow. "You don't just get to *quit*. You don't just walk away from someone you love when the going gets *tough*."

She heard her mother's words fountaining out of her aching throat, powerless to stop them.

He said nothing for a long time, his pale blue eyes gone empty and distant, until finally he drew them back up to her face and said, almost gently, "Isn't that what you did with your husband?"

She stumbled backward, off-balance, staring stunned at Flint as if he'd struck her.

And then she turned and fled.

She walked up the beach in the growing dark, waiting for its soothing calm to work its magic on her taut nerves, but even the gulf seemed agitated, the incoming tide surging aggressively up around her feet, making her stumble to keep her balance. But something in her needed to unfurl its toes into the water, let the wildness inside her bubble out in a primal shout.

She wasn't like the bitter old man. She was *not*. She hadn't just given up because Will didn't do what she wanted him to do. She didn't just walk away with no chance for them to fix what broke. They'd *tried*, but you couldn't bring a child into the world if only one parent wanted it. You couldn't ask someone for a lifetime of that kind of sacrifice. One of them had had to choose, and Marcie wound up being the one who didn't have the courage to stand by what she thought she wanted. Who hadn't wanted it *enough*.

And yet she hadn't counted on the cost—what the choice would exact from her. From the two of them. They'd tried to overcome it, but in the end it was too great a hurdle.

It was different from Flint and his daughter.

Her feet took her to the art studio, dark and boxed up tight. Locked. She pounded on the door, desperate to get inside, to lose herself in something—anything—that got her out of her head. Rattling the knob, she said, "No. *No!*" unaware she was shouting until she heard Jeff's voice behind her.

"Hey, Collage Artist . . ."

She whirled to see Jeff coming up the plank steps behind her. Whatever he saw in her expression wiped the grin off his face.

"Everything okay?"

"I want . . . I want to . . ." She didn't know how to finish.

If he'd touched her at that moment, even only in comfort, she'd have sunk into his arms, clutched at him, taken a step toward an unknown that there'd be no pulling back from.

Instead he pulled a set of keys from his pocket, twirling them once around his finger. "I was hoping you'd change your mind about the party."

So she followed him to his car and they drove.

She was barefoot, wearing the same cheap cotton sundress she'd had on all day, trying to encourage some ventilation underneath the clothes that stuck to her in the dank heat at Flint's. She had no purse, no ID—nothing.

She felt weightless.

Jeff drove them off the island, over the bridge, down the first street they came to, which ran along the other side of the pass. The houses here were sparser than on Marea, even less well maintained, and the residential area soon gave way to huge corrugated-metal warehouses and buildings. Jeff parked in the pocked asphalt lot of one of them, weeds springing up through a veiny network of cracks.

What moon there might have been was hidden by bunched clouds, and in the darkness of the parking lot Marcie heard screams from inside. She realized the sound was laughter—loud and unrestrained—and it gained volume as they walked closer. When Jeff opened the door for her, sound and sights and scents washed over them.

Some kind of funky music played from unseen speakers,

heavy with—strangely enough—accordion and what sounded like a church organ, with distinctive male lead vocals whose lyrics were unintelligible. But the beat was fast and a handful of people bounced in the center of the room on the concrete floor, dancing energetically, if not well. A buzz of conversation—voices raised over the music—accompanied the melody, and Marcie would have sworn she heard a chain saw in the background, but there was none within sight.

In the center of the vast room, dim in the light of only a few torchiere lamps tucked into corners to reflect off the walls, and string lights dangling from the open ceiling, half a dozen more people lounged in an incongruous living area delineated by a huge furry area rug; a long battered leather sofa, a red chaise longue, two upholstered recliners that had clearly seen years' worth of backsides, and several bean bags surrounded a cocktail table made of plywood laid over concrete blocks, the top of it littered with cups and ashtrays, beer and liquor bottles, and what appeared to be a glass smoking pipe.

The room reeked of marijuana, sweat, and smells that fired up long-dormant circuits in Marcie's brain—the heady, headachy scent of acrylic paint and adhesive, the now-familiar earthy odor of clay, the sharp tang of cut wood. And underneath it all, oddly, the distantly pungent odor of fish.

Will would have wrapped an arm around her protectively, turned them around and out the door—this was not their kind of party, too many strangers, too many substances. But Marcie wanted whatever dangers lurked in shadowed corners, didn't care what consequences she might be inviting. The pot she smelled? Yes, bring it on. What else was on offer?

Jeff waved a greeting at several people who called out or gestured him over, and Marcie followed him to the living area, where he introduced her as "My new friend Marcella. She works in assemblage. Marcella—the gang," he said, waving around the room.

There were casual waves and head nods, smiles and "welcomes" and even a couple of shouted names filtering to her over the music, but Marcie didn't worry about trying to remember them. When Jeff poured a splash of tequila into two cups and offered her one, she didn't hesitate, taking it, clacking it against his, downing the liquid in one swallow.

There was good-natured laughter when she coughed at the burn. *Jesus.* High school was a long time ago. Jeff raised the bottle, a question, and she held out her cup for more.

She stopped after the second shot, but only because someone passed her a bottle of St. Pauli Girl, and when the glass pipe made a round and came to her, she had a tiny toke of that too, her eyes watering as she tried futilely to hold in her cough.

The smiles that met her were so good-natured, though, no trace of mockery in them, and Marcie let herself sink into a feeling of mellow well-being.

Someone had thrown open the large steel roll-up door along a side wall, revealing a loading dock leading to an actual dock trailing out over the dark water of the pass, on which someone said Tucker—Marcie had no idea who that was, but was glad to give him the credit he was due—had built a fire in a large, footed firepit. She and Jeff had positioned themselves on the brown leather couch inside, but facing it so they could enjoy the dancing flames and occasional sparks that popped and drifted into the inky air.

"You want to see the rest of the place?" Jeff asked, his head resting against the cushion beside her head.

Marcie had become fascinated with a worn spot on the

cushion next to her thigh. "Did you know this means it's cheap leather? Top grain. Top. Grain." She hit the consonants hard, popping the *P*, as she repeated the term with gravitas. "Just a thin little layer of leather," she said, liking the way the words elided together with a pleasing alliteration.

Jeff looked at her fondly. Yes, indeedy, that's what that smile was—*fond*. He gently took the beer from her hands, replacing it with a plastic bottle of water. "Come on," he said, and then he was standing in front of her, a hand out. "A walk will do us good."

He kept hold of her hand as he led her deeper into the warehouse, to the shadowed edges out of range of the sparse illumination. "This was an old mullet processing plant," he told her as they walked.

"That explains the fish smell."

"Went out of business a while ago—the local mullet population took a hit in 2016—and it just sat here, empty, till eventually it went up for auction. So a bunch of these guys went in together and decided to buy it, and now it's their studio."

Just as he finished, Marcie saw the truth of his words for herself—the walls of the warehouse were lined with artists' work areas: drafting tables and easels and large flat work spaces roughly hewn from plywood; bottles and tubes of supplies littering an array of shelving that must have been Goodwill or salvage finds; rags, brushes, tools of every sort. Sparks flew in a far corner, and when they neared, Marcie realized where the chain saw sound and the wood smell were coming from—a woman wearing safety goggles was working on some kind of elaborate woodwork pattern in what looked like a headboard.

She let out a breath, took in another deep one, letting the familiar, comforting scents fill her lungs, chasing away some of the pleasant fog that had shrouded her. "It's wonderful," she said softly. She turned to Jeff. "Why don't they open part of it as a gallery or a storefront?"

"Practical Marcie." It was the first time he'd called her by her proper name, and she wasn't sure she liked it. "Art's not always meant to be displayed or sold."

She pondered that for a long moment, his fingers still warm around hers. "I actually think it is," she said finally.

"Maybe so," he said agreeably, raising an indifferent shoulder. "But also the place smells like fish."

That gave Marcie the giggles so hard she had to drop his hand and grasp her knees, and after a moment she infected Jeff and he doubled over too, both of them laughing like careless children.

He recovered before she did, little giggles springing from her lips erratically like bubbles till she finally gathered herself together, wiped her eyes, and straightened, her eyes meeting Jeff's.

The music and noise and everything else seemed to recede in the background, like a rack focus, as he held her gaze. His amusement had vanished, something shifted in the air between them, and her heart started to punch against her ribs.

"Now, there's Marcella," he said, low, and it was the only sound in her ears, even with the furniture maker's circular saw spinning thirty feet away. Jeff pushed himself off where he leaned against a butcher-block table strewn with one-by-two strips of framework for a canvas, a nail gun, and spent tubes of wood glue. He took a slow step toward her, his eyes rimmed in shadows in the dim space but still trained on hers, until they were face-to-face—too close—and she had the sudden insane urge to brush his abdomen with her fingers, clutch his untamed curls in her fist.

She waited. Not breathing.

Finally his hand moved to his mouth, and Marcie wondered if he was politely covering a yawn, but when he lowered it his mouth was open and she saw a tiny white disk, almost like a birth control pill, on the end of his tongue.

Without thought, she leaned forward, opened her lips, and melded her tongue to his.

Flint

The wind was just starting to pick up, a low, ominous moaning sound filtering to land from the horizon.

He wasn't able to sleep with the threat of the storm rising, the throbbing of his back from overexerting himself the last couple of days. Thinking about what had happened with Marcie. What he'd told her, what he'd done. Finally he got up and made a pot of coffee.

She'd taken off down the back steps like a Gorgon had been on her tail—not too far off the mark in her view, probably—and hadn't come back yet. Now it was after three a.m., and no sign of her.

There was lightning out on the horizon over the water he saw through the kitchen window—not jagged streaks of it, but pulses of brightness shattering the dark, like distant bombs dropping over an enemy—and with the creaks and groans of the house hunkering down against the rising wind, it had him all jumpy, riled up, raw edged.

She was on foot—her car was still in the driveway—and hadn't even taken shoes with her. Where the hell could she have gone and stayed all this time, barefoot?

What if she injured herself and was stuck somewhere, couldn't get back? Unless she'd had her wallet in her pocket, which he very much doubted, she wouldn't even be able to call a cab.

He dumped his coffee in the sink—the caffeine wouldn't help matters—and let himself out the front door, the screen clattering against the doorframe in the sharp wind. When they got back he needed to secure that. Or hell, let it get ripped off. It was useless anyway—the wood rotting out, the mesh pulled away from the edges in some places, billowing when a breeze blew.

He pulled around her car, heedless of the trenches he dug in the front yard, and out onto Marea. The street was quiet, dark with hardly any moon. Not many people out at this hour, in this weather. Every now and then he'd see a shuffling silhouette hunched over against the wind, and he'd slow down and peer over at it—just to see if it was Marcie—then dismiss it. Beach rats, mostly, homeless bums that just lapped the island up and down, up and down, nowhere else to go. Harmless, most of 'em, but if they'd seen her . . .

The wind blew in gusts into his rolled-down window, strong enough to make his eyes water, the whipping of the palm fronds overhead sounding like flames.

The little building she'd shown him where that artist who was sniffing around her worked was dark as the bottom of a latrine, and so was Tequila Mockingbird, that skank hole where the girl had found a job, both buildings shut up tight, not even the drunks still lurking on the steps out in front of the bar. No sign of the girl.

His heart was beating too fast as he reached the end of the island, flipped a U-turn in a parking lot, and drove back in the other direction, watching the street just as carefully but spotting no trace of her, and the grocery and convenience stores were as dark and locked down as everything else.

Back in his driveway he hustled from the car to the front door, the wind seeming to push him as if hurrying him to get inside. Maybe she'd be there by now, and if she was already asleep, he would wake her up and tell her how many kinds of an idiot she was for being out so late, ignoring the weather.

But everything was the way he'd left it—even the turtles waiting on the kitchen table where he'd forgotten to take them in his haste to look for her. No sign of the girl.

His head hurt, felt like a grenade with the pin pulled, just waiting to go off. That awful moment when you weren't sure how long to hold it—let go too soon, Charlie'd lob it back at you. Hold on too long . . . You could almost feel the pressure of it, like the world narrowed in on the one point where you held the thing in your hand.

This was not in the damn program. The girl was supposed to have come in, gotten on her feet, and gotten the hell out. They weren't supposed to tell each other their deepest-darkest, like some kind of kaffeeklatsch. She wasn't even supposed to have been here in the first place, a lapse in judgment he was paying for. He knew better. Knew when he found her crumpled up like yesterday's trash on the beach that he should have walked on by.

He could call the police . . . but tell them what? The Keystone Kops on this island couldn't do jack, incompetent wannabes who puffed out their chests while they held up noise meters in front of bars and called out the managers who were hardly more than beach drifters themselves—just drunks with dream jobs—to tell them to roll back the volume on the band.

Maybe she'd left. Gone back to wherever she came from. And that was fine with him. What he'd wanted in the first place.

Without her car? his own sarcastic voice asked in his head, but he ignored the logic.

He didn't need her judging him. She didn't like his choices? Fine—he'd never asked her to. You pull open doors you got no business opening, don't be shocked if you don't like what's behind them.

Well, he wasn't going to let it ruin one more second of his life. She wasn't his responsibility and she wasn't his problem, and if she wanted to get herself into trouble—wind up on the beach in a pile of dead this time, instead of just passed out, or go back to the husband who'd done God knew what to her to make her leave in the first place—then she was welcome to do it.

Marcie

The kiss shocked her even more than taking a pill from a virtual stranger when she had no idea what it was.

The last time she'd kissed someone other than Will she'd been fifteen years old in the basement of Brittany Bailey's house, and she couldn't even remember the boy's name now—just that he had saliva-wet lips that felt like worms slithering against hers, and she'd been done with kissing for a while. Until Will.

This was nothing like that. Jeff's lips were warm and dry, his tongue soft, and he'd just touched it to hers—Marcie tasted the slight bitterness of the pill. He moved his tongue gently, as if creating enough friction to dissolve the little disk . . . as if tasting her tongue—and when it was gone he pulled away, Marcie's heartbeat a vibration in her chest.

He took her hand again and pulled her back to the party, getting her another bottle of water—she'd lost hers somewhere—and urging her to drink it all: "I don't want you to get dehydrated."

That was when Marcie started to worry.

"What did we just take?" she leaned over to shout over the music, now something with electric guitar and, weirdly, washboard.

"Ecstasy," he said close to her ear, his warm breath raising goose bumps.

That reassured her a little—for a second she'd panicked she'd just done LSD or meth or something; Marcie wasn't any kind of expert on recreational drugs. She hadn't heard anything too terrifying about MDMA unless it was the bath-salt variety, and hopefully Jeff knew his source enough to trust him. Or her—Marcie didn't want to be sexist about Jeff's drug dealer.

The thought made her chuckle, but it wasn't the tipsy giggles she'd had earlier. The buzz she'd gotten from the tequila shots had already started to wear off and she wouldn't have even thought the tiny pill had taken effect as they talked to some of Jeff's friends and wandered the warehouse and went out to the firepit on the dock. Someone was making s'mores that smelled delicious, but Marcie wasn't in the mood to eat. Almost an hour went by and nothing; she was fine. In fact she felt great—the ache she'd felt in her feet from standing on the concrete floor had disappeared, her slight headache had vanished, and she was filled with energy. Riddled with it, in fact— it was hard to sit still with the strange hybrid music that had been playing all night—part funk, part folk, part zydeco, and who knew what else.

"Who is this?" Marcie asked, voice raised over the music as they stood near a cooler, where Jeff had opened another water bottle and insisted they split it. "I mean the band?"

"Donna the Buffalo."

She couldn't figure that out for a moment and then realized what he'd actually said and started laughing, a joyful effervescence in her chest, in her ears. "Oh, '*Dawn* of the Buffalo'! I thought you said Donna, like that was the name of the buffalo."

He was grinning back at her, sharing the joke. "It *is* Donna. Donna the Buffalo—they're great. On the festival circuit."

Marcie nodded. "I love Donna! I love her voice!"

This time it was Jeff who laughed, a rich, deep sound that fizzed all the way inside her and made her shiver. Marcie let her body shimmy with the sound, and it felt so good to move, she started shuffling her feet in place.

"Her name's not Donna." He was yelling now, someone having cranked up the volume.

Marcie smiled, touching his chest with an accusatory finger. "You just said her name is Donna!"

He shook his head, still grinning. "No, I said the *band* is Donna. The singer is Tara."

Marcie felt her mouth drop open, letting the sheer silliness of that wash over her, and then laughter funneled up out of her again. "That's wonderful!" she said.

He nodded and took both her hands in his. "I know!"

They were standing like that, hands clasped, smiling at each other in pure delight, when another song started, a bouncy, bass-y guitar riff that segued into a funky melody with a violin and a driving drum line.

"Oh!" Marcie shouted, squeezing his fingers and bouncing in time. "I have to dance!"

He leaned closer: "You want to dance?"

"I *have* to!"

Jeff grinned and gave a wide shrug. "That's Donna. That's what they do!"

They pulled each other over to the impromptu dance floor and she let her body sway and move, no self-consciousness, no worries about taking up space as she spread her arms and twirled, felt the air on her cheeks and lips and rustling the folds of her dress against her bare skin. This song was the man's voice, that nasal, unintelligible tone from before just fountaining a torrent of words she could barely understand—something about conscious evolution, but it was perfect. God, she felt so *good*. As if the last weeks fell completely away—the last *years*—and she was young and free again and the world was a bright, sunny, beautiful place. She tipped her head back to watch the twinkling lights overhead as she moved, like strings of stars, and Jeff's strong grip caught her—of course he did—holding her steady while she tipped back farther and let her body lean and sway and move, waving her hands in the air—*Exactly like I just don't care,* she thought giddily—and feeling the music in every capillary of her body.

"They're amazing," she said to everyone—to the air, the world—almost tipped upside down now, as if her body were made of the most marvelous rubber. She pulled herself upright effortlessly, Jeff's hands sliding up her back as she did, and they danced that way, her hands on his shoulders, no space between them, the wonderful warmth of their bodies like a glow.

She started laughing and leaned so close to Jeff's ear her lips brushed the warm shell of it. She let them rest there for a moment, savoring the sensation. "I must be high!" she said finally. "This song feels like it's gone on *forever*."

"It has! They're a jam band. This could go on all night."

That was the best news she'd heard, and Marcie hugged him, squealing in delight.

She had no idea how long they'd been dancing. She could dance for eternity—she wasn't remotely tired, even though she'd lost count of how many songs they'd heard; they had to have been out here for hours, in between trips to the makeshift bar on a drafting table near the front of the room for another couple of tequila shots, and regular trips to the cooler for water.

"Hydrate!" they called out in unison each time, water spurting up and the cheap thin plastic of the bottles crackling as they toasted. Jeff wouldn't let her get back out and dance till she finished the whole bottle, so she drained it like a frat boy pounding a beer, every time, pulling him back out to the dance floor behind her.

Sweat ran down her back and pooled underneath her breasts, the rising heat barely alleviated by gusts of air that blew in from the open rolling door. The sudden cold splash of liquid on her legs and bare feet felt wonderful, just the cooldown she craved, but Jeff stopped dancing and touched her arm, his face furrowed, and that was when she realized it stung a little. Looking down she saw a dark trickle of blood on her ankle.

"What happened?" she asked, still dancing.

"Someone dropped a beer," he said, and then he swooped her up into his arms like Rhett flipping Butler and carried her over to the living area, settling her at one end of the sectional a blond guy in cargo shorts hastily vacated, the guy's shirtless chest as smooth and lean as a greyhound's.

"Thanks, Tucker," Jeff said.

"Oh, you're Tucker!" she exclaimed. "Thank you for the fire!"

He gave a lazy grin, a mouthful of white teeth flashing against the tan of his skin. "Had to put it out—wind kicked up and the sparks are flying everywhere."

"I don't mind," she reassured him.

"We have a first-aid kit somewhere," Tucker told Jeff, motioning to someone behind Marcie.

"And some superglue," Jeff called out after the person, presumably running for supplies.

He knelt on the fuzzy area rug in front of where she sat, her foot propped in his lap.

"Superglue?" she said, liking the feel of his warm hands against her damp skin as he picked out the glass, rinsing the blood away with water from someone's proffered bottle and catching it with a handful of paper towels someone passed over.

"Seal you right up. Get you back on your feet—literally."

"Totally true," a woman standing next to Marcie said, wearing a gauzy maxi skirt and a short black top. Her graying brown hair was half caught into a knot, half spilling in wisps around her face. "It's the same stuff they use in the ER. I dated a paramedic last year," she said.

"You dated everyone last year," Tucker said, and winked— either at the woman or at Marcie; she couldn't tell, but the woman looked pleased as everyone laughed, stretching her arms overhead and exposing a little of her soft, rounded belly. Marcie ran her hands over her own belly, liking its pliant give.

"Here, she needs anesthesia for the operation," Tucker said. He held a bottle out to her, his blond curls outlined against the light like a nimbus around his head. "You want a glass?"

The other people around her laughed; she liked the sound of it. She reached for the bottle. *What is it? What's in there? How many people drank out of that thing?* The voice in her head was Will's and Marcie didn't care; she brought her mouth directly to the lip, tipping back her head. Oof—whiskey. She let its sharp, acrid scent waft up her nose, its burn slide down her throat. She swallowed . . . swallowed again.

"Damn!" Tucker was nodding approvingly at her as one of the other men—Austin? Houston? something in Texas—trotted back with a small white box in his hand, which he slapped into Jeff's like a nurse, and Marcie laughed, holding the bottle back out to Tucker.

"Keep it," he advised. "Jeff's got more bedside manner than surgical skill."

"Fuck off," Jeff said, grinning as he peered at the sole of her foot, reaching out one hand for the bottle.

Their banter washed over her as warm as the liquor, all of it making her part of the little group. When pain lanced into her before she even fully registered that Jeff had tipped the bottle over her foot to let the alcohol run directly into the wound, it felt like an initiation. She gripped something hard and realized it was someone's hand. She didn't know when the woman now sitting on the arm of the couch beside her—"I'm Max," she'd murmured in Marcie's ear—had offered it, but the whole group had moved closer and there were pats on her back, a comforting squeeze of her shoulder, Max's tight grip. Jeff put the bottle back in her hand and she took a swig.

"That's got it. You're good to go." He looked directly at her, his hands wrapped around her calf. "But I hope you won't."

She didn't, her foot indeed feeling good as new—her whole self feeling newer too, and definitely good. The group passed the bottle around some more, trading good-natured insults and references she didn't get, but Marcie just let their high spirits surround her, draw her in as Jeff slapped another bottle of water in her hand and commanded, "Hydrate." Her limbs soft and liquid, her brain light as helium, Marcie just watched the bobbing shapes on the dance floor, became one of them when she couldn't stand to sit still anymore, enjoying the sounds of everyone's good time as if whatever circle of connection encompassed this eclectic little group of artists had spread to her too.

After a while the music turned off, but one of the younger guys—Marcie never caught his name—produced a guitar and started strumming, drawing everyone over to the living area. She recognized "American Pie," which made her laugh—had this kid even been alive when Don McLean went down in that plane crash? No, wait. . . . It wasn't him who crashed. It was someone in the song. Wasn't it? She laughed again because who knew? She hadn't been alive then either, and she and Jeff, hands linked, joined in with the others as they sang along to the chorus . . . and then another song, Nirvana? And another, the music weaving itself around her, *through* her, through the whole group of them, making them some kind of collective entity.

They'd found seats in a corner of the sectional and Marcie thought at first the low moaning sound she heard was coming from her. She and Jeff were leaning shoulder to shoulder, her legs resting across his lap, and he was touching her like a blind man, running his fingers, his palms, the backs of his hands along her feet, her shins and calves, across her knees and higher, drawing shivers up her thighs.

She was content just to lie here, give him access to her body, wondering whether her skin felt as good to his fingertips as his fingertips felt on her skin. Some part of her knew this was the drug's doing, and yet she couldn't find the fault in his sensual, almost innocent exploration. She didn't mind the moans he was drawing out of her—she was glad to give him feedback on how nice this felt—but when she uncapped yet another bottle of water and took a long slug, she still heard it: low wails crescendoing outside the warehouse, where the now-lowered rolling door was clattering against its tracks.

"What is that?" she asked.

A creaking overhead answered her before Jeff did: "Guess we're getting the outer bands of the storm."

The wind surged against the house again now, and the roof emitted another series of cracks and groans. Marcie pushed herself up from her slouch, looking around the room. The crowd had thinned out—she had no idea what time it was or how long she'd been here—but the people left didn't seem too concerned. A couple wedged together into one of the reclining chairs seemed to be sleeping; Max lay farther down on the sectional, wearing earbuds, smoking a joint, and staring up at the ceiling; one lone dancer was swaying to some distant percussive beat. Marcie relaxed back against the cushions, running her palm along the springy hairs on Jeff's arm.

A freight train screamed through the building.

Marcie jolted, the shrieking sound yanking her upright. "That's not just the outer bands," she said, swinging her legs off his lap and letting her feet burrow into the fuzzy rug.

Her head felt tight and heavy, as if something were pressing in on it. The dull thunking she'd thought was part of the music was rain, she realized—splattering against the metal roof with impact. She stood and walked to the little office area up front, the warehouse's only window, but it was too dark to see anything. She put a hand against the glass and was startled to feel it shuddering.

"He was right," she murmured.

Jeff was behind her. "What?"

Marcie took his hand, pressed it to the glass. "Feel that." She could see his hand pulsing like a heartbeat.

"Son of a bitch," he said, low.

The electricity was still on—a shaded lamp on the nearby desk cast a dim illumination, and against it Jeff was a rumpled silhouette, his hair wild and his shirt bunched up at one side, wrinkled where they'd lounged on the couch for who knew how long. With his hand still pressed to the window she had the fleeting impression that he was part of the storm, connected to it, the elemental wildness outside echoed in the man on this side of the flimsy barrier between the two. She wanted to wrap her arms around his torso, press herself into his back, make herself part of that primeval organism that was raging against the house.

Something crashed just outside the window, something heavy and breakable—a planter?—and she jumped back instinctively, reality surging in.

"We have to get away from the windows," she said, pulling at his T-shirt. "Close the shade in case the glass shatters."

"That's not going to help. If Mother Nature wants this building, she'll take it."

Well, she's not taking me, Marcie wanted to shout. *And she's not taking you.* The idea made her panicky—Jeff pulled out a window, sucked up into the storm, gone. One more thing lost.

And suddenly she thought of Flint—alone at his house, his back barely healed.

"The hurricane's hitting. I need to go home." She didn't know whether she meant Flint's house or her own.

Jeff turned from the window, half his face lost in shadow. "What?"

"I have to get back to Flint—the man I've been staying with. He's old, and he hurt himself, and . . . he's all alone."

"It's pretty ferocious out there." He was standing in front of her, blocking her from leaving.

"I know that. That's why I have to get to him." Her voice was loud even amid the groaning of the building. Raw.

"Okay. Okay. I'll drive us."

The wind pushed its way into the warehouse the moment Jeff opened the front door, surging inside, pushing the door into them, swirling napkins and discarded plastic cups along the floor. The warehouse screeched and cracked its protest.

"Outside—hurry!" he said. He turned to pull the door shut behind them, arching his body with the effort. They'd warned the others, woken the sleeping, and they were all gathering their things to take shelter at somebody's nearby house.

Marcie and Jeff hurried to his car, pushing against invisible resistance. This wind wasn't like the clean gulf breezes that blew every afternoon. It was weighted, wet—like strips of papier-mâché—and smelled dark somehow, musty and metallic.

The car door yanked out of Marcie's hand when she opened it, and Jeff quickly stepped behind it, bracing it with his body as she threw herself inside. He pushed it closed, skirted around the front, hunched against the storm. Over on his side he fought to open the door, and once he made it inside, it nearly careened shut on his leg. The car rocked with the force of the slam, the force of the gusts, but it was eerily quiet inside.

Going over the bridge was the most terrifying thing Marcie had ever experienced, the car slewing side to side like a child's remote-control toy, but once they hit Marea the wind settled slightly as they drove at a crawl. The wet streets glowed under shuddering streetlights, rain pelting the windshield in thick drops that continually changed direction, until the lights suddenly extinguished as if switched off, the sound of a cannonade reverberating somewhere distant.

"That was the transformer," Jeff muttered.

In the sudden darkness the deserted street was an unfamiliar slideshow, disturbing images lit briefly in their headlights as they passed.

Downed palm trees crisscrossed the sidewalk in front of the Shark Bar, like a giant game of pickup sticks. The ones still standing bent their heads as if trying to protect themselves from the buffeting wind, fronds streaming backward in a graceless clump. A car that never moved from in front of an ancient faded pink cracker house—a rusted green Charger with one flattened tire—was almost buried under a bank of torn-out sea grape and mangrove and limp fakahatchee grass that had blown up against it. Debris flew past them—garbage and whole branches of spiky palms and one plastic lounge chair that careened directly at the windshield before suddenly changing trajectory and thunking into the hood, then sailing up and into the night like a kite. Marcie could see the shadow of indentation it left in the dim illumination their headlights reflected off the rain.

Her throat felt choked—not with fear, but with aching gratitude. She wanted to reach over, take Jeff's hand, but they were white on the wheel as he fought to hold them on the road, and in the dark expanse between them he was too far away for her to reach.

Flint's house was pitch-dark, like all the others, the metal shutters plastered to the windows like blinders. She pushed open the car door before Jeff had even stopped completely, rain lashing her as she struggled to the front door.

She froze there, a sense of "not right" creeping into her before she realized why—the screen door was missing, torn away and blown off somewhere. She could see the jagged edges of the hinges where age and moisture and salt had rusted them lacy. *Tetanus*, she thought inanely. They'd have to remember to unscrew what was left after the storm so no one sliced themselves open on the serrated edges.

She unlocked the door, and as she turned the knob it was yanked from her hands and flew inward. She thought it was Flint, greeting her with his rediscovered rage, until Jeff pushed her inside and shoved the door closed behind them against the wind that had blown it violently inward.

Complete stillness and darkness engulfed them as he threw

the bolt. With the power out and the windows covered, it was black as a grave. A whistle broke the startling silence. "Solid concrete," Jeff said, his voice at her ear. "This house must be built like a crypt."

She shuddered at his echo of her thoughts. "It pretty much is one," she muttered, then raised her voice: "Flint?"

The dark house seemed to swallow her voice. Marcie reached down, patting the air until her hand encountered the age-softened fabric of Flint's chair, orienting herself. "Herman!" she called louder.

"He's not here," Jeff said. "Come on. We need to get to my place." She felt a tug on her sleeve, but she resisted.

"He wouldn't leave." She moved toward the hall, slowly, one hand in front of her so she didn't face-plant into a wall, her fingers trailing along the left wall. She hit his doorway sooner than she expected, her hand curling around the frame. His door was open, and she stepped inside, anchoring herself in the opening. "Herman. Are you here?" Her heartbeat thumped in her chest.

"Where would he keep a flashlight?" Jeff's voice asked, behind her.

"I don't know. No—kitchen drawer, far-right side of the sink."

"Stay here."

His steps faded in the hallway as Marcie stepped farther into the room. She pictured Flint collapsed on the bed, his back out again, too angry at her still to answer, out of spite. "Herman!" she whispered hoarsely. "Are you in here? Herman!"

But there was nothing. Her heart sped up. His medication—he could have overdosed and be unconscious . . . or worse. Crumpled into a heap in the bathroom . . . the living room . . . anywhere. She could hear the silverware clinking from the kitchen—Jeff didn't know the layout; he must be blindly pulling out drawers. She couldn't wait if Flint was collapsed somewhere, in distress.

"Ow! Dammit!" She'd barked her shin hard on the bedframe but ignored the throbbing. Reaching down to the bed like a blind person, she felt the stiff quilted bedspread, ran her hands along its unwrinkled expanse. He made his bed every day, with tucked corners and perfect creases under the pillows, like a nurse. Like a soldier. She turned back for the doorway and screamed when she hit flesh.

"It's me."

"Jesus!" She rested her hands on Jeff's chest, trying to steady her racing pulse. "No flashlight?"

"Not that I could find."

She remembered the three standing on the counter with Flint's survival supplies. "Let me check the nightstand." Marcie inched her way back to the bed and felt for the drawer of the old wooden stand beside it. Opening it, she felt inside: two paperback books . . . reading glasses . . . something velvety soft—a cleaning fabric—and a cylinder too small to be a flashlight—lip balm, she guessed. Nothing else.

"We need to go." Jeff's tone was tense.

"Wait."

She pushed past him, back down the hallway to the bathroom. Her foot caught on something, and for one stomach-dropping instant she thought it was a body. She reached down—a damp, crumpled towel. It made her uneasy—Flint would never have left it on the floor.

She moved into the tiny room, intent on what she was looking for, and fumbling around with her hands held out before her, she finally located it: a book of matches on the back of the toilet, next to a scented candle that had appeared there a few days after she moved in. One of his oddly considerate gestures.

Or more likely he was just trying to erase the unfamiliar smells of someone else invading his house.

It took three tries to strike the first wooden match; her hands trembled. In the sudden flare of its light she looked around quickly—except for the towel on the floor, nothing unusual. She caught the reflection of Jeff's eyes down the hallway, watching her, just before the match burned out. Marcie lit another one and touched it to the candle wick, carrying it out of the bathroom toward the door to the guest room. Empty—she stepped inside to check the floor on the far side of the bed to be sure.

A clanging sound out back made them both jump as she searched the living room, and then a loud, frantic knocking on the back door.

"He's outside."

"Not if he's as smart as you think he is," Jeff countered, but he was already making his way to the kitchen. She hurried over behind him and saw him reach for the back doorknob in the flickering light of the candle.

A feeling of foreboding crashed over her out of nowhere, and she wanted to shriek at Jeff not to open the door, that some-thing horrible waited beyond it. But when it pushed itself into Jeff with the wind, there was nothing there—just the old wooden screen door that clattered crazily against the jamb.

Her candle blew out.

The wind was louder now, a sinister hiss, but for some rea-son it seemed weaker than before—still harsh, but they could stand against it—and Marcie realized it was the sound of the waves she was hearing . . . too close, bigger than she'd ever known the placid gulf to be. Flint had been right, she thought as she fruitlessly stared into the darkness behind the house:

The water was going to surge all the way up the beach, over the turtle nest.

The turtles.

Without a word she pushed back inside, past Jeff, fumbling for the matches where she'd thrust them into her pocket. Relighting the candle, in its feeble light she quickly scanned the house, verifying that she hadn't seen what she already knew she hadn't: The cooler was gone.

Relief rushed through her as strong as the rising tide: Flint was okay. He'd evacuated. He'd taken the dozens of tiny, leathery turtle eggs they'd dug up and gone somewhere safe.

"Jeff," she called, and he appeared in the doorway from the kitchen. "He's okay. He got out." She could hear her own voice steadying with the words.

"Storm's blowing itself out," he said. "But the water's coming up fast. We need to get out of here too."

Storm surge. Flint's house was going to flood. The candle guttered again as she swung around to his rickety bookshelf, the flame righting itself as she set it on the piecrust table. His books were the only things she could think of that he gave a damn about.

Except for one thing . . .

"I need five minutes," she said into the blackness. "And something to load some stuff into."

"Marcie, it's time to go. The water's rising." His voice was flat in the darkness. "Once it hits the car's undercarriage we're stranded."

"Then go! I'll do it myself!"

"Jesus." She heard his steps behind her, the creak of the front door, which he left open behind him, the sound of his car door opening, the engine rumbling to life.

She hadn't really thought he'd leave. She'd be trapped in this dusty old mausoleum alone while the water rose around her, eight feet left to the ceiling once it swirled inside, in the darkness—

Jeff's headlights blazed into the dark house through the open door, and Marcie had to squint against the sudden flare of light. It shifted as he came back inside, carrying two milk crates he must have had in the trunk.

"Show me. Hurry," he said shortly, setting them on the floor.

Gratitude flooded her surely as the rising gulf waters. "Top two shelves." She pointed. "Be careful—they're old. And valuable. I'll be right back."

She raced into the kitchen, heavy thunks behind her telling her he was stacking the books at top speed.

Jessie's letters. Where had he left them? In the inadequate light trickling in from Jeff's headlights, she scanned the table, the counter—nothing there, but they would have blown off when they opened the back door. She dropped to her hands and knees, looked under the table, the cabinets, behind the refrigerator—nothing, though she noticed the storm supplies were missing. Where had he gone?

She opened every drawer, contents clattering, even checked the garbage in the pantry. Dammit! She headed back down the hall.

"Marcie, come on—" Jeff started.

"One more minute!"

Scrambling in Flint's bedroom, she lit matches to search it again—the closet, the drawers, under the bed, under the *mattress*, did the same in the bathroom and its small trash can.

She fought down the panic rising in her chest, forcing her feet to still, her heart to calm. He wouldn't have taken them with him, she was certain. Where would he have put them? Maybe the trunk of his car—nothing she could do about that, if so; she didn't have a key. Maybe the garbage outside, but when they'd pulled into the driveway she'd seen it on its side, hinged lid gaping open, contents strewn to the wind already.

"Marcie, we're in the eye. We have to go. Now." Jeff was beside her, his voice was loud in the sudden stillness, and Marcie realized the storm had ebbed, the silence piercing after nature's fury.

And in a flash she knew.

She was out of matches, but she didn't need them—she pushed into the girl's bedroom that had become Marcie's own, walked over to the little nightstand in the dark, fumbled for the drawer pull and opened it, and her hands hit unerringly on the stack of paper as if she'd put them there herself. She spun around and hurried back to the hall.

"Okay. Let's go."

"What the hell do you think you're doing?"

Jeff whirled around and Marcie could see behind him to where Flint stood in the glare of the headlights streaming into the living room, his face hard with fury.

Flint

Middle of a damn hurricane and the girl was here. Marcie.

He and Isobel had waited out the first half of the storm in her house's only bathroom—too much like last time, except just the two of them now, the bathtub filled with water and each of them at separate corners of the tiny room, Flint telling himself, over and over, that he didn't care what happened to Marcie. Whether she was safe.

In the eerie silence of the eye he'd heard sounds from outside—an engine starting up, the dull thud of a car door. Someone thinking the storm was over. Isobel'd made him go check on the moron, and he'd seen that the car was in his own driveway, his front door gaping open. Goddamn looters.

Unarmed and old and fucking lame, what did he think he was going to do? But he'd been inside the back door before he'd thought, seen the silhouette of a strange man standing in his hallway, and his rage roared up. If Flint had had his old .45 the man standing there would have been down before he'd said a word.

"What the hell do you think you're doing?"

When he whipped around, Flint saw Marcie standing there, and relief cascaded over him. "Don't you even know enough to get out of the way of a storm, you idiot?"

"Who are you?" the man challenged, blocking Marcie again with his body.

"This is my goddamn house. Who are you?"

"It's okay," Marcie said, pushing past the man. And then to him: "Where were you?"

"You need to get the hell out of here. The island's gonna flood."

"I told you, Marcie," the man said. "Come on."

"You keep out of it!" Flint barked the words.

"Stop it!" Marcie glared at Flint. "Come on—Jeff's car is out front."

"I'm not going anywhere."

"Then neither am I."

Little stick of a thing, arms crossed, jaw set. Facing off with him like a pit bull.

"Suit yourself." Flint turned for the back door.

"Idiotic," he thought he heard that son of a bitch say, and Flint turned around.

"Hurry up, if you're coming. And bring that asshole with you if you have to."

Marcie

arcie carried one of the milk crates, the ribboned pack of letters tucked on top, shoving the other into Jeff's arms as they followed Flint to the back door and outside. By the third step off the porch they were standing in water. Jeff shook his head, but marched along, across what used to be the narrow strip of sand behind the sea grapes—behind where the turtle nest would have been washed away if they hadn't dug it up.

Flint walked around the next-door neighbor's house, past where he had shoved Isobel's dented trash can, but there was nothing there now. He walked up the front steps and let himself inside the front door as if it were his.

He let the screen door loose behind him, and Jeff caught it before it crashed shut in his face, his left hand shooting out while he angled his body to balance the heavy crate. "Great guy," he murmured as he stood against it to let Marcie in.

"Who was it?" The voice was Isobel's, from the back of the

house. She came out holding a small unlit camp lantern and a brown paper grocery sack. She had lights, although they were dim—had to be a generator. Flint moved to take the bag from her, only then turning around to look at Marcie and Jeff.

"The hell you got?"

"Your books," Marcie said, hefting the crate up a few inches as if to show him. "What we could carry. I was afraid they'd get ruined."

"Of course they will. Everything will if the water comes high enough. You gonna eat books? Drink 'em? Foolishness."

"And your daughter's letters," she said as if he hadn't spoken. "You're welcome."

"That was very thoughtful of you." Isobel's eyes were tired but kind. "Why don't you put the crates on the dining table? Herman, give me that back," she said, reaching for the bag. "There's more in the cupboard you can go get."

"Storm's about to blow up again," he countered, but disappeared into the kitchen.

Marcie put the crate down where the woman had indicated, Jeff following suit behind her.

"I haven't met your fella. Isobel Dominguez."

Marcie instinctively opened her mouth to issue a denial—*He's not my fella*. How silly. She was married. But Jeff stepped to her to take the bag, and Isobel put out a hand.

"Jeff Walker."

Marcie looked over at Jeff, startled. How had she not known his last name?

"If the damn cotillion introductions are over, there's a hurricane outside about ready to pick back up." Flint had charged back into the room.

Isobel didn't seem to register his gruff rudeness as she put a gentle hand on his shoulder. "Come on, Herman—let's get these young people into the bathroom before things get too exciting."

Marcie knew the rules of safety in a storm—get to a place with no windows; interior walls near the center of the house and plumbing walls were more structurally sound—but she hated the idea of being caged in a small room with Flint and Jeff posturing at each other like betta fish. That bizarre moaning was starting again faintly, though, and Marcie knew there was no choice. She grabbed the pile of letters as they filed into the little bathroom, where she saw the Igloo cooler they'd packed the turtle eggs into.

"You gonna eat turtles? Drink 'em?" she asked Flint dryly.

"Don't be smart."

A shriek from the house announced the other side of the storm, and Jeff closed the door behind him, pressing himself in the corner between it and the small linen closet, next to Marcie. Isobel perched on the closed commode as gracefully as if it were a Louis Quatorze chair, and Flint jammed himself into the corner where the vanity met the wall, as far from everyone else as he could get in the minuscule space, his arms crossed, his face sour. With four of them crammed inside, the room felt ridiculously tiny—and hot. No one spoke as the groans outside grew louder.

"This what you were doing when you stayed out all night?" Flint's glare fixed on Jeff, but the question was for Marcie.

She looked directly at him. "I thought you didn't care what I do?"

"Didn't say I cared."

"Then don't ask."

"Could be a long night in here," Isobel said pleasantly. "Might as well get to know one another. What is it you do, Jeff?"

"I'm sure we can guess."

"Herman, enough. Jeff?"

"I'm an artist, ma'am. Clay."

"An artist! How lovely. And do you sell your pieces any-where?"

Flint snorted.

"I do—festivals and art fairs. I do some online commissions too." Jeff was pretending Flint wasn't there, like the bratty child the older man was acting like.

"How delightful! I'll have to look up your work. And you, Marcie?"

"I . . ." Suddenly she wasn't sure how to answer that ques-tion. *I'm a hotel event planner* had tripped from her mouth on autopilot for years at networking or corporate events for herself or Will's business, but it didn't feel right anymore. *I'm a waitress* wasn't accurate now either. *I'm an artist* was just silly.

"I'm finding my way," she said finally.

Isobel gave a smile so gentle, Marcie suddenly missed Em-ily, Will's mom, with a fierce pang. "Aren't we all, sweetheart?"

Her eyes heated, and Marcie blinked and looked down to-ward the bathtub, which someone had filled with water.

"How about you, Isobel?" Jeff said into the silence. "How long have you lived here?"

"Oh, goodness. My husband and I came as soon as he was discharged—sixty-five, that was. Ten years before our son was born."

Jeff nodded, and Marcie had an insane urge to laugh at their polite party conversation while crammed into an outdated bathroom, their hostess perched on a toilet seat. "He live nearby?" Jeff asked Isobel.

"Shut your mouth." Flint had gone so quiet that his sudden growl made Marcie jump.

"Herman! That's not necessary!" Isobel didn't raise her voice, but her sharp command might as well have been shouted. "My boy passed away," she said in the same pleasant tone as before, as though they hadn't been interrupted. "Many years ago."

Jeff nodded, his face soft.

This time Marcie couldn't blink the tears away, and they crested her eyes and ran down her cheeks. She wiped them self-consciously, but they kept coming, silently, like a tap left running in a freeze. "I'm sorry," she murmured, wiping again and again. "I'm sorry." She felt Jeff's arm come around her but she shrugged it away. She didn't deserve it. Had no right to the same grief Isobel had over her lost son.

But she let herself take the washcloth he offered. "This is so . . . I'm so sorry," she said, apologizing for her embarrassing unstopped tears, for misappropriating Isobel's pain, for . . . She didn't know what.

She dabbed the cloth uselessly to her face, trying to turn away, but Jeff was to her immediate left and Flint to her right, and there was nowhere to go. And then Isobel's eyes were in front of her, kind and soft as she said gently, "Oh . . . my dear," and took Marcie into her arms, and Marcie was crying for real now, sobs wrenching out of her so hard they hurt her ribs, mortified at what she was doing, saying over and over, "I'm sorry. . . . I'm sorry. . . . I'm sorry," as the woman said nothing, simply held her for what felt like minutes on end.

And then a crash from outside seemed to shake Marcie's very bones, on its heels a shrieking sound like the agonized voice of God. She and Isobel jumped back, the older woman's hands still strong on Marcie's arms as they shared a look of alarm.

Jeff reached for the doorknob before Isobel pulled his hand away.

"Not yet, son."

"But—"

"Not yet."

Another crashing sound followed—still loud but not quite as terrifying—and in the last moment of illumination before the lights went out, Marcie looked at Flint, who hadn't moved from his spot against the vanity, to find him staring steadily at her as if no one else were there at all, and the wrath of nature weren't tearing away at the world outside this room.

Marcie

They waited out the storm in the tiny bathroom, no one bothering to light the camp lantern against the blackness. Isobel's warm presence stayed beside Marcie after Jeff moved to the narrow space between the bathtub and the toilet, he and Flint silent and invisible against the far wall. No one spoke over the howling of the hurricane.

Sometime in the middle of the night it stopped so gradually that it wasn't until Jeff spoke into the darkness that Marcie realized the storm was over.

"Is that it?"

"I think so," Isobel said. "Herman?" A click and then flickering blue light dimly illuminated Flint holding the lantern. He nodded. "Let's get some rest," she said, and her voice sounded strained and tired.

Taking the lantern gently from Flint, she showed Marcie to the spare bedroom—in the thin, cold light it cast she saw a dark coverlet over a full-size bed, wood paneling on the walls with pictures she couldn't make out and was too tired to try. Isobel glanced at Jeff, behind her, then looked back to Marcie, letting her decide. Marcie nodded and said, "Jeff. Let's get some sleep." She braced for a barb from Flint, but he stayed silent, lost in the darkness somewhere behind him. She was on the bed before Jeff closed the door, and by the time the mattress sank behind her with his weight, she was already drifting. He might have touched her, whispered something in the dark, but she didn't register it.

Silence woke her, and Marcie opened her eyes to a stillness and peace that settled over her like a blanket. The room was dark and she thought at first that it was still nighttime, but remembered the boarded-up windows. She sat up, Jeff on his back beside her on top of the bedspread, fully clothed, like her, and sound asleep. It couldn't have been more than a couple of hours since the storm had blown out, but Marcie felt as if she'd slept for a day. She eased out of the bed and opened the door, weak light seeping in from somewhere.

The room must have been Isobel's son's, though she seemed to have redecorated since he died. There were no posters on the wall, no pennants or even the marks and dings in the plaster that a rowdy young boy inflicted like a casually skinned knee. They were painted a neutral beige, the burgundy coverlet matching the curtains. The bed and dresser were plain wood and as nondescript as hotel furniture, and nowhere were the leftover trappings of boy.

But the photos told his story—an open-faced, freckled, gap-toothed kid whose image lined the walls from babyhood to toddler to gangly boy to adolescent, a few of a young man growing quickly into handsome adulthood . . . and then no others.

Marcie moved closer to make out details in the faint illumination. Isobel was visible in the boy's eyes, the angle of his eyebrows, the shape of his jaw and chin. The smile was that of the man digging in the sand beside him; posed with a pitcher's mitt and baseball while the boy, in a blue-and-white uniform, leaned into the crook of his arm; standing proudly with an arm slung around the boy in his black robe and cap. She loved what Isobel had done with her son's space—she hadn't left it as a frozen memorial of her lost child, as Flint had done in his daughter's room. She'd adapted it into something useful for the life she had now, but kept the boy as part of the décor, part of the fabric of the room, her house, everything.

She heard sounds—the clap of a cupboard and the clink of glass—and headed out into the house. Light crept around corners enough for her to see the empty living room and the movements of someone in the adjacent kitchen.

"Isobel?" she called softly, walking in that direction.

She appeared in the doorway, a steaming mug in her hands, shadows under her eyes like thumbprints. "Good morning, Marcie. Do you drink coffee?"

"So much."

"Here." She held the mug out to Marcie. "Take this one and I'll make another."

"Thank you." Marcie took it gratefully and followed the older woman as she turned back into the kitchen. "Is the power back on?"

"I'm afraid not. I boiled some bottled water and made instant. Can't promise it'll be delicious, but at least it'll stave off the headache." Isobel gave a weary smile. "There's powdered creamer if you need it—it won't make instant coffee any more palatable, but it's best not to open the refrigerator as long as we can."

"I'm fine," she said, taking a sip. "Have you been outside?"

Isobel nodded grimly as she poured more water from a gallon jug into a pan on a two-burner camp stove. "I stepped out with Herman earlier this morning. It's . . . not good, I'm afraid. Particularly for his house."

Marcie glanced back at the sofa, a folded blanket and pillow on its arm, and wondered whether Flint had slept there or with Isobel, before the rest of her words sank in. "What happened?"

"Well, first the flood . . . Then the roof blew off. Everything inside is gone. Ruined." Pain dropped over her expression as if long familiar with her face. "I offered to help salvage anything we could, but he didn't want my assistance. You know how he can be."

She did, Marcie realized. Flint was too proud to accept help from anyone, even when he needed it. Even when he offered it to someone else, the way he had when he picked her up off the beach, let her stay in his home. She remembered his expression last night when her tears had finally broken out of whatever numb patina had been over her since leaving Will, his earlier rancor gone, his gaze like a steadying arm keeping her on her feet.

"I think I'm going to head over there," she said.

Isobel nodded toward Marcie's bare feet. "You'll need some shoes, dear. There's a pair of waders there by the back door." While Marcie pulled them on, Isobel poured the boiling water into another mug, dissipating the flower of brown as she stirred, and handed it to Marcie. "Take this to him."

"Jeff's still sleeping," Marcie said. It seemed odd to leave him in the house with a woman he—either of them—barely knew. "I can wake him and—"

"Let him sleep; we'll be fine. Go on."

Isobel opened the back door for her and Marcie gasped when she did. If she hadn't known where she was, she'd have had no idea—the landscape had changed overnight. The house seemed to be sailing on a shallow sea, water surrounding it and as far as Marcie could see, littered with floating debris—beach chairs and frayed, torn foliage, jagged strips of wood and other pieces of things Marcie couldn't identify. Palm trees lay half out of the water like scattered pickup sticks, their tops stripped.

She saw Flint sitting on the top step of his back deck—the only step visible on the rickety deck somehow standing perfectly intact above the water, as though it were made of bedrock, while the house behind it . . . was a stripped skeleton. His feet in the water, he was looking out over the flat, gentle gulf with his back to his ruined house, which was just . . . walls. Jumbled contents spilled out into what used to be the yard, splintered wood and papers floating away. The sun hadn't yet risen, but it was announcing its coming arrival in a lightening sky so delicately blue and cloudless, it seemed to mock the previous night's storm.

Marcie swallowed hard and carried both mugs down the stairs, Isobel's boots sloshing into water on the second-to-last step. The thin rubber would hardly protect her feet from whatever was underneath all that water, but they were all she had.

All she had . . . *Here,* her brain filled in automatically, as an image of their house—hers and Will's—for a moment replaced the ruin in front of her.

She was careful of her footing as she made her way to his house. He didn't glance over as she sloshed closer, climbed the steps, sat down beside him, and held out the second mug.

"It's crap—instant," she said quietly, "but it's hot, and it's caffeinated." He took it without a word, and for a long time they sat and sipped and listened to the faint sound of the placid gulf.

"Is it a total loss?" Marcie said, immediately wishing she could bite back the stupid words. A child could have seen everything was destroyed.

But Flint only grunted and gave a nod. "Think so."

She looked at him, but he was still staring calmly out to sea. "I'm sorry."

"You didn't do it."

"I should have . . . gotten more stuff out."

He took another slow sip of the viscous coffee, not even seeming to register its acrid taste. "Just a bunch of old junk. Should've let it go a long time ago."

The island's quiet was strange—the nearly silent surf, no radios from the beach, even the seagulls seemed still to be sleeping, if they'd survived the storm. It felt like no one was up and stirring except for the two of them.

"So now what?" she asked.

Flint shrugged. "Now we clean it up."

She exhaled a sigh. "What a job."

"It's good to have some of my books, at least. And you got Jessie's letters. Thanks."

He wasn't looking at her, and his tone didn't change—same terse, gruff bark he always spoke in. But something inside of Marcie woke up from a long slumber and raised its head, and she lifted her eyes and followed his gaze out to the horizon, where the sea and the sky came together and led . . . anywhere at all.

She set down her empty cup and leaned, just slightly, to her right, until her shoulder touched his. He let her stay there for a few moments before he shifted, and she straightened away—until the weight of his arm settled over her shoulders and rested there, like an awkwardly perched seabird.

"You can't just leave things where they are with your daughter," she finally said quietly.

"Yeah. I know." He drew her toward him, just slightly, and she let herself lean into his side. "Same goes for your husband."

His shoulder was warm and strong against hers. "I know."

Together they sat and watched the sky brighten as the battered island slowly woke up.

The power was out throughout the island, Isobel told Marcie when she walked back over to the woman's house—Flint had told her to go on; he wanted to sit for a bit longer. The older woman sat in her worn armchair, Jeff now awake and on the sofa, a small battery-powered radio on the coffee table between them that gave scratchy reports of the damage. The bridge was closed too, due to possible structural damage, Jeff added. Not that it would have mattered—even the road was impassable with all of Marea covered by nearly two feet of water, and help wouldn't be coming from the mainland till it ebbed. The island was cut off for the time being, and anyone who hadn't evacuated—which would be most of the residents, Marcie thought, given the storm's original projected path farther north—was encouraged to stay inside until the surge water retreated.

Jeff's car was dead. All the vehicles would be, he told them—ruined by the salt water that had swirled up into the undercarriages. Compared to what Flint had lost she couldn't worry about her car, but she felt the bite of guilt about Jeff's. He hadn't wanted to come back onto the island.

"I'm going to walk back to my place," he said. He clasped Marcie's hand where she sat beside him on the couch, and she gripped his back, a wave of tenderness washing over her. Whatever had kept her feeling deadened all those weeks seemed to have been blown clean with the storm, and she felt like an exposed nerve, sensitive to everything.

"I'll come too, to help," she said, but the idea of the art studio seemed a million miles away. She was thinking of the dilapidated restaurant farther up the island, and oblivious Darla, and the old men who were practically fixtures at the bar. Surely they hadn't tried to shelter at Tequila Mockingbird. The rundown old building looked like a solid breeze would have collapsed it.

"Take water if you need it," Isobel offered.

"There's some at my place," Jeff said. "But thanks."

"I'll be back later," Marcie told Isobel, rising with Jeff. "If . . . that's okay?"

"Of course it is," she said. "We'll all be getting cozy for a bit."

Isobel pressed peanut butter and jelly sandwiches on them before they left. There was something comforting about sitting at her kitchen table, eating the familiar food off a napkin while Isobel bustled about the kitchen. Twenty minutes later she and Jeff were slogging north, toward the studio and his apartment.

Marcie had been worried that water would pour into her boots and weigh them down, but the level seemed lower—the road was slightly higher than the houses along the beach, or else the surge was already retreating. They had to dodge floating debris, and be careful of their footing—there was no way to see where they were walking, and now and then one of them would step on or off a curb, or a dip in the road, or something else—spongy or rigid, unseen beneath the surface—and stumble.

The damage was erratic—most of the structures they passed were fine, windows intact beneath tape, a few boarded up, shingles or roof tiles missing in patches, but otherwise untouched. And then here and there some were totaled like Flint's house, one structure decimated while the buildings on either side of it looked perfectly intact, as though the fist of God had smashed straight down. In front of one of those a gray-headed man and woman stood out front looking at the rubble, the woman lean-ing against the man, his arm around her sagging shoulders.

More people were out now, doors and windows thrown open in buildings along the sidewalk, revealing their inhabitants bus-tling about inside; some sitting outside on porches or lawn chairs barely above the water, idle; one lady standing on a third-story balcony of a hotel, staring down at them with a strangely blank face.

At Pearl Street a palm tree had fallen into a tiny yellow cot-tage, tearing through the awning and barricading the front door. A group of people worked to move the thick trunk, and Marcie and Jeff joined in to help. Together they lifted it on its base like a fulcrum, swiveling it away from the house and let-ting it fall alongside. A ragged cheer went up, and the owner came out through her cleared front door with an armful of so-das and waters, passing them out to her neighbors.

The sun was up in full force now, and the heat was already rising. With the exertion and the humidity, Marcie felt as wet on the top as she did from the knees down. The air smelled heavy and dank, like fish and sulfur.

By unspoken agreement they headed toward the studio first. The building was still standing, the roof and windows intact as though the little studio had decided to simply sit out the storm. The only evidence that it had been part of the hurricane was the askew angle at which it sat—the concrete steps led off-center to the front door, the other half hanging out over the water like the prow of a ship.

"Lifted off the foundation," Jeff said, leaning to unlock the door. He swung himself inside and Marcie followed his lead, holding her breath.

The interior, lit by the sunshine streaming through the pris-tine windows, was like stepping back in time a day. It looked just as it had the last time Marcie had left it—not a piece disarranged, nothing disturbed. It was as though the storm had simply passed it right by. Jeff gave a humorless chuckle.

"Not a scratch inside—and the building's going to be condemned."

She already knew what they'd find when Jeff pointed her toward his apartment, half a duplex squatting directly on the sand. It was situated on a slight decline, downslope from the studio, and unlike the raised building behind it, the concrete-block house sat flat on its foundation.

The kitchen door was open and water swirled seamlessly from the exterior inside. Jeff waded in, the water past his shins, and headed for the back of the small space while Marcie waited in the kitchen.

A moment later he emerged and shook his head.

"Insured?" she asked.

"No. But it doesn't matter—it's just stuff. Everything I cared about is in the studio."

She put a hand on his arm. "Still . . . I'm sorry."

"A lot of people lost more than that."

She nodded. "I have to check on my friends from work. Will you be okay here?"

"I'll come with you. I'd rather do something to help."

She nodded, and in the flooded mess of his kitchen he put his arms around her. After a moment she did the same.

Marcie heard the bar before she saw it. As they approached Tequila Mockingbird she thought she was hearing music, and by the time she'd passed the surf shop in front of the building she could make out the incongruously cheerful sound of the Beach Boys. "California Girls" poured out onto the beach at top volume—almost loud enough to drown out the cacophony of voices buzzing underneath.

Like its grizzled, scrappy denizens, Tequila Mockingbird looked as if it had come through the wringer—huge chunks of siding missing, a few of the windows blown out, with jagged shards still clinging to the edges, part of its tin roof peeled back like a can of sardines—but it was still standing.

Marcie and Jeff walked up the wheelchair ramp—two of the wooden stairs were missing, and one looked completely cracked through—and rounded the corner on the beach-facing side of the restaurant, where the storm surge had begun to recede.

The deck was a mess, some of the picnic tables overturned or blown into a pile—a few had made it over the railing and lay legs up on the sand, like playful dogs awaiting a belly scratch. The sliders along the back wall had been thrown open—or blown off—and the entire back of the bar was open to the surf.

And inside, the bar was packed.

Every table and chair was full, the bar was wall-to-wall, and people stood in nearly every spare inch of floor space. Judging from the volume, the frequent shrieks of laughter, and the couple of people sprawled out on the few standing benches outside, there was some drinking going on.

"Marce!"

The voice was Art's, sitting in his usual spot at the bar, waving his arm frenetically to get her attention, and from his saturnine grin and unfocused eyes, he was feeling no pain. "Beer!" he said happily, lofting a glass.

Beside him, Bink and Petey had followed the direction of Art's announcement and noticed Marcie's arrival. Petey grinned and waved, and held up his own empty glass. "Marcie, check it out!" he said, then swooped the glass to the taps and opened one up. Foam spilled over the top, which he quickly leaned forward and sucked away.

Either Darla had given him special dispensation, or she was dead. Despite her laid-back attitude about the bar, no one touched her taps but staff. Not even the regulars.

A touch on her elbow swung Marcie around, and there stood Darla herself. Out of her lair she always seemed tiny, coming up only to Marcie's shoulder, and her mass of frizzy hair tickled Marcie's nose as the woman wrapped an arm around her and gave an uncharacteristic squeeze.

"The gang was worried about you, girl. Good that you're here. Grab a glass! Power's out and ain't no way of knowing when it's coming back—might as well drink it before it gets warm."

Before Marcie could respond or think to introduce Jeff, Darla was gone again, her diminutive frame melting into the crowd.

Jeff was staring around at the packed house. "Do they even know there was a hurricane?" he asked.

Marcie made her way to the bar, Jeff trailing along. Petey and Arthur gave her sloppy hugs and cleared a tiny space for her to stand between them.

"You guys didn't wait out the storm here, did you?" she asked as Petey slapped a beer into her palm. She passed it back to Jeff, offering quick introductions.

"Not me," Bink said. "The wife woulda had my ass—sorry, Marce—my fanny."

Marcie just stared at him. She'd literally never been here when Bink hadn't been planted at the bar. He had a *wife*?

He went on, oblivious: "Think Darla stuck it out here, though. You know her—I think she thought she could bully the storm outta hurting her bar." He gave a cackle. "Probably did too!" He handed her a second beer, and Marcie took a long, grateful sip. It wasn't as cold as it could have been—as Darla painstakingly ensured it was—but at that moment it was the best thing she'd ever drunk.

She indicated the capacity crowd with her glass. "What's the deal?"

Petey shrugged. "This is how Darla does. When a storm hits and the power gets knocked out, she opens the place up. Food'll go bad anyway, she says."

"We take care of our own." Marcie hadn't seen Darla resume her usual station, but she was leaning against the other side of the bar toward them, a full glass in front of her. "We're gonna fire up a few grills outside later on and cook everything in the walk-in. You and your boyfriend here oughta stick around."

"Hurricane party!" Bink announced.

"I have to get back and check on the friend I'm staying with," Marcie shouted over the crowd. "Just wanted to make sure you guys were okay."

Darla was pulling another beer off the tap. "Invite him over! More the merrier."

Marcie put her half-empty beer down, turning around to Jeff. "I need to—"

He set his own mug on the bar and reached for her hand. "Let's go."

Flint

Flint hadn't moved from his back deck when Isobel rounded the corner twenty minutes after Marcie had left. He didn't know why he was still sitting there, except that looking out to the horizon felt better than turning to see the terrible mess behind him.

She carried sandwiches on two paper plates, and handed him one as she sat beside him on the stair.

"I'm not hungry," he said, taking it anyway.

"Eat, Herman. We've got a lot of work ahead of us."

He took a bite—nothing special, just peanut butter and jelly on whole-wheat bread—but Isobel had always had a way of making anything taste exceptional. He and Jessie used to dissect her meals—literally and figuratively, trying to figure out exactly how she made even the simplest things so delicious. She used the exact right amount of peanut butter, the perfect ratio of jelly, the bread squishy soft.

He scoffed at himself as he chewed. It was a sandwich. No need to get sentimental about it.

"Thanks," he remembered to say finally. She just nodded, chewing her own sandwich.

After they finished she took his plate from him and set them beside her. "Let's unboard my house, since there's no power and we need the light," she said. "That's a quick job, and then we can start cleaning some of this up. You'll stay with me in the meantime."

He wiped his hands on his pants, giving himself time to think before he answered her. He wanted to protest that he didn't need her help, didn't want to stay with her. But he did. On both counts.

"Why are you doing this, Isobel?" he said instead.

"Doing what?"

"This," he said, flinging out a hand to indicate the sandwiches, her presence. She was going to make him spell it out. "All of it. Helping me. Being nice. I haven't given you any reason to."

Isobel smiled softly, and in it he saw the woman he'd known so well so long ago. "You did. Once."

He looked back out to the horizon. "A long time ago. A whole lifetime."

He could see her nodding in his peripheral vision. "Yes. A few people's lifetimes. Robert's. Berto's."

"Don't, Is."

"But not ours, though," she said as if he hadn't interrupted her. "Ours are still going on. We're not through yet, are we, you tough old bird?"

He snorted. "Look who's talking, you ironclad virago."

She laughed at that, the sound light as birdsong, and leaned in to bump his shoulder with her own. "A fine pair, you and I. I always thought so."

He tried to grunt out something skeptical, but it came out as a hum that sounded more like agreement.

"Now get off your ass, old man, and let's get some work done while it's still light out." Isobel stood up and took a step down, not even seeming to notice her feet splashing into a channel of water trapped behind a small berm. She turned around and put a hand out to Flint.

And without a thought, he reached out and took it.

Unboarding was always easier than boarding up. They started on the back deck, Isobel bracing the plywood in place while he unscrewed them, and then together they stacked them on end against the railing at one side. On the side windows, where he had to get a ladder, he simply let them fall, and one of the old boards cracked in half when it hit the floodwater, another floating off down-island. Isobel made to go after that one, but Flint stopped her.

"Those aren't going to be any good for another storm," he said. "It's about time we got you some real storm shutters."

"Those are expensive, Herman," she said, but she had sloshed back to stand near the ladder, shielding her eyes as she looked up at him.

"Let me take care of that."

"Don't be ridiculous. You have your own house to worry about."

Flint lumbered back down the ladder, his knees reminding him he was too old to be doing this for too many more hurricanes anyway. He stood on the bottom rung, and as short as she was already, she was a good two feet below him still. "Isobel, if you want me to stay here until I have a house again—or until you figure out what a sorry idea that was—then you're going to have to let me do a few things. I'm not taking your charity."

"I wasn't offering charity," she snapped back. "And I *will* take the damn shutters, since you didn't have the sense God gave a goat to build up on stilts, and you've spent every storm worth a spit taking shelter at *my* house."

"Good!"

"Fine!" she said, and then she burst into laughter. "Oh, my. I have missed you."

Flint shook his head as he stepped off into the water and headed around the front. "Crazy woman," he muttered, but even he could hear that it sounded like an endearment.

They were halfway through taking the second board off the front windows when one of the people they'd seen passing by now and again where the street used to be sloshed into Flint's driveway and stood staring at his ruined house. A man, backpack over his shoulders and carrying a duffel; early to mid-forties, clean-cut brown hair, lean but not skinny. He moved through the shin-deep water to where Flint's front door used to be, and he stood there with a disturbingly blank look.

Flint caught Isobel's eye. She was holding the side of the board he'd already unscrewed while he worked on the other side. She raised her brows and then moved her gaze back to the stranger.

"Hey!" Flint called. "Can I help you?"

The man looked up, saw Flint and Isobel. "I . . . This isn't . . ." His voice was dry as sand. "I'm looking for Marcie Malone."

Flint stiffened. "What do you—"

A hand on his elbow, softly. "Herman," Isobel said, low.

Flint took a breath. "Yeah," he called shortly to the man.

"Hang on." He finished unscrewing the plywood, and he and Isobel lowered it and moved it across to lean against the other one. He handed her the drill, brushed the sawdust off his hands on his pants, and clomped down the stairs and toward the stranger.

Up close, the man's face looked . . . shattered. "Is she . . . She wasn't in here when . . ."

"Mind if I ask who you are?" he said, keeping his tone level.

"I'm Will Malone. Her husband."

Flint stopped where he stood, four feet out from where the man was still on his front doorstep, as though there were one. He glanced back to Isobel, whose fingertips had flown to her lips.

"Please," Will said. "Just tell me if she's—"

"She's fine," Flint said. "Safe."

Everything in the man seemed to let go, as if he'd been holding himself taut for hours. "Jesus. Thank God. The storm hit, and I couldn't reach her, and . . . and then this." He gestured to the house. "I kept hoping I had the wrong address."

Flint walked closer through the swirling water, made himself extend a hand. "I'm Flint. This is my house. Marcie's been staying with me."

Will stood straighter, his eyes sharpening on Flint. "You're . . . Oh." He glanced over Flint's shoulder; Isobel must have come up behind him.

"I'm Isobel. I live next to Mr. Flint and his friend Marcie." She put a subtle emphasis on "friend." Always setting everyone at ease, Isobel was. "I believe a cell tower got knocked out in the storm—or maybe the lines are just too busy, but in any case, there was no way to make any calls. You must have been worried."

"You have no idea, ma'am."

"Well, Marcie's gone to help some of the people she knows

on the island, but she'll be back before long, I'd expect. Why don't you come into my house? That's where we all weathered the storm—Herman here, Marcie, and me."

Isobel squeezed Flint's arm as she listed three names, not four. He didn't need her prodding not to fill in the last blank, for Christ's sake—he wasn't a complete ox. He left her arm tucked into his as they led the man up the stairs to her house.

"You can leave your things by the door for now, son," she said as they walked inside. "Have a seat." She indicated the living room, and Will lowered himself to the sofa. Flint followed, standing facing him at the end of the couch until her strong hand pressed into the small of his back, pushing him toward the armchair.

"Why don't both of you just relax?" she said as Flint sank grudgingly into Robert's chair. "You must be exhausted if you've come through the storm, Will. I can't offer much in the way of hospitality, but would you like something to drink—perhaps a sandwich?"

"I actually missed the storm itself, ma'am. It went straight across the peninsula and blew out over the Atlantic. Something to drink would be welcome. Thank you."

"Isobel, please," she said. "I'll be right back, gentlemen." Behind Will's head she fixed Flint with a hot look as she walked toward the kitchen, as if she didn't trust him not to chew this kid to pieces.

Women.

Will was looking around the room, as if hunting for traces of his absent wife. Flint cleared his throat, drawing the man's attention. Marcie's husband leaned forward, elbows on knees, and seemed to be hunting for words.

"Can I ask you . . ." he said finally, then stopped, gave a slight shake of his head, rubbed his temple. "Just . . . how is she?"

Flint stared at the man, trying to get his measure. A husband she'd run from—hard enough to wind up near dead on the beach when he'd found her.

"Island's flooded. How'd you get on?" he asked instead of answering. He heard the abruptness of his question a moment too late. Maybe Isobel wasn't totally off the mark to doubt his rusty social skills, but he wasn't giving away a damn thing to this man until he knew what Marcie wanted.

"Oh . . . yeah. They're turning people back at that bridge. I think it got damaged. Anyway, there's a street running along the other side of this bay back here. They weathered things a little better than you did, by the way. I parked there and walked till I found a house with a little dinghy on their dock out back—rang the doorbell and offered to buy it."

Huh. He was scrappier than he looked.

"How'd you track her down?"

The man looked confused. "I didn't. I had the address." He reached into a pocket of his jeans and pulled out a crumpled piece of paper, torn from a larger one. "I . . . She'd asked me to send her some things."

So she wasn't trying to hide from the guy, at least. That told him something.

"Where's the dinghy?"

He looked perplexed again, as if Flint were asking the wrong questions. "I left it on the dock I found at the end of one of these side streets. Pearl, maybe?"

"Gonna get stolen."

"I don't really care." His tone had sharpened, and Flint was glad to see some backbone in him. He couldn't see Marcie with a milquetoast.

Isobel came back into the room and some of the tension fled in her wake. The guy looked relieved not to have to deal solely with Flint anymore.

"I went ahead and put together something to eat. In case you want it." She set a plate down on the cocktail table—a real plate this time, not paper. Even in the aftermath of a hurricane, Isobel always had class. It held sandwiches cut delicately into diagonal quarters, some kind of chips, carrot sticks. She offered the glass of water she held directly to Will. "Nothing fancy, but it'll take the edge off."

"This is more than kind, ma'am—Isobel," he corrected himself. "Thank you."

She sat beside him on the sofa, a buffer between him and where Flint glowered at him from the armchair.

"You picked an unfortunate time to visit our little beach town," she said conversationally as Will picked up one of the sandwich triangles and finished it in two bites. He took another one immediately as he nodded his response—despite his averral, he must have been starving.

"Yes, ma'am, I can see that." He pushed his gaze over to Flint with a clear effort. "That's terrible about your house."

Flint grunted.

"What will you do now?" he went on.

Isobel shot Flint a soft smile that brought a strange prickling warmth into his chest. "Herman is staying with me for a while. We go very far back together, he and I."

Will nodded again, reaching for another segment of sandwich and making a clear effort to be polite and not wolf it down. "And . . . Marcie?" Her name bubbled out of him, as though after Flint's earlier shutting down of that line of inquiry it had been an effort not to ask about her. "Will she . . . Have you invited her to stay as well?"

"Of course, dear. She's welcome here too."

"Marcie has a home anywhere I am. Anytime she needs it."

Flint didn't mean for it to come out as a threat, but he heard it in his words.

Will simply met his gaze. "Thank you," he said quietly, and that was all.

Flint shifted uncomfortably in the armchair. He needed to get out of here before he actually started liking the son of a bitch. He pushed himself up and started for Isobel's front door.

"Herman?"

Her voice stopped him. "Need a little air," he said to the front door. "I'm tired of sitting around, Is." He turned around to see her standing, Will getting to his feet too. Her face was drawn into lines of concern.

What the hell was he thinking? He couldn't leave her alone with him. He stood a moment longer, then walked slowly back toward her living area. "I'll stay."

Isobel met him halfway and put a hand on the inside of his elbow. Without thinking he put his own on top of it, and the feel of her skin was a jolt—softer than he remembered, like worn chamois, the skin papery thin over plump veins, but the feel of her fingers so familiar.

"No, you're right," she said, and her eyes were shining with something that felt like approval. "Why don't you take a bit of a walk? You might even run across Marcie, and let her know her husband is here."

Jesus. He hadn't been thinking. Marcie would show back up with that . . . well, with the *fella*, as Isobel had called him. And find the husband she'd fled sitting here waiting.

He wasn't going to let her walk into this situation ignorant.

He patted Isobel's hand gently, gave her fingers a squeeze, and let go. "Right. You're okay here?" He was looking only at Isobel as he said it, and her firm nod eased his tight shoulders a little.

"We're just fine. I'm sure Will could use some time to relax after his trip, and all that worry. And you won't be long . . . ?" Her voice lifted just a fraction at the end, enough to tell him that she wasn't quite as sanguine as she appeared. Not concerned about herself or her own well-being, though, he realized. Marcie's.

He put a hand on her shoulder to reassure her.

"Thank you, Herman," she said, low enough for only his ears.

He nodded shortly, shot one last warning glare at Will—who met it unflinchingly—and then brought his eyes back to Isobel's, for one moment wishing he were the kind of man who could take her face between his hands and tell her something tender and reassuring. "I won't be long," he grated out instead. And more gently: "I promise."

He waded up an island gone soggy and humid, debris everywhere, pieces of damaged buildings and cars and trees floating past or damming up against other debris. The water had mostly receded now, though, and as always, the locals had begun the laborious process of cleaning up and starting over.

He checked the little art studio she'd shown him first, the building intact but askew on its foundation—no way to fix that. The door was locked, and no one answered his knock. That yahoo she had with her, the artist . . . she said he lived near the gallery, didn't she? There were houses on either side, and a duplex behind it near the street with a similar paint job as the art building, but the first two yielded shell-shocked tourists who'd never heard of the guy, and the third was flooded out and deserted.

He slogged farther up the beach until he reached the Tequila Mockingbird sign—half a block south of the actual building. Nearing the place itself he was surprised to hear loud music and voices—the place was packed to the gills, like the bar wasn't literally hanging in strips around them. A few mismatched charcoal grills were going on the back deck, every inch of their surfaces covered in meat, and someone had covered a picnic table in a few inches of wet sand and a layer of what looked like tinfoil and built a bonfire on it, and on a metal stand over that, a couple of old guys were tending what looked to be a huge pot serving as a makeshift deep fryer, a third one filling up red cardboard baskets with whatever was coming out of it and passing them around to the crowd.

Sweet Mary. A hurricane had ripped through town and these people were having beach blanket bingo like they didn't have a worry in the world.

He pushed his way through the crowd until he could get close enough to the bar to shout to the little blond troll of a woman behind it, "Hey! Marcie been here? Malone?"

"Hey—Gramps! Welcome back. She sure has, baby. Want a beer?" She grabbed an empty mug from under the counter and poised it under the taps, bleached-out eyebrows raised for his reply.

"No . . . thanks. I'm just trying to find her."

The woman looked around the room, as if searching for Marcie—like Flint hadn't already done that—and seemed surprised not to see her. "She *was* here—with that man cake of hers. Musta left."

No shit. But at least he knew she'd been here. If she was already on her way back to Isobel's, she'd be blindsided.

"Any idea where she was headed?" he asked.

The troll offered him a grin, gapped teeth white against the leather of her skin as she pulled the tap and poured the beer she'd offered Flint, then took a sip. "Back to you, darlin'. She was worried aboutcha."

Two weeks ago he'd have snapped back that he didn't need worrying over, but all that came out was "Yeah. Okay. Thanks."

"And hey, you find her, y'all come on back. Ya gotta eat, right?" She cackled, hacked, held out a hand. "I'm Darla. You're welcome here anytime, big guy. Any friend'a Marcie's, am I right?"

Flint looked down at the tanned hide of her wrinkled hand for just a moment before he took it, engulfing it with his. For all her withered size, the woman had an iron grip. "You're right. And . . . thanks," he managed. He'd said it more times today— made more physical contact—than he had in the last twenty years. "I'm Herman."

Darla smiled at him, her eyes narrowing to squinty little commas in her face. "*Mucho gusto*, Herman. FYI, I ain't gonna remember that later, so let's make sure to do this again then."

He left her bent over the bar, resting her weight on those shriveled strong hands, laughing and coughing at the same time.

Marcie

The afternoon sun was braising Palmetto Key, heat rising up in a heavy, wet sheet off the saturated ground.

By now everyone still on the island—which, given the lack of warning of the hurricane's abrupt path change, was pretty much everyone—seemed to be outside as Marcie and Jeff walked back toward Isobel's house. But for all the activity, there was little for them to do. Bewildered tourists could do nothing but stand outside their hotels and condos, staring dazedly at the vacation paradise that had turned into a water-logged prison overnight, while locals seemed to have gathered in clumps, waiting for the sea to recede before beginning the slow process of putting their lives back in order.

Marcie and Jeff stopped a couple of times—once to help a woman search for her dog, along with several other neighbors who combed the street until the animal was found, trembling and curled up underneath a torn-off piece of siding four houses

down. When the dog—a midsize mutt who looked even more of
a mongrel with his fur wet and matted—saw his owner, he un-
coiled himself in one fluid move and raced to her like a shot, the
woman crouching to enfold him into her arms and letting him
joyfully lick her face and neck. The second time they veered off
the road toward one of the bungalow hotels along Marea, where
a slight young guy wrangled to clear the debris packed around
his car to get inside while a petite woman barely out of girlhood
held an infant and watched from the raised porch. Marcie stood
with the girl and the baby while the two men tossed aside
branches, palm fronds, and trash until the kid could wrest one
door open. He ducked inside and came out with a baby carrier
and a box of diapers, and his wife laughed and started to cry.
Marcie rubbed the woman's arm, her fingers grazing the baby's
velvet skin, lifted her hand and cupped the fine hairs at the
back of the child's neck for a moment, and the mother smiled at
her through her tears and offered to let her hold the baby. She
did, the little girl's bare torso like silk against her arms. She bent
her head to touch her lips to the chick down on top of the baby's
head, smelling Johnson's Baby Lotion, then held the child back
to her mother and rejoined Jeff on the sidewalk as the parents
called their appreciation.

   He took her hand as they walked on toward Isobel's, and the
warm, full feeling that had flowered in Marcie's chest last night
at the party spread its tendrils. The island wasn't devastated—
for the most part the buildings and most of the trees had weathered the storm, and the beach would recover from the flooding.
The islanders didn't give up so easily—she saw it in Darla and
the Mockingbird gang, in Jeff's sanguine acceptance of the
water flooding his house, in every person they'd passed or stopped
to help. From Isobel, and from Flint. Hurricanes were a part of

living at the sea's edge, and the people of Palmetto Key accepted the bad with the good, and held steady.

When she heard someone calling her name from somewhere down the street, it didn't even feel surprising—of course people here knew her. She was one of them. She recognized the voice just as she realized that most everyone she knew on the island was either with her, behind her at Tequila Mockingbird, or before them at Isobel's. She looked over toward the beach side of Marea to see Flint walking toward them faster than she'd ever seen him move.

"Dammit, woman," he called, splashing across the street to where she and Jeff had stopped. "Where you been? I've been looking for you." He was out of breath.

"What's wrong? Is it Isobel?" she asked, alarmed.

"Isobel's fine." He bent at the waist, rested his hands on his thighs to catch his breath.

"Are you okay?"

He straightened. "I'm fine. Everybody's fine. Your husband's waiting for you at Isobel's."

Despite the smothering wet heat, Marcie felt a chill prickle her hands, her face, her feet. She saw Jeff take a step back from the corner of her eye, heard water squelching as he did.

"What?" she whispered.

"Will, right? Will Malone?"

One hand seemed to float up in front of her mouth, and she felt her breath bouncing against it and washing over her face. "Will is here?"

"Marcie?" Jeff was back at her side, a hand on her arm. She touched his fingers absently, but stared at Flint.

"He's there now?" she said, though Flint had already said he was.

He nodded. "What do you want me to do? Do I need to get rid of him?"

"No, I . . ." She turned to Jeff, remembering he was there. "I'm sorry, I have to . . ."

His eyes were gentle. "I know."

Tears pricked her eyes—she didn't know why. "Thank you," she said. "For . . . everything."

He looked at her for a long moment, and then one side of his mouth lifted in an almost-smile and he nodded. "See you around, Marcella." A half wave, and then he turned and started wading back toward his house.

Marcie watched for only a few steps, then turned to Flint.

"Okay," she said. "Let's go."

It should have been a shock to see him after so long. After . . . so much. Or at least some kind of impact.

But when Flint held the screen door to Isobel's house while she went inside, it was almost as if Will had always been there, was supposed to be there. The shape of his head, the way he stood at the sliding glass door, which Isobel and Flint had taken the plywood off of, looking out at the gulf, the movement of his body as he turned and saw her, and his face . . . his face as familiar as her own. It was less like reuniting than it was almost like looking into a mirror. *Of course. There you are.*

His head looked smaller somehow, but then she realized it was that his face had thinned, his neck, his eyes more noticeable in his face, larger.

Their expression had changed too. When Will used to look at her it was like a magnetic field drawing her in, grounding her. But his eyes were uncertain now, guarded. Separate.

She didn't know she'd stopped in the doorway until she felt

a gentle pressure on her shoulder, realized Flint was trying to come in behind her. She took a step forward. Another.

"Herman," she said in a voice that felt rusted. "This is Will. Will—"

"We already met," Flint said at her side.

"Oh. Right. Of course you did." She stood immobile, at a loss now that the platitudes were taken care of, she and Will just staring.

Flint took a step forward so he was in her line of sight. "We can sit down here"—he moved a hand to indicate Isobel's living area—"or outside . . . or I have some things I can go take care of. . . ." He was looking directly at Marcie now, as if Will weren't in the room. What did she want? He was asking her without saying it.

"I'm . . . I think Will and I will go for a walk."

"You sure?"

She almost wanted to laugh at Flint's protectiveness—from Will!—and the way he wasn't even trying to disguise it in politeness. She raised a hand and touched his shoulder without thinking. "I'm fine. Thank you."

Flint reached to move her hand—no, he clasped her fingers for the barest moment—and then he nodded and stepped away. "I'll see if Isobel needs some help. We'll be right here." This last was directed at Will with a finger jabbing out toward the kitchen, less a statement of location than a threat.

She caught Isobel's head popping out as Flint rounded the corner into the kitchen, hushed whispers trailing behind them.

"We'll be okay," she called after him, realizing she didn't know if it was true.

Marcie

She'd wanted to walk on the beach as they talked to make it easier—so they'd have other things to look at besides each other, be side by side instead of face-to-face. The water level was lower now—she'd noticed it was receding as she and Flint had walked back—but it was still nearly up to the steps, so they sat on the back porch at Flint's, even though there was no house there anymore.

"You've lost weight," he said in the thick silence that had fallen over them since they'd left Isobel's.

"So have you."

His gaze dropped to her hand. "You aren't wearing your ring," he said stiffly.

"Oh . . ." She fingered the place where it should have been, realizing she'd left it on Jessie's dresser. It was long gone now. Her throat ached for the loss. "It got lost in the storm."

What else was there to say? She could see from his expression that Will filled in the blanks—she hadn't been wearing it.

Marcie looked out to the gulf, gulls wheeling overhead, a kingfisher plunging straight down and arrowing into the surf with a plop she imagined she could hear. Life as usual, right back to normal as soon as the storm had passed. Except for her.

It was odd to have Will here, in a place and a life that had nothing to do with him, where she'd become someone else. And yet it was so natural to sit beside him like this, Marcie had to keep from waiting for him to take her hand, from leaning her head on his shoulder. But the space between them was too wide for that, in every way.

"How did you get here?" she said instead.

He shrugged. "Drove down through the night. Took a little motorized dinghy across the bay this morning."

Of course he had. He always looked after her, took care of her. Would do anything to make sure she was okay. Tears backed up behind her eyes and made them feel swollen, and her throat was tight. For a moment she wished she could erase the last months—go back to before the lima bean, when they were happy and uncomplicated and the thought of not being together was as bizarre and incomprehensible as removing an arm. She would look at the pregnancy test and it would be a single line instead of two, and regret would pinch her for just one second before she ran in to show Will so they could laugh together at being over forty years old and scared as teenagers of finding out they were knocked up. They'd talk wistfully for a few moments about the life they might have had if they'd taken another path, been slightly different people, had a passel of kids together. And then they'd laugh it off, go out to a nice dinner somewhere, maybe plan a vacation. Things were so much simpler.

"You didn't have to do that," she said.

"I was worried about you. The storm."

"There was no phone service." But the truth was, she hadn't thought to call.

"I know," was all he said, and she wondered if she'd spoken that last thought aloud.

The beach was full of sound now—the shushing waves, screaming birds, a plane, the chatter of neighbors addressing the damage—but silence fell smothering and heavy between the two of them.

"I thought—"

"Do you—"

They both stopped after talking at once, but didn't laugh.

He looked out toward the water, and she saw what she hadn't noticed before—the lines around his eyes were deeper and more pronounced, and there was gray above his ears that she'd never seen before. In so short a time.

"I've been trying to make sense of why you left," he started finally.

Marcie gave a short humorless laugh. "Me too. Honestly, Will, I didn't intend to. It really just . . . I think I got to a breaking point and I didn't know how to handle it."

He looked at her as if seeking something in her face he couldn't find. "Did you ever imagine this could be you and me? Sitting here like this? Struggling?"

"I did, actually. I thought it all the time."

His head jerked back as if she'd slapped him.

She tried to explain, feeling out the words as she spoke them. "One of the things I've realized here is that it was my biggest fear for most of our lives—losing you. It's why I let go of a lot of things I shouldn't have."

"But I never asked you to—"

"You didn't—I'm not saying that. It was my choice—every time it was my choice." It was true—when they were first married, thinking they had a child on the way, Will had never asked her to give up anything, even as hard as things were then. Together they drew up their long-range plans—Will would start college first, at night after work, and Marcie would take care of the baby. As soon as he got his degree, Marcie would go, handing off child-rearing duties, with Emily on hand to help both of them.

After she lost that pregnancy, with money so tight, they stuck to the original plan for college for Will to start first ("Because you're a man and you'll make more," she joked, except that it was true), while she got a job working the front desk at the Bonafort.

When it came time for her to go to college, she thought about her art—she'd never thought of going anywhere but art school—but by then she was establishing herself at the hotel and realizing hospitality offered a much more secure living. Art school felt like a foolish indulgence, one she'd outgrown. So she accepted Claus's offer to supplement her degree for the hotel and studied global hospitality management at Georgia State, telling herself she'd made the right choice as she worked up the ladder at the Bonafort, both of them making steady salaries with benefits that once seemed far out of their reach.

And then Will's father died, and Emily spiraled into a scattered, forgetful depression that they both worried at first was dementia, and that was when they'd scrounged together every dime for a down payment on the cheapest house in the nicest new development they could find where Emily could also buy a small house just steps away so they could take care of her, check in on her. She thought about her art from time to time, scrolling through Pinterest projects that sparked a momentary fire inside her, but almost as if it were a childish thing left behind with adulthood, like king of the hill or make-believe.

But maybe Will's fire had been banked by life too. She remembered his dad getting stung by hornets while mowing the lawn when she and Will were juniors. They hadn't realized he was allergic until then, but when his throat closed up and his face turned a terrifying shade of red, Emily called the paramedics, and they'd slid a needle into his dad's heart and then took him to the hospital for two days. Will had told her about it the next day, eyes rimmed red. Mowing the grass was one of his chores, but his dad had finally done it after Will had been putting it off one too many times for football practice. *If I'd just done what I was supposed to do,* he'd told Marcie, voice choked.

She remembered his thirtieth birthday, when Will had been miserable working as the tech manager for a food-service distributor. Marcie gave him a loaf of Wonder Bread wrapped in a gift bag and told him, "Quit. I'll be the breadwinner till you figure out what you'd rather do." He'd cried that night a little bit, pulled her to him and told her he loved her. But he'd never done it, worried about the mortgage and their retirement and the newly widowed Emily, who might have needed financial help.

What parts of himself had Will given up along the way, worried about doing right by everyone else?

"Having a child was an experience I wanted us to have, an unknown adventure," she said slowly, finding her way. "But I was afraid."

"You never seemed afraid. You seemed so certain. That was part of what scared me—that you knew so thoroughly what you wanted, that we could handle it, and I didn't. All I could think was that I was going to let you down. Let you both down." He raised his hands, let them drop to his lap. "And I did."

Heat filled her eyes. *Oh, Will.* So much weight he always

carried. She shook her head. "You need to know something, Will. I scheduled an abortion."

It was so hard to say it out loud, and a fresh ache bloomed in her chest, her throat.

He stared at her, not comprehending. "No, that's not what happened." As if he were correcting the story. As if she could possibly have it wrong. "You . . . I was there, Marce—I remember when the bleeding started, and the doctor told me—"

"The miscarriage happened the day before the appointment." Silence pulsed between them like a heartbeat.

"Why didn't you tell me?" His voice was raw.

She lifted one shoulder. "I didn't know if I was going to go through with it. And . . . I was so angry at you."

"Because I didn't . . . because of the way I reacted. Because it took me so long to accept it. I couldn't get on board for you."

That was true, at least partly. For the weeks until she had decided what she had decided, she'd waited for Will to come around, to share the thrill she'd felt from the moment she realized that they had created something together that grew— actually *grew*—inside her. But he hadn't, the prospect filling him with such visible dread each time Marcie mentioned buying baby things, or creating a nursery, or even got sick every morning like a first-trimester cliché, that finally his reluctance started to seep into her. Every worst-case scenario, every primitive fear, every story on the news about older mothers, or Down syndrome, or autism or multiple sclerosis or even fetal alcohol syndrome, for God's sake, weighed on her heart like cement. Every plan she and Will had made that had to be abandoned now—early retirement, buying an RV, traveling for months at a time—had begun to feel like a painful sacrifice. Every young mommy at the grocery store or the mall reminded her that she

would be ridiculously out of place among them at a playground
or baseball field or school play. And those fears wove together
until she felt she was suffocating underneath them, and was
paralyzed with indecision.

She waited now for the wave of venom to rush up her throat
and choke her the way it had when she'd told him she was pregnant and his face had fallen like a dynamited building. The way
it had eaten at her after the miscarriage—the fury that grew in
her like a cancer, aimed at Will with all the force of a fire hose,
until she finally had to get away from him because she couldn't
imagine ever being able to look at him and love him the same
way when she was so filled with hate for him.

Only to realize once she got away that it wasn't Will she was
angry with after all.

His face seemed to collapse from the inside. "Oh, Marce,"
he said finally, so low the words seemed part of the breeze. He
reached to take her hand and she let him. "I'm so sorry. I'm so
damned sorry for it all."

"Me too," she said ruefully. "We were both so full of fear. It's
all I could consider. I wish I hadn't let it dictate my choice—any
of my choices: art school, travel, work. But I can't go back, can't
undo a single one of those decisions. I can't 'make it right'—
neither of us can. But I can *not* make that choice again."

"What does that mean?"

"What happened to me wasn't really about the pregnancy.
Or not wholly anyway. That was just . . . what? I guess an *experience* I wanted to have. And I'll never get that same chance
again. I'm not even sure I'd want to," she cut him off when Will
made as if to protest. "But I don't want to miss out anymore on
embracing experiences. I realize how much I've been operating
from a place of fear—what might happen, what could go wrong,
what I might lose. *Who* I might lose." She squeezed his hand,

then pulled her own back to her lap. "I don't want to live like that anymore—according to the negatives. 'What-if' has felt like a cautionary tale for me, a warning—for both of us—instead of limitless opportunity. But living 'safe' means you always stay where you are, in one place." She smiled softly. "In your toad hole."

"What?"

She shook her head. "Something someone at work told me."

"What about work? What did you tell them about—"

"I'm not going back to the hotel."

She hadn't known it until the words came out of her mouth, but even as they did she knew the truth of it. She was done there.

"What do you . . . You mean, you want to change jobs? To go back to school? Do you want to adopt a child? Whatever you want, Marce, I'll support it. I promise. I—"

"I don't know what I want yet. But I know I don't want that anymore—not just the hotel but all of it, living my life stuck in place, afraid to take chances. I can't do it. I want to live forward, outward. Open to anything. Diving into the unknown. If the worst happens, then it does—I can handle it. I know that now."

His head shook back and forth, slowly, like a windshield wiper trying to clear the screen. "I don't know if I can live like that."

"I'm not asking you to."

In a sudden lull of the breeze it felt as if all the oxygen in the world had been sucked away.

"What . . . what does that mean?" Will scraped out finally.

"Will . . ." She reached and took his hand again, cradling it in hers on his thigh. "I've spent the last twenty-five years so grateful for having you that I've been terrified of losing you."

"You're not going to lose me, Marcie—"

"You can't promise that. No one can. But even if you could, I have to find out what else matters to me—just me—besides making sure I have you in my life. I can't imagine it without you." She squeezed gently, took a breath. "But I think I need to—at least for a while."

His face twisted in on itself like a house with the studs removed. His brows were pulled low, his mouth tight, and after a moment she saw he was trying not to cry. The realization nearly undid her. "I screwed up, Marce."

"We both did."

"You didn't do anything," he said. "Nothing wrong. It was me. I was selfish and stupid and—"

"Will—"

"I'd undo it if I could—I'd go back and be who you deserved, and be strong enough for you, and not—"

"Will, don't . . ."

"—not be so lost in my own fear that I wasn't there for you, before or after, that I made you feel I didn't want . . . I was weak when you needed me to be strong. Afraid when I should have been fearless." His mouth was twisted in self-loathing Marcie recognized like an old antagonist.

Will had been blaming himself for what happened. Marcie had been blaming herself. And as they sat behind Flint's ravaged house, looking out over an island washed over with garbage and detritus, she realized the futility of all of it. What caused the devastation didn't matter. It happened, nothing more. Trying to cast or assume blame accomplished nothing but inertia. Will had done what he had done—he couldn't help how he felt. Loving him as she still did—as she always would, she saw now—how could she not forgive him for simply feeling what he had felt? And Marcie, she finally began to see, had done the same.

Will would never move forward if he didn't forgive himself. And he wouldn't do that unless she could forgive him. Forgive them both.

The poison inside her that she'd gotten so used to for so long was gone. She let go of his fingers and reached her hand to his cheek, an oddly maternal gesture. He turned his face toward it, his lips in her palm. "We did the best we could, my love," she said softly.

"But it wasn't enough?" The words were whispered against her skin.

She shrugged gently. "I don't know. It's all we had."

He shook his head, and she saw that his eyes were wet. "Will we get past this?"

She lowered her hand, didn't know how to answer him. On some level she felt that his coming here, their finally talking about it, all of it . . . that they finally *were* moving past it. What she didn't know was whether they would be doing it together.

He seemed to hear what she didn't say: "What about us?"

She shrugged again. "I don't know. I know that I love you, Will. I can't remember a time that I haven't. I can't imagine a time that I won't."

He looked at her with searching eyes. "Will that be enough?" he asked again.

This time Marcie smiled sadly at him. "It's all we have."

They sat there for a long time afterward, and after a while Marcie started to tell Will about her life in Palmetto Key. About Flint, and how he'd found her on the beach. About her job at Tequila Mockingbird, and Darla and Art and Petey and Bink, and the strange sort of family they had all created for themselves, pieces of driftwood washed up together on the same beach. And finally she told him about the studio . . . about Jeff—but only that he was an artist who rented the building and was offering her a place to work on her own art.

Color leached from his cheeks. "Is that what this is about? Someone else?"

She shook her head. "No. I mean, he's been a part of all this"—she swirled the air in front of her chest—"that's been going on with me, but not the way you . . . I'm not sleeping with him, Will."

"But you're not just friends."

She didn't want to hurt him, but she couldn't lie. "He isn't part of this."

She could see that it bothered him—that a lot of her stories did, to think of her helpless on the beach in that state, alone, or waiting on rude tourists—but he let her talk, even smiling at certain parts, like the regulars standing up for her to the mouthy teenage boys.

"You've done so much," he said when she stopped, the sun slanting over the gulf and into her eyes.

"It seems easier here. It's sort of . . . a time-out place. I don't think I have to be me here." She laughed self-consciously. "That sounds weird."

But he was nodding slowly. "You know that little art shop in St. Simons?"

She smiled wistfully. "Of course." That was where he'd bought her the tourmaline ring.

As if she'd summoned it with the thought, he reached into his pocket and pulled it out, the teal-and-pink stone lighting up in the sunlight.

Marcie blinked back tears, inexplicably relieved as she accepted the ring from him, running her fingers over the stone. "I wondered if you'd sent it."

"I couldn't. But . . . I get it. That time-out feeling." He'd shifted so he wasn't looking at her anymore, instead watching a gray-blue heron do its delicate tippy-toe walk near the sea grass behind Flint's house. The water was still receding, Marcie realized—it came just a few inches up the bird's stalky legs. "For just that second I almost asked you if you wanted to stay there. On the island. Like we could just pick up everything, leave our jobs and our home and all of it, and go live in paradise, like beach bums."

"Why didn't you?" she said quietly. "Why didn't you ask me?"

He turned a hand palm upward. "It seemed ridiculous."

"It wasn't."

He simply nodded, and for a moment Marcie felt a tendril of that same strong thread of connection to him that she'd felt since she'd first seen him running off the field in high school.

They stayed there on the empty slab of porch for a long time, talking. It was almost as if they were both afraid to stop, afraid to get up from where they were, sitting on the empty stoop of a nearly razed house, in between their old life and whatever was in front of them.

A dull knock came from her left, and Marcie looked down to see a stray boogie board had floated into Flint's yard and banged up against the wooden stairs their feet rested on. The sound seemed to start time again, and Marcie slipped the ring into her pocket as they stood to walk back to Isobel's house.

Flint

They scrounged up enough pairs of gloves for everyone—gardening gloves and work gloves, even dish gloves and an old pair of Berto's leather bike gloves Flint couldn't imagine why Isobel would have held on to, considering—and began to clean out the worst of the wreckage. Will threw himself into the work, lifting up two-by-fours and sheets of plywood with Flint, which surprised the hell out of him—when he and Marcie had come back inside from their long talk, the man wore a look Flint recognized, like the first time a grunt staggered out of a foxhole when some of his buddies didn't.

While Isobel and Marcie sifted through the rubble underneath for anything worth saving, Flint and Will gathered the debris and started piling it at the street for the pickup Flint knew inevitably followed in the days and weeks after a storm. Lean as he was, Marcie's husband was surprisingly strong, and he worked like a damn ox, steady and quiet, standing ready by the next chunk of house to be moved before Flint could even direct him. Flint had even slapped him on the back a couple of times.

They worked for the rest of the afternoon, mostly in silence except for instructions or strategies from Will or Flint as they labored to move an especially heavy or awkward fragment, or the occasional exclamation from Isobel or Marcie when they discovered something intact as they sifted through what was revealed—a bizarrely untouched stack of books; Flint's favorite boiling pot, nicked and dusty, but still usable; even an incongruously shiny wrench occasioned a shout and a moment's break for everyone to admire it. When your life was reduced to broken pieces, apparently the tiniest part of it that survived intact was cause for rejoicing.

He'd carried an armful of splintered wood out to the porch and let it drop onto the pile they were making there, and was standing, stretching out his back, while Will moved a mattress off a clump of soggy, flattened boxes in what used to be Marcie's room—Jessie's room—when Marcie gave a cry of triumph.

"The turtle!" she crowed excitedly, holding up the little piece of pottery.

Big deal—the house is kindling, and it's not the Ark of the Covenant. But the words never made it up his throat, blocked by an unexpected lump as he moved to her side and let her lay the smooth clay figure, one leg missing, in the palm of his hand, a twist of gratitude wrenching something loose in his chest.

They worked for hours, their movements slowing with fatigue. By the time the sun was hovering over the gulf, lighting it up golden orange, they were winding down when they heard a sharp whistle and a gravelly call of "Ahoy, the house!" from the front.

Marcie stood from where she'd been kneeling sorting through what seemed to be the entire contents of the hall closet—some sodden jackets, a ripped duffel bag emptied of whatever it had held—he couldn't remember—the upright portion of his vacuum cleaner with the bottom half sheared away—and her look of mild startlement melted into a grin as she saw something through the stripped shell of his house. A second later that husk of a woman from the bar appeared around the side, followed by three old derelicts he'd seen installed there like fixtures when he went looking for Marcie, their arms laden with shopping bags that seemed in danger of overbalancing them.

"Workers of the world . . . you gotta eat," the woman announced.

"Darla! Hey, gentlemen." Marcie stepped toward the edge of the porch. "What are you all doing here?"

She looked up at Marcie. "Still had all this food left after today, and we figured you might want a hearty meal after a day's work. You—cute boy," she directed at Will, "come on over and help a lady out."

Will hastened over to the group, jumping down from the porch and taking one of the bags as she barely broke stride around the back and up the steps. She looked around and whistled again, this time a low single note, and turned to look at Flint. "Halle-fuckin'-lujah, Ahab, that bitch ate your house."

Introductions were made. Darla lifted an eyebrow when she met Marcie's husband, and gave a hoarse widemouthed laugh, winking at Marcie. "Nice goin', girl!" she chortled. Flint shot a glance at Will, whose expression didn't change, and he wondered how much the man knew about his rival. Then everyone followed Isobel back to her house and out onto her patio, the only place where so many people would fit. As the sun disappeared into the gulf, a breeze kicked up behind it, and the air seemed cooler, fresh. Isobel and Marcie went inside to bring out drinks, while Will set the bags down on the picnic table and Darla started pulling out paper-wrapped bundles like endless eggs from an illusionist's mouth.

"We got roast beef"—*plop* onto the table—"ham"—*plop, plop*—"coupla turkeys, but I don't advise 'em at this point." These she rolled out of their paper and torpedoed over the back, their contents separating midair and then exploding on contact with the wet sand. Avaricious gulls and petrels came swooping and running over to peck at the bounty.

Darla was still producing items from her bags: "I got a few weird sammies I put together outta chicken fingers and cole-slaw and pickles, but I had one and they ain't bad. This one here's vegetarian pimento cheese—any tree huggers in the mix? Then there's whatever random shit I had leftover. You got your spinach dip, your potato salad, your coleslaw. . . ." She looked into the last emptied bag as if surprised that it contained noth-ing else.

Marcie came through the slider with Isobel behind her, their hands full of a pitcher of lemonade, bottles of water, a few cans of soda. Marcie balanced a stack of green plastic cups upside down over one can. Flint and Will reached to help them, and they set it all down beside the food.

"Well, what the hell are we waitin' for?" Darla said after a moment's inactivity. "Dig in!"

He hadn't realized how much of an appetite he'd worked up until he took the first bite—Darla was right about the chicken finger sandwich; even cold it was good. For a few moments the patio fell silent; after the long day they'd had—in every way—it seemed like everyone was starving. But once they all got a few bites into them, conversation started back up.

It was odd having Isobel's porch full again like this, voices

talking across one another, the occasional laugh, the confusion
of hands reaching for more food or another drink. Back when
Berto was alive it was like this a lot—only full of boys instead
of old men like him. Isobel would put out platters of sandwiches
and plastic six-packs of cold soda, Berto and his friends sprawled
like sea lions across the furniture, not yet grown into their lanky
bodies. Jessie was always hovering nearby, wanting to be part of
the group. And more often than not the boys had included her,
like some little pixie mascot for their adolescent army. "Hey, no
Coke for you, pipsqueak," Flint had heard Berto's friend Josh
tease her once out on the patio while he and Is were in the living room. "Ms. Dominguez, can we have some milk?"

"Better bring it in a bottle for big baby Josh, Ms. Isobel," his
girl had fired back, and he and Isobel shared a glance, Flint
grinning while the boys had roared.

He looked around at the odd assemblage—Isobel and Marcie, Will and Darla, three ancient relics that anyone observing
the group would have lumped Flint right in with. Except for
Isobel he hadn't known any of these people a few weeks ago,
and here they were, offering what little they had. For no reason
he could think of . . . except for Marcie.

The day caught up with everyone after dinner, and conversation quieted until finally Darla stood up and announced that
she was headed home. The old men obediently stood and shuffled out after her, all of them, who Flint had found out had also
been in the service, clasping his hand on the way out with loud
smacks and strong grips.

That left Isobel and Flint, and Will and Marcie. An awkward arrangement if there ever had been one.

Flint held out a hand to Will. "Thanks for pitching in."

"More hands lighten the load." When they broke the clasp, Will's gaze moved to Marcie, and he looked as uncomfortable as Flint felt. "I'm going to head out too," he said, and gave a halfhearted chuckle. "I'm guessing there's a lot of hotels with vacancies."

Flint wanted to know what had happened with Marcie and Will, where things stood. They'd worked practically side by side seamlessly, but also mostly wordlessly, at least directly to each other. So far they'd been pleasant but impersonal, like casual coworkers rather than spouses. He'd like to ask her about it, but he wasn't some gossipy old crow who needed to know every little personal detail about someone. And anyway, there hadn't been any opportunity for private conversations today, not with everyone working so steadily.

And then there was a hilarious moment of boomeranging eye contact between Isobel and Marcie where Flint suspected a lot more was said than he or poor Will could possibly pick up on. Finally, as if something had been decided between the two women, Isobel pronounced, "Nonsense. You'll stay here. I hear the sofa's quite comfortable." She sent Flint a smile.

And suddenly it dawned on him that Will on the sofa meant . . . Flint would be in with Isobel. Didn't it?

And didn't that just blow his mind.

Isobel brought out fresh bedding and made up the sofa while Marcie slipped a pillowcase onto the thin pillow. She'd clearly had a hand in her husband's being asked to stay, and she seemed to want him there, but it said something that she didn't invite him into her bedroom. Flint almost felt for the guy—for the life of him he couldn't figure out what message she was sending, and he doubted the other man could either.

The women took the first turns in the bathroom, getting ready for bed by the light of the lantern they'd used in there during the storm—how could that have only been this morning? And then Flint stood from the chair where he'd been making stilted chitchat with Will.

"Guess I'm off to bed too," he said offhandedly, but his heart was tripping like a teenage boy's.

Ridiculous that a grown man—an old man, for Christ's sake—would be so damned unsettled at walking into a woman's bedroom. He headed off down the darkened hall, ignoring his heart's pounding.

At the last second, before his hand hit the doorknob to her room, he detoured into the bathroom and pushed the door to behind him. *Coward,* he spit at himself. Standing in the half dark, he could hear the long breaths he was sucking into his lungs.

And over that sound he heard something else too—a click and then a slow scrape—and in an instant he went back twenty-five years, more, and remembered lying with Isobel in that room that he'd just bypassed, a smoother version of her sleeping in his younger, stronger arms, while Jessie was curled up on that same sofa, a tiny angel in slumber, and Flint listened to Berto trying to sneak undetected from his room to meet up with friends, or a girl, or whatever it was he liked to do now and then in the middle of the night. Flint, remembering his own younger days, had turned a blind eye to his nightly peregrinations—it was a covenant between men that only Flint was aware of, because he didn't think Berto had ever known he knew.

The noise meant Marcie was coming out of Berto's room, probably headed back to the bathroom, and here he was sitting in the dark like a terrified little kid.

But her footsteps went the other direction. After a moment Flint heard her soft voice, and the lower pitch of Will's answer. But he couldn't make out what they were saying.

He eased the door open and slipped out, taking silent steps into the hall. But he couldn't quite get close enough without being spotted to let their quiet murmurings coalesce into words.

Then suddenly Will's oddly calm voice came as clearly as if Flint were sitting in the same room: "You are my family, Marcie. And I will not give up on us."

A flash of compassion for the man shot through him. Will seemed like an okay guy. And it sounded like he was losing her.

Did that mean she was staying?

More than anything Flint wanted to peer around the corner and see what was happening—where the two were sitting, whether they were touching, what their faces looked like. But before he could convince himself it was worth risking being spotted, he heard the crack of a door opening, and knew Isobel was standing in the doorway and had caught him eavesdropping like a girl. He scooted guiltily past her into her room, and she closed the door behind him—cutting off Marcie's response to her husband.

He expected Isobel to call him on his intrusion into the couple's privacy, but instead she simply came into his arms. Flint closed his eyes. He didn't know now why he'd been so nervous earlier; Isobel felt as natural in his embrace as if she'd left it twenty minutes ago, instead of more than twenty years.

"You really care about her, don't you?" she asked quietly.

He opened his eyes, didn't even try to shrug it off. "Yeah. I do," he said. "She's so much like Jessie, isn't she?"

Isobel pulled back, meeting his eyes. "But she's not Jessie. You know that, Herman."

He blew out a breath. "Yes."

She stepped away, but took his hand and led him to her bed—the only other pieces of furniture that fit in the tiny room were a dresser and nightstand—and they sat on the edge together, their legs touching. "You must have missed her so much." He knew they were talking about Jessie now, but Isobel's tone carried no judgment, just a plain sympathy that made his throat tighten. "How nice it would be to be part of each other's lives again . . . wouldn't it?" she added gently.

He took his hand back, clenched his fists, made a sound that bore no resemblance to language. Finally he pushed out, "I wouldn't even know where to find her."

"She's in Washington, DC."

His heart froze in his chest. "What?"

"And her son, Nathaniel—your grandson."

"My grandson? I have a grandson?" Of course he did—that made sense. But he felt as if his brain were encased in ice.

Isobel was watching him carefully. She nodded. "You do." She stood, went to her nightstand, and pulled out a stack of papers—postcards and greeting cards.

Isobel held the stack directly in front of him, and he had no choice but to take it. He flipped one open. The same handwriting as the ones his daughter had written him over the years from wherever he'd sent her for summer—neater, but still so unmistakably hers. "There are pictures too," she said briskly. "Mostly just from holidays, but you'll like them. She's married, and her husband loves her son like his own. Even adopted him. You are welcome to read these if you want to."

He was still holding the pile aloft in front of him, at arm's length, like a first-time father straight-arming an infant, the papers' edges trembling. "She writes you?" he said in a strange small voice.

"Mostly at Christmas, and always on my birthday, and Berto's. And I write to her. I even met up with her and Nathaniel once years ago, when I went to DC for vacation."

Nathaniel . . .

Nate Mosley had saved Flint's life in a sugarcane field in Quang Ngai Province in 1967. He must have told Jessie the story a dozen times—a nostalgic old veteran with no one else to recycle his old stories to except his daughter. She knew Nate like an uncle, though she'd never met him. Flint never saw him again after the war. Never tried to look him up. She couldn't have been thinking of that story when she named her son. Could she?

Washington, DC. What did Jessie do there? What was her life like? He kept picturing his daughter the last time he'd seen her—eyes huge in her pixie face, which was so crumpled with anger and betrayal. She'd been a kid then, though. She'd be all grown-up now. No—in her thirties. And her son . . . her son would almost be an adult. Grown-up, and his own grandfather had never known him. Never tried to know him. A wave of loathing washed over him, and Flint thought he was going to be sick.

"I fucked up my whole life," he ground out bitterly. "Hers too. Everyone's."

"You've got a mighty high opinion of your capabilities, old man. Jessie's doing all right. So's Nathaniel."

"And what I did to you, Is. The way I cut you out . . ."

"I'm doing all right too. Always have." She sat back down beside him, not touching now.

He turned to face her, looking at her for a long, long moment. "You're better than I deserve, Is."

She nodded, and her crisp expression softened. "That's true. But I happen to like you. For some godforsaken reason, Herman, I might even still love you."

He could feel his jaw clenching and unclenching, and a ballooning feeling inside his chest that moved swiftly into an ache, and then a sharp pain. A heart attack. But the hot wetness in his eyes told him that wasn't what it was. His throat worked to push out words, but he couldn't—he'd cry like a goddamn baby. He forced them out anyway: "You know how I feel about you, Is, don't you? How I always have." His tone was sandpaper, his face was wet, and his words weren't enough. Not by a long shot.

But Isobel smiled—that smile. "Of course I do, you stupid old man." She patted his arm, almost a slap, and the sting of it brought him back to himself. She was a hell of a woman, Isobel. So much more than he deserved. But by some miracle he had her anyway.

"You think she'd want to hear from me?" he grated out. "To . . . know me again?"

Isobel's brow furrowed, her lips pulled in as she thought about it. It was one of the things he'd always liked about her— she didn't just fire off an opinion right away. Isobel thought things through. "I think the only way you'll find out is to try," she said slowly.

He had to look away from her sharp gaze then, down to the floor. "I can't do it alone," he muttered.

She gave a chuckle, as if what he said amused her. "You don't have to, you fool."

He felt a touch against his shoulder, and then the solid pressure of Isobel's hand at his back.

He leaned into it, welcoming her support.

Marcie

~~~

t took a week to get the power back on across the island, the process stalled by the three-day wait while the city inspected the bridge and finally pronounced it safe for traffic.

Those three days were like a time capsule, the people on the island when the storm hit stranded there, cut off, isolated to themselves. They had no one to count on except one another, and they showed up. The island was a hive of activity every day, no one wanting to stay boxed inside in the hot, still air with no A/C, and so everywhere bustled with islanders—and even the tourists—pitching in full-bore on cleanup for neighbors, clearing debris from the street and storefronts, and at the end of the day, reverting to circadian rhythms without the daylight extension of artificial light, people gathered at houses or restaurants or on the beach, sharing food, water, supplies until the sun went down. The devastation of the storm seemed to wash them backward in time for a brief, suspended period, and built bonds of community, support, friendship. Out of disaster came something unexpected and lovely.

Will stayed—he had no choice, his dinghy having disappeared as Flint predicted. "Someone must've needed it," he said, but he'd wanted to stay and help anyway. Marcie wanted that too. His presence was a comfort, even with things so unsettled between them, and whatever came next, she wasn't quite ready to let him go. The chrysalis of frozen time was welcome in that way too.

Two days after the hurricane, when the gulf had retreated to its boundaries, while Isobel and Will made sandwiches, Marcie and Flint re-dug the turtle nest, as close to where it had been as they could. Adults returned to the exact spot where they were born to lay their own eggs, Flint told her, and while a few feet one way or the other probably wouldn't make much difference when any survivors came back one day to dig nests of their own, the odds against them were high enough already.

As they placed them gently back into the hole in the sand, Marcie tried to sense movement inside, some indication of life—that the baby turtles, despite all the uprooting of the last week, were still forming inside their leathery shells.

"No way to know till we know," Flint told her, laying a hand on her shoulder. They smoothed the sand back over the eggs, Marcie feverishly hoping for the best.

They knew the bridge had been cleared when Red Cross trucks showed up along Palmetto, navigable now because of the tireless efforts of the islanders, distributing water and first-aid supplies, hot meals and snacks—rare in the absence of anything dry enough to burn on the island—and, laughably in the stifling heat and humidity, blankets.

Will left the next day.

Art had shown up to pick Will up with his nephew, who

lived on the mainland, in the kid's enormous white F-150. Most every vehicle on the island had been totaled by the storm surge, salt water destroying the engines, but they'd already heard that Little Neck Pass Road had stayed dry—another hidden blessing of the storm that Will had been forced to leave his car there. Marcie's was among the totaled, sitting useless in the driveway along with Flint's.

"I don't want to leave you without a car," Will told her on the beach that morning when they walked for miles, trying to find a way to say good-bye.

"It's okay. I don't really need one right now. And I'll buy one when I do."

He squeezed her hand where they were linked between the two of them as they walked. "I don't want to leave you at all," he said, his voice constricted.

Marcie stopped, pulling him to a stop with her. She wrapped her arms around his waist, letting her head rest in its familiar spot against his chest, her throat tight, an aching behind her rib cage. After a moment his arms came around her and they stood like that for a long time, listening to each other breathe against the backdrop of the surf and the plaintive seagulls, feeling each other's hearts beat.

When Will finally spoke it was a rumble against her ear. "This isn't over between us, Marcie." It was a promise rather than a threat.

She closed her eyes against wetness. "It'll never be over between us, Will. Not entirely."

She'd call him, she promised. She'd call Emily too, find a way to try to explain, to apologize, and hope the woman could forgive her for hurting her son, for vanishing from Emily's life without a word too. Whatever happened, Emily had been a mother to Marcie, and she could no more fathom a future without her mother-in-law in it in some way than she could without Will.

When the time came for him to climb into Art's nephew's truck, a grenade of panic detonated inside Marcie's chest. *No!* she almost cried. *Wait.* . . .

But that was fear talking. Fear, and grief, and the pain of what was lost. It was time to look forward, not backward. Sometimes you had to let go of some things to discover others.

After

~~~

This was her favorite time of day—when the island was still dark, the sun yet to crest the horizon behind her, and the gulf still an inky smudge visible only in the streaks of phosphorescing waves as they broke on the sand. Everyone was still asleep in the house behind her—she'd fallen into Flint's habit of waking early, walking with him along the shore, watching the island slowly put itself back together and checking for new turtle nests. But oftentimes she got up even before he did, her busy mind prodding her awake long before dawn, and she'd bring her first cup of coffee out onto Isobel's back porch.

That was one of her prime requirements when she'd started looking for a place of her own—something on the beach with a sitting area out back for mornings like this. She'd had to wait a while after the storm—city engineers were methodically checking the buildings for structural damage, and blue tarps stretched over rooftops here and there—but she'd finally found something last week, a small two-bedroom stilted house just down the street. The owner was a friend of Isobel's, temporarily relocating to the other coast of Florida to be closer to her daughter when she had her baby. She'd be back sooner or later, but that suited Marcie just fine for now—she wasn't making long-range plans just yet. She'd move into the new place in a couple of weeks, just before the woman's grandbaby's due date.

As she did every morning, she tiptoed down the steps and walked over to check their turtle nest, but so far there'd been nothing: no sign of movement, no indication that the hatchlings had survived—had even been alive when they replanted them all those weeks ago.

Too many weeks, she knew.

Their turtle was a Kemp's ridley—itself an endangered species—and incubation took around forty-five to sixty days. They were on day sixty-two now. Sand temperatures affected the incubation period, Flint told her—cooler sand slowed things down, and the storm surge had no doubt notched the sand temps down at least a few degrees.

Marcie had been clinging to that hope, checking the sand for any minute disturbance—the hatchlings would carve themselves out of their eggs with a tiny temporary horn when it was time, but it could take up to three days for them to dig their way out. This morning she hovered over the nest behind the bare flat slab where Herman's house had been, eyes fixed on the surface in the dim predawn, looking for any tiny movement. Finally she gave up and went back to the porch to wait for the sky to lighten, for the household to awaken.

Herman and Isobel were headed to DC this afternoon.

He'd been almost comically nervous as Marcie and Isobel helped him pack—three days ago, Herman unwilling to take any chances on not being ready for the trip. He'd been even more nervous in the days immediately after the hurricane, working up the courage to reach out to Jessie. Late at night Marcie heard him and Isobel in their room, still talking through how to contact her, when, what he would say. He'd started with a letter—Marcie never saw it, but she'd watched him and Isobel work on it for almost a week before he felt it was right—and then she waited with them in almost unbearable suspense for Jessie's reply.

It came in the form of a phone call six days later, Herman almost dropping his cell—which Marcie had driven him to the AT&T store in her secondhand Toyota to buy—when he saw the area code.

He took it onto the porch, and when he didn't come back inside for long minutes, she and Isobel peeked their heads out to check on him and saw the cell phone abandoned on a chair outside, Herman a diminished figure on the beach in the distance, walking away.

When he came back nearly an hour later, they were waiting in the living room with iced tea and a cheese plate Isobel had put together, both of them nervous as debutantes as they waited to find out what had happened.

Isobel rose to her feet as he came in, Marcie gripping the armrest of the sofa where she sat. He stared at the two of them, at the polite little spread of hors d'oeuvres. "What's the occasion?" he said gruffly.

Isobel took him by the shoulders and shook him. "What happened?"

He scanned the food, the icy pitcher, his gaze meeting Marcie's and then moving on to Isobel's. He took in a long, shaky breath and let it out. "She's not ready yet," he said finally. "But she wants to see me when she is," and air gusted out of Marcie with the force of a blown tire as Isobel hooted in relief.

Over the next weeks he and Jessie had talked often, at first just for a few minutes at a time, and gradually longer, and finally they'd set up a careful visit: Herman and Isobel booked a hotel near Jessie's house so they could meet on her terms, take their time getting to know each other again after so many years.

He was a wreck. But more vitalized than she'd ever seen him, as if he'd shed years over the last weeks—and dropped a weight from his shoulders.

Marcie was driving them to the airport later, but this morning everyone was coming with her for her third showing of a gallery space—she wanted their opinions before finalizing the lease. It wasn't perfect—the building wasn't on the beach, as she'd hoped for, but across the street on Marea, not far from Tequila Mockingbird. But it was in the busiest part of the island, and raised up a few feet—Marcie wasn't eager to risk another flood—yet still low enough that passersby would be able to see into the expansive front windows, which were brand-new, thanks to the storm having blown out the old ones.

The space was much bigger than she'd wanted too—nearly twelve hundred square feet—but old enough that the owner was willing to bargain on the rate, especially when Marcie offered to make needed improvements herself. And the extra space brought with it opportunities—there was room to section off a small working studio along one side, with a low wall so patrons could enjoy the artists as they created some of the pieces that would then be for sale in the shop. Marcie had been looking into storage and work-space solutions that would accommodate a variety of media—including her own collage work.

She'd been talking to the artists from the warehouse party for the past few weeks—Tucker and Max and Dallas, almost all the others who were interested in showing and selling their work—

discussing which of their pieces they might want to display in the shop, negotiating consignment rates.

She'd imagined Jeff's pottery featured in the display windows—their uniqueness and visceral appeal would be a wonderful draw—and when she'd gone by to see him almost a week after the hurricane, she'd found him working inside the off-kilter studio, the door thrown open to let in whatever hot breeze puffed occasionally off the gulf. He didn't notice her at first, and Marcie stood in the doorway, watching him bend over to retrieve pieces of his pottery and set them gently into a cardboard box.

As if he felt her eyes on him, he looked up and straightened, going still at the sight of her. "I wasn't sure I'd see you again," he said. "With your husband here."

"He went back home."

His face cleared. "You're not going back. Are you?"

She shook her head. "No."

He smiled. "I thought you would."

"Why?" Her tone wasn't confrontational; she simply felt curious.

"I don't know. I think I was afraid it was easier for you than the unknown."

She walked all the way into the room. "It probably would be. But right now . . . it feels like it would be a lot harder to go back."

He lifted the box he'd been carefully placing pottery in, placed it on a shelf, and moved closer to her. Marcie inhaled the smell of him: the tang of the ocean that seemed to linger on his skin, the musk of sweat, the dark, sweetish scent of weed.

"Have you ever been to northern California?"

She smiled. "No. What's it like?"

"It's like an artist invented it. Gray-blue ocean with froths of white on top of the waves that crash in against these crazy cliffs—every shade of brown and black and gray and beige you can think of. Dark green trees, rushing rivers—the Russian River, in fact. There's a little town along it called Guerneville that looks like an alpine village plopped down in the middle of California. It's like living in the trees."

She could see it in her mind as he described it, like a painting. "That sounds . . . unbelievable," she murmured.

"Come with me."

Marcie gave a tiny laugh. "What?"

"As soon as I leave the North Carolina festival, that's where I'm headed. It's an artists' haven—lots of tourists, but it doesn't have a tourist-town feel, not like this place. The nicest people you could imagine. Land so beautiful you can forget how bad we've screwed up most of it."

"What about here? Your studio?"

He gave a broad gesture around him with both hands. "Here is done. The building's going to be condemned—probably both of them. This island's played out for me. I'm ready for something new too. What do you think?"

For just a moment she allowed herself to picture it—the redwoods and the mountains . . . the ocean, a more primal cousin of the gentle gulf. A bohemian community of artists where maybe she'd let the gray threading into her hair grow out, and wear gauzy skirts and go barefoot. She already knew what her answer was, though, and she could see in Jeff's eyes that he did too, even as he said again, "Come with me, Marcella. It'll be an adventure."

She smiled sadly, knowing this would be a path not taken, an experience she wouldn't have. Not now anyway. "It's not my adventure, Jeff."

"Because of your husband?"

"Because of me." She shrugged. "I'm figuring out what I want. And right now I want to do that here."

Jeff reached out and brushed a flyaway hair out of her eyes. "California's there anytime you change your mind."

She nodded, knowing she wouldn't. She'd helped him finish packing up his pottery for the festival, and left him to pack up everything else. A few days later he'd been gone.

The sky was just barely lightening now, deep indigo slowly fading out, and the dawn threw rippling shadows from the water to the sand below her.

Marcie sat up straight, her coffee sloshing onto the plank floorboards. She clanked her mug down on the railing and hurried down the stairs, her heart thumping. When she convinced herself she was seeing what she thought she was seeing, not just wishful thinking, she ran back upstairs and into the house, almost barreling over Herman in the kitchen.

He steadied the coffee he'd been pouring from spilling. "Whoa, girl—where's the fire?"

"The nest!" she said, forgetting to keep her voice down. "It's moving."

Immediately he set the mug down, forgotten. "I'll go get Isobel. We'll meet you outside—keep an eye on it."

She ran back out and down the steps, over to the nest, where the sand was definitely churning.

A tiny dark spot appeared on the surface, and Marcie dropped to her knees. A head. A little perfect turtle head, small as the miniature sculpture of Jeff's that sat on the ledge in Isobel's kitchen.

She glanced up at the squeak of footsteps on the sand to see Herman and Isobel headed over, and they joined her at the perimeter, watching in awed silence as the first tiny body emerged, pushing itself awkwardly with minuscule flippers. It seemed the most inefficient means of propulsion Marcie could imagine, the fins so small, the turtle's body much heavier by comparison, but the creature kept at it, and little by little he made it all the way out and started heading toward the sea.

She looked at Flint and saw he was grinning in a way she'd never seen, one hand clamped firmly around Isobel's. She knew she wore a goofy grin of her own as their eyes met.

As if the first turtle had given the signal to the others, a handful of other tiny bodies poked out of the sand now and eked their way out and onto the beach. And then more . . . and still more, and Marcie couldn't believe the nest had held so many. A breeze kicked up, and the coolness on her face told her it was wet with tears she hadn't realized were there.

"Wait," she said in a whisper, and, "Wait." She scrambled to her feet, swiping a sleeve over her cheeks, the tourmaline ring on her right ring finger catching in her hair, and ran—back around the house, up the stairs, and in through the door, where she went straight to her bedroom.

In his sleep, worn out from driving in late last night for the weekend, Will looked like the boy he'd been when she'd first seen him.

He'd been coming down every couple of weeks, first sleeping on Isobel's couch and then, as they found a rhythm together, migrating into the spare room with her when he spent the weekends. He'd helped her run the lease numbers on the gallery space, vet contractors for the renovations. Things weren't back to "normal." Maybe they never would be. Marcie wasn't sure that was what she wanted.

She touched his face. "Will," she said softly. "Will. Wake up."

She was still smiling—couldn't take it off her face—and the moment his eyes fluttered open and he saw her, he smiled too. "Marcie." One hand came up to clasp her fingers.

She squeezed. "Will, get up—you have to see this."

She practically pulled him down the stairs and to the back.

She brought him to where Flint and Isobel still knelt together next to the nest. "Look," she said. "Look at that."

Now they could see a wave of movement exiting the sand like ants from a kicked anthill, dozens of little bodies pushing their way against gravity to the sea that they'd never known, but that called them.

"My God," Will whispered.

"This is the hard part," Flint said. "This is when most of them get eaten by seabirds, or fish, or crabs."

Marcie's throat tightened as she watched the tiny turtles push toward shore with everything they had. They were beautiful—perfect—and most of them wouldn't make it past tonight. Yet they pushed on toward the sea, because that was the only way they even had a chance to survive—despite all the obstacles, despite predators, despite the limitations of their own immature bodies.

Suddenly she heard a roar, like a feral animal, and it was only when the noise startled her that she realized it was coming from her own throat. She shot to her feet and ran down toward shore, careful to make a wide arc around the trail of turtles streaming in the same direction. A susurration surrounded her, and she saw a flock of birds take flight, their white wings tinged peach in the dawning light. "Go!" she screamed. "Hyah!" She windmilled her arms and zigzagged through the sand, shouting nonsense syllables as if she were scattering wild horses.

She heard a lower-pitched echo of her own noises and saw Will beside her, gesturing and shouting like a crazy person, shooing the birds along with her. He looked ridiculous—just as she must—and Marcie started to laugh. Will looked over at her, a wild grin on his face, and he was laughing too.

"Goddamn birds!" she said to him.

"Goddamn birds!" he agreed, his smile wide.

Marcie turned back to see Flint and Isobel standing near the makeshift nest still belching out a stream of turtles, their hands clasped. A few silhouettes farther down the beach told Marcie their shouts had woken some neighbors, and she waved, feeling giddy. She turned to look back at her husband, who still wore the same foolish grin she felt on her own face, and then she whooped again, lifting her hands into the air and darting around to clear away the birds as fast as they settled back on the sand. Will joined her, and together they ran around the lightening beach, trying to shorten the longest of odds.

Acknowledgments

Writing and publishing a book are never done in a vacuum, and I have so many of the usual suspects to thank.

I've been lucky to have generous feedback and encouragement on this story, which took much longer than most of mine to develop. Thanks to the Novel-in-Progress group of Austin, whose members critiqued and encouraged the very earliest versions of it, and to my well-beloved Penheads—Kelly Harrell, Amber Novak, and John Jones—for reading subsequent drafts ad nauseam, yet still urging me to stick with it. Gentleman John Jones was a particular and relentless champion of the story for many years, and while he passed away before he could see it in print, I got to share my delight with him when I got the publishing contract for it. John, you're on every page of this book (and you can check out his own beautiful novels under his pen name, John J. Asher). Thanks to Kathryn Hera Haydn, Marcie Walter, Richard LeMay, Dr. Duana Welch, and Karin Gillespie for reading various versions and offering insightful feedback. If I've left anyone out it's entirely inadvertent, and I will make it up to you with homemade cookies.

My special thanks to two talented, generous-hearted, and brilliant authors, Leila Meacham and Sarah Bird, dear friends whose books I adore, both of whom took time to read an advance copy despite writing their own newest books, and Leila also navigating enormous personal challenges. Asking them to read my book was like asking Kobe Bryant to check out your free throw.

Thanks to author Camille Pagán, whose books are so good you should go read them right now, for the perfect title when the one I'd had my heart set on since I first started a prototype of this book, *Falling Together*, got snagged by Marisa de los Santos in the nearly fifteen years it took me to fully find the story (I forgive her, as she is another of my favorite authors).

My agent, Courtney Miller-Callihan, has doggedly and unflaggingly shepherded this book into publication, and also offered welcome expert editorial feedback in the seemingly endless iterations of revisions.

I'm so very grateful for the team at Berkley who has such faith in me and my stories and makes both shine: my patient, insightful, delightful editors, Cindy Hwang and Angela Kim; the superstars in marketing and publicity Bridget O'Toole and Daché Rogers, who help get my books into readers' hands with determination and creativity; art director Rita Frangie and the design team at Berkley, who created a cover I love so much I want to enlarge it and use it as room décor; and production editor Dan Walsh and the unsung heroes of copyediting and proofing whose eagle-eyed expertise saved me from embarrassing errors.

Thanks to the reviewers, bloggers, Instagrammers, podcasters, booksellers and especially indie bookstores, librarians, bookfest staff and volunteers, and all those who help books reach readers. You're the lifeblood of this industry. And to the readers who pick up our books—stories don't fully come to life until they're in your hands, so thank you. I'm also so grateful to the author community, particularly in the genre I write in. It's an endlessly warm and supportive group I'm privileged to be part of.

I know it's weird, but this is my book, and if you can't thank your dogs in your own book for lying faithfully at your feet for hours on end, day after day, offering company and comfort, love and laughs, then where can you do it? Alex and Gavin, you're such good boys! Now go lie down.

Thanks to my husband, Joel, for all the things, always.

And a special shout-out to my mom, Carole Hlavin Yates, who taught me any number of valuable life lessons, but two in particular have shaped my life and this book: Life is a series of choices, and happiness is one of those choices. Thanks, Mom. You know I love you.

Photo by Korey Howell

Phoebe Fox has been a contributor and regular columnist for a number of national, regional, and local publications, including HuffPost, Elite Daily, and SheKnows. A former actor onstage and on-screen, Phoebe has been suspended from wires as a mall fairy, was accidentally concussed by a blank gun, and hosted a short-lived game show. She has been a relationship columnist; a movie, theater, and book reviewer; and a radio personality, and is a close observer of relationships in the wild. She lives in Austin, Texas, with her husband and two excellent dogs. This is her sixth novel.